Caird, Janet
  The umbrella-maker's
daughter.

I've travelled the world twice over,
Met the famous: saints and sinners,
Poets and artists, kings and queens,
Old stars and hopeful beginners,
I've been where no-one's been before,
Learned secrets from writers and cooks
All with one library ticket
To the wonderful world of books.

THE UMBRELLA-MAKER'S DAUGHTER

In 1832 Mary Tullis and her father, the umbrella-maker, arrive from Glasgow to make a new life in the Scottish town of Dyplin. It will be a hard year for the townsfolk: cholera comes, so do the resurrectionists stealing bodies from their graves. The new young minister is profoundly tested as he falls under the spell of the attractive newcomer. Meg Annan, of the stained reputation, is also in love. But much of the love—and the hate—is misplaced, culminating in the May Burning, in which the tensions of the community are tragically released.

JANET CAIRD

The Umbrella-Maker's Daughter

Complete and Unabridged

ULVERSCROFT
Leicester

First published 1980 by
Macmillan London Limited

First Large Print Edition
published April 1983
by arrangement with
Macmillan Ltd., London
and
St. Martin's Press, Inc.
New York

British Library CIP Data

Caird, Janet
  The umbrella-maker's daughter. — Large
  print ed.
  (Ulverscroft large print series: general
   fiction)
  I. Title
  823'.914[F]   PR6053.A36

  ISBN 0-7089-0943-4

Published by
F. A. Thorpe (Publishing) Ltd.
Anstey, Leicestershire

Printed and Bound in Great Britain by
T. J. Press (Padstow) Ltd., Padstow, Cornwall

To
MARK, KATY and ANNA

1

AS the gig turned the corner, they met the procession head-on, just as the band struck up afresh. The horse shied and Macpherson pulled it to the side of the road, jumped down and held its head, making soothing noises to it, while casting a sardonic eye at the marchers. His passengers, the man in front, the girl behind, stared down wonderingly at the band and the tramping men and the banners. The banners had been hastily constructed: one or two already had corners flapping wildly in the breeze and, as they bellied out and in like sails on a crazy ship, they distorted the noble sentiments they carried. "LIBERTY, EQLTY, FRATNITY", said one; "BRITONS EVER NEVER SLAVES", said another; "RFORM", said a third; but the last tautly and triumphantly announced: "1832 Year of Glory" to two disgruntled pipers bringing up the rear. Everyone else was smiling and cheerful and greeting the gig with waving caps and shouts of, "it's a wonderful day". Macpherson returned a reluctant nod of the head. The man in the front of the gig waved back, the girl did no more than lift a timid hand, even though they raised a cheer "for the lassie".

When the road was clear, Macpherson set the gig going once more.

1

"A lot of havers," he said. "Them and their procession! I tell you, Mr. Tullis, they've gone daft over reform in Dyplin."

"You're not in favour yourself?" said Tullis.

"I'm neither one nor the other. It doesna affect me, for I'm no more qualified tae vote noo than afore. But the way they're going on, you'd think Paradise on earth was roon' the corner. Ye'll no be a political man yersel?"

"Not really. If I can make a living, and have some comfort by my own exertions, I'm quite pleased."

"Aye, aye, just so. Ye'll be an umbrella-maker? Mistress Campbell at the Knowe said her new neebor was an umbrella-maker."

"Yes, that's me."

"Frae Glasgow?"

"Yes."

"I'd hae thocht ye'd mak mair money frae umbrellas in Glasgow than Dyplin; it's no' a vera big place."

"I hope I'll make a living. And I felt it was better to move from Glasgow; for health reasons."

"Health reasons. M'hm. Yir chest, nae doot. They tell me the air in Glasgow's no fit tae breathe."

"It is certainly clearer here."

"Aye. It's a braw bit o' the country. It's a pity the lassie has tae sit wi' her back tae us, fur in a meenit we'll hae a fine view afore us. See! The hale valley, and the hills beyond. Turn ye roon, lassie, and tak a look."

2

He pulled the horse to a halt, and Mary Tullis turned to look. They were driving down a low ridge to the south of a broad valley, chequered with fields, through which a little river meandered. On the far side rose a range of steep, rounded hills, honey-coloured, Mary thought, over which moved the blue shadows of the light, high clouds. Woodlands were green along the foot of the slope; and almost opposite them, she could see the ruin of a medieval keep in a fold of the hills; below it, a huddle of red-tiled roofs ran up to the end of a road that rose into the heights. Macpherson seemed disappointed by her lack of reaction.

"Is it no a bonny scene?" he asked, but all she said was:

"Very bonny."

He gave a little shrug of his shoulders and then pointed with his whip.

"Yon's Dyplin. An' if ye look close, ye can see your hoose—thon white yin up at the top o' the hill."

Mary looked eagerly, and saw a white cottage at the top of the cluster of houses.

"I see it," she said. And then, "I wish we could fly to it, right over the valley."

Macpherson was amused. "Aweel, ye canna. We'll juist hae tae tak' the usual way—doon the Braes, past the bleachings and up tae the turnpike."

"That's what I mean," said Mary. "I'd like to miss the houses and people and go straight there, near the hills."

"That's nae wey for a bonny lass tae talk! Ye should be eager tae meet the fowk. That there's the auld toon, of course. Doon below, on the level, there's whit they ca' the new toon—big braw hooses built maistly fur the teachers at the schule. Ye'll hae heard tell o' oor braw new schule?"

"I have," said David Tullis, as they moved on.

"Aye. Ye'll be hoping tae dae some tred wi' yir umberellies wi' they fowk. But umberellies is no' the things fowk buy every day. Ye'll hae tae sell an awfu' lot."

His quick inquisitive eyes slid round to David Tullis and back. For all his gentleness, David was a shrewd businessman. "I think I'll find sufficient custom," he said, mildly. "Of course, I'll be wanting to go round the countryside making myself known, and for that, Mr. Macpherson, I hope I shall be able to call on the services of your gig."

"Oh aye, certainly, certainly," and Macpherson lapsed into silence and concentrated on driving.

The horse took the downward slope at a walking pace and, when they reached the valley floor, resumed a reluctant clumping trot, weary after the long drive from the coach halt at Inverforth. They came to the flat grasslands by the river and saw acres of ground covered with great lengths of linen pegged down on the grass to whiten in the sun and wind. They rippled under the moving air and shadows passed up and down the whiteness. Macpherson indicated the fields with a jerk of his whip.

4

"The bleach-field. Ane o' the maist modern in the country, they say. Nooadays some o' the whitening's done wi' a chemical—gey smelly stuff tae, but the linen still hes tae be pit oot in the sun. It's a shair sign o' summer here when ye see the cloth bein' pit oot on the grass."

They came to the turnpike road that ran along the valley to Kinross and beyond. Here they saw the "braw hooses" Macpherson had mentioned, comely buildings of grey sandstone. The street was empty; they saw only one woman. Macpherson explained: "A' the men are awa' in the procession; and the weemen are busy ben the hoose."

Presently they turned off the main road and trotted up the side of the burn, which ran straight through the village and was crossed by three bridges. At the top bridge, beside a small woollen-mill, they had to get down from the gig, for the climb up to their house was steep, and the horse tired. A few yards up, the road forked in front of a low red sandstone cottage—"the Red Hoose", said Macpherson; they took the left-hand street and climbed up steep cobbles to their cottage, past neat two-storied white-harled houses, separated from the pavement by a foot or two of garden, where roses climbed over the walls. Macpherson pointed out their attractiveness.

"Thir's no many places roon aboot wi' as mony braw stane hooses as here. We hivna mair nor twa turf-hooses left in Dyplin, barring the miners' hooses, and they'll no be here lang. And here we

5

are, at yir hoose. They tell me yir furniture's already come by the carter, sae when I've lifted doon yir box here, I'll say guid-day."

While her father and Macpherson dealt with the box, Mary opened the door and went into the house. It stood on a terrace, built to counteract the slope, with a little garden in front. Inside the door there was a small hall, with a cupboard opening off it. She went into the room on the right. It was the kitchen, with a window back and front. Someone had lit a welcoming fire, and on the iron swee above the flames an iron kettle was gently swinging. In the window on the north side, looking out to the hills, was a sink with a pump, a sight to rejoice Mary's heart. In Glasgow, comfortable though their flat above the shop and workroom had been, the water had had to be fetched from the pump in the back yard. She was fingering the pump when her father came in.

"Well, Mary, what do you think of it? You see, indoor water. There is a good well in the garden."

"This is a good room. Look at the hills out there! Think of working at the sink and seeing that! It's wonderful."

"I thought you'd like it. Come, I'll show you the rest of the house."

The room to the left of the front door was as big as the kitchen, but less bright, not having the through windows. A door opened from the rear wall into a small room which had been added at some time, and was little more than a closet.

6

"This will be my office," said David Tullis. "It will hold my desk and chair and a set of shelves."

"And where will you work?"

"Didn't you see from the kitchen the out-house in the garden? Come, I'll show you."

They went back through the kitchen and out the back door. The garden, long and narrow, stretched about fifty yards from the house, ending in a low stone dyke, and separated on the left side from the next garden by a high hedge, and on the right by a dyke from a grassy field. Against this dyke stood a low stone out-building. It held a carpenter's bench, some planks, and had a fireplace and a good wooden floor. "It will be ideal for the work," said David. "It was a joiner's shop once." He pointed to a neat little wooden shed beside the hedge. "And that is the closet. A good earth closet, like the one in our garden when I was a child."

Mary wasn't listening. She was looking up to the hills, and when her father touched her arm she said, "Father, I can't believe that we are to live here. It's Paradise. It's what I used to dream about. It's . . ."

He shook his head. "Lassie, lassie, no place is Paradise. Dinna begin with too high expectations. It's people, not hills, that make a place. Now, what about something tae eat?"

But when they went back to the kitchen, they found a woman putting a lump of coal on the fire. She turned when they entered and said, "I saw you coming, and came to bid you welcome."

"That was kind," said David Tullis. "Mary, this

7

is Mrs. Campbell, our neighbour. I told you how she had undertaken to see to the placing of the furniture when the wagon delivered it."

"I hope it's to your liking," said Mrs. Campbell, as she and Mary shook hands. "It's no easy to place anither body's gear. I put it where I thocht it looked best to myself."

Mary looked round vaguely, but said gratefully, "It looks very nice. Thank you, Mrs. Campbell."

"And I've a cup of tea and a scone ready for you next door, if ye'd care to come in. Unless you'd like something stronger than tea, Mr. Tullis."

"No, thank you. Tea will be most acceptable, won't it, Mary?"—for he could read her face, and knew that if he didn't speak quickly she would utter an offending refusal.

Mrs. Campbell's house was very similar to the Tullis's. Her kitchen was not so large, space being taken up by the box bed built into the wall opposite the fire.

"As it's no a formal meal, I've just set it in the kitchen," she said, and then proceeded to give them scones hot from the girdle, butter, jam, and a boiled egg. "Seeing ye're just off a journey." She and David talked of the weather, the state of the roads, the prices of food—potatoes at a shilling a bushel, and butter elevenpence a pound. Mary should have shown interest at this point, especially as Mrs. Campbell was bent on recommending the best places to buy eggs, chickens, butter, but it was left to David to take it all in—a fact which didn't escape

Mrs. Campbell's shrewd and appraising eye.

"Thon lassie's no' much of a housekeeper, I'm thinking," she confided to John Campbell later that evening. "It came out she's been at a braw school for young ladies in Glasgow and she's right well-spoken. I can see he's no just depending on his umbrellas for a living. Nice enough folk—but there's something there!"

"Havers," said John comfortably. "Why should a bonny lass be wanting to discuss the price of eggs and tatties? Oh aye, I ken she's bonny. I saw her when the procession passed Macpherson's gig. Why not tell her about the dancing on the Knowe tonight? That's more in her line."

For the triumphant Reformists, having marched bravely round the parish, were to round off the celebrations with a torchlit dance on the Knowe—a little green plateau just above the west bank of the burn, where all the celebratory bonfires and merry-making of Dyplin took place.

"I'll go in and ask them myself to come," he said. "Get your work done quickly, Alison, for we want to be there at the start."

"Och, I'm past dancing," said Alison, "but I'd like tae see it. It's a fine night for it, now the wind's gone."

She busied herself in the house, while John, wearied with his marching, settled down for a snooze by the window. He ran a prosperous joiner and undertaker's business; by nature a jovial extrovert, he could, when professionally necessary, adopt an air of solemn awareness of the fleetingness and vanity of life. His father, when he had carried on the business, had occupied a flat above the workshop, but Alison had strongly objected to living "above the coffins". So she and John lived away from his place of business, which was at the foot of the village. They had no children, but their regret at this had passed, and Alison cherished and spoiled her John.

While Alison was getting ready to go to the Knowe, John went next door to invite their new neighbours to come with them, but was soon back without them.

"Mr. Tullis says they're too tired, and mebbe he's right, though it would have been a good way for them tae meet the folk."

"What about the lassie?"

"I don't know. She didna say a word. She's vera quiet. But bonny; aye, bonny."

"Bonny," said Alison a trifle tartly, "is as bonny does. Are we going to that dance or are we not?"

"I'm ready." And they went.

Later that evening, Mary and her father sat by the fire while the long summer twilight drained from the room. She stared into the embers, her chin on her hand, her dark eyes dreamy and lost. David spoke:

"Mary, can you be happy here?"

She did not answer at once. Then, slowly, "Perhaps. I don't know. Tonight I can't help

10

wishing—I don't always feel like it—but tonight I can't help wishing he had lived."

Tears were running down her cheeks, and it tore his heart.

"Oh, Mary, Mary—it was for the best. Try to believe it. It was for the best. Look. We have come away. You can begin again. Mary, I did all this for you."

"I know. This will pass. I don't cry so often now. It will pass."

She rose to her feet. "I think I'll go out for a little. Did you know there was a gate in our back wall? I'll go up towards the hill. Not for long, I promise."

She put a shawl round her shoulders, and went out by the back door. As she opened it, she heard the faint music from the Knowe, and from the garden she saw the glow of the torches. Climbing up through the meadow beyond the wall, she came to a little knoll and, standing on it, she looked down on the dance: a ring of blazing light, and people gathered round watching the dancers doing a reel, with a noise of careless voices and music. Looking down on it all, she had the old familiar feeling she had known as far back as memory stretched; of wanting to be part of it all, and knowing she was not and would never be . . . not unless someone came and took her by the hand and said, "Join us". Suppose one of the young men whirling round in the reel down there were to dash through the burn, and bound up the slope, and catch her by the hands

11

and pull her down with him and over the water and up to the lights and the music . . .

Only one or two of the dancers noticed on the skyline the distant figure of the umbrella-maker's daughter.

2

ALISON CAMPBELL'S forebodings as to Mary's housekeeping capacities did not seem to be justified. Casting a monitorial glance through the hedge, Alison could see washing being hung out just as it should be and rugs being shaken; and she could smell good soup cooking. Mary did show herself appropriately grateful for advice on shopping and even accepted an offer from Alison to accompany her round the shops. For the most part, these were situated in a little square halfway up the hill where the street forked at the Red House. Here were the butcher, the grocer, the dry-salter and, a little way along the street running to the south, the baker's; the shop in front, the bake-house behind and always the warm smell of baking. As they walked down the cobbles to the square, Alison gave brief sketches of the owners.

"Ye have tae watch Mrs. Walker here," (as they approached the grocer's). "He's all right, but she's no above putting a thumb on the scales. She's from Dunfermline; her sister married a teacher at the New School here and she fairly fancies herself. Their father died of drink, poor man . . . Good morning, Mrs. Walker. This is my new neighbour, Miss Tullis. I'm just showing her the shops. . . ."

Between the Walkers' shop and Johnston the

butcher, Mary learned that Mr. Johnston was a nice man, but prone to bouts of drinking and that Mrs. Johnston really ran the business. Miss McArdle, who kept the dry-salter's where Mary bought candles, left a spinster when her young man was trampled by a runaway horse, was "an ill-tongued besom"; but Peter Robertson, the baker, was in every way estimable and so was his wife.

"All the bakers I've kent," said Alison, "have been good folk. Mebbe it's something to do with their work—making good things for folk tae eat. Mind you," (feeling perhaps that she was painting an over-rosy picture), "they say there's mair mice than there should be in the bake-house, but whit's a few mice?"

In the baker's shop a pleasant bright-eyed girl, wearing a spotless starched apron, served them. "Mrs. Robertson's niece, and a real nice girl," whispered Alison, before voicing aloud polite enquiries after the health of the Robertson family.

As they made their way back up the hill, Mary said, "Does everyone know everything about everybody in Dyplin?"

"Just about," said Alison. "I expect it's the same in all small places. I found it strange at first—I come from Perth—but you get used to it. But I'll tell you one thing: if you want to keep anything to yourself here, do not tell anyone at all. My John taught me that. He belongs here, and he knows. Especially money. Never tell a soul about your money.

Naebody here kens a thing aboot John's affairs; and never will."

She was silent for a minute and then said, "There's another side tae it. Once ye're accepted, folks are kind and helpful here. But for all that, unless ye're born here, ye're aye an incomer. Like masel, though I've lived here fifteen years. . . ."

"But suppose you weren't 'accepted'?"

"Och, everyone is, sooner or later. Weel, almost everybody. I mind . . ."

"Yes?"

"Och, a while back, a man and wife came—he was a doctor; from England. But it wasn't that—they were different. She was musical, and had a braw piano, and he used tae look for fossils—mebbe now it would be all right, with the New School: some o' the teachers there are no' just ordinary—but the doctor and his wife were aye outside things: right tae the end she would ca' Dyplin 'Dieplin', instead o' 'Diplin', and it pit folk's backs up. She used tae be 'at home' once a month and naebody went. I was sorry for her. Aweel, after a couple of years they went. Frozen out, ye could say." She glanced at Mary's still face and downcast eyes. "But maistly they like new folk coming."

When they parted at the gate, Alison went in, faintly uneasy, not knowing why. Mary, having put her basket on the table in her kitchen, moved to the window and stood looking up to the hills, thinking of the poor woman who played the piano and had been so surely rejected. After a few minutes she

15

gave a shrug of the shoulders and went about her chores.

Soon her father came in and they sat down to their midday meal. Mary could be a more than adequate cook, and David, pushing his plate aside, said: "That was a good dish, lass. How have you spent the morning?"

"I went to the shops with Mrs. Campbell."

Something in her voice made him glance at her, and the anxious expression which was habitual with him now when he was with her, returned. But he said nothing.

"They're very inquisitive, the people here." She was clearing the dishes as she spoke. "Everyone knows everything about everybody. . . ."

David pushed back his chair. "It's always like that in a small place. I remember in Kilreggan when I was a boy. . . . When I went to my apprenticeship in Glasgow I realized what a relief it was to be one of the crowd, and not spied on by everyone. But it's not a thing to worry over, Mary. Keep a close tongue in your head, be pleasant—and give nothing away." He laid a hand over hers. "It's all right, lass. Nobody need know."

She gave a faint smile and said, "When will the rest of the gear be here?"

"Tuesday or Wednesday next week. Then I'll get working. I've two or three orders already—I went down to the New School today and made myself known. I think all will go well, Mary."

But Mary was washing dishes and didn't answer.

16

That afternoon, while her father was busy setting his workshop to rights, she set out to climb the hill behind the house, a low hill, an outcrop of the main range, called, as she had learned from Alison, Gloom Hill. Soon she had reached and clambered over the drystane dyke bordering the field, and was out in the dry tawny grass of the hillside. As she climbed, the air grew keener and the breeze stronger, and her spirits lifted in response. When she was half-way up, she saw the figure of a woman on the crest of the hill, her skirts flapping, her shawl held tight across her shoulders. She was making her way down the slope at right angles to Mary, to join the road to the castle, skirting the hill to the west. She passed close enough for Mary to see her bright red hair blown and dishevelled in the wind. She looked neither to right nor left, and when she reached the road, walked a few yards down towards the village, and then went into a small poor cottage with an untidy garden where straggly stalks of kale grew.

Mary had stopped climbing to watch, and now went on, wondering. No doubt Alison would be able to tell her all about the woman, and she frowned, uneasy again at the thought of the ceaseless monitoring by the community. But only for a moment. As she climbed, the sky grew larger, the wind more exciting, and when she reached the crest and turned to look down, she forgot everything in the delight of what she saw. Below her, Dyplin: the red and grey roofs running down to the burn: and beyond the mass of the New School, a low grey building set in a green field, with young trees marking the perimeter. Beyond, the river flowing west, and beyond that the ground rising to the Braes—and then fields and woods blending in the distance, with a glint of water that must be the Firth; and, far away, blue hills rippling along the horizon. Eastwards, the woods and hills closed the view, but westwards she could look down the whole rampart of the hills, to the low ridge above Stirling, and see the smudge of distant smoke that must be Inverforth. She had never seen anything like it before. Going down to Greenock to visit cousins, she had seen the Highland hills across the water of the Clyde estuary, but she had never before looked from a hilltop on the world below. Twice a year, she had gone into Ayrshire, to her uncle's farm in the village where her father had been born, and had looked on these holidays as times of delight, away from the noise and crowds of Glasgow, where she had been born and grown up. Not that she disliked Glasgow or her home—but in Ayrshire, she felt a quickening of the senses, a lightness of heart, and most of the verses she wrote were rooted in that countryside. Now it was as if what she'd felt in Ayrshire were multiplied a hundred times, offering her a great cup of delight—and she sat on the turf with her hands clasped round her knees and her eyes on the view, rapt, beyond thought.

So it was that she was totally unaware of the

approach of the man who came striding up over the hill from the little glen beyond, his footsteps muffled by the tussocky wind-flattened grass. When he spoke, she jumped, her vision shattered and, looking up with startled eyes, saw Daniel Rutherford for the first time.

A tall man, his dark-red hair, flecked with grey, blown in the wind; a pointed beard, heavy eyebrows and dark, almost black, eyes. He was looking down at her almost with amusement and, as she scrambled to her feet, he put out a hand to help her. But she ignored it, and he said, "I'm sorry if I startled you. You were admiring the view?"

And when she didn't answer, he said:

"I think I know who you are: the umbrella-maker's daughter."

Surprise made her speak. "How did . . . ?"

"I saw you in the gig on the day of the procession. Besides, everyone knows everyone here."

"I don't know you."

"Ah. Pardon me. I am Daniel Rutherford, teacher of infants at the New School."

She made as if to leave him, and he smiled and said:

"Don't run away, I won't hurt you. Besides, you're in sight of your home down there."

His voice was kind, interested, reassuring, and as she turned towards him, he went on:

"Do you think you will like living here?"

Mary looked back over the valley. "Oh yes. It is very beautiful, and peaceful, and quiet."

19

He smiled. "Ah, but appearances can be deceitful. Dyplin has known terror in its time. You can just see the top of the castle tower back there; it was burned down by Montrose in the wars of the seventeenth century—and they not only burnt the castle, but every house in the village except one, and that was the inn. And look there, down in the valley, that clump of trees—that hides the Martyr's Bridge—and the man who put it up in the sixteenth century was burned at the stake in St. Andrews as a heretic. . . ."

"You know a lot about this place."

"It is my hobby. Come, I'll show you something. Over here."

She followed him over the grass to a place where the turf was worn and pebbly. On the ground were three pieces of rock, as if a boulder had been split, linked into a triangle by three short lengths of thick iron chain.

"There," he said, "that marks the place where they burned a witch in the eighteenth century. Can't you see it? The smoke and the flames, and the good people of Dyplin looking up at the hill."

Startled and shaken, she whispered, "It's horrible, horrible. I know about these witches; poor, simple, old, daft women; there was one in a close near us in Glasgow, and the children used to shout 'witch' at her. It was wicked, wicked."

"It was indeed. But the witch they burned here was young and bonny, not old and simple. We have the full report of her trial; she 'sang and danced on the Sabbath', among other things, and wore 'claes that were ower gliskin for her station'. In other words, she was different; and they destroyed her."

He spoke with detachment, telling facts of antiquarian interest, tapping the stones with his stick as he did so. But Mary interrupted him with a cry:

"I must go back, I must indeed!" and, picking up her skirts, she fled downhill to the house.

He watched her go, surprised and puzzled: a strange girl, but bonny. Her eyes, widening in horrified interest at his story, had seemed to fill her face; and the wind had blown her dark hair entrancingly across her cheeks, glowing from the strong air. . . . He made his way down to the road, thinking of her.

Mary ran like a deer down to the wall, her heart thudding, full of strange terror that had seized her at the tale of the burning. Once off the hill, and in the garden, she felt calmer. Her father was in the shed, and called to her:

"You had a good walk, Mary."

"Yes. You can see the whole countryside up there. And I met the infant school master. He knew who I was. He was telling me something of the history of the place. Do you know—" for all she could do, her voice changed and trembled—"they once burned a witch up there? A young lassie."

"Dear, dear. Aye, they got up to bad things in the auld days. Lassie," he looked at her, "ye're not crying for her? It was long, long ago."

21

"I know. It was just—oh, you know how I get upset about things like that."

"Ach, ye'll never learn. Keep your tears for when they're needed—and Mary, I could do with a cup of tea."

But the story haunted her. That night she tried to make verses about it, but they wouldn't come.

The faint smell from the wick when she blew out her candle mingled with her sleep, so that she dreamt confusedly of fire and smoke.

22

3

TWO days later, Mary and David made their first public appearance before Dyplin, at the kirk. They went with John and Alison Campbell, not altogether to Alison's satisfaction. But John insisted. "They'll no' ken where tae sit, and if they land in the wrang pew alongside some folks, they'll be glowered at and fairly frozen out." So on Sunday morning, he and David in their Sabbath black clothes and tile hats preceded Alison and Mary down the hill to the kirk. Alison was in dark grey with a sober black straw bonnet. Mary, to Alison's relief, was also in grey, albeit of a lighter shade, and the shawl over her shoulders was black, though it had a border of brilliantly embroidered flowers; but her bonnet was light straw, threaded and tied under her cheek with a brilliant green ribbon and with a cluster of pink roses under the brim: "unseemly", was the word that came to Alison's mind. But she said nothing, and she and Mary walked behind the two men in decent silence.

Dyplin kirk stood on rising ground on the east side of the burn. It had been built on the site of an older church, and in the churchyard to the south of it old table-stones stood arthritically and unevenly on squat, bandy legs. From the little bell-tower on the west gable the bell clanked purposefully as the

Campbells and Tullises made their way downhill. On the way, they overtook others, and exchanged silent nods of the head, and well-drilled liftings of tile hats. Worshippers approaching from the west climbed up from the road by the burn, past the little session-house with its two small windows keeping a sharp look-out on the graveyard. The Campbells and Tullises took the path from the east that led past the high wall bordering the Manse garden to the front of the church. It was a glorious morning, the sun shining from a cloudless sky, the hills honey-coloured, the land to the south shimmering. To Mary, used to the sombre Glasgow Sabbath, with the awesome hush in the streets, the stillness of the heavy stone houses in their Sabbath seclusion, it was intoxicating. She forgot the silent dark figures moving among the tombstones and, turning to Alison, said, too loudly and gaily:

"Is it not a most beautiful day?"

Alison's reply was a tightening of the lips. One did not discuss frivolities like the weather on the way to the Lord's House—one did not discuss anything—not if one was aware of the proprieties. Mary flushed a little and was silent. They were now at the church. It was set east and west, and in the south wall there were three doors: the centre one was the Minister's door and led directly to the pulpit steps. John Campbell led the way through the east door to the pew in the corner under the gallery, opened the door, and stood aside to let Mary go in first, next her father, then Alison and then himself. The tile-hats were unostentatiously placed under the narrow wooden seat, the heads bowed for a moment's prayer, and then they sat upright and silent, eyes fixed in the approved manner on the back of the pew in front. But Dyplin had long since perfected the art of seeing a lot, even with lids lowered. By the time the minister had climbed up from his door to the pulpit it had been established among the men that Mary was a very bonny lass, with long dark lashes and beautiful hair and a clear, warm skin, and the women had satisfied themselves that though "no' bad looking", she thought herself a cut above other folk (the bonnet and embroidered shawl). Curiosity thus so far satisfied, they addressed themselves to the business of worship.

The Reverend Matthew Glendinning was young, in his first charge, and still an idealist. Every Sunday, when he looked down from his pulpit on the tight-packed congregation (for the church was really too small for the growing town), he felt a genuine glow of love for them—his people, the family of God. He had once tried to express something of this to his mother, who kept house for him in the manse, but her reply had been, "Don't forget they're not always in the kirk, Mattha." And it was true, of course, that, looking down at the Johnston pew, with Willie Johnston and his wife and the three children, immaculate in dress and deportment, it was really hard to remember that he himself had piloted Johnston home only three days ago, having found him wandering through the Manse shrubbery in a state of happy inebriation. But perhaps when they came into the church, they did, for a time, become a family of God, within the secluding walls of the building, in front of the Table—he was rather ashamed of this feeling, for it was rank bad theology to ascribe to stone and mortar a mediation of grace. Matthew knew his theology, but was uncomfortably aware that his heart all too easily betrayed his theological head. He had not that sense of brooding and surrounding sin with which his fellow members of Presbytery seemed endowed: and was aware they knew it. But, on this sunny morning, with the light from the windows on either side of him, he found it hard to be condemnatory and gloomy. Once the opening psalm, with the resonant help of Joseph Harvey, beadle and precentor, was safely launched, he looked round as he always did, to see who were and who were not present, for Matthew Glendinning was well acquainted with his congregation. All the regulars were there, including Daniel Rutherford, his four children and his small, plump, sharp-eyed sister who kept house for him. Matthew's charitable glow dimmed a little as his eyes flickered over the tight, rounded cheeks, the pursed mouth. Her eyes were on the psalter, but he knew they were sharp and small. Still, she was a good housekeeper, ran her brother's house well and kept the children neat as new pins. Daniel Rutherford he scarcely knew, in spite of frequent meetings and much talk. A

26

strange man, always wary. But losing his wife so suddenly and grievously—drowned in the burn one winter spate—would make a man withdrawn. Matthew's mother had a way of pursing her lips when Daniel's name was mentioned that indicated disapproval of some kind—but she refused to be drawn on the subject . . . for Mrs. Glendinning had made it a rule she would carry no gossip from the town to the Minister's study. Matthew's eyes moved now, noting absences, noting presences and, finally, came to rest where a shaft of sunlight reached under the gallery and played on Mary's green bonnet ribbon and embroidered shawl.

More than one noticed how his glance lingered and, by the time the psalm was finished, and though he did not look that way again, the whisperers were already poised, when time and place permitted, to murmur that the Minister seemed fair taken on with the umbrella-maker's daughter.

Matthew's sermon was on the text, "Judge not that ye be not judged", and he preached with eloquence, but only for thirty-five minutes, as Joseph Harvey noted with mild disapproval. Forty minutes sermon time, for Joseph, was the minimum permitted: forty-five was better. He sometimes wondered if the Minister was quite up to his position—not but what the sermon had been good enough, well argued, not lacking in sharp and pointed admonitions, very apt to the congregation, for Joseph, born and bred in Dyplin, knew it to the core. The trouble was, did the Minister know just how apt it was? That was one thing about old Dr. Gillies—fond of the bottle he might be, tyrannical he might be, but he knew his flock, and when on form, could summon hell-fire and damnation into the kirk with a thunderous roar of his voice. Still, Glendinning was a good young man, and doubtless would learn: "and I hope the learning'll no' be ower hard," thought Joseph, standing with bowed head for the Benediction.

Once Matthew had left the pulpit and gone out of his door, the congregation spilled out into the churchyard, and there neatly divided itself—the boarders and teachers from the New School, Dr. Munro, Mr. Paterson the banker's family and one or two others making their way down the west path, and ultimately to their fine new houses round the school and along the turnpike road. The rest, now relaxed and ready to talk, made their way past the Manse. Alison and John Campbell met up with Peter Robertson and his wife and three children, and Annie Young, Mrs. Robertson's niece. There were introductions and Mary and Annie walked up the road together. Annie was fair, blue-eyed and cheerful.

"Will you like living here?" she asked.

"I think so," said Mary. "It is a very beautiful place."

"Och aye, in this weather. But come the autumn, it rains and rains, and the clouds come down and blot out the hills. It's no sae nice then. Will you not miss Glasgow, and the people, and the shops?"

"I'll not miss Glasgow." The emphasis in her voice made Annie look at her.

"I was only there once and I liked it fine."

"It rains there too, and the streets are wet and muddy, and the traffic splashes you."

"But there'll be more to do there. It's very quiet here."

"I like quiet."

Annie, feeling snubbed, said no more, and the two girls walked in silence to the parting of the ways.

Back in the house, David took off his black frockcoat, now oppressively warm, hung it carefully over the back of a chair, and said, "They seem nice enough folk in Dyplin. We should be all right here. Eh, Mary?"

She caught, as always, the undercurrent of anxiety in his voice, and wished she could reassure him. But the need for truth was too great. "I don't know, Father. If not, it'll be my own fault, no doubt."

She paused as she lifted the pot of potatoes to hang on the swee above the fire. "I find it hard to get to know people, to be friendly . . . that Annie Young—she was being friendly, and I put her off. Why?"

"You don't have to be friends with everyone."

"I know that. It's just—they all seem to have a place in things, and to be pleased with it."

"And you're not?"

29

"No. You know me, Father. You have your trade that you like and make a living at. I keep your house—and it's not enough. But other girls seem to find that all right. So it's something in me—and it makes me feel I don't belong."

"But you won't always be keeping house for me. If it pleases Providence, you'll marry, and have children. . . ."

She put out a hand. "Don't, Father—don't."

"But we're here to make a fresh start, Mary. It's all in the past. Don't cut yourself off from people." He took her hand and held it for a moment.

"I'll try not to." She shivered suddenly. "Unless they cut me off. . . . When did you say the rest of the gear was coming?"

"Tuesday, or perhaps Wednesday."

"Good. I'm missing the books."

"And I want to start work."

On Tuesday morning the cart, hauled up the hill by two horses, stopped at the Tullises' door. Alison, from a strategic position at a window, where she could peer out over the white lace screen and herself be invisible, watched wide-eyed as the bundles of long delicate canes, the thicker sticks for handles, the bales of black cotton and silk and delicate coloured sunshade materials were carried in, as well as chests of goodness knows what, and vices and turners and tools beyond her recognition. Last of all two small book-cases and two boxes were lifted in. In due time, the driver, who had helped with the unloading while his horses munched at their nose bags, came out with a bucket of water, gave them a drink, then climbed onto the driving seat and drove away. Alison waited for a decent interval, picked a bunch of lavender from the bush beside the rhubarb patch in her back garden, and went round to the Tullises' door. Mary opened it to her, flushed and excited, looking, as Alison later said to John, more alive than she'd seen her before.

"I brought some lavender," said Alison. "But I see you're busy."

"Yes, but come in just the same. The books have come!"

She led Alison into the parlour on the left. To the oval table in the centre of the room, the six upright chairs and the two upholstered fireside chairs, the glass-fronted cupboard with the best china in it and the little davenport desk, had been added two book-cases—one under the window, one beside the fire. In front of and on top of one, books had been hastily stacked, and on the floor was a box. Mary flung back the lid. "There," she said, "there's the rest of them," and she looked with pride on the books neatly packed inside.

Alison had never seen so many books at once in a private house, outside old Dr. Gillies's study, where they were to be expected. "Your father must spend an awful lot of his time reading," she said.

Mary shook her head. "They're my books, most of them." And, smiling at Alison's astonishment, she said, "Does that surprise you?"

31

Alison was startled into frankness. "Yes. Women don't usually have time to read—not women like us. Maybe Mrs. Innes at Griffton—but she's gentry."

"Well, I'm not gentry." The lid of the box clicked shut, a little louder than necessary. "But she's been kind to me," thought Mary, "I mustn't be angry." And leading the way to the little room that opened off the parlour, she said, "Would you like to look at these?"

The bales of material were neatly stacked on a table, and Alison fingered and admired. A sprigged rose cotton took her fancy. "I'd fine like a parasol made of that—but och, when would I need a parasol here?"

"It's mostly the gentry buys them," said Mary, not altogether without malice.

Alison looked at her with a half-frown and then smiled. "Aye. I deserved that, lassie. You read your books as much as you like, but I'll not bother with a parasol." She looked round. "I had no idea that all this was part of umbrella-making."

"It's a very skilled trade," said Mary, "and my father is a master at it."

"Well, well," and Alison departed, full of thought.

"She's a nice enough lass, but she's a good conceit of herself, I'm thinking," she confided to John over their tea that night. "Her and her books! If she was doing all her work richt, she wouldn't have time tae read."

"Havers," said John. "If you didna spend

as much time on knitting an a' that . . ."

"And where would you get socks if I didna?"

"Where does David Tullis get socks?"

"Mary knits them. I've seen her knitting up the garden."

"Aweel then. If her father gets his socks all right, and she seems tae feed him well enough, and the house is aye clean when I've stopped by, why should she no' read?"

"It's just—it's just . . ."

"It's just this, Alison—the women canna bide another wumman no' being just the same as themselves. Nae room for difference or change. If the women had had onything tae dae wi' it, we'd never have had the Reform Bill. . . ."

"Mercy on us, how have we got to the Reform Bill?"

"I'm just saying, men are mair tolerant than women. Look at Sandy Craig up at Grey Wisp farm. They say he's got hundreds of books thonder. Naebody thinks he's less o' a sheep farmer for that."

"Oh aye, the men are very tolerant—especially when it's a braw lass in question. But I tell you this, John Campbell, once the men do turn against a body, they're far mair harsh than women."

"Aye weel, mebbe you're richt. I'll take another scone, Alison, they're extra guid the day."

Alison, fully aware she was being mollified, passed the plate of scones and the subject was dropped.

4

FOR a week or so, Mary and David were the subject of Dyplin's careful scrutiny. David was soon summed up. He hired Macpherson and his gig to drive him round the village and the countryside, leaving business cards and gathering orders. It was evident he was a good businessman, and in all probability a good craftsman. The shrewder inhabitants of Dyplin agreed that he was not entirely dependent on umbrella making for a living, and in this they were right. David owned more than one snug property in Glasgow, and was partner in two profitable little businesses, the one dealing in leather goods and the other in flour-milling. As far as money was concerned, he need not have made umbrellas at all. But he loved his craft, and could not have lived in idleness.

Mary was less easily categorized than her father. It was very soon clear that she was no spendthrift. But then, neither was she mean; and she was always ready to spend more for better quality. But where David was easy and genuinely friendly towards all he met, Mary had a certain aloofness. Her politeness—and she was always perfectly polite—had a chilling quality. Annie Young said bluntly that she was a "stuck-up thing". She said it to young Hugh Walker, who had seen her talking to Mary after church, and who made a special visit to Peter Robertson's baker's shop to ask Annie about Mary, and then annoyed Annie by saying she was jealous of Mary's fine bonnet.

"Jealous? Me?" Annie tossed her head. "Why should I be jealous? I dinna need a fancy hat wi' wee pink roses tae hae the lads look at me."

Hugh laughed and went away. Next day he waited for Mary to come out of his father's shop, and offered to carry her basket for her, but was coolly and courteously told it was quite unnecessary. Annie, who had seen this manoeuvre from her place behind the bakery counter, met him later.

"You didna get very far wi' the umbrella-maker's daughter, Hugh."

He laughed. "You were right, Annie. Come, let's be friends again."

So Mary, it was decided, thought herself a cut above the rest of the world; in which case, the world of Dyplin was happy to leave her alone.

Not that Mary was even aware of being left alone. She was for the moment content with her books, with the countryside so close at hand. She would not have called herself happy, but neither was she unhappy.

One late afternoon, there was a knock at the Tullises' front door. It was Daniel Rutherford, come, he said, to see about having an umbrella made. Mary asked him into the parlour.

"If you will wait here, I'll get my father. He is in his workshop."

"There is no great hurry. I see you have quite a collection of books. Are these your father's?"

"Some of them."

"Then they are mostly yours? It is not usual—at least, not in Dyplin—to find a young lady with so many books. And such books!"

He bent to study the titles. "Byron; you read poetry?"

"Yes." She was on the defensive.

"Why not? So do I. You know the work of Keats?"

"Yes—but I must tell my father you are here."

David took the news of a customer calmly. "Tell him I'll be with him in a minute or two. Ask him to sit down and wait. I can't leave this just at the moment."

When Mary went back to the parlour, she found Rutherford standing by the window reading a small grey book. He turned, smiled, and said, "You do not only read poetry. You write it—isn't it so?"

He held up the book. Mary reached for it. "Please give it to me. I did not want anyone to know. . . ."

"But why not? Not everyone has published a book of verse so young. Are you not proud of it?"

"No. I would not write them now. Please, you must not tell anyone—I thought the book was hidden. . . ."

"Ah, but you must know, if I think a book is being hidden, that is the one I choose. So when I

36

saw this little volume tucked carefully away . . ."

"Please, please—say no more. And please—tell no one."

An odd child. The poems were no works of genius—but not rubbish either. They showed a sensitivity to nature, a feeling for landscape, a certain sensuousness and the capacity for expressing it. He turned the page slowly, glancing at her as he did so. A woman beseeching he always found exciting. Distress had deepened and darkened her eyes. Her outstretched hands had a sculptural quality; she was, for the moment, beautiful; he had, after all, been justified in coming to the house on the absurd pretext of ordering an umbrella. (He had two already.)

He smiled. Mary saw his smile, not the eyes above it, as he said, "All right, I won't tell." For after all, it was of no importance, and he gave promises lightly.

She took the book from his hand, and placed it at the back of the bookcase. When she turned, David was there, and took Daniel Rutherford into the back room to discuss styles and materials. Mary fled to the kitchen.

Presently David came through, rubbing his hands as he did when pleased.

"He ordered two—one for himself and a sunshade for his sister who keeps house for him. He seems a pleasant man. They say he's a wonderful teacher of the infants. Well, I'll get back to the workshop. Are ye all right, Mary?"

"He saw the book. My book."

"Well, well, what of it? You used to be proud of that book."

"Not any more. I didn't want people here to know. I asked Mr. Rutherford not to say anything to anyone."

"Aweel, I daresay he'll not. But I wouldn't worry aboot it. It doesn't seem to me—" for David had his own shrewdness—"that folk here would be all that interested in poetry."

"But they'd think it queer. . . ."

Not quite understanding, but sensing her distress, he laid a hand on her shoulder. "Lass, ye can only be yourself. I don't know where your poetry-making comes from, unless from your mother's side, but if it's in you, then don't keep it down."

"I'll never write poems again." But at this David merely smiled and went to his workshop.

All the way home to his new house by the new Infant School Daniel Rutherford thought of Mary. An intriguing girl and, moreover, desirable—very much so. How old would she be? Not much past twenty, if that. Her mother was dead, he knew. That dry old stick of a father, with his silk and cotton, his bamboo or rosewood—what a life for a girl! No wonder she took to books and poetry. . . .

Later that week, Daniel Rutherford and his sister Susannah were invited to an evening at the Rector's house. The Rector of the New School was a leading figure in Dyplin—remote but very present, and a party at the Rector's house was an occasion.

Nevertheless, as he and Susannah made their way to the Rector's house, Daniel was less than enthusiastic. None of his colleagues was particularly congenial; one or two he disliked; and he was aware that, as teacher of the Infant School, he came low in the ranking order—not that this worried him. He knew that intellectually he was the equal of any of the staff, and he took a secret pleasure in noting their lapses and, occasionally, exposing some crasser stupidities.

Susannah, on the other hand, unsure of her position as, not a wife but a housekeeping sister, was wondering aloud why they had been asked to the second party, rather than the one given the previous week.

"The Drysdales were at last week's party. Of course, he teaches Latin in the big school. And the Gruebers—but I don't see why two foreigners should be asked to the first party, and not us. And Mr. Fraser, the writing master . . ."

"They come farther up the alphabet than we do, Susannah. The Thompsons, the Youngs and the Woodrows are all going tonight."

"Oh. Oh, then I expect you're right," and visibly cheered, Susannah quickened her step.

Daniel glanced at her with some distaste. She ran his house well, in the sense of keeping the servant girl up to scratch, seeing to the meals, caring for the children. But her interests and such pleasures as she knew ended with the house; she had a constant girn

39

about life, and towards her neighbours was malicious and tale-bearing. On the other hand, she had not had much of an existence—caring for their parents till she was past forty, and now caring for his family—and terrified, he knew, in case he married again, and she was left without a home. Women were vulnerable to fortune. What had they to offer but their sex? And, once the bloom was gone, was it any wonder they turned to gossip and malice? Thank God, thought Daniel Rutherford, I was born a man . . . and became aware Susannah was addressing him.

"I wonder if the Minister will be there. Dr. Munro was at the last party."

"What does it matter? Can't you enjoy yourself without bothering who has or has not been invited?"

Susannah, huffed, was silent, but recovered her spirits when she walked into the Duffus's drawing-room and saw Matthew Glendinning and his mother; for in her eyes, the Minister ranked above the doctor, and if the Glendinnings were at this party, then all was well.

The evening took its all-too-predictable course. Miss Agnes Duffus, the Rector's younger daughter, sang. So did Miss Matty Woodrow—a dark-haired vivacious girl who had the reputation of being "sprightly". Young Mr. Lambert, a newly-appointed member of the staff, was prevailed upon, after some decent hesitation on his part, to give a martial recitation about a gallant officer at

Waterloo. Miss Methven, Dyplin's one teacher of music, obliged with two solos on the piano. As the Minister was present, there was no card-playing. Daniel Rutherford felt himself being swallowed up in a morass of boredom. He was sitting between sharp-tongued Mrs. Thompson and Mrs. Woodrow, amiable, placid, plump and with not an idea in her head. In the intervals of the music, the usual enquiries as to the health of the families were exchanged. The music over, he made an effort to escape by rising to his feet to help serve the Madeira and cake. But this was foiled by Mrs. Duffus's firm announcement that the maids would serve—no one need bestir himself. So he had to sit down again. The ladies had now found a satisfactory topic of conversation. Both their husbands had ordered an umbrella from David Tullis.

"Are you thinking of getting one, Mr. Rutherford?" asked Mrs. Woodrow, who was rather afraid of Daniel, and wished he would sit somewhere else.

"Yes, I have ordered one for myself, and a parasol for my sister."

"Really? Well perhaps she may find a use for it. The weather has been fine of late." Mrs. Thompson was not afraid of Daniel and disliked Susannah.

"I believe Tullis and his daughter were in church," said Mrs. Woodrow.

"Yes, the young woman in the very conspicuous

41

bonnet," said Mrs. Thompson. "Quite unsuitable. But I hear she rather puts on airs."

Something in Daniel snapped. "She is a remarkable woman," he said, "and has published a volume of verse."

"Really?" The two ladies spoke together—Mrs. Woodrow astonished, Mrs. Thompson scornful. She raised her voice. "Do you hear that, Dr. Duffus? We have a poet in Dyplin—the umbrella-maker's daughter!"

Daniel spoke into the silence. "She does not want it to be known. I should not have said anything. . . ."

"But why not?" Matty Woodrow was all interest. "It's all so interesting. Fancy an umbrella-maker's daughter being a poet!"

"I do not think," said Matthew Glendinning's gentle voice, "that it is more remarkable for an umbrella-maker's daughter to write verse than anyone else. I mean, her father's occupation has nothing to do with it."

"Perhaps not. But I was sure she must be an unusual person when I saw her on Sunday. . . . You noticed her too, didn't you, Mr. Glendinning?"

Matthew felt himself blushing—he blushed, he knew, all too easily—as he said, too coldly, "I did observe her."

Agnes Duffus came to his rescue. "Everyone notices newcomers in Dyplin. Matty, shall we sing that new duet?"

After the duet, Daniel managed to escape from

42

the two ladies and join a group of men round the Rector, who were engaged in manly talk about Reform and voting qualifications. But the Rector interrupted the conversation to say, "An interesting young woman, the umbrella-maker's daughter, by all accounts. You know her?"

"I met her when I went to place an order. She has a remarkable library of books. I was wondering if it would be in order to introduce her to our school library."

"Oh certainly, certainly. The trustees are anxious that the townspeople should avail themselves of the library."

"Then I will tell her of it."

The party soon broke up. Walking home, and closing his ears to Susannah's prattle, Daniel felt a nagging guilt. But why? He had done no harm. It was a silly whim on Mary Tullis's part to keep her poems secret. Besides, he had done her a good turn in securing her access to the library. He would go himself and tell her—and into his vision of Mary's eyes lighting up as he told her, came Susannah's voice.

"Are you listening, Daniel?"

"Yes. What is it?"

"Matty Woodrow is setting her cap at the Minister. A very forward girl."

"Nonsense. Last week you told me he was casting eyes on Patty Macbeth."

"Oh that was just surmise. But didn't you see her . . ."

At the same moment Mrs. Glendinning, walking with Matthew along the dark avenue to the Manse, was saying, "I thought Matty Woodrow was very pert to you, Matthew. After all, you are the Minister. Agnes Duffus is a nice girl. She—she will make a good wife to someone . . ."

The gravel ground beneath Matthew's heels as he halted his steps. "Mother, I have told you before, that I do not feel it is the Lord's will that I should marry yet. It is a matter to be left in His hands, and I ask you now not to speak of the thing again."

"Yes, Matthew." Mrs. Glendinning was all meekness. She had no intention of hindering Matthew's progress towards marriage, but it was satisfactory to know he was heart-whole. It was too dark for her to see that he was blushing again. Nor could she know he had just convinced himself of the necessity for paying a pastoral call on the Tullises.

5

BY next day, the secret of Mary's authorship was public property. Mrs. Woodrow made it her business to call in at her sister, Mrs. Walker's, shop to pass on the news gathered at the Rector's soirée. She always did this after an "evening", thereby allowing her sister to share in social glory beyond her reach, and gratifying her own sense of pride in having married a master at the New School. So it was that when Alison Campbell went into the shop, Mrs. Walker was able to say, while her thumb hovered over the pound of Belfast ham, "You didn't say the umbrella-maker's daughter had written a book of poetry when you brought her to the shop."

Alison could only look her disbelief.

"Ye didn't know?" ("And fine she kent I didn't know," said Alison later to John.) "Oh aye. My sister heard all about it at the Rector's house last night. Mary Tullis had been reading her poetry to Daniel Rutherford. They must be well acquainted. Aye. That'll be five shillings and sixpence in all."

Alison, curiously upset, decided to postpone further shopping and went home. Mary was in the back garden, and Alison, holding aside branches in the privet hedge, hailed her.

45

"Busy, Mary?" for Mary had insisted on her using her first name.

"Yes. Well, no. I'm pulling up some weeds. I could not bear being in the house, it's such a beautiful day."

Alison came to the point. "You never tell't us you wrote poetry. . . . Lassie, it's no' a crime!" seeing the look on Mary's face.

"Who told you?"

"Nellie Walker in the shop. Her sister Nan Woodrow—her that's married on the teacher—heard it at the Rector's last night. It seems ye've been reading your poetry to Daniel Rutherford. . . ."

"Did he say so? It's not true, it's not true. I asked him not to tell anyone—he found the book by accident."

To Alison's consternation, for she was quick to respond to human distress, she saw tears in the girl's eyes.

"Oh, Mary. It's not all that serious a thing. Come on over and have a cup of tea—the kettle's on the boil and John's up-country on a job so I'm in no hurry." And, as Mary hesitated, she said, "Come on. See, come through the gap here. Did ye no' ken aboot it?"

She pushed the branches farther aside, and revealed a gap in the bushes, masked by small branches, but wide enough to slip through.

"Years ago, when the hedge was growing, there were two wee girls lived here, one in each house. And the gap was left for them to slip through, and it's aye been kept. So come on through, Mary."

Mary went. Alison had the wit not to re-open the subject of the poems, and over the tea-cups she talked of weather, gardens, John's work. Gradually Mary relaxed, and it was she herself who mentioned the poems.

"I asked Mr. Rutherford not to say anything about the book."

"Ach, it probably slipped out before he thought."

"It was treachery."

"You're making too much of it, Mary. What's the harm anyway? Mony a body would be proud to have a book in print."

"Maybe. I didn't want anyone to know. It's caused me enough trouble already. I just want to lead an ordinary life among ordinary people."

Alison smiled.

"I'm thinking you're not just quite an ordinary lass yourself. Maybe you would call us ordinary folk here in Dyplin. But I'm not sure if there's such a thing as ordinary people. Take my John. Tae most people he's just John Campbell, joiner and under-taker, good at his business. But John didna want tae be a joiner. He wanted tae go tae sea. But his father wouldn't hear of it, and he was an only child sae he just went into the business. But he's read just aboot every book you could find on seas and ships; and he kens mair aboot riggings and sails than mony a mariner." She paused for a moment. "Come on. I'll show you something."

She led Mary through to the front lobby and up

the stair. At the top a door opened into an attic that ran over the kitchen below. Alison flung open the door.

"There," she said, and waved a hand.

Mary could say nothing. On the bench which ran round the walls were ships, schooners, clippers, men o' war, merchantmen, in full sail, each spar, each rope, each tiny piece of bunting perfectly miniaturized; so that every model spoke not only of skill and craft, but of love and longing.

"Aye," said Alison, answering Mary's look. "John made them all. When the mood comes on him he spends hours up here. But mind you, there's no' mony ken aboot all this. He's kind o' shy aboot it. Ye might say," (with a flash of insight that astonished herself) "these are *his* poems."

Mary was going from one to another, laying a gentle finger here and there on the exquisitely worked wood. "They're beautiful," she said. "He must love ships very much."

Alison looked at her with respect. "Aye, he does." She fumbled for words. "It all comes out in these—all that he wanted to do and didn't. But you're not to let on I showed you them. He wouldn't like it."

"I won't," said Mary, "and *I* mean that."

Back in the kitchen Alison went on, "You see what I mean by people not being just ordinary. There's Sandy Craig from the farm on the hill there—an ordinary sheep farmer you'd think—but they say he's got hundreds of books up there and that he's writing a history of the world . . . and puir Willie Johnston, when he's no' in his cups, can play almost any tune you like on his whistle . . . och, I could tell you o' lots of them that's able tae dae things that's not ordinary at all."

"They're all men," said Mary. "What do the women do that's not ordinary?"

Alison looked at her and then laughed. "Aye, it's true. The women don't seem to go in for things like that. Too busy, maybe. They all knit, embroider and do sewn pictures if they've time; the only one I can think of that's not ordinary is Meg Annan—and she tells fortunes."

"Who's she?"

"She lives in the last house in the road going up to the castle—a red-headed woman. And fortune-telling isn't all she does." Alison's voice was dry.

"Does she make her living from fortune-telling?"

"No. She does sometimes work on the bleach-field—not all the time, but when she's needed; and she'll help out with sewing if the dress-makers have too much to do. And silly girls go to her for their fortunes—and sometimes, they say, for a love-potion. Och, it's all havers. She's an incomer—came here about twelve years ago. A braw young woman she was, but there was a mystery aboot her. She gets her cottage at a small rent from the estate at Griffton—they say her mother had a connection there. But don't you have anything to do with her. She's—not respectable."

And Alison, who had firm views on what was and

49

what was not suitable for a young woman's ears, abruptly changed the subject.

Mary went back to her own house less distressed but no less angry. So when she answered a knock at the door that afternoon and saw Daniel Rutherford, she flushed and frowned. He knew at once what was wrong, and said gently:

"May I come in? I want to explain something and apologize."

She stood aside silently and he preceded her into the parlour. When he turned to face her, she still said nothing, but looked her indignation.

"I know what you are thinking," he said. "I should not have said anything about your book. For I think that is why you are angry with me?" Perhaps a direct question would get her to talk.

But she only bent her head stiffly.

"The words slipped out. I—it was in answer to a criticism. I meant well."

"A criticism of me?"

How could he have thought of her as a meek and timid girl? Her eyes were positively flashing, her voice cutting. She was momentarily quite splendid. Perhaps something in his eyes warned her, for she lowered her eyelids and said more gently:

"It was unkind of you."

He took advantage of the change of tone to say, "I am sorry. But perhaps I can make up for what I did. I have arranged with the Rector of the New School that you should use the library there. . . . They have a fine collection of books."

50

But she was not to be so easily mollified. "I have plenty of books of my own, and can buy more."

He had not expected this steeliness in her. "I am truly sorry. Come, let us be friends."

Before she could answer there was another knock at the door, and she left the room. He heard her say: "Mr. Glendinning! Please come in," and in a second she was showing the Minister into the parlour. He looked surprised to see Daniel there, but they exchanged polite greetings. Mary went to find her father and the two men were left together.

"I called to tell Miss Tullis she was free to use the library at the New School if she wished." Yet why, thought Daniel, do I feel the need of giving an explanation of my presence? Matthew Glendinning always had this effect on him, of making him feel he must justify himself; and yet he rather despised Matthew as young and callow, unworldly and innocent. Old Dr. Gillies, now, he had respected him, felt at ease with him, even almost liked him, although by all accounts he was more a preacher of the word than a doer. . . .

Matthew, looking round at the bookshelves, said, "I should have thought Miss Tullis had enough to read here: poetry, I see, and novels . . . well, we must not expect the ladies to be too serious in their interests."

The man's a fool, thought Daniel, all sense of guilt vanishing; but the return of Mary and her father prevented a reply, and he took a polite departure, knowing well that a pastoral visit from

51

the Minister was not to be encroached upon by a mere lay acquaintance.

David Tullis greeted Matthew with the respect due to the Minister and the friendliness due to a much younger man.

"Mary," he said, "make a cup of tea for Mr. Glendinning. No, no," as Matthew made a polite protest, "you are not taking me from my work. I am happy to make your nearer acquaintance. Pray sit down."

Mary came and went, laying a fresh cloth on the table, bringing out the good china, getting the jam and butter, the scones she had baked that morning, the fruit-cake. . . .

That her father was enjoying the visit she knew by the tone of his voice and the uninterrupted flow of conversation. She heard little of it, her mind being taken up with Daniel Rutherford's visit. Angry she still was, but not with the fierce indignation she had felt at first seeing him on the doorstep. She knew quite well that she would end up, if not quite forgiving, at least ready to talk and have acquaintance with him. He had twice said he was sorry, and she thought it would not be easy for him to say he was sorry—and, remembering how he had looked at her, she felt for a moment uneasy and almost afraid—and hastened to carry the tea things through to the parlour and sit down.

Her father and Matthew Glendinning drew their chairs round the table. Matthew asked a blessing, and said:

"Your father tells me you like living in Dyplin."

"Oh yes, I do. It is a very pretty place."

"It is. We must thank God for His mercies in setting us in such pleasant surroundings." For Matthew took his pastoral visiting as a serious duty and both he and his parishioners took for granted a solemnity of speech which they felt only right and proper, coming from the Minister—though it had been a change after old Dr. Gillies who, when he did pay a visit, was abrupt, downright and even earthy in speech.

Mary said nothing; public talk of God tended to make her feel ill-at-ease. Matthew, however, having talked at length with David, was determined to have talk with Mary too. Was it not his pastoral duty to get to know the minds and hearts of his flock? So he told himself, aware how little he had tried to learn of the heart and mind of Miss Susannah Rutherford, from whose conversation he fled as quickly as possible.

"I see you have many books," he said. "Your father tells me you are fond of reading."

To which Mary's sole response was a flash of the eye in her father's direction.

Matthew tried again. "I trust you do not confine yourself to the reading of poetry and novels. Lord Byron is not quite what I should have expected a young lady of good principles to have on her shelves. . . ."

Mary reddened. "Lord Byron is a great poet, sir. I read poetry for the pleasure and the truth of it. If I

53

want instruction in principles, I should read sermons. But sermons I find dull."

"Mary!" David shook his head at her, but she was already feeling repentant.

"I beg your pardon, Mr. Glendinning. I should not have said that. But it seems to me that poetry is in a different world from principles . . . and I must tell you that I did not find your sermon dull."

Her smile, her appeal for pardon, were irresistible. Matthew smiled back and said, "I am sure your principles are strong enough to resist Lord Byron's influence. I understand the novels of Sir Walter Scott could be a good influence." He turned to David. "I had a letter from Edinburgh today with mention of his sadly failing health. But the cholera there is abating. By the mercy of Providence we have so far remained free of it here."

The conversation moved to affairs of politics and commerce, in which David talked and Matthew asked questions. Mary did no more than fill tea-cups and pass eatables. She would have been astonished to know that not a gesture, not a movement of her head, not a lift or fall of her eyelids went unnoticed by the Reverend Matthew Glendinning. Of her mind and heart he learned little: of her outward self he learned much. Before leaving, they knelt and he led them in a simple prayer. When he left, all Mary remembered of him was that he was slightly built and had fair hair. But she could have drawn a portrait of Daniel Rutherford.

6

MARY shut the door behind the Minister just in time to miss seeing Dr. Munro's gig, coming down from the high road along the hills, stop at John Campbell's gate. The doctor spoke to Alison at the door, but did not go in, and left her wiping her hands nervously on her apron and looking worried. When John came in, she gave him the message.

"You're to call at the doctor's. An undertaking job. And ye're no tae say anything tae anybody, but just go quietly and at the back door and he'll let you in. John, I dinna like it."

"Noo, Alison, we've had this out before. If it's a smallpox job, ye ken fine I've done it often enough and nae hairm. Noo, whit's for my meat?"

But he returned from his visit to Dr. Munro's visibly shaken, and very unwilling to tell Alison what it was all about. Only after extracting a promise of total secrecy did he explain.

"It's a job up at the Torlinn Inn. The doctor was called to two visitors, a brother and a sister travelling in the Highlands on holiday. They came from Perth, and they took ill—and—and died. Both."

"Oh, that was terrible, John. But why you? Have they no' a man up at Maukin tae coffin them?"

55

"Oh aye. Wee Paterson. But he'll no' touch it. Ye see, Alison, it was cholera."

Alison dropped the pan she was scouring with a clatter.

"Oh John—oh John. Must ye dae it?"

"Aye, I must. Ye see, Alison, they were people like oorsels. And young. And they've a richt tae be given proper burial. . . . Forbye, Dr. Munro says if I dae the same as with smallpox, and wash weel, and mebbe burn the things I've worn, there's no' that much danger."

"But the cholera . . ."

"Aye. It's a bad illness. I'm thinking we've no' just realized here in Dyplin just how bad it's been in the land. The doctor was telling me it came up the Great North Road from London, and it's been bad in Edinburgh. Ye ken he went away for a week or twa—well, it was tae Edinburgh he went, tae see just how they dealt with it there."

"And how dae they?"

"Just as weel as they can. It's no' an illness they can dae much for at all. No' everyone dies that's smitten. But the doctor said it's mair a matter o' Providence if a body lives than onything man can dae. No' but whit there's things they can try—and whiles they seem tae wark."

"Such as?"

"He didna say. It's been in Inverforth, and it's in Perth, but as far as he kent, in between had been free o' the malady. Until today. He's no' wanting folk to ken, for that would just start a panic. If

there's nae mair cases, naebody need ever ken. An'
if it does come here, that'll be time enough for folk
tae worry. At least, that's what he thinks.''

Alison had seated herself at the table to listen.
Now she said, "When do you go?"

"In half an hour. The doctor is coming for me in
his gig. If anyone says anything to you, ye'll just tell
them I'm away on a job up-country and he's giving
me a lift. Sae get me the auldest pair of trousers I
have, and shirt and jacket.''

"But the gear?"

"Oh, wee Paterson's makin' the coffins—just
rushing them up. The doctor wanted it a' done as
quick as possible. . . .''

It was long past midnight when Alison, lying
sleepless in bed, heard the sound of hooves on the
high road. They stopped at the gate, and she heard
a murmur of voices. The gig moved on, and she
heard steps go round the end of the house and
waited for the sound of the back door opening. But
the house remained silent. She flung a shawl over
her nightdress, went downstairs and opened the
back door, calling softly:

"Is that you, John?"

From far up the garden she heard his answer.

"Aye. Fling me oot some claes. I'm burying these
I've got on. And Alison, get back tae your bed, and
dinna come doon till I tell you. I'm gaun tae wash
frae heid tae foot. Ye'll hae the kettle on the fire?"

"Aye, John. There's hot water. I'll pit claes by
the door here for you."

She got a shirt, trousers, jacket, socks and boots and put them by the door. Then she went back to bed, and lay shivering between the sheets, for all that the night was mild.

It seemed hours before John came to the foot of the stair and called, "It's all right noo, Alison."

He had put coal on the fire and was sitting with his hands stretched to it, as though he too was chilled through. When she saw the look he turned on her, she went to the little cupboard by the window, took out the bottle of whisky, poured three good fingers into a glass, added hot water from the kettle, and put it into his grasp: all without a word. He cupped his hands round the glass, and took a long mouthful; and she heard his teeth clink on the glass. Then he gave a long sigh and said, "You're a good wife, Alison."

"Was it bad?"

"Aye. Bad. I've seen mony a grievous thing on the job, as ye ken, Alison. But naethin' like yon. The filth o' it—the stench. Oh, Alison, it'll be an ill day if it comes tae Dyplin!"

At last she persuaded him to leave his crouching over the fire, and come to bed. Even then he was troubled and nervous as she had never seen him. Finally, she put her arms round him as if he had been a child, and murmured and soothed him into sleep. She lay awake till the light crept through the curtains.

Three days later, the carter from Perth drew up at the Tullises' door to deliver material to David. He was slow in getting down from his seat behind the two Clydesdale horses, and staggered as he made for the end of the wagon to lift the bundle. David went to help him, and Mary, standing by the door, thought how tired the man looked. He put the bundle on his shoulder and began to walk up the flagged path that led round the end of the house to the workshop. He was so unsteady on his feet that Mary wondered if he was drunk. David, coming behind him, put out a hand to steady the bundle. But it was too late. The man lurched, let go of his burden which rolled into the flower-bed, and fell face down on the path, vomit pouring from his mouth, and filth staining his breeches. That was at mid-morning. At midnight, watched by Dr. Munro, Mary and David, he died, on a mattress in the closet by the Tullises' back door, where Mary and David had carried him. The cholera had come to Dyplin.

7

TUCKED away under the hills though it was, Dyplin had from time to time known upheaval and, sometimes, disaster, like the attack of Montrose's men when Dyplin was almost destroyed and had to rebuild itself and, more recently, the non-violent but possibly more profound change brought by the building of the New School and the arrival of a totally new group into the community who built themselves fine new houses, demanded a different quality of goods in the shops, brought new ideas—without them Dyplin would not have been perfervid for Reform—and filled the gap between the Inneses of Griffton and the tradesmen and workers in the farms, bleach-field and coalmine. Dyplin had in twenty years come from being a lost sleepy village to being, as one of the incomers put it, "a rural pleasance with the graces of the town", where those same incomers gracefully maintained a division between school and town which they would have denied ever existed.

Now cholera had come to Dyplin. Dr. Munro, cautiously finding his way down the steep street from the Tullises' after the carter's death, had no doubt in his heart that this would be another of the harsh dislocating episodes in Dyplin's story, though he had once again, making such arrangements as he could for the discreet disposal of the body, impressed on John Campbell the necessity for secrecy on his part and on the part of Jock Rennie, the grave-digger, and Joseph Harvey. They were to be roused as early as possible so that the burial could take place, if possible, secretly. He himself had undertaken to contact the Minister very early in the morning. But now, as he reached the road past the Manse, he saw a light from the Minister's study window. Why not get hold of him now? He made his way along the dark drive between the shrubs till he could look in through the unshuttered window and see Matthew sitting at a table, a Bible before him, by it a pile of weighty books, paper and a quill in front of him and two candles burning steadily. He appeared to be preparing a sermon but inspiration seemed to have failed; he was leaning back in the chair, his hands clasped behind his head, staring dreamily at the blank wall opposite. Dr. Munro tapped on the window; Matthew jumped, came over and peered out, nodded when he saw the doctor and went out of the room. Presently the bolts of the front door were drawn, the vast key grated in the lock, and soon Dr. Munro was in the study. Matthew was shocked by his news.

"Poor man! Taken so suddenly, and with no time to make his peace with God! Truly, we know not the hour."

To this the doctor said nothing, for though by no means an unbeliever he defined the Minister's sphere of interest and his own very precisely: Matthew's concern was with the fate of men's souls in the after-life; his was to keep their souls as long as possible in this. Matthew, having in all sincerity paid a tribute of thought and concern to the unknown dead, now asked with, the doctor noted, considerable concern, about the Tullises.

"And Miss Tullis—and her father, are they in danger?"

"I cannot say they are not, though both showed remarkable calmness and presence of mind. And Miss Tullis tended the man with great humanity. She is a remarkable young woman."

"I am sure she is." Perhaps Matthew was aware of the fervour in his voice, for he went on hastily: "And will the infection spread?"

"Again I cannot say. The Tullises' is the last house on that road. I have asked them not to go into the shops for some days for fear of carrying the contagion. But I do not think we can avoid it. It has been rife in Inverforth and Perth; and I fear what measures we can take are of doubtful value."

"We must put ourselves in God's hands, Dr. Munro."

"Well, yes. Indeed," and the doctor prepared to go, "there is not much else we can do. You will be ready at five in the morning, then? At first light?"

"I shall. And I shall keep it as secret as may be."

The next morning, just as the sky was growing light behind the hills, John Campbell drove his gig up the Manse drive. David was beside him. In the back, a heavy blanket covered the carter's plain unvarnished coffin. Jock Rennie and Joseph Harvey met them and the four men carried it through the Minister's gate in the wall, and lowered it into the grave dug between the wall and a group of cypresses. There Matthew was waiting to say the committal words. And in half an hour, Jock had the grave half-filled and the others had gone. No one appeared to have seen them.

For four days all in the know waited and wondered. On the fifth day after the carter's funeral, Dr. Munro was called out to the miners' cottages in the little valley to the east of Dyplin and found a man dying. He drove a coal lorry to and from Inverforth. He had been ill for two days before his wife, desperate, had sent a ragged and grubby child to the doctor's door; and even as the doctor was examining him, he died; and when the doctor left the house, another distraught woman was waiting to beg him to go to her house where her man was "bad with the flux". By nightfall, all Dyplin knew that cholera was among them.

Or not quite among them. The colliers in Dyplin were a race apart, living in their own cluster of miserable, wattle-and-daub, thatched cottages in a little valley by the stream which marked the parish boundary to the east. They were not among the very poor, it being possible for them to earn three shillings and sixpence a day by working very hard and, even though they only worked nine days in a fortnight, their wages compared favourably with the eight shillings a week earned in the bleach-field. Nevertheless, a bleach-field worker was totally accepted into Dyplin; the colliers were not. Perhaps because glimpses of them, black-faced with red-rimmed eyes, were disturbing; perhaps because their work in the dark bowels of the earth marked them out as different. Every time a collier got drunk at the Thorn Bush Inn and went staggering and shouting down the road, heads shook and tongues wagged, though Willie Johnston's lapses were met with tolerant shrugs. Very few of the colliers were known by name; and their wives, silent, anxious women with black shawls over their heads, moved quietly in and out of the shops. They were never seen in the kirk, but expected, and got, Christian baptism, marriage and burial from the Minister. Old Dr. Gillies moved among them with complete assurance, and they liked him, sensing in him a rough toughness of character that matched their own. Moreover, he made no effort to entice them to the kirk, seeing no reason for forcing them into a situation where they would feel awkward and ill-at-ease. Matthew, on his first arrival in the charge, had seen in the colliers a fruitful field, and for some time tried hard to get them to come to the services, but came up against an undeviating "Na, na, the kirk's no' fur the likes o' us" that finally defeated him. He did, however, go down to the houses every week to teach the children the catechism, and to read, but even this was disheartening; only two, a girl and a boy, had so far learnt to read, and their

parents refused to send them to the New School—
indeed, they had no clothes fit to go in. The colliers
remained obstinately apart and their little clachan,
Kellyton, a ghetto.

The first reaction to the news that cholera had
broken out among the colliers was relief that it was
there, in a place apart, not right in the midst of
Dyplin. With the relief went indignation—the
colliers, dirty, coarse people, needn't have caught
cholera, if only they'd been cleaner and more sober;
did not *The Scotsman* quote authorities as saying an
indulgence in strong drink was a contributing factor
to catching the disease?

After the relief and the righteous indignation
came the fear—and a determination to keep the
disease where it had started.

So it was that the next time a collier's wife slipped
quietly into the Walker's shop and prepared to
stand with customary patience waiting to be served,
Mrs. Walker turned sharply from serving Miss
Susannah Rutherford and said:

"Ye needn't wait. I'm not serving anyone that's
carrying the cholera."

The woman lifted her basket as if to go, then
turned and said, "But there's nane in oor hoose ill."

"Mebbe no. But it's in Kellyton."

"But a' the sickness is at the ither end o' the
street."

"That doesna' matter. Out with you."

The woman hesitated for a moment, and then left
the shop. Mary, who had been waiting her turn, for

the doctor had told the Tullises he now saw no good reason for them not to move freely, followed her out. The woman was standing on the pavement as if uncertain what to do, her basket on her arm, her hand, rough and black-nailed, clutching a scuffed little leather purse.

"I'll get your messages for you," said Mary. "What do you want?"

The woman stared.

"Ye're no' feart?"

"No. Come, tell me what you want."

"Three pounds of oatmeal and three of barley and a bottle of whisky. But ye needna ask fur that if ye dinna want tae."

"It doesn't matter to me. I'll get it."

She turned, but the woman said: "Here, tak' ma purse."

Back in the shop, all eyes were fastened on Mary.

"It's your turn now, Miss Tullis," said Mrs. Walker, coldly.

"Before I get my own things, I want three pounds of oatmeal and three pounds of barley and a bottle of whisky for the collier woman," said Mary, "and I'll pay for them first."

She opened the shabby purse, but Mrs. Walker put out a forbidding hand.

"I'm touching none of her money," she said.

Mary's cheeks reddened. "But I expect you'll touch mine," and she repeated the order.

Having paid for it, she made her own purchases and left, the whole transaction having taken place in complete silence. But above the tinkle of the bell as she closed the shop door, she heard the clatter of voices beginning.

The woman was no longer alone. The Minister was talking to her and, when Mary came out of the shop, he said, "Mrs. Linton here tells me you were getting her messages."

"Yes." She put the oatmeal and barley and the bottle into the woman's basket, and handed her back her purse.

The woman opened it and cried, "There's naethin' oot it!"

"Mrs. Walker wouldn't take the money."

"But ye'll tak it."

"No. I don't want it."

The woman reddened. "Ye're feart tae touch ma money tae?"

"No, I'm not. If you really want me to, I'll take it."

"Aye, I do want. Ma man's a guid worker and we're nae paupers."

She handed over the money, and then, ashamed of her outburst, said gently, "Thank you," and went away on the path that led to Kellyton.

Matthew was full of concern and admiration.

"The colliers must not starve because of the fears of the shopkeepers. I will go and see Dr. Munro and try to find a way. . . . You are a brave woman, Miss Tullis."

He thought Mary hesitated, and then she said, "No, I am not. Good day, Mr. Glendinning."

He was still looking after her when Susannah Rutherford and the others came out.

"Did you see what happened, Mr. Glendinning?" Susannah's little eyes were sharp. "I don't think Miss Tullis has any right to run the risk of spreading the contagion by putting herself in communication with people from the colliers' houses."

"Miss Tullis has just performed an act of true charity," said Matthew, "and I've no doubt will receive the protection and blessing of Providence which it merits. Good day."

He lifted his hat and strode off, indignation in every line of his black ministerial coat.

"Well!" said Miss Susannah to her companion, Mrs. Woodrow. "It appears ministers are as easily influenced by a dolly face as ordinary men!" And the two ladies sped on their way, choking with such a tale to tell.

Matthew did go to Dr. Munro and put the case of the colliers. The result was the calling of a meeting of the men of Dyplin. A fair number, mostly trades-men, turned up at the old school by the burn below the Session house. After much talk and much quotation of "what the wife says", it was decided that a representative of the colliers should come to the far end of the bridge over the burn that flowed between Kellyton and the fields round Dyplin, and shout their requirements. These would be put at the other end of the bridge, and credit given till the crisis was over. And the colliers were to be told that they were not to come into Dyplin.

"If we keep apart, we'll surely no' run much risk," said Peter Robertson, the baker.

"Will you do without a doctor, then? For I must go to Kellyton. I will not leave these people unattended."

Charles Munro spoke calmly and incisively, and made a startled silence. When no one spoke, he went on, "You see, it is not possible to cut them off entirely. But I promise you I will do all I can to avoid carrying the contagion. For yourselves, all I can say is keep everything as clean as you can, wash your hands before touching food, teach your children to do the same, and boil your drinking water."

"Hoots, doctor, there's nae need o' that." It was Willie Johnston speaking. "Oor well has the purest water in Dyplin."

"Hoo lang is it since ye tasted it?" said some anonymous wag.

Willie grinned sheepishly. "Noo, noo, fair's fair. Forbye, the wells are all good."

"I can only give you my advice," said the doctor. "It's up to you to follow it or not."

"There's another thing." Samuel Walker was ill-at-ease. "My wife says she hopes the Minister will see it's his duty not to carry the disease into the congregation."

Matthew rose to his feet, his face white with anger. "I shall follow the dictates of my conscience,

Mr. Walker, which tell me that if I failed to take the comfort of the gospel to the dying, whoever, wherever, and from whatever cause, I should be miserably failing in my duty as a Minister of Christ."

But Walker was a dour man. "Ah well, Mr. Glendinning, ye'll no be surprised if the attendance drops."

Three of the teachers from the New School were at the meeting, and now Daniel Rutherford rose to his feet and said smoothly, "I think we have discussed all that requires discussing. As far as possible, contact with the infected area will be avoided. The Minister and doctor will, I am sure, take every precaution to avoid bringing back contagion. I propose we close the meeting."

This was agreed to with relief, and the meeting broke up. John, reporting back to Alison, said, "They're all feart, Alison." He chuckled. "Naebody thocht tae ask if I might bring the disease. And oh, ye should have seen the Minister! Fair blazing, he was. I didna think he had it in him tae be that angry."

"Afore this is all by," said Alison, "we'll all learn a lot about a lot o' folk."

For a time it seemed as if the cholera could be contained in Kellyton. There it raged, working its way downstream from the top hovel where it had started. After the first five, they buried the dead in a plot of level ground at Kellyton, given by Mr. Innes

70

of Griffton, owner of the colliery. Matthew Glendinning and Dr. Munro toiled hard, scrupulously carrying out the régime of changing clothes and washing laid down by the doctor. John Campbell made the rough deal coffins but did not go into the hamlet—the survivors in a household did what was needful, bundling the dead out of the way and into the earth as quickly as possible. The doctor and Matthew got into the way of going together. When the doctor found at his door yet another distraught woman or child or a man dumb with misery twisting his woollen cap in his blackened, chapped hands, he called for Matthew on his way, for as likely as not it would be comfort for the bereaved that was needed, not help for the living. So Matthew saw filth, squalor, human wretchedness as he had never known it; and the doctor faced a grinding sense of self-reproach, face to face with those seeking help which he could not give. They lived for a time in two worlds, and on the Sabbath, Matthew, looking down on the decent godly congregation, somewhat depleted, the Woodrows and Walkers being conspicuous by their absence, and others too, fearful of contagion, found it hard to understand how the two communities could exist so near to each other.

But the distinction was soon to be blurred. One of the mining families was the Millars, who lived in a cottage second from the lower end of the hamlet. It was a Millar brother and sister who had learnt to read; there were seven children, father and mother, and they were noted amongst the colliers for their good looks, being all tall, fair, blue-eyed. The father was a giant of a man, like a Viking pirate, and even at his grimiest his blue eyes flashed like sapphires. The whole family worked at the mine, either cutting coal, or picking it over, or loading waggons. The second son, Jamie, was courting Peggy, the Woodrows' maidservant. No one approved of the affair, neither her parents, labourers in an upland farm, nor the Woodrows. But Peggy deeply loved her handsome collier. After a fortnight's separation, she could no longer endure not seeing him, and they met in the woods above the mine. Peggy told no one, justifying herself by the evident fact that Jamie was in splendid health, and that the sickness was several houses removed from his home.

Three days later Jamie was at death's door. He recovered, but by the time the sickness had burnt itself out in the house, his clever little sister and two brothers had died. His mother was left crawling round the house, a broken woman, and the Viking pirate sprawled on his bed, never sober.

And Peggy? Peggy sickened too; and died, and sprightly little Matty Woodrow and her mother too; and Dyplin's ordeal began.

First reaction to the tragedy in the Woodrow household was fear. People stayed in their houses, scuttled out to buy necessities, hurried back to close doors against the lurking menace. But when a second household went down, the sense of shock was succeeded by a feeling of outrage. Was not this the age of progress? It was thirty years since a steam paddle-boat had begun navigation on the Forth and Clyde Canal; and twenty-one since the Comet had puffed its way across the Clyde; and railways were coming, that was certain. It was no time since the march of triumph for the Reform Bill—and now a strange and particularly filthy and degrading disease had fallen on them; one that reduced a human being to a dehydrated stinking grey slab of mortality with appalling rapidity. Against it they were powerless; and all Dr. Munro could do was prate about boiling drinking water and applying bags of hot salt to patients when they reached the deadly stage of cold and coma. Dr. Munro was too honest to pretend a curative skill he did not have. So it was not surprising that people turned to any measures which were thought to help. Blethering Bob, a pedlar who for years had gone the rounds of the villages selling laces and pins and thread and ribbons and other gew-gaws, and had earned his name because of his ceaseless patter, appeared in the square, but this time, in addition to his usual wares, he had a supply of bright pink pills, guaranteed to protect against all infectious ailments including "the Asiatic cholera". "I am an honest man," said Bob, "and I do not say these amazing pills cure that dread disease. No. But they prevent it. And prevention, my friends, is better than cure. And as I do not wish to make a profit out of such a terrible plague, I am selling these at the ridiculous price of a penny a pill. A course of six preventive pills for sixpence!" Of course he sold them, handful after handful. The numbers round his little folding stall grew; hands and money reached towards him.

"Remember, one a day, at night. Not a cure. I do not say a cure. But a preventative measure. That is why I have made it my duty to go round all those places where the disease has not yet struck to bring the people these amazing pills."

"But we've got cholera here." It was an anxious woman's voice. "Does that mean the pills'll no' work?"

"What? Oh yes, yes, they will work. Cholera here? Dear, dear." Bob's sharp sly face was suddenly paler. He pulled out his big silver watch. "Friends, I regret I must now leave you and proceed on my way. Besides," he glanced into the round black box on his stall, "the pills are finished." And, disregarding all cries of protest, Bob hastily folded up his stall, bundled it into his little pony-cart, and set off up the turnpike road as fast as his horse would trot.

He spread the word. The number of travellers into Dyplin dropped. Carters bringing the flour and meal, the sugar, tea and coffee, the pots and pans and durable goods, left their packages outside on the pavements of the shops and drove away with all speed. The farm people, bringing the eggs and butter and milk and poultry, let it be known that they would leave them by the roadside to be picked up. Dyplin was driven in on itself, knit together by fear and a sense of being deserted. Then a third household went down; so the trouble, they saw, was to be long and drawn out. They began to think of fighting back.

Dr. Duffus sent home or to relations most of the fifty-odd boarders at the New School, but did not close the school entirely and classes continued. Some families moved to stay with friends in the country. Daniel Rutherford sent Susannah and the children to their aunt's house deep in the Border country near Broughton. To give Susannah her due, she did not want to go. "Supposing you are smitten," she said, "who will look after you?"

"I will have to get better by myself or die by myself. From what I hear, nursing makes little difference. And if you and I both died, what of the children?"

So they went, and Daniel lived in two rooms in the house and on the whole found it a not unpleasant experience.

Suggestions for preventing infection passed rapidly from one household to another. For some days, a pall of nauseous smoke hung over the lower part of the town, because Monsieur Grueber, who came from Alsace, had read in a French paper that burning a barrel of tar was a proved way of purifying the air round a dwelling. Other people burnt shovelfuls of sulphur in their front halls. Some people solemnly drank whisky and water every night. Others abjured all alcohol and took to infusions of boiled lemon. Dr. Munro, appealed to for his opinion on all these and other prophylactics, could only say he had no medical reason for thinking them effective. He still repeated his simple advice to boil water.

John Campbell, meeting him one day coming wearily out of a house where a boy of fourteen had died, and three others were ill, asked him if the boiling of the water was really essential.

"I think so, John. But not all medical men would agree. It is certain that the disease flourishes most in the dirtiest quarters—though not only there. And the wells here in Dyplin may be good enough; but we also have cess pits and pools in the soil. Might the filth from them not travel to the wells? I don't know, John, I don't know. It's just an idea. But we boil all the water in our house."

But mostly Dyplin found boiling water too simple a remedy, even though the Minister preached a sermon on Naaman's scorning of the prophet's advice to bathe in Jordan, and drew an analogy with the doctor's simple recommendation; a sermon which was held by some of his elders to touch too much on worldly as against divine matters. It was a fine thing when the house of God was used to recommend the boiling of water! Besides, a'body kent the water was fine hill-water. . . . But Matthew redeemed his reputation as a preacher when, bewildered by the loss and suffering he met daily, he, like his fellow-divines throughout the land, could find no better answer than the wrath of God, punishing a sinful world, nation, town. This approach the elders could take approvingly in their stride, being comfortably aware of the sins of others, and some of them aware that, with the cholera, sin had indeed extended its sway in Dyplin.

For if pressure from without made Dyplin a more closely bonded community, pressures within loosened bonds. The strands of the web of custom and attitudes were broken, differences diminished under the common undiscriminating menace. So it was that, in the Robertson's shop, Alison found herself quite naturally joining in a conversation with Meg Annan, with whom she would have scorned to exchange more than a distant nod. Meg, her red hair coiled at the nape of her neck, bare-headed, wrapped in a black shawl over a checked skirt, was a sober enough figure. She was always pale, it was her dark eyes that gave meaning to her looks; almost black, mostly half-lidded, for Meg tended to look down most of the time. When Alison arrived in the shop, she was talking to Annie Young, who was serving, and the topic was, of course, the cholera.

"It's in the shoemaker's house," said Annie. "My uncle left the bread at their door this morning, so that naebody need come tae the shop."

"Yes, it's a bad time," said Meg. She turned to Alison. "Ye're all well yourselves, Mrs. Campbell?" And Alison, without thinking, answered, "Yes, I'm glad to say we are."

"It's a bad time," Meg said again. "Would you believe it, some of the lasses have been at me tae ask fur something against the sickness! But I tell't them that if it's a wee love-bottle they're wantin', I'll dae it; or a charm against the warts, but naethin' fur the sickness. Aweel, guid-day tae ye."

For a moment Alison met the full gaze of her dark eyes. "And it fair gave me a turn," she said to John. "She's a bold woman, thon."

"Aye," said John, non-comittally.

"Her lettin' on aboot her charms and love-bottles! The Minister should have pit a stop tae it long ago."

"Aye. Weel, old Gillies juist wisna bothered. And as fur Mr. Glendinning, I doot if he kens much aboot Meg Annan. At least, I hope he disna," and John gave a little chuckle.

"You should be ashamed of yourself, John Campbell, and you an elder, talking aboot the Minister like that!"

"Like what?" John was all innocence.

"Ye ken fine what I mean. You shouldna even joke aboot Meg Annan and the Minister. Ye ken fine she's—she's a bad woman!"

"That's as may be."

"No 'may be' aboot it! The women in this place are no' blin', or deaf either, and ken fine there's mair goes on in Meg Annan's hoose that makin' up bottles o' biled nettles and water for silly lasses! Furthermore," said Alison, who knew her Bible too, " 'thou shalt not suffer a witch to live'."

"Hoots, woman. Ye're not suggesting they tie Meg Annan tae a post and burn her, juist because—

because some of the lads is mebbe a wee bit ower free wi' her. . . ."

Alison was ashamed of herself. "Na, na, I didna mean that. I was carried away. God forbid there should ever be such a thing again as a witch-burning. Ye ken, old Mrs. Bowman, her that lives doon by the river? She telt me once that her mother, when she was a lassie, saw a witch burnt—and said it was the worst thing she ever saw in her life."

"Aye. I'm thinking the world has grown better. But mind you, Alison, a time like this makes fowk dae queer things. I saw Geordie Matheson hammering up a horse-shoe over his door yesterday, and when I asked him why he was daein' sic a superstitious thing, he muttered something about cold iron keeping out the devil and the sickness. . . . Folk are frightened, Alison."

"I'm frightened tae, John. Fur it's spreading everywhere."

People had cause to be frightened. Like a gathering wave, the sickness grew. More than half of those afflicted died, and the stricken households were left to battle it out on their own, for none was willing to risk self and family in helping others; and this in Dyplin, where neighbourliness had been accounted the greatest social virtue. Those who suffered were fiercely jealous of those who escaped. Bitter rumour and whispered accusation replaced the old clash about births and marriages, drinking, meanness, extravagances and the daily complexity of living. The mechanics of daily life broke down.

When the Walker family was smitten, the shop stood unattended, and the supplies of meal and flour, butter, eggs, bacon, tea, sugar, remained on the shelves. The situation was saved when Patrick Woodrow roused himself from the stupor he had sunk into after the death of his beloved Matty and his wife, and went to serve in his sister-in-law's shop, indifferent to any risk from the Walker family lying ill in the flat above.

The New School was closed officially, just at the point when its organization was collapsing, and the fine new building stood silent and empty, the big windows looking blankly out over the wide lawns. A silence fell on the town, for children were kept round their own doors and only the most essential traffic came and went as speedily as might be in and out of the streets. So the slow clip-clop of the horses drawing the hearse to the churchyard sounded all the louder, and was to remain a memory for always. At first the decencies and due rituals of death were maintained; but there came a time when that was no longer possible; Jock Rennie could not dig the graves fast enough. So a long wide ditch by the north wall of the churchyard was made, and they put the coffins in and covered them quickly; and Matthew said the necessary words over two or three at a time.

With the coming of the cholera, Mary Tullis became of little importance in Dyplin. Even the incident with the miner's wife made small stir. With realities like illness, bereavement, death, suddenly a part of life, Mary's difference was unimportant. She and her father, newcomers living at the top of the town, were outside things. David worked away at his craft, building up a stock for the time when normal life would return; Mary, thankfully aware that she was no longer of interest to Dyplin, came and went quietly from the shops, did her work, read, walked on the hill, and listened to Alison who was worried and anxious about John, and found relief in talking. For the sickness isolated her. People were afraid of contact with the wife of the man who might have handled the dead victims, and her friends and acquaintances avoided Alison. She was too sensible a woman to be hurt by the way her old friends shunned her. "I'd do the same myself," she said, over the hedge, to Mary. "But I'm glad I have you tae talk wi', for I've aye been fond of company. No' like you, Mary. I'm thinking you could be right happy all by your lane. But then, I'm no' keen on books like you. It's real people I need."

She would not come into the Tullises' house nor let Mary come into hers, but if Mary went into the garden to hang washing or gather kale, Alison would come out to speak, over the hedge. But one morning, before Mary had David's porridge on the table, Alison came to the front door, her face grey with fear and her voice hoarse.

"Oh Mary, John's ill. It's the sickness. What'll I do, oh, what'll I do?"

Mary laid a hand over the fingers twisting and

turning in Alison's apron. "Wheesht, my father will go for the doctor. And I'll come in. Go back. I'll be with you in minutes."

When Dr. Munro arrived at the house he found Alison sitting by the fire in tears, rocking herself back and forth.

"Alison Campbell, are you not with your man?"

She lifted a tear-stained face. "Mary from next door is with him. She sent me down here. She—she seemed tae ken whit tae dae. Oh doctor, will he die? Will he die?"

"I can't say yes or no to that, Alison."

He found Mary busy with water and towels cleaning up vomit.

"What are you doing here? This is a job for his wife. You risk yourself and your father."

For a moment she kept her back to him, still busy about the bed, and saying nothing. Then she faced him, and almost, he thought, as if admitting a fault, said, "I do not think I risk myself. I have had the cholera."

"What!" He couldn't believe it. "When? Where?"

"Last year, when I was in London."

"And your father?"

"No. He was not there."

She turned back to the bed, and went on with her task.

"So if you tell me what to do, I will help Mrs.

82

Campbell nurse him. She is, just now, too distressed to do much."

It was clear she would say no more, so Dr. Munro gave such instructions as he could. As he was leaving the bedroom, Mary said:

"I would ask you not to tell anyone what I have told you."

"I won't tell anyone." And the doctor went down to give what comfort he could to Alison. He found her moving round the room, putting it to rights. She had dried her eyes.

"I'm better now, doctor. Sitting about greeting's no' going to help John. Tell me what I must do."

"I've told Miss Tullis. She will help nurse him. You're a lucky woman, Alison, to have such a neighbour."

"But she canna! She might catch it!"

"As to that, you must speak to her yourself. I'll look in again, but Mary Tullis knows what to do."

Alison, having seen him away, went upstairs and into the room. Mary was sponging John's face, calm and composed; at the sight of him tossing and turning, retching, Alison's fragile composure cracked and she drew a sobbing breath. Mary looked up.

"I'll stay and help you."

"You can't. You must not. It would not be right. He is my man, and it's my duty to care for him—not yours."

Nothing would change her. Alison had clear-cut ideas of right and wrong. And to allow another woman to risk death to nurse John was wrong. At last Mary had to say, "I am not in danger. I have had cholera; in London. But you are never to tell anyone. Do you hear? Never. Now will you let me stay?"

Alison, speechless, nodded. So Mary moved in beside Alison, leaving David to fend for himself and, such was the upheaval in the ways of Dyplin, no one thought it worth noticing that he, a man, should be doing the household errands. Alison and Mary set themselves to the task of keeping John in life. Everything the doctor advised, they did, not allowing themselves to doubt its usefulness. They mixed salt and mustard in warm water and forced him to drink it and waited to catch the vomit. When he was lying exhausted they gave him laudanum in toddy; and all the time, he asked for water and more water, till his body was empty and only a stinking fluid came from him: till he lay cold and comatose, his face withered and pinched, and Alison thought he was dead. But they went on doing as they had been told, and the bricks David had brought from the workshop yard they heated in the oven, and wrapped in flannel and put to his feet and sides; and Mary heated salt in a girdle on the fire, and filled old stockings with it, and laid them over and round him; and they wrapped him in heated blankets up to his ears and folded tight round his neck. Then they could do nothing more, but sit in the candle-light and watch.

And it worked; or John's natural forces worked;

or Providence took a hand—who could tell? But when daylight was beginning to dim the candles, John opened his eyes. They had won.

8

UNTIL John's illness, Dyplin had managed to maintain a grip on the established way of life, torn and distorted as that might be. They still had a basic ritual left, to commit their dead with some decency to the cleansing earth. But with John laid aside in sickness, it all became a hasty hugger-mugger, a wrapping of bodies in any convenient covering, a dumping of them, uncoffined, in the gaping ditch; a final abandonment of the decencies. Dreadful rumours spread of movement seen just as Jock Rennie and his assistants flung in the first shovelfuls of earth. Nothing Dr. Munro said or did could stop the stories. Matthew preached in vain of trust and repentance to a pitifully small congregation. In the face of the catastrophe, people simply gave up the effort of maintaining decency and order. So wontedly sober men reeled home from the Thorn Bush, brazenly, at all hours. Noted housewives let their houses go dirty and their children grubby; and in attics and outhouses, young men and girls, abandoning the strict code in which they had been reared, coupled not in love but in fear, seeking forgetfulness of the grimness round them. Meg Annan came and went with a new confidence.

There were some who could not find an escape in

drink or fornication; and there were some who would not; most of them were among the wan, white-faced little group Matthew faced from his pulpit on the Sabbath. Others were driven into a solitary way of life.

Until the New School was closed, Daniel Rutherford had had to admit to himself, guiltily, that it was a relief to have Susannah and the children out of the house. He had his work, which he liked and was good at; he had contact with colleagues. The servant lass, from up-country, had been called home by her parents when the sickness broke out, but Susannah arranged for a woman from the bleach-field to come in and clean for him. But the New School was closed; Mrs. Finlay went down with cholera; and Daniel found himself alone in his large house, cooking miserable meals, keeping a fire burning, trying to wash his own linen. For now no neighbour was ready to offer meals and help, as would have happened in normal times. One day, he looked out a volume of Cowper's poems and went up to the Tullises to offer it on loan to Mary; but she was not at home. All he could do was leave the book, and go on to walk on the hill, hoping he might see her there.

He climbed up and over Gloom Hill, and down to the track that led to the castle. It was a long time since he had been into it, not since he had climbed up with Emma, his wife, that first summer they were in Dyplin. He had not thought of her for months. What love had been left from the early desire that had driven him to marry her had, by the time of her death, turned into a tired kindness, and not always that. Very occasionally he allowed himself to wonder if it really had been an accident—or if she, for she was a nervous woman, prone to fits of gloom, had thrown herself into the burn, that bleak, wet day when it was running brown and foaming in spate. . . . He shook his head, tossing memory aside, and went up the track to the entrance to the castle. It belonged to the Inneses of Griffton, and they maintained it sufficiently to allow access to the great square keep, which was the nucleus of the building, and its oldest and strongest part. In the wing that joined the tower to the great wall stretching the width of the courtyard on the south there were two rooms, wind and weatherproof, and here the Inneses had installed an old woman, Betsy Black, to act as a caretaker. She was paid a tiny pension, having been a dairymaid at Griffton, and was quite happy to live in solitary state in the castle, with a cow and some hens, which scratched about in the courtyard. In the summer, visitors of a romantic turn who climbed up to the castle, gave her money which she hid in a box in a ledge in one of the great empty fireplaces in the tower. Once a month or so she went down into Dyplin for essential supplies, where the children gave her a wide berth, as she strode along with her long stick, her big woven basket and her old-fashioned brown cape.

When Daniel entered the courtyard under the dark archway he saw her standing at the door at the foot of the tower. As soon as she noticed him, she disappeared into the darkness behind her. By the time he reached the doorway, she was in her room, peering through the door which was barely ajar.

"Dinna come near me. I'm no wantin' the sickness. Ye've no been near it yersel?"

"No."

"Aweel, ye can gang up. But keep awa frae me."

And the door was shut fast.

Daniel climbed the narrow stone stair. There were three big rooms one above each other in the tower, each with a big wide fireplace, each with windows to east and west and south. The windows increased in size with the distance from the ground—a simple defensive measure. In one room there were stone window-seats in the window recess, and a view out to a high valley and the hills. It was a bare, timeless scene, with only the sky, the hills, the stream. Daniel sat for a little and looked, and thought of men and women in the past three hundred or so years who had sat there too, and looked out on the same scene. He shivered a little and rose to continue climbing up the stair.

Through the low door in a little square turret he stepped out onto the roof of the tower. It was surrounded by a low parapet and, seeing it, he was again reminded of Emma, who had no head for heights and could only look over if he held her firmly. He looked southwards over the beech and oak and birch of the glen to the houses of Dyplin, peaceful in the sunshine. Beyond rose the Braes, and beyond that a gleam from the water of the Firth, and farther still a dim blue line of hills. He walked over to the west wall, and looked down into the little valley that the burn on that side had carved through the hills. At one point it disappeared into a deep pool between high cliffs—the boys from the New School used to swim in it—it was icy cold, and the water poured out of it in a violent waterfall. To the north, there was nothing but bare hills. This had been the most vulnerable side of the castle. The walls were thickest here, and pierced with narrow slits for arrows and muskets. He put a foot on the parapet, laid an arm across his knee, and stood imagining the approach of armed men up the slopes and the sudden cry of the watchman on the tower.

"Tak care ye dinna fall, Mr. Rutherford."

Daniel swung round. Standing in an angle of the little turret was Meg Annan, her red hair lifting in the wind, a bright patterned shawl round her shoulders instead of the wonted black. She was not smiling, but her dark eyes were gleaming.

"How long have you been there?"

"I followed you into the tower. And when you went into one of the rooms I came ahead of you up here."

"Do you come here often?"

"Oh aye. I'm no' that welcome a sicht in Dyplin—or wisna', till the sickness came. A body

90

maun walk somewhere. I've seen ye on the hill masel'."

"I have seen you."

"Aweel, we're acquainted, then. Ye ken me?"

"Oh yes." For who in Dyplin didn't know her?

She moved over beside him, and for the first time he stood close to Meg Annan. The first thing that he noticed was how scrupulously fresh and clean was everything about her. Her hair was shining and had a fragrance in it; her shawl was spotless; her black dress neatly ironed, every button in place. Her hands were work-scarred, but clean, her nails immaculate. From her there came a sense of fresh-laundered linen that mingled with the perfume of her hair. He was to learn later that she was fanatically clean, forever washing herself, her clothes, her hair, and rinsing it in water in which she had dipped sweet-scented herbs. But now it came with a shock of pleasant surprise. Because he had only seen her, casually, briefly, mostly at a distance, and because she always wore black, and because her hair was always, as now, less than tidy, with strands blowing over her face, he had taken her to be a slattern.

Now she was smiling at him, and her teeth were strong and white.

"Ye're all alane the now. Are ye no' eager for company? Ye'll no' be able tae tak your usual ride doon tae Alloa tae visit Margaret Johnston."

She was no longer smiling. The dark eyes were

malicious as she turned away and gave him a sideways glance.

Daniel was startled—too startled to dissemble.

"What do you know about Margaret Johnston?"

"Enough. But where's the hairm? Naebody—naebody wi' ony sense, that is—would expect a man like you, wi' the strength that's in you, tae be wi'oot a woman. But ye didna need tae gang that far."

He caught her in anger and drew her round to face him. "Have you told anyone this?"

"Me? Na, na. Meg Annan is no' one tae tell secrets, especially that kind of secret."

She was laughing. The wind blew her hair across his face, he breathed its perfume, her black eyes glowed. Daniel caught her to him.

But she pushed him back. "Na, na. No' here. Whae kens whae's seein' us up here on the tower?"

She caught his hand and led him down to the great vaulted room beneath. And there he took her.

When he left, alone, Betsy Black's claw of a hand was through the chink of the door as he passed.

"Dinna forget the caretaker, sir."

He dropped money into her hand, and heard her chuckle.

"Thenk ye. Ye're a guid giver. But it's a braw, braw view frae the tower, is it no'?"

And the door closed on a cackle of laughter.

Four days later, Alison, who had for the first time since John's illness gone down to the shops, came back into the bedroom full of news. John, weak but well on the way to recovery, was propped up on his pillows.

"And what's going on?" he asked.

"Good and bad. Wee Walter Walker is dead and Annie Young in Robertson's shop at death's door. I canna tell ye it all, John. Naethin' like this ever struck Dyplin before. An' the town's quiet; hardly a thing stirring; an' a smell of smoke and sulphur from folk burning stuff tae try and stop the sickness. And poor Patrick Woodrow there in the shop, handin' things oot as if he wisna half alive. I said something aboot the smoke and the smell, and d'ye ken whit his answer wis? 'It's the stink of hell, hell's where we are'. It fair made me grue."

"Ah weel, the man's had a sair trial, Alison. We've muckle tae be thankful aboot. I'm just feart ye'll catch it."

"That's as may be. I dinna think it's likely. Tho' I could see the twa-three that cam tae the shop didna come in when I wis there—except Meg Annan, and she . . ."

"Aye?"

"John, ye'll no' believe this. She was buying oatmeal, and I heard her say—'Mr. Rutherford likes his porridge made wi' the coarse meal.' "

"Sae dae I. Whit's wrang wi' that?"

"John! D'ye no' see? She must be makin' his breakfast. Meg Annan!"

"Oh." Light dawned on him. "Aye. I see whit ye're gettin' at. Weel, the man's been all alane since Tib Finlay was ill. He'd be needin' a housekeeper."

"But Meg Annan! In his hoose! And him the teacher o' the Infant School! A maist respectable family! Oh, she's a bad yin!"

"Noo, noo, Alison. Ye've nae proof there's anything wrang. The man would be needin' a woman about the place. . . ."

But, aware he was approaching delicate ground, John was silent.

"It's no' juist whether there's onything wrang, John. Afore, Meg Annan would never have thought of going tae be a housekeeper like that. I tell you, everything's been put topsy-turvy by the cholera. An'—an' naethin's being done richt. Oh, John, they're juist pittin' them awa in the ditch happed in blankets—"

And Alison, who had found silence and fear everywhere, whose friends and acquaintances had hurried past with averted faces, collapsed in tears on the chair by the bed. Here Mary found her.

"What is wrong, Alison? Are you ill?"

Alison shook her head, unable to speak. John spoke for her.

"She's upset by everything, Mary. She's been to the shops; and hearing aboot all the folk that's smitten, and the way things are, and them no' being buried richt—it's upset her."

Mary took Alison's hand.

"Don't cry so, Alison. It is horrible in the town, but it will pass. Time makes things pass."

Alison sniffed, and wiped her eyes.

"But it'll never be the same again. Will it?"

"Dyplin had changed already," said John. "Ye ken that, Alison. When the New School came it made changes."

"Aye. But these—" she groped for words. "These were good changes. They were—they were forward changes. What's happened noo is bad."

"Weel, things canna gang backwards, can they, Mary?"

"I don't know," said Mary. She took Alison's hand again. "You're tired. We just have to wait till all this is past. And it will pass."

And of course it did. Gradually the infection lost its hold. Slowly the number of new cases decreased. There came a day when they filled up the dreadful ditch in the churchyard and went back to the old orderly procedures. By this time John was back to work. At length, when there had been no new cases for a fortnight, they held a service of thanksgiving in the church.

To the elders and to Matthew it had seemed unthinkable not to give thanks for Dyplin's deliverance. But as Matthew looked down on the congregation and remembered the faces now gone for ever, and saw the heavy black mourning clothes, he had to stifle a whisper of doubt whether there was cause to give thanks, and there came into his mind Patrick Woodrow's words: "I'll not be at any thanksgiving, Mr. Glendinning, for I have nothing to be thankful about." Perhaps it would have been better to make it a mourning service—but was that

95

thought not a questioning of the ways of Providence?

The time had proved a sore trial of faith to more than the afflicted. Matthew wished he had more of the fixed theological principles of his fellow ministers in the Presbytery. He could just imagine how the Reverend Mungo Bethune would have dealt with Mrs. Matheson when she had said, defiantly, that she prayed every night for her two children who had died within hours of each other. Matthew, face to face with a grief like that, "Rachel weeping for her children", could only murmur that it was not needed; they were in the divine care. The Reverend Mungo would have seized the opportunity for a stern theological expostulation on the sinfulness of prayer for the dead. . . . Miserably aware of his own weakness of faith and doctrine, Matthew would have been astonished and even alarmed to know that the congregation now looking up at him, bleakly unmoving, held him in infinitely greater respect than before the disaster; for Matthew had been tireless and fearless in his ministry to the sick and dying. Joseph Harvey, staring stonily at him, thought, "Aye, he's developing. He'll mak' a grand minister yet," and then he rose, as precentor, to lead the singing of the twenty-third psalm; and was hard put to it to keep his voice firm, for he had lost a daughter and two grandchildren.

But if there was more of mourning than thanksgiving in the church, there was comfort too.

After the weeks of separation and suspicion, people could shake hands, talk and walk side by side down the path through the churchyard. The horror was behind them. Life would now get back to its normal routine.

9

ON the surface, it seemed as if this was happening. One change was permanent. The toll of the cholera among the miners was so great that the mine was closed. The survivors moved elsewhere, and the row of clay and wattle houses was left to crumble away, deserted and unvisited. But the shops were soon back to their usual ways; the carters loitered and gossiped as of old. Blethering Bob once more set up his stall, congratulated his potential customers on the passing of the cholera, and was sure his pills had contributed to that happy outcome. The New School was to remain closed over New Year; otherwise the normal surface of life seemed restored. Even Alison's doubts were resolved when Susannah and the children came back from the Borders and Meg Annan cooked Daniel's breakfast porridge no more.

But the doctor was not so sure that all was as it had been. He had sent his wife and family away at the beginning of the epidemic, and had been left to the care of Kirsty Purdie, who had been a servant in his mother's house and had come to the doctor's when he married. Kirsty fed and tended him, grumbled and scolded, waited up for him at nights, rose at dawn for him. When Elspeth and the children came home, Kirsty was sent off to her sister's house up-country for a holiday. The doctor refused to go away. Elspeth pleaded.

"Things are back to normal. Why not?"

"I don't feel like it. As for 'back to normal'— have you noticed something, Elspeth? No one ever mentions the name of any of those who died. Never, never. It's as if they were pushing the memory of what has happened away out of sight as being absolutely unbearable. They don't even go to the churchyard on Sundays any more, and there's not been a flower laid on a grave."

"I hadn't noticed. But, yes, I see you're right. And once or twice people have made cutting remarks to me about those who went away . . . though they've little cause to say anything to me considering all you did." And angry tears came into her eyes.

"That's what I mean, Elspeth. They're hitting out at anybody and anything. And the division between old and new Dyplin is widening. The teachers and the others in the new bit of the town didn't suffer so much—I don't know why: maybe the houses are better, the wells cleaner—and the older inhabitants resent it. This morning Mrs. Robertson the baker said something about incomers to a place 'aye getting the best of it'. She felt Annie Young's death very badly. If all this bitterness and anger is kept down and hidden, I fear it will come out some way, against someone, against something."

But no one else seemed concerned. Daniel

Rutherford had always been one for walking on the hills. So no one thought it odd when they saw him striding up the road to the castle; and no one but old Betsy knew that Meg Annan as often took the narrow slippery path up through the glen; and Betsy was not one to tell.

"We'll no' can meet here come the real winter," said Meg one blowy late October day, when the clouds raced and scuds of rain blew past the old tower. "Ye'll need tae find a quiet way tae my house."

Daniel said nothing. Meeting in the castle was one thing; creeping into Meg's house with all the risk of discovery was another. It might be necessary to break it off with Meg. She would surely understand that the teacher at the Infant School could not be known to have dealings with her. But now, as she turned to him, buttoning up the bodice of her sober black dress, and said, "Ye'll no' stop seeing me, come the winter?" there was a note almost of pleading in her voice, so different from her usual flaunting ways that, for a moment, he wondered if the solution would be so simple.

Her tone hardened. "Ye'll no' can gang tae puir Margaret Johnston. The cholera took her."

"Yes, I know. Come, Meg, it's not real winter yet. There's time to think things over."

Twice Daniel had gone to the Tullises' house, hoping to see Mary. Twice she had been out. He began to wonder if she were avoiding him, but this was not so. Mary had not seen him all the time of the cholera. She seldom thought of him, and when she did it was with a feeling of resentment at what she still considered to be his treachery. The volume of Cowper which he had left she pushed angrily aside, it lay untouched on top of a bookcase. With the dying away of the cholera she had fallen into a placid routine of shopping and housework, reading and writing poetry again, putting into her poetry something of the terror and horror, the sadness, the sense of a bewildering chastisement that all felt, herself too, in spite of her immunity; and she found in voicing all this pain a sense of healing for her own private wound, for the disaster that had driven them to Dyplin. Now, coming and going from the shops, exchanging quiet greetings with the passers-by, she felt a sense of reassurance, that at last she was fitting in, was part of the background, and was no longer of any particular interest.

But it was not so. Somehow it had leaked out that the first case of cholera had not been in the miners' houses, but in the Tullises'. It was there it had started. They had taken in a man with cholera; they had brought it to Dyplin. The resentment was not against David—"a decent man, just quietly doing his trade". "She was the one that had to play the kind angel of mercy and nurse the man." "All very well being that kind tae strangers; but whit aboot putting the rest o' the place at risk? The Minister, that was different; it was his job, tho' mind you he didna need tae be all that zealous . . . but as for Miss

101

Mary Tullis, wi' her airs and graces *and* her poetry . . ."

Thus the murmurs over tea-cups and across counters. Alison heard nothing, at least at first, it being known she was "very taken up with Mary Tullis". Nor, of course, did either Mary or David, and they entirely failed to catch the drift of any innuendoes.

Mary felt she was happier than she had been for a long time; or if happier was too strong a word, then at least that she was beginning to feel that happiness might be possible again; that the frozen numbness was passing, and she could allow herself to feel more than a cringing desire to feel nothing. The new spring of poetry was surely the first sign of this thaw. That her poetry had changed and deepened she knew; but whether it was good or bad she could not judge. And who was there to tell her? Even supposing she could have found it possible to show it to anyone.

During the time of the cholera, she had walked much in the countryside, and had explored into the valley as well as up on the hill. One of her favourite walks was to go down to the Martyrs' Bridge. An old and narrow road breaking off from the turnpike led down to the bridge. There the river had cut through the rock, and ran very deep and dark and still. Thick woodland grew on either side, and the place was shady and could seem gloomy. Mary loved it for its very shadiness and remoteness. With the making of the turnpike little traffic went that way, and she had never met anyone on her walks there.

One late November afternoon she went down to the Bridge, walking briskly and enjoying the low sunshine that cast long shadows across the stubble and the roadway. The bridge was in the shadow of the valley, a little chilly. But she stopped to lean on the parapet and look down into the dark water. When she turned back to take the homeward track across the fields, she saw that a man was standing under the trees looking at her. He moved forward. It was Daniel Rutherford.

She faced him in silence, frowning. He raised his hat and said, "Miss Tullis. I am glad I have met you. I have called once or twice at the house with books, but you were from home."

"Yes."

He was still unforgiven. He looked at her appreciatively. She wore a dress of some light woollen material, a dove-grey, he supposed it might be called, and over her shoulders a short cape of a bright tartan whose reds and greens glowed in the subdued light under the trees. Over her head she had tied a little white shawl; it showed up her dark hair and the curves of her firm round cheeks and small pointed chin. Everything about her indicated orderliness and control; as she stood there gazing unsmiling at him, he had a sudden desire to break down that control, to find out what lay beneath it.

He moved forward again and said, "I see you have not forgiven me. Come, much has happened since we last met. You escaped the cholera, I know. So did I. I am sure my careless words must have been long forgotten by everyone. Can we not be friends?"

Mary hesitated. But it was of course true. In view of all that had happened, to continue bearing a grudge because of his heedless words was petty: besides, of all her small acquaintance in Dyplin, he was the only one who had not seemed to find her interest in books and reading either odd or unimportant. So she said gravely:

"Very well."

"Ah, but I shall not feel truly forgiven till you say it with a smile."

"Very well," and she smiled. Perhaps because Mary was not a prodigal smiler, when she did smile, it was like a transformation, and Daniel thought, "She is beautiful after all."

He stood beside her and they both looked over at the water. "You come here often?" he asked.

"Quite often. I like it here."

"Some people would think it dark and gloomy. After all, it commemorates a man who suffered a dreadful fate."

"Yes, I know. You told me when we first met, on the hill."

"Yes, I did." So she remembered that first meeting. He went on, "If one knows the story, then surely one must remember it here."

"I remember it as being a memorial to a very

brave man, who wouldn't give up what he thought right."

He sensed again a steely quality in her. "But there are other gloomy associations here. Not long ago—some ten years ago—a murder was committed here. A farm servant shot the baker when he was driving past here in his cart, and killed him and took his money bag. They traced him because he paid for everything he bought in pennies and ha'pennies."

"And what happened to him?"

"He was hanged at Perth; and a fair number from Dyplin went to see it."

"Oh, that's horrible. Don't you know any stories about Dyplin except the fierce and the cruel?"

"Oh yes, I think so. It's just that the fierce and the cruel seem to be what is preserved. But I can tell you a pleasant thing about this very spot—whether true or not I can't say. Do you see where a little trickle of water runs down the rock there?"

He pointed downstream and to the right, where a bright orange streak stained the rock.

"Yes."

"Well, it comes from a little spring in the wood there, and the story is that it was blessed by a holy man, long before the days of the Martyr, and that the water has healing powers. The farmers come to get it to give to sick horses; and some people in Dyplin will come and take away a jug of it for medicine. It probably has minerals in it—you see how it stains the rock."

105

"Perhaps that's what Meg Annan uses for her love potions."

He was startled, and looked earnestly at her; but her eyes were innocent of any guile, and she was laughing.

Nevertheless, he said abruptly, "I must leave you now, for I have some way to go. A child who was at my school has had an accident and I want to see how he is. But I am forgiven?"

"Oh yes. Good day, then. I must be going back."

Daniel went over the bridge and up into the trees. Mary took the track over the fields. From behind the huge tree that had hidden Tom Brigg when he shot the baker, Meg Annan watched them go.

10

HAVING re-established contact with Mary, Daniel followed up two days later by calling at her house. This time he found her at home and was invited into the little parlour. He made only a brief stay, saying he had simply come to ask if she would care to go to the library in the New School with him on the following day, the Trustees having decided that the library should be open although the school was to remain closed till after New Year.

"You are not short of books, I know," he said, "but at the library you may find books which you would wish to read but not necessarily purchase."

David added his voice. "You would find it interesting, Mary."

She saw the familiar anxious look in her father's eyes and knew it would please him if she agreed, for he could not help, every now and then, urging her to go about more, get to know people, not keep herself shut in a corner, reproaching himself for not doing more for her. So she said:

"Yes, I'll go. At what time?"

"I will meet you on the steps of the New School at two o'clock tomorrow."

The library of the New School was the centre of the building, a handsome square hall, rising up the full height of the structure to a dome. It was a beautiful room, and Mary, entering it for the first time, stopped in the doorway with a little exclamation of admiration.

Daniel responded quickly, "It is very fine, isn't it? And you see the shelves are full."

Mary's eyes were glowing. She moved over to the shelves.

"May I?"

"Certainly. Choose what you want. I will have a word with Mr. Fraser, who is on duty today."

Certain of the teachers at the New School took it in turns to act as librarian. Walter Fraser was the writing master, and one of the older members of the staff, having been the first appointed after the Rector. While Mary moved round the shelves Daniel went to the table and spoke to him.

"I've brought Miss Tullis, the umbrella-maker's daughter, to join the library. She is interested in books."

"Ah, yes. The poetic young lady. She is very welcome to join."

He rose from behind the table and he and Daniel went over to Mary. Daniel introduced her to Walter Fraser, who said kindly, "I welcome you to the library, Miss Tullis. Can I help you, or would you rather choose for yourself?"

"Choose for myself," said Mary too hastily, and then added awkwardly: "Thank you."

Walter Fraser smiled. "I prefer to do my own choosing too."

He went back to the table and sat down again to read the *Edinburgh Review* open before him. But his attention wandered back to Mary and Daniel, who had not taken Mary's hint and was going round the shelves with her. He took a book from the shelf, and opened it, pointed out something; they began discussing it. And so it was that when two ladies—wives of staff—came in to change their novels, the first thing they saw was Mary and Daniel Rutherford in animated conversation. Neither Mary nor Daniel noticed them. The two ladies returned their books, and then went to choose new ones.

"Good afternoon, Mr. Rutherford." Amelia Drysdale had a resonant voice. Daniel turned and bowed.

"Good afternoon."

"You have found an interesting book?" This was Madame Grueber, a graceful French woman, not entirely popular with the other New School ladies. Her eyes were on Mary with cool appraisement. Daniel did not like either lady.

"May I introduce Miss Tullis? Mrs. Drysdale and Madame Grueber. Miss Tullis and I were looking at Dugald Stewart's *Philosophy of the Active and Moral Powers.*"

"Indeed." Madame Grueber was condescending. "Miss Tullis is interested in philosophy as well as poetry. An unusual combination. I'm afraid I have no time for any reading beyond something pleasantly relaxing."

Mary's colour heightened. "One can always find time for what one is interested in."

"Indeed. But few women, if any, would find philosophy of interest."

She bowed graciously and the two women moved over to a shelf of recent novels.

Mary watched them with tight lips and sparking eyes, and said, "I don't think I want to borrow books from this library."

"Oh, come," said Daniel, "you mustn't let two stupid women turn you from the library. See, here are the works of Sir Walter Scott. Surely there is one of them you would like."

She hesitated, looked, and succumbed.

"Yes. *The Heart of Midlothian.* I haven't read it."

Walter Fraser, as he entered the book in the list of borrowings, said kindly, "I hope you will make full use of the library, Miss Tullis."

For he had overheard, and appreciated, the little encounter with Madame Grueber, whose pretensions to cultural distinction were not a little trying to her acquaintanceship among the New School staff.

Outside, on the steps of the New School, Mary held out a hand to Daniel and said firmly, "I am going to the shops now. Thank you for taking me to the library."

He was being neatly dismissed. As he took her hand, he admired the cool competence which she drew round her like a cloak. Watching her walk quickly away past the rows of teachers' houses, he determined to find out what lay beneath the cloak.

Once having tasted the pleasures of the library, Mary continued to use it and the quiet figure standing reading in the shadow of a pillar became a familiar sight to the other users. Daniel, knowing his colleagues and, more important, his colleagues' wives, was careful not to be seen too often talking to her as she wandered round the shelves. Nevertheless, through him and through Walter Fraser, who was interested in the quiet gentle girl who could talk about the books as none of the other women could, she met a number of teachers and their wives, maintaining always a cool politeness and reacting very swiftly to any touch of the patronizing or condescending. Kind Mrs. Fraser would have asked her to tea but, as she said to Walter, "She's so independent. I'm afraid to ask her. And I don't know why she should be. After all, she's only . . ."

Walter filled the pause. "Only an umbrella-maker's daughter? You're wrong there, you and your friends. She's a great deal more. Just see how she's got the lot of you wondering about her!"

Occasionally the Reverend Matthew Glendinning went to the library, generally to look at *Blackwood's Magazine* or the *Edinburgh Review*—a little guiltily—he was never sure he was not succumbing to worldly temptation in wasting his time thus. Sometimes he would take out a book on travel, Mungo Park's *Travels in the Interior of Africa* or Heber's *Journey through India*. It was while searching for Burney's *Discoveries in the South Sea*

111

that he met Mary, standing by the pillar in her usual place, lost in Susan Ferrier's *Marriage*. She was so absorbed in the book that she started when he spoke to her.

"I beg your pardon. Did I startle you?"

"A little. I was lost in my book."

"May I ask what it is?"

She told him, and asked if he had read it.

"No. I do not read novels."

"Oh, but why not, Mr. Glendinning? They teach one so much about people."

"But novels are false-telling. They are not true."

"Not true in fact, but true in spirit."

"Truth is truth, Miss Tullis. I do not distinguish kinds of truth."

"So you have never read any of Sir Walter Scott's novels?"

"None."

"Oh, I pity you. Not to know the nobility of Jeanie Downs—I have just read *The Heart of Midlothian*—and her resolve to maintain her principles in the face of the strongest temptation—she was a splendid character."

"I can, and have, read of noble women in history: like Madame Rolland. How can you learn better about people than by reading the lives of those who have really lived and struggled? Like the travellers battling on in the face of danger and despair, and yet achieving their goal. Or those who kept their faith in the face of torture and death. . . . But I am preaching, and you, I remember, dislike sermons."

112

Mary looked self-conscious, but all she said was, "But you do not consider it wrong to read novels? It is not a sin?" She looked at him demurely.

"Not a sin," said the Reverend Matthew Glendinning. "A weakness."

"Then I am very weak."

Could she be laughing at him? There was a hint—the nearest touch—of teasing at least. Matthew Glendinning was quite unused to being either laughed at or teased. He rather liked it. Smiling, he said "A pardonable weakness, but a weakness." And then had to leave her in answer to a "Good afternoon" from Miss Susannah Rutherford.

On his return from the library Matthew astonished his mother by asking her to invite Mary and her father to tea at the Manse in the near future.

"Mary Tullis and her father! Whatever for? They're newcomers, and there's many a family in the congregation mair meriting being asked to the Manse than them."

"Nevertheless, I would like you to ask Miss Tullis and her father to tea."

She recognized the note in his voice. It meant that he had made up his mind and would have his way. But she made one last effort.

"But Mattha, if we ask just them—folk'll talk."

He frowned. Matthew seldom frowned. A little tremor ran through Mrs. Glendinning.

"And why should they 'talk'?"

"You know fine. A father and—and his un-married daughter. You know fine . . ."

Her attempt at provoking him to a declaration of interest failed.

"There would be no 'talk' if we asked others with them? Then ask others."

"But who?"

"I leave that to you." His frown cleared. "You arrange it."

But Mrs. Glendinning knew better. She came to him an hour or two later.

"I thought John and Alison Campbell, and the Robertsons, and Joseph Harvey and Maisie?" for the beadle and his wife were solemnly entertained at the Manse from time to time.

Matthew considered. "I should like one or two of the teachers from the New School."

His mother stared. "But—but . . ."

" 'But' what?" The frown again.

"David Tullis is only an umbrella-maker and . . ."

"And Miss Tullis is 'only' the umbrella-maker's daughter? Ah, but she's a lot more than that."

"Well, Mattha, you must choose the party yourself. I'm taking no more to do with it."

"Let us think it out together. The Campbells, yes, but not, I think, the others. What about the Frasers? They know and like Miss Tullis. And perhaps Daniel Rutherford?"

But Mrs. Glendinning could be strong-willed too.

"Never! I will not have that man in my house,"

for she knew all about Meg Annan and Daniel's porridge. Matthew was, of course, quite unaware. Sometimes she was exasperated by the way he remained ignorant of what went on round about him. He was, of course, professionally convinced of the fallen state of man, but seemed often unconscious of human folly and ill-doing among his neighbours. Now he was surprised at her vehemence.

"Why not? He knows Miss Tullis and her father."

Mrs. Glendinning folded her lips, but she was not without cunning. She was aware of how her son felt about Susannah.

"We can't ask him without his sister; and you know yourself how ill-tongued she is. Why not ask the doctor and Mrs. Munro? He kens a'body."

So it was decided. Alison was elated at being invited to the Manse, an honour which did not come too often, and was much intrigued when Mary said casually that she and her father had been invited too. By various subtleties, she discovered who the other guests were to be, and was all the more exasperated that she and John could not accept, being already trysted to go to the induction of her nephew as minister at Forgandenny near Perth.

"It's very aggravating, John. I'm that curious tae ken what it'll be like at the Manse. Fancy them being invited, just newcomers, and alang with the doctor and the Frasers! If it comes tae that, fancy us being invited with them. Ye should have seen Maggie Walker's face when I let drop we'd been asked!"

"I don't see onything extraordinar' in us being asked. The doctor and I ken each other fine. And Walter Fraser's father was a tile-maker in the West and I'll back a guid joiner against a tile-maker ony day. Besides, it's the age of democracy. Have ye forgotten woman, I've noo got a vote? Aye, an' I'll be using it tae afore long."

"Och, you and your democracy! Ye ken weel folk have their place. . . . Mind you, I wouldna wonder but the Minister's mebbe taking a notion tae Mary."

"What?" John lowered his three-day-old copy of the *Scotsman*. "Oho! That'll rouse the clash! Mind you, I'm no' shair she's the richt one fur a minister's wife—no' because she's am umbrella-maker's daughter, but . . ."

"Aye. I ken what ye mean. I canna juist see Mary being the lady o' the Manse—and yet she's a kind good girl as you and I ken, John."

Quite unaware that there could be anything out of the way in their being invited to the Manse, Mary and her father turned up at the appointed hour and were shown into the parlour, where they found the Frasers and the doctor and his wife already seated by the blazing fire. It was a dull and chilly day, but here all was warmth and welcome, the flames dancing on the brass poker and tongs and shovel, and flickering in the glass of the corner cabinet.

The curtains were striped red and grey, the carpet was red, the chairs solid and upright, but comfortable enough and polished so that the firelight glimmered on them too. The candles were already lit, burning clearly and steadily.

Matilda, wearing her best cap and apron, announced them with a little bob curtsey, and then hurried to the kitchen to brew tea. Mrs. Glendinning welcomed them and introductions followed. The doctor already knew David. Mr. Fraser was interested to meet him. Neither felt it strange that the umbrella-maker should be asked to meet them. Both the ladies would have firmly denied that they entertained feelings of superiority towards their fellow-men, but both were secretly surprised when Mary and her father were announced. Mrs. Fraser knew Mary from meeting her in the library. Elspeth Munro shook hands with interest. She had heard of the "odd" young woman, the umbrella-maker's daughter. What she saw was a well-dressed young lady. Mary was wearing a light grey dress, and a shawl patterned in grey and pink. Her summer best bonnet with the offending green ribbons had been replaced by a winter one of black velours with a ruching of pink ribbon under the brim—it was no more sober than her summer one and had also provoked comment. Mrs. Glendinning took her bonnet and shawl and Matthew settled her in a chair by the fire.

As always happened at Dyplin tea-parties, the men and women grouped themselves apart. Soon

117

the men were deep in discussion of the coming elections. David was well read in politics, but chary, for business reasons, of making his political allegiance obvious. The doctor and Walter Fraser, while both on the side of Reform, had differing ideas as to how and how far it should be carried out. Matthew did not say much, but sat back a little and watched Mary as she joined in the women's talk. They discussed the price of butter, the difficulties of getting coal now that the mine was closed, and new crochet patterns. Normally Myra Fraser and Elspeth Munro would have discussed their respective families but, anxious not to exclude Mary from the conversation, they did no more than voice polite enquiries. Mary had learned, in Glasgow, the necessity for playing her part in such social exchanges, and she did so with a good grace.

When they moved through to the dining-room to the tea-table, it was different. Mrs. Glendinning prided herself on her tea-table. On an immaculate lace-covered white linen tablecloth gleamed her white and gold wedding china, carefully cherished through the years. There was the expected spread of thin bread and butter, three kinds of scones (she and Matilda had been hard at it all morning in the kitchen), dark sticky ginger-bread, sultana cake, shortbread and a sponge almost ready to float away, it was so light, sandwiched with a delicate layer of raspberry jam and dusted with pink caster sugar. Only the bread came from the baker's. Tall crystal jam-dishes held home-made strawberry, raspberry, plum and blackcurrant jam and in the butter-dishes was a choice of fresh or salted butter. On a tray before the hostess was a silver tea-set, bequeathed to her by an aunt, and her most cherished possession. In this room too, candles were lit and a fire blazed.

They sat at the round table, alternately men and women, and now the conversation had to be general; that is to say, the women dropped their domestic topics to play audience to weighty masculine talk. It was still of politics and the elections. Mary asked:

"When will the election be?"

"It cannot be long now," said the doctor. "There will be an open-air meeting, a vote will be taken by a show of hands and acclamation. But either candidate can then claim that a ballot be held."

"It will be a great day," said Mrs. Fraser. "I should like to watch it."

"I should rather be voting," said Mary.

There was a silence.

"Voting? But women do not vote," said Walter Fraser.

"I know. But I can't see why not."

"But—but politics and such things are not for women. They are too—too . . ."

"Too what?"

"Too difficult. Is that not so?" he appealed to David.

But David shook his head. "I do not think they are too difficult. Too unpleasant, perhaps."

Walter Fraser looked at the women. "Myra, you don't want to vote, do you?"

"Not particularly, because I know nothing about politics. But I expect I could learn."

"Mrs. Glendinning?"

"I don't know much about it either, but it seems to me ridiculous that any fool of a man, if he has enough property, can vote, and I can't."

"Mother!" Matthew was astonished and startled.

"I'm sorry, Mattha. I shouldn't have spoken so strongly."

"Will you be voting, Minister?" asked Doctor Munro.

"No," said Matthew. "It's a matter of conscience. I will not vote."

"But that's so unfair." Mary's eyes were bright with indignation. "I should like to vote, and cannot. And you can, and will not!"

Matthew smiled at her. "Even if I wanted to, I could not give you my vote. Why do you want it so much? It is for men, surely, to concern themselves with the ordering of the State, under God, and for women—" meeting her look he faltered—"for women to support and strengthen the men."

"I see." Her voice was dry. " 'He for God only, she for God in him'."

"Is that in the Bible?" asked Mrs. Fraser with interest.

"No, my dear. It's from *Paradise Lost*," said Walter, smiling.

"Oh well, that's the next best thing," said Myra placidly.

But Mrs. Glendinning had decided it was time to change the conversation. "We ought, I'm sure, to feel thankful that we're all able to be sitting together like this," she said, "after the terrible time of the sickness."

There was a murmur of agreement round the table.

"Indeed yes," said the doctor. "But the effects are not past yet. I don't mean there will be more cases. I am thinking of changes in the way people think and feel and behave. Have you been conscious of this, Minister?"

Matthew looked troubled. "Yes, I have felt something. There has been a falling-off in the attendance at Divine Worship. . . ."

He caught his mother's eye.

"But these are matters for the Kirk Session. As the Proverbs of Solomon say, there is 'a time to keep silence and a time to speak'. Come, Mr. Tullis, and Miss Tullis, how do you find life in peaceful little Dyplin after Glasgow?"

Some time later, as the guests were leaving, Mary turned to look into the parlour, glowing with fire and candle-light. After the conventional expressions of thanks she added, with an unexpected intensity of tone, "I am glad to have been here." Then she stepped out into the dark autumn night.

Mrs. Glendinning went back to the parlour,

shaking her head. "She's a strange girl. I can't make her out."

Matthew was standing by the fire, looking into the flames. He turned to his mother. "I want to make her my wife," he said.

"Oh, Mattha! Mattha!"

"Why not?"

"She's not the girl to be a minister's wife."

"Why not?"

Mrs. Glendinning braced herself to go on. "Ye ken fine, Mattha, that a minister's wife is not just a wife. She—she represents the Manse. . . ."

"And why should Miss Mary Tullis not represent the Manse?"

"She's too—too different; too thirled to books and poetry—too taken up with things that don't concern a woman."

"But once married, once with a family, she would put aside her books and poetry, I'm sure. She is a good housekeeper. If you were to visit her, you would find a well-run house. But the truth is, I love Mary Tullis."

Mrs. Glendinning had long since learnt when it was useless to argue with her son, so all she said was, "She is a fortunate woman."

"Ah. I said I wanted to make her my wife. It does not follow I will succeed. I do not think she thinks of me at all—or only as the Minister, prone to sermonizing."

" 'Only' as the Minister? Oh, Mattha, has she made you scorn your calling?"

"Not 'scorn'. But a minister is also a man. Come, we'll say no more about it. Will you bring me my plaid? I must go up the Braes to Malcolm Dunbar's house. Dr. Munro told me he was so near to death."

The little group of guests split up at the end of the Manse drive, Mary and David going up the steep street of the old town, and the others making their way towards the New School.

"I don't see her as the Minister's wife," said Mrs. Fraser.

"Miss Tullis? Is there any likelihood of her being a minister's wife?" said her husband.

"Why do you think she was asked to the Manse? Besides, didn't you see how the Minister could hardly take his eyes off her?"

"Nonsense. He hardly spoke a word to her. Do you hear this, Doctor?" He called back to the Munros, who were walking behind. "Myra thinks the Minister wants to marry Mary Tullis! Did you ever hear such nonsense?"

The doctor smiled. "Women are always ready to marry off their unmarried friends."

Myra Fraser and Elspeth Munro looked at each other. "It's not nonsense," said Myra. "I think Mary Tullis is a trouble-maker—no, that's not the right way to put it. She doesn't make the trouble— it gathers round her."

"You women!" Walter shook his head. "Here's a quiet, pretty young woman, and because she catches you out on a quotation from Milton, you decide she's not fit to be the Minister's wife! Admit it, Myra."

Myra smiled. "You know that's not the reason. Of course I haven't read *Paradise Lost*, and I don't think it matters in the least whether I have or not. As for Mary Tullis, Mrs. Munro here knows what I mean, don't you?"

Elspeth nodded. "I think so. But it was interesting meeting her."

11

ALL Dyplin soon knew of the tea party at the Manse.

Matilda told her friends and family, "That Mary Tullis was real braw; weel dressed. If you ask me, she's castin' an ee on the Minister. And she's some queer notions. They were talking aboot the elections and I heard her say she'd like tae vote. Imagine!"

Dyplin did just that. Mary, the superior bluestocking, also became the rampaging vote-seeker; and over the tea-cups and round the fires, the talk grew.

For it was the high season for gossip. As the last of the leaves fluttered down, the dreary autumn rains came. Day after day the low cloud lay on the hills, so that a stranger would not have known they were there. The rain poured ceaselessly. The road past the Tullises' house was a torrent, and the surface wore down to gravelly runnels until it was like the map of some strange watery country. Dusk fell early. People gathered thankfully round the fire and the wet woollen cloaks and plaids hung and steamed in the background and filled the house with the smell of sheep. The women knitted or sewed; the men read and smoked thick tobacco till the room was full of haze. John Campbell went up

125

to the attic to work on a model boat. Willie Johnston whittled away at a new whistle and sat happily practising a new tune, while his children played with the wood shavings (the little girls made curls from them to dangle against their cheeks), and his wife clucked resigned disapproval. Now was the time when the Thorn Bush Tavern flourished, and this year more than ever, for those that had found the way there in the sickness did not forget it, and children learned to listen for the uneven steps and get out of the way.

For them it was a time for all the indoor games that had been forgotten during the long summer days. They played at houses under the table. The boys who were lucky enough to have them fought battles with their lead soldiers, and the girls endlessly dressed and undressed their dolls; and they peered at picture books, while the jumping candle flames made the pictures change and come alive; and spent time staring into the fire and making pictures from the crumbling embers and telling stories. This year they had been cheated of their Hallowe'en; but there was New Year to come and the summer days to dream of; and meanwhile, there was hot bread and milk with brown sugar and, for a treat, a scattering of hundreds-and-thousands on it.

For the older people, for the children, the short days had compensations. But for those in between it could be a weary time. This was the season when the custom was for the girls to take to sewing. Some of them worked at pictures and found satisfaction in choosing colours and seeing the design grow beneath their fingers. One or two were happy to lay aside the pictures and work on their wedding-gear, sewing shifts and petticoats, and long nightdresses, edging them with fine crochet, made for them more often than not by their friends and bridesmaid-to-be. Others, less skilled with needle or crochet hook, knitted long fine white woollen stockings. They met in the bride-to-be's house, and sat round the table in the mellow candlelight and, when their eyes were tired, laid down their work and told stories.

For the boys, work finished early in winter and, once they had washed off the glaur and dirt, some would join the girls round the table and tease and ogle. One or two were fiddlers and, if the mood took them, and the household was not too strictly ruled, they would strike up a reel and the table and chairs would be pushed back for a dance; or they would play sad tunes of the old days while the listeners hummed the melody with their eyes on the past and long ago. On Saturday nights there was the dancing-class when little Mr. Brotherston came from Inverforth with his wee fiddle and the young from the more worldly families went to the long attic room above the Thorn Bush to dance the reels and jigs that he had been teaching for years.

That was how it had been. But not this year. Little Mr. Brotherston had died in the epidemic, and no one had replaced him. For some there were weary problems instead of the fun of the dancing as

127

in previous years; for the desperate coupling of the cholera-time was bearing fruit, and there were girls who chose to sit in the shadows far from the fire, wondering how to tell and what to do. Lucky for them, the days of the repentance stool were past, and in time shamefaced weddings at the Manse plastered over the disgrace. There was not one betrothed girl in Dyplin; too many young men lay in the churchyard, and those that were left, having seen the normal pattern of marriage, home and children so often shattered by the sickness had no mind for serious courtship. The fiddle-players were among those who had died and there were no more songs and reels. The gatherings round the table were dreary affairs, the sewing too readily put down, the heads bent low round the candle flame for murmurings and mutterings, tales of death and apparitions and old stories of witchcraft and the power of Satan.

No one knew for sure who started it. Grizel Wauchop, one wet and dreary night, ferreting at the back of her grandmother's closet, came on a tattered leather-bound book printed in the old way with "ss" like "ff". It was *An Attack on the Abominable Practices of Necromancie and Witchcraft*. Among his denunciations, the enthusiastic author had printed a series of spells "to show the lewdness and foolishness of such wicked doings". Grizel, hiding the book under her shawl, took it to her friend Jenny Niven's house; and there the young people, being in the "best room" and their elders in the kitchen, laid the book on the table and giggled over the incantations and spells. But it was never clear who was the first to suggest they try raising the devil.

It involved salt and flame, and drawing a pentacle on the floor, and making ritual gestures and circling widdershins and repeating strange words and names—but they would not, they decided, say the Lord's Prayer backwards. Clearly, the rite could not be carried out in the house. But at the foot of Grizel's garden, there was an old stone out-house, once a weaver's shed, with an earthen floor, now used for storing spades and forks and gear cast out from the house. Here was the place.

Two nights later, eight of them met in the out-house, six girls and two older boys, who professed scorn and scepticism but were drawn by a reluctant curiosity. They stuffed the little windows with sacks to make sure no light escaped and then lit two candles and set them up on a barrel. Grizel laid the book between them and gave directions.

"You must draw a thing like this, with a stick on the floor," she said, and showed them the pentacle. "But we'll need to clear a space. There's too much straw and sticks about. There's a broom in the corner. And you can just do the sweeping, Dougie Johnston, instead of standing there laughing."

Dougie set to with the broom to clear a space and, when he had swept the ground, Grizel drew the pentacle with a pointed stick on the earthen floor.

"Now we put a candle in the middle. Have you the salt ready, Jenny? Put out the other candle.

Now we have to join hands and walk round here and say—" she glanced at the book—

"Be the Horns, the Handstaff and the King's Ell,
Be the Pole and the Planets and the signs all Twell
Be the elements all that our craft can compel
Be here, O Satan, frae the Pit o' Hell."

Now that it had come to the point it stopped being a frolic. The candle-light left the corners of the shed full of darkness where ill-defined shapes lurked. The air was thick with the dust and mustiness raised by Dougie's energetic sweeping. The candle flame, lighting them from below, jumping in the draught, made sinister masks of the familiar faces. Bessie Niven, Jenny's sister, and only thirteen years old, began to whimper.

"I don't like it. I want to go away."

Jenny snapped, "I told you not to come. You're spoiling it. Be quiet."

Bessie began to sob, but Sandy Todd, a kindly boy, much enamoured of Jenny, took Bessie's hand.

"Don't be frightened. It's just a game, like Hallowe'en."

"Are we ready then?" Grizel was impatient. "Now, mind and say the words right. And when we've said them, Jenny will throw the salt on the candle . . ."

"And Auld Nick himsel' will be here!" said Dougie. "What's stopping us?"

They circled the flame widdershins, holding

hands, muttering the horrid jingle, half-ashamed, half-expectant, nerves taut. At the end of the incantation, Jenny flung salt on the candle. There was a momentary blue flame: then darkness. In the seconds of stillness and silence that followed something moved among them. Bessie began to scream.

"Be quiet." Jenny's voice was like a lash. "Do you want Grizel's father out here? Grizel, light the candle."

There was a spurt of flame that died. Grizel had to try three times before she got the candle upright and lit. They lit the second one, and only then could look at one another and talk.

"Something came," said Jean Stott. "I felt it move."

Bessie began to whimper again.

"Me too," said Sandy. He looked at Dougie. "You weren't up to any tricks?"

"No' me. I had half thocht o' makin' juist a wee rumpus, but I swear I did naethin'. A' the same, I think it's mair likely tae hae been a rat than auld Nick. Nae deevil wud come for a han'fu' o' saut and a silly wee poem. I'm thinkin' ye'll need a mair powerful spell than thon."

His robust commonsense was comforting.

"Oh well, it was a good ploy," said Grizel. "We could try again. That's not the only spell in the book. But mind you, not a word to a soul. Mind that, Bessie."

"Bessie'll not say anything," said Jenny. "She knows what would happen if she did."

Bessie never did say anything, and never again took part, but the others couldn't resist whispering to their friends. Next time they met in the shed there were twelve of them and soon fifteen or so were in the secret. Their elders remained unaware of what was going on, easily convinced their sons and daughters were "just going down to Jenny's—or Grizel's—or Jean's—for a while". Perhaps in other times they would have been more concerned about the on-goings, but there was an apathy in Dyplin, a weariness, a readiness just to let daily life take its course without bothering much beyond appearances. So as the days shortened towards the turn of the year, the group met three or four times a week. A hierarchy developed; Jenny Niven was the leader, not consciously chosen, but assuming the position by force of personality, even before Grizel who had found and kept the book. For the time being, there were no more attempts to raise the devil; for something *had* moved among them . . . and although none of them would have admitted to believing it was the devil, still. . . . They turned to trying to see into the future—dropping a white of egg into water, and reading the shapes it formed; or staring into water in a glass bowl and waiting for an image to grow in it. Dougie Johnston brought a grubby pack of cards, and Grizel, whose aunt "read the cards" would spread them out and predict good or bad fortune. Inevitably, some predictions came true, or were made to seem true by them, anxious to believe. They told each other it was harmless; they were not hurting anyone, it was just "a good ploy"—words comfortingly minimizing the strange excitement that swept them as they crowded round the bowls of water, or peered at the cards, while the candle flames swayed and the air whispered under the door.

As time went on, the tension and excitement grew. The boys' hands were bolder, feeling for the curve of a breast through the girls' stiff woollen bodices. The girls less sharply slapped down their exploring fingers. There were kisses snatched and returned in the dark corners of the old shed; and a sudden breaking apart of young bodies startled by the onrush of forbidden sensations; for as yet the bonds of upbringing held. Some of them, Grizel herself, at one and the same time wanted it to stop and wanted it to continue.

Once, on a night of rain and tempest, when their numbers were fewer, Jean Stott said, "Maybe what we're doing is bad. My father says it's wicked to try to see the future. They were talking about the second sight last night. My Aunt Cassie says she knows it's true, but my father got angry and said it was all wicked havers."

Jenny had an answer. "If it's havers, then it's harmless. Besides, it's in the Bible. Saul asked a witch to help him see the future. And if it's in the Bible, it must be all right."

They wanted to be convinced, and were. The meetings went on.

12

MARY, brought up in a large town, was not a gossip-monger; being aloof from the community, she was not among the tale-bearers and whisperers round the fires. She listened politely to the news Alison loved to retail, but seemed to forget it as soon as she heard it—to Alison's exasperation.

"She's no' interested in what goes on," she complained to John. "She's that ta'en up wi' her books that real life doesn't mean anything to her!"

"Weel, if she likes it that way, why not? It's not," said John, who, since his illness, would not hear a word against Mary, "a sin no' tae be pryin' into your neighbour's affairs. Forby, if it's stories she wants, she's better reading her books than listening to clash, the maist o' which is nae mair true than the novells she reads."

John always called novels "novells". To which Alison would only answer: "It's no' natural."

Mary enjoyed the drumlie days of autumn. She read voraciously, using the library more than anyone else in Dyplin, stealing quietly in and out with her little pile of books. She discovered the poems of Crabbe, and found in his bitter realistic pictures of rural life a piquant contrast to her beloved Byron. Reading Crabbe sharpened her eyes to the life around her. She even wrote one or two sketches of life in Dyplin in his manner and discovered in herself a hitherto unrealized capacity for sardonic comment on her fellow-men. For Alison was wrong in thinking Mary was not interested in people. She was, but she also had a dislike of spreading tales and rumour. Here in Dyplin the foibles, the weaknesses, the subterfuges were clear for all to see. The strengths and goodness were not so clear.

Mary did not know that each time she went up and down from the house to the shops or with her little pile of library books, eyes and tongues followed her; and that Daniel Rutherford was often on hand to help her choose her books was known and noted. Matthew's visits to the Tullises roused little comment. It was the Minister's duty to visit; the house was at the top of the village and comparatively out of observation; and Alison was careful to say nothing about the frequency of his calls. David enjoyed Matthew's visits and their long and involved discussion on points of doctrine, for David, born well into the previous century, had been firmly grounded in the church's tenets. Mary took no part in these conversations; to her it was remote word-mongering, with no bearing at all on her ideas of God and goodness. Matthew did not find this strange. It was not for women to discuss sanctification, justification and predestination. What he did find disturbing was Mary's talk of books and poetry, themes and characters that, to

135

him, were dangerous or even immoral, and not the stuff a good manse wife would talk of. But Mary's own life was as modest and unassuming as could be. He fell more and more in love, until he had to wrestle with himself not to go to the cottage more than once a week, lest he be tempted to neglect his other duties.

Mary regarded his visits as pleasantly relaxing for her father, mildly boring for herself. David, however, gentle and quiet as he was, had a sharp eye where Mary was concerned.

"The Minister doesn't come just to crack wi' me, Mary," he said one day after Matthew and he had been talking for an hour or so.

"Why, then?"

"For you, lass, for you. I think he's growing fond of you."

Her reaction was sharp. "Don't say that. I don't want to have anything to do with that sort of thing again. It brought me only sorrow and trouble."

"But it's all behind you. You'll find someone who will be a good husband to you," said David, voicing his dearest wish.

"Never. I don't want to love anyone. I want to be just myself, with you, quiet, undisturbed."

"It's not always in our choosing to love or not," said David, thinking of her mother who had flashed into his life like a kingfisher across a dark pool and sped out of it to death in two years. "It's not natural for a young woman to be cooped up with an old father and a wheen books."

136

"Books are safe, father. Books can't hurt." She took his hand. "Not even you know what all that did to me. I can't go through it again."

Her vehemence should have made him ponder; for Mary's visits to the library were not the placid pleasure they appeared to be. Daniel Rutherford was too often there for her peace of mind. He had a way of smiling when she came in, as if he had been waiting for her, which at once attracted and repelled her. When he walked round the shelves with her, she was conscious of every movement of his hands, every tone of his voice, and found it hard to raise her eyes to meet his: yet if he was not there, she was disappointed—and scorned herself for it. She no longer went to the Martyr's Bridge, having met him for a second time on the road to it. She had encountered him once on the road from the castle, but he had passed her swiftly with a hurried greeting, seemingly ill-at-ease. To avoid him, she kept more to the lower slopes of the hills behind the house, although the weather was not good for hill walking.

On a day when the mist had at last lifted, she set off from the garden, over the wall and onto the hillside. She had shortened her skirts to well above her ankles by tying a cord round her waist, had put on strong boots, crossed a shawl over her shoulders and under her armpits and tied it at the back, and tied a smaller shawl over her hair. She put her head into David's workshop as she passed and said, "I'm going up the hill."

"I see you're in your climbing gear. Keep an eye on the weather. The mist comes down fast up there."

He turned back to his work. He was carefully cutting a silk delicately patterned with rosebuds into panels to be fitted onto a light cane frame. The sunshade was to be a present from Mrs. Innes of Griffton to her favourite niece. Mary lingered, thinking, "He looks happy. He looks happiest when he is in his workshop."

"You like making umbrellas." She lingered in the doorway.

David turned to her in surprise. When she was a little girl, she had often come to his workshop, collecting the scraps of material, wrapping her dolls in them. But for years now she had not seemed interested in his work. He would have been astonished had he heard her words to Alison in his praise.

"Aye, I like it." He hesitated, then continued. "Each one's different—and it's good to have a skill that uses brain and hands and eyes. And umbrellas are good things to make. This one here—it'll hae a braw silk fringe when it's finished—will mebbe make a bonny lass look that much bonnier. That big black one there for the doctor will shelter him on many a day when he's on his way tae some sickbed. . . . I like tae think I'm making something that shelters folk . . ." His voice trailed away. "I'm havering. Away tae the hills. But take care."

Mary was thoughtful as she went up the path to

the gate in the wall. Her father had never before spoken of his trade like that. How little she knew of his ways of thought. Perhaps here, when they were much more alone together she would get to know him not just as her father, but as David Tullis. . . . Meanwhile, ahead the hills beckoned.

She walked with long swift strides over the lumpy grass, enjoying the feeling of free movement, for she had taken off her heavy flannel winter petticoat. She skirted the top of Gloom Hill; she never went there, having a horror of the three chained stones that marked the burning place of the poor young witch. Behind Gloom Hill, a wide shallow glen ran eastwards, with a burn tumbling among boulders, and to the north of the burn the smooth bulk of Grey Wisp, one of the higher hills in the range. On the south side of the burn, a path led through the hills to join the main road to Crieff, through Glendoonan. She had followed this path for some distance on a previous walk. Today, under the first blue sky for weeks, she was in a mood to take to the open hillside beyond the burn, where there were no footpaths, but only the little inches-wide sheep-tracks.

She found a place where she could cross the burn by jumping from boulder to boulder. Above her rose the great whale back of the hill. She would climb it, right to the top. Before setting off, she turned to look down. Below, she could just see the castle tower and, away to her right, high on the hillside, where the easy slope changed to the steepness of the hill, the steading of Craig's farm, the legendary Craig, the man who had "at least a thousand books", whom Alison had pointed out to her once in the village, a grey-headed, broad-shouldered man, wearing a checked plaid and carrying a long shepherd's staff. Her eyes lingered for a moment on the group of buildings before she turned and breasted the slope. It was steep, but she had learnt that by following the zig-zags of the sheep tracks she would find the easiest way up. She knew, too, to avoid the tumble of scree away over on her right, above which rose a little precipice of bare black rock with the shine of water on it. She moved strongly, pulling on tufts of honey-coloured grass where the slope was steepest, enjoying the movement, feeling the thrust and pull of her leg muscles, gulping the sharp keen air. She would not look back till she was at the very top. She kept her eyes on the ground, with an occasional glance up to the crest, curving against the wintry blue sky. At last she reached the top, only, of course, to find it was not the top; the ground still rose, though more gently, to where a little tumble of stones, a rough cairn, marked the true summit. Here the going, though less steep, was rough with pockets of mossy bog. She kept her eyes on the ground, lifting her skirts to jump the patches of water and reeds. At last she was by the cairn, a rickle of large pebbles and slabs of rock. Panting, she stood by it and looked ahead.

A great curling wave of mist was filling the

hollows and curves and rolling towards her. Intent on her walking, she had not seen the cloud piling up ahead of her, and now she looked at it with incredulous disappointment that became chill dismay as the first cold wisp coiled round her. Shuddering, she turned to run and stumble down the slope. She reached the steep descent while the air was still clear round her but, as she scrambled down, the cloud reached her, and she was curtained by damp billowing blinding greyness, cutting off sight and hearing. She stood panting and panic-stricken, remembering how the cloud could rest for days, even weeks, on the hills. She drew two or three deep breaths, waiting for the racing of her pulse to steady. Panic was useless; she must think.

Before the mist had reached her, she had seen the scree and precipice far down on her left. So she must try to go straight down; or bear right. She tried to think of any features of the ground that might guide her. But nothing came to mind.

She was cold, and damp was clinging to her shawl. She began to feel her way down; but going straight down and never to the left was not so easy. She had to step aside where tiny rivulets trickled past her feet, or to avoid the bright green marshy places. She found a sheep track that slanted down to the right, but it soon swung left and she was afraid to follow it. She walked slowly down into blankness. The mist was thickening and the light lessening. Or was it the early winter dark falling? She began to run, and fell as her foot twisted on the coarse tangled grass. She scrambled up and stood, her head forward, peering and listening. She could hear only her gasping breath and the beating of her heart. But through the greyness something loomed, tall and dark. She stretched her neck, staring, and called softly:

"Is someone there?"

Her voice muffled and died. The shape remained. She groped forward, one hand outstretched, and felt cold stone. It was a tall errant boulder left aeons ago by the glaciers. But she could not remember seeing it on the way up.

She leant against it for a little. It at least was fixed and solid in this dreadful world of drifting cloud. As she leant, she heard the sound of running water; not the tinkle of the little runnels, but the sound of a burn. Perhaps she was near the burn she had crossed on the way up, though she did not think she had come far enough downhill. But it was impossible to tell how far she had come. Over the burn, if it was that burn, was the track; and once on the track she could find her way home.

She listened, her hand on the boulder. The sound came from over on her right—how far away she could not tell. Reluctantly she took her hand from the comfort of the boulder, and moved towards the sound. After four steps she could not see the rock; and the noise of the burn was fainter, though still audible. She felt her way in its direction like a blind woman with hands outstretched. Now she could hear it clearly, now it faded. No; there it was, quite clear, just ahead. . . .

She stepped into space and felt icy water swirl round her knees and tug at her skirt. The burn was not more than five or six feet wide, but running strongly. She was in a little pool among boulders, and she used them to pull herself across to the steep bank. She clawed her way up and lay shivering and gasping on the grass, very afraid. For it was not the burn she had crossed in the morning, which ran quite gently along the valley. This one careered down the hillside. She had absolutely no idea at all of where she might be.

The cold was creeping up round her from her sodden boots and skirt. She stood up and wrung out as much water as she could. As she straightened up, she thought she heard a dog barking. She froze, pushing back the shawl from her ears. Only the hateful sound of water. Should she move away from it, and so, perhaps, hear other sounds more clearly? But away from the burn she would again be without any guiding line at all in the swirling and deepening twilight. She decided to follow the burn.

A sheep track went down by the water, and this made the going easier. But the cold, and her tiredness, and the wearisome peering into the mist were making her light-headed. She followed the track almost mechanically, hearing always the water drumming on her left. It was growing louder; it was a continuous rushing; it was like a waterfall. She stopped abruptly and looked. Yes; the water

143

vanished, narrowing and tumbling over a ledge, and disappearing into the mist. The sheep track swerved suddenly to her right. Ahead, the ground vanished. Willy-nilly, she would have to leave following the burn.

She found a pebble and tossed it into the mist ahead. She heard it fall among stones and judged the drop was not so very great. Nevertheless, it was impossible to go straight on. She must follow the track; and within moments she was once more aware of nothing but the ground beneath her feet and the surrounding cloud. And then she heard it again. Somewhere, ahead of her, a dog was barking.

As long as it led towards the sound, she would follow the sheep track. It might well enough lead to a sheep-fold, or even a shepherd's cottage. So she stumbled on; heard the dog again; quickened her pace; and suddenly out of the mist came a dry-stone dyke, a gap with a hurdle, and beyond a glimmer of light as from a window.

She clung to the wall sobbing with relief and exhaustion. Then she pushed the hurdle aside and stumbled up a rutted path towards the light. It came from a small window set deep in a grey stone wall. To the left was a door. She groped along the wall to the door and knocked; a feeble knock, for her hands were numb, but it set up a fierce barking from within. She heard a voice reproving the dog, but no one came to the door. Over her shoulder she saw the mist wreathing towards her, and suddenly she was banging on the door and shouting. The door opened, she stepped forward, tripped and fell. She felt herself being lifted, carried into warmth and set in a chair. Light flickered through her eyelids and she opened them. A fire was blazing on the hearth before her, and a man, grey-headed, broad-shouldered, was kneeling by the chair and looking at her in astonishment.

"In the name of God, where did you come from?" He shouted over his shoulder. "Mirren! Stop what you're daein' and come here. We've a visitor."

A small, rusty-haired woman with a broad high-cheeked face came through from the back of the house, wiping her hands on a rough apron of sacking. She stopped when she saw Mary and raised her hands.

"Guid sakes, Craig! Whae's that?"

"I'm not sure yet, Mirren. But come here. The puir lass is wet through and cauld as daith. I'll get some hot whisky and water. You bring dry stockings and change hers. Quick noo."

Mirren was used to obeying without question. From a chest of drawers at the back of the room she took a pair of black knitted stockings, pulled off Mary's sodden boots and stockings, put on the dry ones and pushed onto her feet a pair of rough leather shoes. Craig came back with a tumbler of hot water and whisky which Mary drank thankfully. It stopped her shivering and she began to feel better. The heat of the fire set her wet skirt steaming, and Mirren said:

"The lass's skirts is dripping. Gin she doesna change them, she'll catch her daith."

"Hae ye onything she can change tae?"

"Aye, I have. Gin ye'll tak yersel' tae the kitchen, I'll get her changed."

Craig went to the kitchen and Mirren brought out from the chest of drawers a heavy woollen skirt and a flannel blouse and, disregarding Mary's protests, took off the steaming skirt and shawl and put her own things on Mary.

"They're nae that grand," she said, "but a queen's couldna be cleaner. Noo I'll hang yours in the kitchen and they'll nae be that lang in the drying."

Left to herself, Mary looked round the room. It was lit by two three-branched candlesticks, one on the mantelpiece above the fire, which also helped to light the room, and one on the round table in the middle of the stone floor. In front of the fire was a heavy rag rug. She was sitting in a big black leather-covered armchair. A smaller chair stood opposite her. Round the table were set four wooden chairs. At the back of the room was a chest of drawers with brass handles that gleamed in the candlelight. All round the walls were tall bookshelves, full of books. She would have liked to walk round and look at them, but the drink and the warmth, after the cold and fear, had made her lethargic, and she was content to rest her head on the back of the chair and look dreamily at the shelves. Presently Craig came in carrying a steaming jug and a glass on a tray. He insisted on pouring Mary another small drink, filled his own glass, and said:

"I think I ken who you are. The umbrella-maker's daughter. But your name?"

"Mary. Mary Tullis. And you're Mr. Craig."

"A'body calls me just 'Craig'. Aweel, Mary, can ye tell me hoo ye cam tae walk into the house on a day of mist like this?"

"I went for a walk on the hill, and climbed to the top; and the mist caught me."

"Aye. It happens. It was a good thing you found your way here. Folk have died on the hills here, caught by the mist, and tumbling and breaking a leg and lying till the cauld did for them."

"I heard a dog barking."

"Aye, that was Riever. He was shut out at the back. Weel, noo, whit'll we dae wi' ye?"

"I must get home. My father will be worried."

"I well believe it. I can tak ye doon tae Dyplin. Even in this I could find my way. But I'm thinking you would be better to rest for a wee: at least till your clothes dry. Mirren! Mak' a cup of tea and bring in something tae eat. Then we'll see about taking the lassie hame."

He said no more and Mary was happy to sit in silence, looking into the fire, while from the kitchen came the sounds of a meal being prepared. Soon Mirren had the table laid for two with bread and butter and cheese, milk and sugar, last of all bringing in a pot of tea and plates of ham and eggs.

"Come awa'," said Craig, "and eat. That'll mak'

ye feel a lot better and keep off the cauld tae."

Mirren poured out tea and then retreated to the kitchen.

"Is Mrs. Craig not eating with us?" said Mary.

"Mirren? No, no, she'd rather bide in the kitchen. Forby, she's no' Mrs. Craig. She's ma hoosekeeper."

Something in his tone brought a little flush to Mary's cheeks, but all she said was, "I've heard about you and your books. You have a lot of them."

"Oh aye. My books are one of the wonders of Dyplin." He spoke drily. "Spending money on books is a very queer thing tae dae, tho' naebody would think it queer if I spent it in the Thorn Bush."

"I've got books too. Not as many as you, but quite a lot."

"Have you now?" He looked at her under his thick eyebrows. "And what kinds of books would a lassie like you have? Nice wee love stories, nae doot, with a beautiful girl and a brave young man and a wedding at the end!"

Mary smiled for the first time since she had entered the house.

"I've a lot of Sir Walter Scott's books, and Maria Edgeworth, and Fanny Burney, and Jane Austen and Susan Ferrier."

"Oh aye. But ye'll no' have *Tom Jones*?"

"I do. And *Amelia*."

"You don't say? They're no' juist books I would

expect a young lass tae read. What does your mother think aboot them?"

"My mother died when I was born."

"I didna ken. . . . Your father then?"

"My father lets me read what I like. Why not?"

"Why not, indeed? But no' juist usual. And whit else dae ye have on your bookshelves?"

"Poetry."

"Aweel, ye hae me beat there. I havena much o' that, except Milton and Shakespeare and Robert Burns—an' I canna say I read much o' them, except whiles Robert Burns. Weel, weel. A young woman that reads *Tom Jones* and poetry. . . . Whit dae they think o' that in Dyplin?"

Mary reddened and frowned. "I don't care what they think."

"Aha. That means they think you're a queer one tae. Weel, I wouldna worry. I dinna."

"But you are lucky. Up here, away from people, with your books all round you. . . . Do you ever go to the library? I do."

"Na, na. I like tae read my ain books. As lang's I can, I'll buy my books for mysel! Eat up, lassie, and then we'll hae a look at them."

He had a fine collection. If Mary did not share his interest in astronomy and botany, she could appreciate the history and travel; and wonder at the fine edition of Milton. More than from the books themselves, perhaps, she got pleasure from watching his way of handling them, lifting them from the shelves with gentle care, stroking them

149

with tenderness. She wandered round the shelves, touching and listening, not speaking. Mirren moved out and in, clearing the table. The room was full of warm light, and Mary felt such peace as she had not known since coming to Dyplin.

She suddenly turned to Craig and said, "I wish I could live like this, far away from everyone, with books all round me, and no people to bother me."

"That's no way for a young lass tae talk. Books are fine. I couldna live without mine. But they're not life."

"I don't like life. Books are safe."

He looked long at her. "So that's the way o' it. Ye've been hurt . . . na, na, I'm no' asking any questions. I'm just saying ye'll maybe find safety in books, but you'll miss living. Books canna tak the place o' fowk."

"I hate most people."

"Hoots, lassie, ye dinna hate them—ye're afraid o' them."

"Are you afraid of people?"

"There was a time when I was afraid of the hurt fowk could dae tae me—and I turned tae my books. And noo I canna dae wi'oot them."

"But if you're happy?"

"Happy enough, in a subdued wersh way. No' what you should tak' for happiness. Sometime I think books are a snare, like drink. They're a' richt for an auld man like me. I can make them the better part o' my life and nae hairm. But you—you should tak' care they dinna get a haud o' you at the expense

150

of life. . . . This is a queer talk we're hae'in. I've never met a lassie like you afore; I can weel understand that ye'll no' just fit in wi' life in Dyplin. . . . See, is this no' a braw book? Just feel the binding on it—smooth as glass."

But the magic had gone, and Mary was quite glad when Mirren came in with her clothes. "These are dry noo."

"Then I must go. That is, if it's possible."

She felt a pang of guilt that she should so completely have forgotten the anxiety her father must be feeling.

"It's possible," said Craig. "It's just a question o' keeping on the track from the steading to the castle road. I doubt if the mist lies much below the castle. So get ye changed and I'll get a lantern and we'll go."

Outside, there was not a gleam of starlight to lessen the blackness, but Craig was unperturbed. He gave his long shepherd's stick to Mary, held the lantern in his right hand and made her take hold of his left arm. The lantern, held low, showed them the track, and it was not hard to follow it, though they had to go slowly. Craig was right. Not far below the juncture of the rack with the castle road, the mist thinned out. The lights of Dyplin shone below, and soon they were crossing the field behind Mary's house.

At the gate in the garden wall, Craig said, "I'll leave you here. Yonder's your father at your back door." For David had opened the door and they could see him dark against the light.

"But won't you come in?"

"Na, na. I dinna visit much in Dyplin. I haven't been in a house there these ten years. I might come across some time and hae a look at your books, but no' the nicht. Awa' tae your faither."

He turned and was striding up the slope before she could thank him. She found David torn with anxiety and as near as he ever came to being angry with her.

"I told you to watch for the mist, Mary."

"I didn't hear you. And I'm sorry. It happened so quickly and it was horrible. . . ."

"We didna know what to do. John said to wait for a bit to see if the mist would lift before we got the men together for a search—and there was no point in going up in the mist. But I thank God you're safe, Mary."

"If I hadn't found Craig's farm, I think I'd have died of the cold."

"Don't say it, Mary." He took her hand. "It doesna bear thinking of."

She felt again the weight of his love and anxiousness.

13

APART from the Campbells and her father, no one in Dyplin ever knew of Mary's escapade on the hill. John would never have thought of mentioning it, and Alison had learnt to keep quiet about Mary.

She herself thought much about her encounter with Craig. His suggestion that books, her refuge and shelter, might be a trap, disturbed her. Was she afraid of Dyplin, afraid of people? She was an outsider in Dyplin and had told herself she wanted it that way, hugging to herself a comforting feeling of superiority. Was she, in reality, afraid? And what did she really know of the people of Dyplin?

But getting to know Dyplin was not easy. The village, Alison grumbled, was dead.

"I don't believe there'll be anything doing at New Year. I've never known the place as dull and dreary. Whit the young folk find tae dae these lang nichts I don't know."

However, change was on the way. One day John came in from a business visit to Inverforth and said, "Ah weel, Alison, ye'll no can grumble ony mair aboot the dullness o' Dyplin. There's tae be great high jinks here."

"What high jinks?"

"Whit wud ye say tae a Parliamentary election?"

153

"An election? Here? Ye're no' serious."

But John was. Dyplin lay almost in the centre of the new electoral district. To the west lay the coal-mining and industrial area; to the east it was rural and agricultural. Mr. Brownlie, the sitting Tory member, drew his support from the west. General Robert Wedderburn, the "Reform" candidate, came from the eastern side. Feeling ran high, and it was felt that a small, fairly "neutral" place would be best for the actual election. Dyplin was mid-way between the two areas. Mr. Innes of Griffton, who was by his lights a good landlord, and was aware of the apathy and misery that had hung over the village since the sickness, had persuaded the powers-that-be that Dyplin was as good a place as any for the polling; and hoped that this would have a revivifying effect on the place.

Alison pondered John's news, and said grudgingly, "Weel, it might make a bit of excitement for the men. But I don't see it having much in it tae interest the women."

"But they say there'll be a grand ball fur the electors, and a procession, and all kinds o' high jinks."

The *Inverforth Gazette* confirmed John's news. The election, it said, would be held in Dyplin, "for a quiet place, removed from pre-election hurly-burly, is, by both sides, considered to be the best location for the important and historic event". Accordingly, the two candidates, Mr. Brownlie and

154

General Wedderburn, would there present themselves to the electors early in December.

Overnight, Dyplin was transformed. All the old political fervour revived. Those who had the necessary property qualifications to be electors assumed airs of weighty responsibility which were infinitely galling to the non-voters, provoking a stream of sardonic, not to say slanderous comment, which greatly added to the gaiety of life. As Dyplin was, almost to a man, for the General, there was little party animosity; the tension was between voters and non-voters; but the revivifying effect was there. The women, voteless themselves, lined up with their menfolk; and the small boys found a new ploy in sticking up bills exhorting their elders to "VOTE FOR WEDDERBURN AND LIBERTY" and tearing down those (put up furtively at night) proclaiming "BROWNLIE FOR ORDER AND STABILITY."

For the first time David found himself taking an active part in community affairs. He had always been very much a political man, had been an adherent of the Reform movement in Glasgow, and the lack of any political activity in Dyplin was one of the things he missed most. Now he came into his own, was on the committee set up to make arrangements for the election, and undertook to go round the outlying farms and hamlets to persuade voters to turn up on the day. David had recently acquired his own gig and horse, sharing stabling and grazing with John Campbell, and was no longer dependent on Macpherson's hired gig for transport; which may have had something to do with Macpherson's remarks, from behind a cloud of thick tobacco smoke in the Thorn Bush, about "Incomin' fowk no' a year here—I mind the day the umbrella-maker came—that mak' a leevin' frae us and then think they can organize oor lives as weel."

Sometimes, when David went round the farms, Mary went with him and glimpsed again the kind of life she had known in her childhood holidays in Ayrshire. There were the uncommunicative men who could nevertheless be eloquent enough when the talk turned to cattle-beasts or barley; and the women with reddened cheeks and thick bare arms, as often as not wearing a sacking apron and heavy boots, who cooked and baked (and many a scone, hot from the girdle, with the butter spread generously by a thumb, and melting lusciously, were they offered), and washed and swept and milked and churned, and helped with the farm-work if need be—she looked at them with new respect. Craig, she felt, would have approved of them. They certainly hadn't fled from life; and she would come back from such an expedition to her house with its quiet rooms and gently flickering fire and the furniture in order and her books waiting and for a time would feel that it lacked some dimension. She tried to say something of this to Alison, who responded with her usual commonsense:

"Hoots, Mary, you're not trying tae tell me you could live like one o' the Hepburns up at Lawfoot;

156

you wi' your books and learning! I couldna dae it—I like my comforts and conveniences. My mother's people had a wee farm—sae I ken something aboot it. And it's a hard, hard life. Mind you, I'm not saying it's an unhappy one—fowk hadna much time tae be mindin' whether they were unhappy or no' " (with a shrewd glance at Mary), "and I daresay there was a sense of satisfaction in gettin' a' done that had tae be done—just as it's a good feeling when I get my apple jelly made, or the blanket wash finished. . . . But there's more tae life, surely—as I would think you would ken."

"Och yes, you're right, Alison. I would be driven mad if I had to live like that. All the same, there's a kind of reality about them—I listen to my father and your John with all the talk just now about liberty and justice, and the golden age they seem to think is coming, and then my father and I go to the Hepburns—and while he and Tom Hepburn are talking their politics, I see how Lizzie Hepburn is living, and all she does, and their politics just seem like bubbles on the water."

"Aweel, the men aye like tae think that's important. It keeps them happy. We're not a' made happy with the same things. But folk aye think their way is the only way—and then are aye wanting other fowk tae be happy their way. I'm not very good at explaining what I mean . . . but you understand?"

"Yes, I do," and, moved by a sudden impulse, Mary leant forward and kissed Alison's cheek—to

Alison's vast embarrassment—before returning home.

It was at a meeting of the committee held in David's house that Mary met Alexander Torrance, editor of the *Inverforth Gazette*. He had lately succeeded his uncle as editor, and had ideas of enlarging the appeal of the paper beyond the mere chronicling of news and advertisements. He had, in fact, visions of being a patron of literature. He arrived early and, while waiting for the members of committee to assemble, he had wandered round Mary's bookshelves—and had found, pushed in at the back, the little volume of her poetry. He read the verses with mild interest, then turned to look again at the author's name—Mary Tullis—could it be a relation of his fellow committee member? When David came in, he asked him, and had to be told it was David's daughter.

"The young lady who showed me in?"

"Yes."

"I should like to talk to her about her book."

"I don't think she would like that. She is very reluctant that it should be known that she has published. . . ."

Nevertheless, when the meeting was over. Torrance lingered behind and spoke to Mary. "Miss Tullis, I should like you, if you will, to contribute some verse to the *Inverforth Gazette*. I have recently become editor, and I should like to introduce a literary element to the paper; and encourage local writers. . . ."

158

"No, I couldn't. It's impossible."

"But why? Have you stopped writing?"

"No; but I don't want it to be made public."

"But why? Surely every poet wants his work to be known."

"I—people think it strange that I write poetry."

"But you could do it anonymously. I promise, no one would ever learn from me of your authorship."

Mary hesitated for a moment, then shook her head.

"They would find out."

"Not from me, Miss Tullis, never from me. Think about it."

Mary did; for of course Alexander Torrance was quite right. She would have liked to see her poems in print, but dreaded near-ridiculing comment. Her father was wise enough to say nothing. The upshot was that one morning there arrived in the *Inverforth Gazette* office a postal packet addressed personally to Mr. Alexander Torrance. Inside there was an unsigned letter; and a poem. The letter said:

"Dear Mr. Torrance,

I have thought over our conversation. I am sending on a poem I have since written. It is in a different style from those that you read in my house. So you may not wish to print it. I rely on you to keep your word as to anonymity."

If the letter, not at all what he would have expected from an apparently shy and hesitant young woman,

159

made Alexander Torrance raise his eyebrows, the poem sent them up to his hairline. Instead of the rather slight if quite charming verse about scenery, mainly waterfalls, streams and autumnal woods, which he expected from his cursory glance through Mary's book (though if he had read with more care he might have found traces of thought and passion among the verdure), she had sent him a sardonic poem on rural life and the contemporary euphoria about Reform, in which the high-flown posturings of the politically-minded were set against rural life as lived on the little farms round Dyplin. Her reading of Crabbe had borne fruit, and Torrance recognized his influence. He printed the poem, himself personally posting the letter of acceptance to Mary so that no one in his office could know that he was in correspondence with her. To his satisfaction, the poem produced a reaction in the form of letters from Reformers protesting at the cynicism of the work; and from anti-Reformers rejoicing that Reform was apparently shown as "mere surface tampering with the status quo". In Dyplin the poem was read with mild interest. The only comment which Mary heard was that of John Campbell to her father, who was as ignorant as any of the authorship.

"Hae ye seen the poem in the *Gazette*? A gey sharp jab at the Reformers—but mind you, there's something in it. Forby, it's the kind o' poetry I'm no sweirt tae read—it's aboot real things and people and no' fal-lals aboot rosebuds and falling leaves."

But Dyplin had other things to think of. The two candidates with their supporters were to converge on the village in mid-December for the "nomination" of the candidates. A show of hands would then be demanded which could in theory decide the election, but it was generally expected that the defeated candidate would demand a poll. Even the non-voters were drawn into the excitement. It was to be a day of festivity and spectacle. Processions were promised, and flags and banners, and for days beforehand the children of Dyplin marched round their houses with whistles and drums and rags tied to sticks, "being electors".

If the actual election was to be the voters' finest hour, the women were to come into their own with the Ball. Whichever candidate won, there was to be a Voters' Ball. Dancing on the green, dancing at weddings was a matter of course. There were, occasionally, balls at Griffton, but these were for the gentry. A ball like this Reform ball, was something unheard of, and the excitement and anticipation correspondingly high. A new dress for the Ball was, of course, a necessity; and it was generally agreed that it must be a proper ball dress, not simply a muslin or silk version of a day dress. The ladies of the New School were set agog by the designs in a magazine which Madame Grueber had sent to her from Paris. There was endless and delightful discussion of styles and materials. Women in Dyplin were for the most part good home dressmakers, and were quite ready to try their

161

hand at concocting a ball dress, and Mr. Wilkie the local draper had shrewdly laid in a stock of suitable materials. But not every woman felt capable of such a task; and there was also a certain cachet in having a dress made by a professional dressmaker.

There were two dressmakers in Dyplin. The leading one was Madame Laporte (neé Amelia Jones; widow of one Aeneas Sinclair, a good-looking ne'er-do-well who had drunk himself to death after four years of marriage and left her with two children). Amelia, who had a flair for dressmaking and some basic training, having heard of the opening of the New School in Dyplin, had bought a house near the new turnpike, called herself "Madame Laporte", sent out a few cards announcing her qualifications as being "skilled in all the refinements of elegant dressmaking" and soon built up a nice little business, with a comfortable fitting room where a fire glowed in winter and ladies could retire behind a Chinese screen to disrobe. Even Mrs. Innes of Griffton had been known to patronize Madame Laporte. So when the Ball was mooted, orders flowed, and in addition to little Nellie Saunders, her apprentice, whom she bullied but was also training very soundly, Amelia had to take on two extra hands.

Even so, she could not deal with all the orders. So in desperation some of the ladies had to turn to little Miss Leah Beattie, Dyplin's other dressmaker, for help. Miss Beattie, having looked after her parents till their deaths, was left with a neat cottage, a tiny

162

amount of savings and no visible means of support. So she took to her needle, and made hard-wearing winter dresses and summer gowns for Dyplin's more prosperous ladies. Make a ball gown she could not but, by lowering the neckline of her standard pattern, widening the skirt, daringly cutting off the sleeves at the elbow and adding a frill or two, she managed to produce something sufficiently removed from the everyday to satisfy her clients. She was making a dress for Alison, who was surprised when Mary said to her:

"When you go to have a fitting of your dress, may I go with you? I'd like to ask Leah Beattie if she would make a dress for me." She paused. "A dress for the Ball."

"But I thought you didn't like going to such affairs."

"I've never been to one, so how do I know? My father would like me to go. He's always telling me I should be meeting people. Besides . . ."

"Yes?"

"I've been thinking—I haven't really tried to get to know the people here and perhaps I should. So I said I'd go."

"Well, I'm glad of it. You may be a bit late in asking Leah, but we can try."

So one chilly afternoon they went to a little cottage up one of the lanes off the High Street.

As she lifted the iron knocker, Alison said, "We'll not say a word about a dress for you to begin with. I'll just say you've come to see mine."

Leah Beattie, small, anxious, her nose pink-tipped with cold, ushered them into the fitting-room which was also her bedroom. It was a chilly room. In the grate was a tiny fire where one lump of coal glowed timorously under a blanket of dross. The bed was covered with a spotless white bedspread, across one corner of the room hung an equally spotless curtain. In the window was a table with pins and needles, reels of thread, scissors neatly arranged in order. Round the walls hung dresses in various stages of completion.

"Miss Tullis has come to see my dress," said Alison. "You don't mind?"

"No, not at all," said Leah. She offered Mary a chair, and Alison retreated behind the curtain. "Please to remove your winter petticoat," Miss Beattie called to her, and took down from its place on the wall an ample gown of silk checked with black and pink.

Mary tactfully kept her eyes on the fire till Alison said, "You can look now," and Mary could make appropriate sounds of admiration; which was not difficult, for the dress was becoming. Miss Beattie's air of anxiety dwindled and she even looked momentarily happy.

Alison judged it a good moment to say, "Miss Tullis is hoping you could make her a dress."

Leah's gentle gloom returned.

"Oh dear—I have so much to do—I don't think—unless . . ."

"Yes?"

"Well . . ." she reddened. "Please do not let this be known generally. But I have had so much work— I had to do something—so—so I asked Meg Annan to help me. She is a good seamstress and—and she has been making up some of the dresses for me. Oh, not yours, Mrs. Campbell; I did not give her yours."

Alison stared, and then smiled.

"Och, Miss Beattie, I'm not so particular as to think I'd get ony harm from Meg Annan stitching my dress!"

Miss Beattie looked relieved.

"I'm glad. But some ladies would. Meg Annan is not . . ." she looked at Mary—"is not . . ."

"Aye, aye. We ken what she's not. And we ken what she is. But I know for a fact she's done sewing for Griffton, so I don't think you need worry aboot her stitching a dress for the likes o' the rest of us. Noo, are you trying to say that if Miss Tullis here doesn't object, Meg Annan will make her a dress?"

"I would cut it, of course; but fitting and sewing—I really have not time."

"What do you say, Mary?"

"By all means. If Miss Beattie tells me when, I'll go to Miss Annan's for fitting."

Both Miss Beattie and Alison looked shocked.

"No, no. You cannot go to Meg's. But she will come to you."

So a few days later, Mary opened the door to Meg Annan, who was carefully carrying a large package. Mary had been measured by Leah Beattie, had chosen her material, and now was to be fitted by Meg, who was doing the actual sewing. Meg was very quietly and neatly dressed, her red hair soberly braided and smoothed. Meg got a certain pleasure out of playing the ultra-respectable sobersides, aware that this deceived no one. Half-consciously, the two women summed each other up. "A wee mouse," thought Meg, her eyes flickering over Mary's small neat figure, swathed in a white apron, for she had been baking. "What splendid hair," thought Mary, "and her eyes! No wonder she is what she is," for the discreet lowering of voices, the glances to and fro, had made all too clear what Meg was; not that that in any way startled the reader of Byron and Crabbe. . . .

"I have come with the dress, ma'am," said Meg, all submissive politeness.

"Come in," and Mary showed Meg into the parlour where the fire danced in the grate. "I'll just go and take off my apron."

Meg undid her bundle and laid out the bits of the dress on the chairs, put her pins on the table, and could then look round. Books! So it was true. She had heard about the umbrella-maker's daughter and her books. She was just a wee mouse, living with shadows and not a right feeling in her body. No wonder she'd chosen the stuff she had—and Meg flicked a scornful finger on the plain brown silk of the dress. If she'd been going to the Ball, she'd have had a dress that would have lit up the ball. She walked over to the bookshelf and ran her fingers over the books. When had she last read a book? *The Lady's Magazine* sometimes—the cook at Griffton occasionally passed one on. And in Daniel Rutherford's house she'd picked up *Frankenstein* and read it. His house too had been full of books: but no one, least of all herself (a little shiver ran through her) could say he put books in the place of life—not like the mouse. . . .

Mary came in and the fitting went on, Meg competently pinning and unpinning, letting out, taking in. There was no mirror in the room, but Mary brought one from the kitchen and managed to see herself piecemeal.

"Yes, that is quite as I would like it," she said, aware of a certain almost disdainful aloofness on Meg's part. She tried to make contact. "I chose this colour because I don't like bright colours in dresses—for myself, I mean."

"Yes, ma'am," said Meg. She carefully removed the pinned up bodice and sleeves and helped Mary out of the wide skirt. "I will be back in four days to fit it again."

"All that sewing in four days? You must work hard."

"I try to do things on time." The lowered lids hid a little flash of resentment.

"And when do I pay . . ."

"You pay Miss Beattie, ma'am."

Four days later, Meg returned with the dress completed. Mary tried it on; it was in every way satisfactory. This time she had moved a long mirror

167

into the room, and so could see the complete effect. Round the neck and sleeves was lace, a deep cream, almost coffee coloured. It had belonged to Mary's mother. The whole effect, to Meg's eyes, was one of self-effacing timidity: a poor effort at a ball-dress— but if that was what the mouse wanted. . . . Mary had turned to her and was saying:

"I like it. What do you think of it?"

"It fits you very well. But it is very plain for a ball."

Mary looked again. "Do you think so? Ah, but wait. I'll show you something."

She went from the room but was back in a matter of seconds. Meg looked at her in amazement. Mary had put on a pendant—an amethyst pendant, a beautiful, large gem, surrounded with pearls. Against the clear skin of her throat it glowed; the prudish dress became a foil for the jewel; the jewel was a signal to notice the neat head, the dark eyes, the shining hair.

"You see?" said Mary. "This was my mother's. It makes a difference, don't you think?"

"Oh yes, yes indeed," said Meg, her eyes on the jewel. "It does make a difference." She gathered up pins and packaging and prepared to leave.

"Thank you for doing my dress so promptly," said Mary.

"No need for thanks," said Meg. "I like to do things promptly. I will tell Miss Beattie the dress is to your satisfaction."

Leah, as she paid Meg, said: "Did Miss Tullis

like the dress? She didn't find it too dark? I tried to make her take a lighter material, but she wouldn't."

"She's got a bit of jewellery that lights it up a bit," said Meg. "Just as well. I call it a mousey dress. . . ."

That night, as Meg sat sewing another dress for Leah Beattie, there came the well-known knock on her door. Without raising her head, she said, "Come in," and in a moment Daniel Rutherford was standing in the doorway.

"Meg! You are a picture," for the material, a rich sea-blue satin, fell in folds round her knees to the ground, and the bright candlelight by which she sewed, and the dancing firelight, for Meg kept good fires, set her hair glowing. He moved forward, laid down his hat on the table, put his hands on her shoulders and buried his face in the nape of her neck where the heavy coil of hair brushed his forehead. She looked up at him and smiled.

"You'll be jabbed by my needle, gin ye're not careful!"

He stepped back. "I can't stay just now, Meg. I'm on my way to a meeting of the election committee. But I saw your light and just had to come in. That's a braw stuff you're working with."

"Oh aye. It's fur Mrs. Drysdale. Fur the ball."

"You would look like a queen in a dress of that. I've hardly ever seen you in anything but black, except for a shawl or two."

"Satins and silks are no' fur me." She smiled, a sly sidelong smile, and looked up at him with narrowed eyes. "I'm not needing bright colours nor braw stuffs tae catch my man."

He chuckled. "Indeed not. You in your black woolsey are worth them all, even if they wore the rainbow itself! Leah's kept you busy, though. Have you much more of her work to do?"

"Not much. I finished the dress for the umbrella-maker's daughter yesterday and delivered it today."

"Miss Tullis? Is she going to the ball?"

"Aye, but in a gey dull dress. Brown. Like a wee mouse."

He laughed. "Ah, but you can't always judge the person within by the outward covering. They tell me the nightingale is a drab bird, but think of its song!"

"Ah weel, I don't think the umbrella-maker's daughter is any nightingale." She put down her needle and caught his hand. "Will you come back after your meeting?"

"I dare not. My sister Susannah watches my goings-out and comings-in like a hawk—and she could cause much trouble. I will come when I can."

She pouted. "It was better in the summer time, up at the castle."

"Summer will be back. Meantime, I'll come when I can. Just make sure the road's empty just now."

Meg looked out. "Aye. Safe enough." Suddenly her mood changed. "Ye're feart tae be seen coming out my house."

But he could deal with her moods. He laid his

hands on her shoulders and kissed her. "Now, Meg, we've had this out. If it got around I was still seeing you . . . the cholera excused a lot, your coming to housekeep for me . . . but I've my post as a teacher here to think of." He held her at arm's length. "I shouldn't go on coming . . . but I can't help myself." He drew her to him and held her close, the fragrance from her hair in his nostrils, her cheek soft under his lips. And suddenly thrust her back and went into the darkness outside.

Meg went back to her chair and lifted her work again, but soon laid it down, for her eyes were blurred.

14

ON the great day of the nominations, excitement began early. A platform had been put up in the square in the centre of the older part of the village, where the official business was to be enacted. At first light there was a sound of bagpipes, and a straggling procession marched onto the square, composed of miners from Inverforth. They had, of course, no vote, but had been recruited for a fee of three shillings a head to support Mr. Brownlie in any useful way which might present itself. On arrival, they squatted on their heels behind the platform to eat the bread and cheese which had been issued to them. Then they dispersed to wander round the town, reluctantly passing the door of the Thorn Bush, it being understood that the three shillings would be forfeited if anyone took drink before the business was completed.

An hour later, the cheerful sound of fifes and drums, and Mr. Brownlie's gigantic face swelling and swaying above the crowd, on a banner surrounded by the hopeful words "Prosperity for All", announced the arrival of the official Brownlie procession. In a carriage decorated with bunting and evergreen rode the Brownlie family; Mrs. Brownlie, a sad, dim little woman peeping out from

172

a bonnet of enormously be-feathered splendour; two subdued daughters in their teens, brilliant in furs and satin; a pert small boy in a checked overcoat and shiny stiff cap, flourishing a toy coachman's whip, sitting on his father's knee; Mr. Brownlie himself very impressive in a well-cut dark coat with gleaming buttons and a tall hat which he held in his hand and waved graciously to the crowd, all the while smiling a vulpine smile. Behind came more carriages full of his supporters; more banners and flags; a brave sight, and impressive, until the General's supporters arrived.

Not for nothing had the General been a General, trained to deploy his forces to the best advantage. Two processions of his supporters converged on Dyplin from east and west along the new turnpike road. Each was proceeded by a band of drums and trumpets and bugles and fifes: and bands brought up the rear. Each procession was headed by a horseman carrying a Union Jack. Behind the first band was a scarlet banner with Liberty on it in huge gold letters. The General's carriage headed the procession from the west, with his wife, considerably younger than himelf, gay and smiling and blowing kisses all the way, their two boys, aged about nine and seven, with them, dressed in miniature uniforms of their father's old regiment. There were twice as many carriages as in Mr. Brownlie's procession, and whereas Mr. Brownlie's humbler supporters had walked, the General's were one and all mounted on horses, shaggy and ill-groomed, but in the mass making a brave show. The whole affair, given the small area of the square, and the steepness of the streets, might have become a chaotic traffic jam. But the General had reconnoitred his ground and drilled his underlings. The horsemen dismounted and marched up to the square behind a band, the horses being held by specially recruited non-voters; there was room for the carriages to be drawn up in front of the shops and houses; the bands halted in the approach streets; and when all was in order, Mr. Brownlie's supporters looked uncommonly like a small guerilla army on the point of being efficiently eliminated by the forces of civilization and good government.

It was clear to all who must win. Nevertheless, the formalities must be observed. Mr. Brownlie spoke first, mouthing great platitudes about stability and order and the good of the country. As the *Gazette* put it (Torrance was firmly for Reform), "his undistinguished oration was listened to with the silence of unenthusiasm". This was not strictly true. There was vociferous applause from the miners, out to earn the promised three shillings. When the General began to speak, the same miners booed, shouted, and stamped, in what the *Gazette* called "a puerile and ineffective attempt to render inaudible the stirring and patriotic words of the Reform candidate, General Wedderburn".

The show of hands clearly confirmed that the General had the support of the majority, but Mr. Brownlie, "unwilling to yield to the evident verdict of the vast majority of the voters" demanded a poll. It was agreed this would be held and the result announced the following week, on December 24th. There was cheering and shouting; all the bands played at once, the banners dipped and swayed, the processions re-formed, the Thorn Bush was invaded, and Dyplin went home to recover and to prepare for the celebratory ball on the day when the poll would be declared.

The triumphant party were determined that the General's election would be marked in no ordinary manner. After the poll had been declared—and the declaration of the poll, a foregone conclusion, was a much less exciting occasion than "Nomination" day—there was to be another procession round Dyplin, and someone—was it Mr. Drysdale, who taught Greek and Latin in the New School?—had the brilliant idea that the victorious General should be carried in a triumphant chair at the head of his rejoicing supporters—always, of course, provided that the weather permitted. So, with some help from John Campbell, a large chair was mounted on poles, to be carried on the shoulders of eight of the strongest young men of Dyplin. It was, as the *Inverforth Gazette* put it, "ingeniously and beautifully decorated with evergreens", and when the poll was announced, in the square where the show of hands had taken place, and the General was declared to have won by four hundred and thirty-seven to one hundred and fifty-six votes, amidst "a prolonged burst of enthusiastic cheering", the

General—and his two small boys—were invited to seat themselves in the chair which was then, not without some anxious moments, raised from the ground and carried round Dyplin. The two small boys clutched the arms of the chair very tightly for at times it swayed and dipped in unexpected ways, but the General maintained throughout an appearance of "ease and confidence", even when, as they crossed a bridge, the bearers stumbled and he found himself tilted over the brightly rippling water of the burn.

By early afternoon, the procession was over, and the General and his family had gone to Griffton to prepare for their appearance at the Grand Ball at night. Cards of invitation had been issued to all voters, irrespective of whom they had voted for, but Mr. Brownlie and his friends had let it be known they would not attend; and indeed, Mr. Brownlie, as soon as the poll was declared, had slunk home, where his wife and daughters were waiting with meek foreboding.

The trustees of the New School had agreed to the Assembly Hall being used for the Ball, and it had been decorated with evergreen and red, white and blue bunting, patriotism being very much the sentiment of the hour. Three fiddlers and two pipers had been recruited to provide music, "an elegant cold collation" was to be served in adjoining rooms at which, "in true democratic fashion as befitted the occasion", the newly-elected member and his family and friends would mingle with the

176

voters, "with no ceremony or standing on rank".

David and Mary, with Alison and John Campbell, went together to the ball. Fortunately, the fine dry weather had persisted all day and they could walk down, the women wearing lacing boots and carrying their slippers. (Johnny Bradley the bootmaker had been nagged by his wife into extending his range of goods to include neat kid slippers for the ladies and pumps for the men: and against all his own gloomy prognostications, made a handsome profit on them.) David and John wore their Sunday suits, but Mary had persuaded her father into wearing a fine lawn frilled shirt, and this, and John's resplendent waistcoat, dark red velvet and very handsome, gave them a sufficiently festive air. Alison was secretly rather proud of her new dress, which John had agreed was becoming, but had misgivings about Mary's, which she had only seen laid out on Mary's bed.

"It's no' like a young woman's dress—mair like for a married woman. Brown—juist plain brown— awful dull. And Wilkie had such a bonny silk— straight frae France, he said—white, wi' wee roses and a green stripe. But she wouldna' hear o' it."

"Weel, she's the one that's tae wear it," said John. "Ye're aye worrying aboot the lassie. When she first came, ye went on aboot her hat being ower fancy. And noo ye're going on about her dress being ower plain. Furby, she's—she's no' the kind fur stripes and rosebuds."

"And whit dae ye mean by that?"

177

"I'm no' sure. But I am sure that Mary kens best what suits her."

When Mary and Alison joined their men before going into the hall, John stared, and then whispered to Alison, "I thocht ye said Mary's was an awful dull dress?"

"It looks better on her," said Alison. "An' I didna know she was to be wearing a necklace like yon."

The General, with all the beaming benevolence of success, welcomed the voters as they arrived, shook them by the hand and presented them to his wife, who gave each a gracious nod of the head. The gentry, including the Inneses of Griffton, were seated on the platform: the personnel from the New School for the most part clustered to the right of the hall: the Tullises and Campbells joined the Robertsons and the Johnstons and other trades-people and farmers to the left. There was desultory conversation and an eyeing of gowns, and an occasional glance up at the gallery which ran round three sides of the hall, where some of those unqualified to attend had come to watch. Among them were Madame Laporte and Leah Beattie, sitting together, united by professional interest, and not at all divided by commercial rivalry, for each clearly understood where her sphere of activity lay; and indeed, Leah looked up to Madame Laporte with some deference. Now, from the front row, they gazed down on their handiwork.

"That's Mrs. Campbell there, in the black and pink," said Leah. "It looks quite well."

178

"Yes, not bad at all, Miss Beattie. Did you advise her on material?"

"Oh no." Leah was quite shocked. "I wouldn't dream of it. I just make up what they bring. . . ."

"Ah. Well now, I try to guide them. Do you see Mrs. Westerton, there on the platform? You know her, I suppose?"

Leah had to confess she did not.

"Her husband is Mr. Westerton of Devonton House. That stout lady in the grey moire silk—with the pink feathers in her hair—you see? *She* wanted a rose-red satin—can you see her in it? Like a great side of beef—I had quite a time persuading her to change and had to allow her the pink feathers to compensate . . ." She leaned forward.

"Who's the young woman in brown?"

"That's Mary Tullis, the umbrella-maker's daughter. I—I cut the dress, but it was made up by—by someone else."

"You mean Meg Annan? Very sensible of you, my dear. Meg is a very good sempstress. Unfortunately, *my* ladies wouldn't have anything to do with anything she touched. Very stupid." She leaned closer, and a warm breath of Madeira wafted over Leah, for Madame Laporte had been quietly celebrating the completion of her orders by having a glass or two of her own good wine. "You and I, Miss Beattie, as dressmakers, see and know enough of the ladies to know that whatever Meg Annan may do or be, she is not unique."

She looked meaningfully at Leah with raised

eyebrows, and Leah, deliciously flattered by this assumption of her knowledge of the world, murmured gently, "Oh yes, indeed."

Madame Laporte was looking down again at the company. "That brown dress . . ."

Leah interrupted anxiously.

"It is dull, I know, but that was what she brought me. I couldn't . . ."

"Miss Beattie—" Madame Laporte shook a finger. "That is the most successful dress on the floor. It suits its wearer to a T, and the jewel makes it remarkable. I congratulate you."

"Oh," said Leah. "Thank you. I—" but Madame Laporte was intent on someone else, and the two ladies settled down happily watching and gossiping.

The stately splendour of the Reform Ball was for years a landmark in Dyplin history. Long afterwards, old ladies would date births, deaths and marriages from the Ball and they could calculate ages with uncanny accuracy.

"I mind her at the Reform Ball," they would say. "She would be about thirty, for she didn't marry till she was twenty-five. Wee Jimmy died in the cholera, and he was four, and Mary Ann was just a wean, and Freddie a baby. She's no' a day less than fifty-six."

But it was the sense of a new beginning, the obscure feeling of history being celebrated, that gave it its importance. It had not the abandoned relief of the dancing on the Knowe when the news of Waterloo came; or the fun of the bonfire in the

180

summer when the Bill was passed. It had more the air of a state occasion; but the *Gazette's* predictions of there being no standing on rank were not strictly fulfilled. True, the ladies and gentlemen did descend from the platform to mingle with the others on the floor and the General danced with every woman present, and asked them all the same questions as to family (if married) or paid the same decorously jovial compliments (if single). His wife graciously accepted requests to dance and managed to keep smiling even when an unskilled heavy boot came down heavily on her satin slipper. She enjoyed most her dance with David Tullis. In his youth, David had been a fine dancer, and had not entirely lost his skill. He partnered her skilfully through a Scottishe; it was a long time since he'd held a comely young woman in his arms; and at the end, when she said: "Thank you, Mr. Tullis, I did enjoy that," there flowed between them a ripple of warmth that indeed disregarded rank and ceremony.

Not that the Ball was not enjoyable: it was. The cold collation was in every way satisfactory; the fiddlers played well and tirelessly, and the gaiety, though subdued, was nonetheless real.

Daniel Rutherford, standing with a group of teachers from the New School, was unaware of Mary's arrival till Susannah, who was sitting with her back to the wall, resplendent in midnight-blue satin, said:

"There's the umbrella-maker's daughter. What a very odd dress for a ball!"

He swung around. Against a background of bright silks and satins, Mary stood in her brown dress, the amethyst glowing beneath her throat. She was looking down but, as if she felt his gaze, she raised her eyes to meet his. Even across the breadth of the floor, he could see her colour deepen as he bowed, and she gave a little curtsy in acknowledgement. They did not dance together for some time. Daniel had to dance with Susannah, with colleagues' wives, with one or two of the ladies from the platform. It was not until after the collation that he could ask Mary: but he had noticed every partner she had had; twice young Innes had danced with her; and George Brownlie, a farmer from beyond the Braes, had had her up three times and seemed never away from her. But at last, he could ask her. It was a waltz, and not many couples were on the floor, such dancing not being well known in Dyplin. The gentry came down from their height for it and some of New School staff, but Mary was the only one from her side of the room.

So at last Daniel held the small firm body in his arms, could glimpse the curve of her breasts under the tantalizing lace of her dress, see the glow of the amethyst against the pale skin. Her eyes he could not see—only the lowered lids and the dark lashes, for she did not look at him. She danced beautifully, following his movements effortlessly. They did not exchange a word.

From the first moment of recognition, she had known that sooner or later Daniel and she would be partners; that her efforts at avoiding him were over; and that she was glad it was so; for, since her first encounter with him on the hillside, all those months ago, and even when her anger against him was at its height, he had been daily in her thoughts. It was as if she were being drawn into a whirlpool—she had struggled against it—for she had been in the whirlpool before and had vowed never to be caught in it again.

Now, decorously and publicly circling the floor, she knew the whirlpool had caught her.

After that they danced many times. George Brownlie retired to sulk in a corner; young Innes realized the situation and turned his attentions elsewhere. By the end of the evening, Daniel was dancing with no one else, and the tongues were wagging round the room. Alison, desperate, made an effort to change the situation, and twice sent John to forestall Daniel and claim Mary as a partner. And each time Daniel did not dance with another woman, simply stood and looked on. Finally, she went to David and said, "It's drawing near the end. I think we should go." David, uneasy himself, noting Mary's flushed cheeks, a glow in her eyes which he had not seen for months, and which filled him with foreboding, agreed readily. So when Daniel brought Mary back after a reel in which she danced as in a dizzying dream, they found Alison gathering up her things preparatory to going.

"I think we'll be for home now, Mary," said David. "I've to be working tomorrow, and so has John."

"But there are only two more dances," said Daniel. John felt Alison's elbow in his ribs.

"Aweel, I'll have a last turn with you, Mary," he said, "if you've any breath left."

"Oh, I could dance for ever," said Mary, and off they went.

Alison refused David's offer of dancing and, as Daniel stood silently looking on, she whispered, "Take her yourself, David, for the next."

Which David did. Mary showed no dismay at dancing with her father; and Daniel, after a moment's hesitation, took Susannah. So the Ball ended with sufficient decorum to soothe Alison's anxieties a little. They sang God Save the King and gave three cheers for Liberty and Reform. And then the great occasion was over.

Up in a corner of the gallery, Meg Annan had watched Daniel and Mary with pain and fury.

15

SO the era of Liberty and Reform was inaugurated with ceremony and celebration. But next day, as dresses were put in the wardrobe to hang unused for many a long month, and then be ignominiously "altered" to suit more prosaic occasions, life did not seem at all different. The election and the Ball had broken the gloom that had hung over Dyplin like the lowering mist on the hills; but now it rolled down again. At the best of times, feeling at New Year swung dizzily between sadness and gloom for the past and the uncertain future, and relief at the anticipation of fresh beginnings. This New Year gloom prevailed, and guilt at the momentary forgetfulness of the year's dreadful toll which the Ball had provided.

Not that Mary felt like that. She woke up the morning after the Ball gayer and happier than for a long time. That Daniel Rutherford did not come near her for days did not at all upset her; whether he was in love with her or not for the moment did not matter. It was sufficient for her to feel again what she had thought would never happen, a wonderful sense of release and vitality, physical and mental. And the third issue of the *Gazette* after the Ball carried a poem in which democracy, as practised on that occasion, was given tart treatment.

It amused young Innes very much, who wondered if that schoolmaster fellow, Rutherford, wrote it.

By the day after the Ball, Mrs. Glendinning had, of course, heard all about the attention paid by Daniel to Mary; much to her secret relief. If Daniel Rutherford was indeed "just on the point of spiering" for Mary, there was hope that Matthew would be diverted from his ridiculous idea of marrying her. But her attempts to bring conversation round to the Ball met with no success. Matthew had been given to understand by his fellow members of Presbytery that he should have denounced the Ball from the pulpit; and had not been mollified that his not doing so had been understood and excused as due to "youthfulness and inexperience in things spiritual". So at his mother's first tentative mention of the Ball, he cut her off with a lofty "Do not speak to me of profane feastings and dancings. They would have done better to mark such a step in the nation's destiny by going up to the House of God," strode into his study and firmly shut the door, every inch the Minister. It was a mood which did not come on him often. When it did, Mrs. Glendinning went about silently till it should pass. But she hoped he would not feel impelled to declaim against the Ball next Sabbath. It seemed a useless exercise, since it was now past history . . . and he would just have to find out in his own way about Mary Tullis and Daniel Rutherford—and that might take long enough. . . .

If Matthew had had any idea of preaching against

the Ball, it was replaced by another theme which had the comforting advantage of allowing him to release his accumulated irritation on a topic to which no one could take exception.

On the Friday after the Ball, there was a death in Dyplin. An old woman, long widowed, who lived in the cottage next to Leah Beattie, gently and decorously died of pneumonia, having fulfilled her three-score years and ten and more; the kind of death which briefly saddened but in no way grieved the village. Her nearest relative, a grandson, lived in Glasgow. It was impossible for him to get to Dyplin before Monday for the funeral. So Tibbie would lie till then in her little house, watched over by kindly neighbours. It seemed a simple enough arrangement, but John Campbell, coming in for his dinner, had to report otherwise.

"He's a queer one yon, the Minister," he said, rubbing his hand over his hair. "I went to the Manse tae confirm the arrangements for Tibbie Maclachlan's funeral, an' I just happened tae say, 'It's a peety she's tae lie over the Sabbath; they'll be saying there's sure tae be twae mair deaths', an' he bristled up and said, 'What's this? Who says any such thing?' An' I said: 'Oh, it's just an auld superstition here, that if a body lies over the Sabbath, there'll be twae mair deaths.' He looked that fierce that I added, 'I'm no sayin' I believe it. It's just a superstition,' but he fairly opened up. 'Superstition is a wicked disbelief in the over-riding law of Providence; and not far from the sin of

187

sorcery; and I believe there is too much of it in this place.' So I said nae mair, but cam' awa."

"Oh aye." Alison dished up the potatoes. "He's mebbe heard aboot Daniel Rutherford dancing a' that much wi' Mary."

John put down his knife and fork. "And whit has that tae dae wi' superstition in Dyplin?"

"You'd be surprised," said Alison.

Matthew had not heard of Daniel's dancing exploits, but he fell with relief on the topic of superstition for his Sabbath morning sermon. If his brethren of the Presbytery ever heard of it, they would not be able to accuse him of laxity on this subject. So the congregation on the Sabbath morning, settling back comfortably for an end-of-the-year homily, heard a voice of thunder announce the text: "I perceive that in all things ye are too superstitious", and were then invited to consider irrationality, lack of faith, paganism, blasphemy, and the general wickedness of superstition: Old Testament texts on divination from Numbers and Deuteronomy, Saul and the Witch of Endor; the young woman soothsayer in Acts—the words rolled round their ears. At the end, Matthew drove his theme home with a special blast at the ungodly superstition in their midst, that the lying of a body over the Sabbath would mean two more deaths.

When he finished, Matthew had to admit to a certain feeling of exhilaration. It was the first time he had preached a denunciatory sermon, and he could feel the attraction: but also the temptation. So when Joseph Harvey, easing him of his robes, said: "Minister, yon was magnificent," Matthew said nothing.

But his nascent spiritual pride received salutary correction the next day. On Monday morning came word that the night before an estate worker and his son at Griffton had been drowned while trying to rescue a sheep from a deep and treacherous river. So Tibbie's funeral on Monday was followed by a more grievous one on Tuesday, on a day when gusts of wind drove the rain among the gravestones and the silent black-clad men in the churchyard drew their cloaks and plaids closer and felt mortality hang heavily on them. For Andrew and Walter Jamieson had been hale and strong, and who would have though of them carried away like that? It was a gloomy ending to a sad year; heads wagged over the justification of the old superstition, and there was an uneasy feeling of dark forces at work. Even Matthew had to fight down a little irrational tremor: and, having at last heard of Daniel's attentions to Mary at the Ball, had to struggle hard to face the last night of the year with thoughts sufficiently solemn and detached from merely personal concerns.

Never in living memory had there been such a Hogmanay as this in Dyplin. Not that Hogmanay was a riotous affair, but it was a time of laughter, of going from house to house, of the candles burning till the late dawn, of giggling in the dark shadows between the houses, and lanterns bobbing through the streets; not a sober time either, but good-humoured mostly, and if men tripped over into loud aggressiveness there was always someone to divert them from coming to blows. But this year, people for the most part stayed huddled indoors; not going to bed; it was unthinkable to be in bed when the New Year came; but sitting round the fire, talking of the past; and there were tears when the New Year came. Some of the younger people went visiting, driven out by the gloom within. Grizel went to Jean Scott's, and then the two of them on to Jenny's, but there was none of the fun of previous years. A few of the drouthier men went from house to house and achieved their usual state of fuddled good-humour; but for the most part, Dyplin was dark and silent.

Up at the top of the town, Mary and David sat by the fire, the kitchen all scrubbed and spruce. They were both reading, but towards midnight, David let his book rest on his knees, leant back and looked at Mary. She too had stopped reading and was gazing into the fire, happily day-dreaming. He thought of the previous Hogmanay, when he had been alone, and Mary far away in London, and the world had been very black. Now, seeing her there, quiet, happy, he should have been happy too. But Alison had dropped hints about Daniel, and David, as always, was anxious for Mary.

He glanced at the clock ticking on the wall. "Mary lass, in five minutes it'll be the New Year."

She rose and put glasses on the table and the jug

of whisky, and shortbread. When the clock showed midnight, David filled the glasses, they kissed each other, and drank to the New Year; and had scarcely put down their glasses when there was a knock at the door. It was John and Alison.

"A guid New Year," said John, as he handed David a bottle. "We couldna be sitting next door, there, and no' come in tae first-foot ye."

"We're glad tae see you. See here, Mary, put more coal on the fire." And David went into a bustle of filling glasses and passing shortbread, and putting up chairs to the fire.

While David was busy, John brought out from beneath his coat-tails a parcel, and handed it to Mary. "Here's your Ne'erday," he said.

Mary, looking surprised and pleased, untied the string and took off the paper. It was a model boat, carved with all the skill John could muster, and fully rigged. She turned to him, her face alight.

"Oh, it's beautiful. Thank you—thank you."

"It's but a little thing, Mary. Alison and I can never thank you enough . . ."

But she interrupted him in some distress. "You must never thank me for anything. I could do nothing else. . . ."

But now David had everything in order, and was raising his glass.

"Your health, John Campbell!"

"And yours."

They sat talking and sipping the good whisky. John and David launched into a masculine review of the past year, in which votes and Reform figured largely. Alison did not say much, nor did Mary. She sat with John's gift on her knee, running her fingers over the wood, feeling the curves and smoothness of the carving, and John watched her with pleasure. After her second glass, Alison became more talkative, and began to tell tales of New Years at her own home in her girlhood. John added his stories, and David and Mary listened and laughed. The candle flames swayed; the fire glowed; the wind brushed the shutters and sighed in the chimney; the room was a warm shelter; when a knock came at the door, they jumped.

David went to open the front door. They heard his surprised greeting.

"Mr. Rutherford! Come in!"

Seconds after, Daniel stood in the doorway.

"A Happy New Year." He bowed to each in turn. "I was passing and saw the light, and felt I must give you my greetings." He put his hand in the pocket of his long-skirted coat and brought out a little stone jug with a cork stopper. "This brings my good wishes, Mr. Tullis."

"I thank you," said David. "Mary, a glass."

John broke the awkward little silence that fell on them while Daniel was drinking. "Are there many folk about, Mr. Rutherford?"

"Very few. I had undertaken to visit friends, otherwise I think I should have remained at home too. But it is a time for friendship, is it not? Though this New Year people seem to have small heart for it."

He scarcely took his eyes off Mary, who had moved her chair back a little from the circle of candle-light, and kept her eyes for the most part lowered. When she did look at him, they shone in a way that made the observant Alison tighten her lips.

Daniel did not stay long. After some commonplace exchanges on the year past and what might come in the year ahead, he rose to take his leave, and shook hands all round. When he took Mary's hand—she had not spoken a word directly to him—he said:

"Miss Tullis, I have not forgotten the pleasure of our dancing at the Ball," and raised her hand to his lips. She blushed rose-red, and dropped her hand, turning aside as David showed him out.

Alison was indignant. "It was not decent," she said to John when they were back in their own house. "Mebbe the gentry kiss hands and all that, but we dinna. Makin' the girl all confused—she was fair upset."

"I'm no sae sure," said John. "Ye can turn red wi' pleasure as weel's confusion. But I could wish she had set her heart on someone else—if she has set her heart on him. Mebbe it's just a passing notion."

"I hope sae too. But he cam tae the hoose deliberately. 'Just passing' indeed! Hoo could he be 'just passing' the last hoose in the place? And him wi' the wee jar o' whisky all ready."

"Mebbe he's taken a real notion o' her."

"Ye mean, fall in love? No fear! It's just—just . . ."

"Aye?"

"If you ask me," said Alison, driven to unheard of bluntness, "if you ask me, it's just carnal desire!" And she pretended not to hear John's whistle of astonishment.

It had been a good move, thought Daniel, going down the road from the Tullises, to call in. How she had reddened when he kissed her hand! He'd never have done it but for the warmth of the good drink in him. Poor Mary! Sitting there with her dull old father, and these neighbours—Alison, a stupid housewife and, God help her, John Campbell with nothing in his head but footrules and coffins—and the dull little room. No wonder Mary had turned to books for escape. She was beautiful; he felt again the enticing lightness and warmth of her dancing. His light-headedness set him dreaming: he would take her away overseas; somewhere warm and sunlit; out of cold, dreary little Dyplin; but as he turned the corner to go to Meg's, the wind, blowing from the hills, caught him coldly in the face and banished the fantasy. There were his children, there was Susannah, there was a living to earn. His escape must be otherwise.

Meg was waiting for him, the fire bright, two candles lit, glasses and drink, shortbread and cake waiting. She helped him off with his coat, drew him to the fire, poured him his drink, and then sat on a little stool, resting her head on his knee.

"Ye'll can stay a while?"

"Oh yes. I saw Susannah to bed, and said I'd go first-footing. And I have, to one or two."

"Ye've no been here for mair than a week."

"I couldn't. I've told you, Meg, I have to be careful. Come, no complaints tonight."

"I'm not complaining. I'm glad you're here."

He ran his hand over her hair and said idly, "Did you get all your sewing done in time for the Ball?"

"Oh aye."

"It's a pity you can't see the ladies wearing the fine things you make for them."

"But I did."

She felt him stiffen, heard the wariness in his voice.

"You were there?"

"Aye, up in the gallery." She turned and looked up at him. "You seemed tae be enjoying yoursel'."

"Up to a point."

"Ye danced a lot wi' the umbrella-maker's daughter."

"Well, she was the youngest woman there. I did my duty dancing with all the others. You should know, Meg, my taste is not for the good married ladies of Dyplin."

"Mebbe no." She was still looking up at him. "They're saying in the place that you're thinking tae marry her."

195

He drew himself up sharply and his voice was angry. "Who says so?"

"Everybody." Then, seeing his eyes flash, she added, "One or two in the shops. They were all talking about the Ball."

"Now listen, Meg. I danced with Miss Tullis because she was the only woman worth dancing with. But that doesn't mean I have any special interest in her. And certainly not that I've any ideas of marrying her. You should know how tittle-tattle flies round Dyplin like a whirlwind."

"But you could marry her—I mean, you being a widower." She turned her head aside, lowered her voice. "You could marry anyone."

Daniel looked down at her head, a little frown pulling his brows. What was she saying? Surely she could never think . . . but no, their relationship was simple and clear-cut and well understood from the beginning. He stroked her hair again, relishing as always its resilience beneath his hand. "Come, Meg, it's the New Year now. Don't let's waste time in foolish talking."

She looked up at him again in the old teasing way and rose to her feet. "I'm not for talking." She blew out the candles and left the glow of the fire.

16

AFTER New Year, the weather changed. The mists lifted from the hills, there were flurries of snow and then came a bitter frost, and Dyplin was transformed into a shining Alpine village, with the hills white under a clear sky and every pond and lochan frozen. Even the burn was stilled, the boulders padded with thick green ice, and the banks with a fringe of icicles, and only a dark streak of water here and there showed that underneath the water was flowing as always. The bright climate roused the spirits of Dyplin. People took time to look up to the hills, to pause on the bridge and peer down at the curves and hollows of the ice. It brought problems too. Dr. Munro had a steady trickle of broken wrists and ankles and even a fractured leg or two to deal with, where people had stepped too boldly onto a frozen step or pavement. Some of the older people tied canvas rags round their boots to give a better grip on the treacherous cobbles; and the cold forced them to wrap up in anything that would keep them warm, so that they were transformed into bundles of wool, and some of them shuffled around like great black bears. The road up to the top of the village was impossible for man or horse. Alison and Mary, going to the shops, had to take a path over the fields towards the turnpike and then double back, and David's supplies had to come a long way round by the hill road.

For the youngsters it was a splendid time. Every street and lane had its slide, tended with loving care, and even secretly watered at night to keep the surface perfect. There was a code that children could have one slide in a street, any more and the grown-ups were angry and threw ashes on them and threatened to do away with all slides. There was a little lochan, not much more than a pond, safe and shallow, where the ground dipped to a hollow between Gloom Hill and the hill. This froze solid, and the privileged few (mostly teachers and a few boys from the New School) who had skates, went skating there. Only two women ventured— Madame Grueber and Mrs. Munro, who had been at school in Switzerland. The doctor could skate too, and he and his wife went up to the lochan whenever possible. Elspeth Munro loved it: up there, out of sight of any houses, under the clear sky and with snowy hills above, she felt, as she told the doctor, back in Switzerland, before she had any worries or responsibilities.

"You mean before you were married to a troublesome old codger like me."

She smiled. "How did you guess? Skating is like escaping into another kind of life—isn't it? It's like being a bird," and she sped away from him, her skirts flying, and looking indeed like a great bird. Mary, who had climbed over Gloom Hill to watch, envied her, sensing even from her stance on a tussock, something of the skater's exhilaration and freedom.

Elspeth Munro noticed her, and glided to the verge beside her. "Miss Tullis! How are you?"

"Well, thank you. I was wishing I could be on the ice too. But I cannot skate."

"You must learn." For a moment Elspeth was silent, looking at her. "I have an old pair of skates at home I could give to you. I never use them. You have strong boots?"

"Yes. Yes, I have. But would you teach me?"

Elspeth laughed. "The doctor and I will teach you. Tomorrow afternoon I shall be here. And the doctor too, if no one needs him. Wear your strong boots!"

So next afternoon Mary gingerly hobbled onto the ice, between Elspeth and the doctor, who fortunately was able to come, and for the first half hour she stumbled and clutched, and fell, and knew she would never, never do it. And then suddenly, all alone, she moved over the ice, and knew she would do it. In fact, she learnt quickly; her lightness, her sense of balance made it easy for her. By the end of the afternoon, she could skate round the pond, slowly, not too assuredly, but at least remaining upright.

"But I shall never be able to fly round like you," she said to Elspeth as they untied the thongs of their skates.

"Oh yes you will. Not this frost, perhaps, but

next time. Once you've learnt to skate, you always can. But the frosts are so short here. That's why I come every day: I'm neglecting my house: and Kirsty shakes her head at me every time I come out; and I'm sure all the good housewives of the place are nodding their heads in disapproval." She removed the second skate and stood up. "I like Dyplin. I am a happy woman. But out on the ice here, skating on my own, I feel a release from the world. . . . What nonsense I'm talking! It's a good thing the doctor went on ahead of us!"

"The skates . . ." said Mary.

"You are to keep them. I don't need them any more. And they're too big for the children. Come again tomorrow."

But the main social activity during the frost was not among the select few up at the skating, but at the curling. Down at the bleachfield there was a shallow rectangular pond, occasionally used for some process in the work, of just the right size to make curling possible. It froze early and solid; and was always the venue for the local curlers when the climate allowed. So now, as soon as it was clear the frost had really set in, the curling stones were hauled out from cupboards and outhouses, and lovingly polished and dusted; the brooms were sought out too; and as soon as the pond was bearing, the men of Dyplin were on it: among them David and John Campbell. Before she began to skate, Mary went down one afternoon with Alison to watch the curling.

The pond was on a stretch of level ground between the bleach-field building and sheds and a lade which took water from the river to supply the bleach-field. There was ample space round the pond for people to stand and watch: and planks had been laid between piles of bricks for seats. In winter there was little doing at the bleach-field, for the sunshine of summer was needed for the linen-bleaching even with the modern improvement of chemical whiteners. Maintenance work to the buildings and vats was done by the permanent workforce of men but the women were paid off. So some of the bleach-workers' wives who lived in a row of low little brick cottages attached to the main building had been quick to profit from the curling, and were boiling kettles on glowing braziers, and making hot whisky punch, and cooking girdle scones and selling them hot-buttered. So there was a general sound of laughter and loud talk, as well as the shouts of "soop, soop", from the players running up ahead of their stones and sweeping the ice to encourage them forward. Mary was amazed.

"I've never seen people in Dyplin look so happy," she said. "They're all laughing and smiling."

"It's aye like this at a curling," said Alison, "unless one or two take ower much and get quarrelsome. Ye see, with the frost, it's not possible tae dae much wark, in the fields, or here. Sae they're forced tae tak a holiday. And the weather's extraordinary,

201

and folk feel a kind o' lightening o' life. You understand?"

"Oh yes," and Mary wondered once more at the way Alison, practical commonsense Alison, could suddenly see into things. By now they were standing at the edge of the pond and could watch the players. There they were, launching their stones up the ice with a great forward sweep of the body that brought them almost down on one knee. And then their partners coaxing the stone up, brushing the ice ahead of it, addressing it imploringly, or profanely. Alison shook her head. "You'd think it was life or death. Whiles I think men never grow up. And d'you see auld Angus Reid there? Him that totters doon the street on a stick, and one hand at his back? And leaves his wife tae dae everything. There he is, prancing up the ice with his broom like a frisky stirk."

"And there's my father and John," said Mary, laughing. David and John, both bent almost double, were skipping up the ice, their brooms swishing speedily to and fro. "You'd think they were doing a savage dance. And who's that?" as a tall figure, wearing a flat bonnet well pulled down over his ears, a long grey muffler wrapped round his chest and tied at the back, mittens on his hands, and a look of ferocious glee on his face, watched his stone slide unerringly up the ice. "It's Joseph Harvey!" And indeed it was, all his dignity as beadle forgotten.

Mary and Alison walked round for a little,

greeting acquaintances, and Mary even persuaded Alison to eat a hot girdle scone, disregarding her murmured protests that it wasna' the thing to eat in public. John and David came off the ice and found them, glowing and high-spirited. Mary had not seen her father so bright-eyed and cheerful for months and months. John opened his eyes wide when he saw Alison's buttery scone.

"I never thought tae see the sicht! Is't Mary or the weather's persuaded you tae eat a scone in a crowd like this? Come on, Davy, we'll hae one ourselves."

When he came back with four scones, the Minister was talking to the others. Matthew was wearing his usual sober black clothes, with the addition of a heavy black muffler folded round him under his coat. But he looked pinched and cold, and even a little red-nosed, and John, seeing him, said:

"Minister, you look cauld. Here, tak one of these scones."

"John!" said Alison, scandalized at such familiarity.

"Whit's wrang wi' that? Will ye, Minister?"

"No thank you, Mr. Campbell."

"Weel, here's one fer each of us. Ye'll no, Alison? Ah weel, Davy and me'll split it between us. Alison, Mr. Glendinning thinks it's no genteel tae eat in a crowd. But Mary here kens better."

Mary, biting greedily into her scone, and licking the butter from her lips, smiled at Matthew and said innocently, "Are you going on the ice, Mr. Glendinning?"

"Mary!" Alison was scandalized again.

"But why not?" Mary looked up at Matthew. "There is nothing wrong about curling, is there, Mr. Glendinning?"

"No indeed. It is a wholesome and a healthful pastime," Matthew heard himself being pompous. She always made him sound pompous. He blundered on. "But can lead to excesses . . ."

"Yes?"

"Such as the taking of strong drink and . . ."

"And buttered scones?" She swallowed the last of hers, licked her fingers and waited for his answer. He raised his hat, said "Good-day" and moved away to greet others.

"Mary," said David, half-seriously, "you were unkind."

"You shouldna' tease the Minister," said Alison.

"Why can't he be like the others," said Mary, "not always reproving. Why can't he go on the ice, and eat scones? There's no harm."

"It's like this, Mary," said John. "He's a guid man and no' feart, as he showed in the sickness. He's—he's young tae; it's his first charge. He's no juist sure o' himsel'—like an apprentice that's juist newly turned journeyman. He's awfu' ta'en up with the dignity o' his calling and the Kirk. And rightly sae. Old Gillies, noo, he was on the ice like the rest of us."

"Weel, you might show mair respect tae him

yourself," said Alison, "offering him a buttery scone!"

"Ach, he's human tae," said John. "But what's that?"

There was an appreciative roar from the spectators round the pond. They moved back to watch. Daniel Rutherford was on the ice, and had just played a splendid shot. He had a bright woollen bonnet on, a red scarf, his face was glowing above his red beard and he had all the assurance of a man exercising a skill in which he knows he excels. He was a splendid curler—"the best in the coonty," said John, and the crowd round the pond thickened as he played. When he had finished, and as he turned to come off the ice, Mary pulled Alison's shawl.

"Let's go now," she said.

"But he's coming over here. He's seen us," said David.

"I'm cold," said Mary. "And so is Alison. We'll go now."

She and Alison walked home almost in silence. Mary gently but firmly rebuffed Alison's attempt to talk about Daniel Rutherford: which did nothing to reassure Alison.

To Grizel and Jenny and the other dabblers in spells and incantation, the cold brought another problem—where to meet. They had outgrown the joys of sliding; they had no skates; they were too young to be curlers. Their meetings were precious to them, but the shed at Grizel's house was where her father kept his curling-stones and besom; so they had to clear from it the traces of their activities and stop using it. Where could they go? It was Jenny, recognized as leader of the group, who solved their problem. In a strip of woodland a short distance to the east of Dyplin a burn had cut out a little glen, a miniature of the glen that led up to the castle. This was the burn that ran through the miners' clachan when it reached the level ground, but the little glen itself was unfrequented, the banks being steep and difficult. Half-way up the glen a huge stone, rectangular, with a concave surface, lay just above the burn. It was known as the Devil's Cradle, and it was generally felt in Dyplin that Spootie's Glen was an uncanny place; all the more so since the miners' cottages had been left lonely and deserted. The first Saturday afternoon of the frost, Jenny and Grizel and Sandy Todd had scrambled up Spootie's Glen. On the other side of the burn from the Devil's Cradle a huge oak-tree grew, its roots exposed by the spate water of the burn. They crawled in among the roots, and Sandy, who was in front, called back:

"There's a hole here!" And then, "Come and look! It's a cave!"

And so it was: a cave the size of a small room, high enough for them to stand upright in the middle; drifted deep with dead leaves, feeling dry and, by contrast with the cold outside, warm. The light filtering from the entrance let them see each other as dark, whitefaced figures as they looked round.

"I never knew this was here," said Sandy.

"I think this is the Highlanders' Cave," said Grizel. "My granny told me that when she was a little girl, her father told her that when the Highlanders were coming back from Derby with Prince Charlie three of them were hurt and sheltered in a cave, and the girl from the farm up the road there looked after them."

"Like enough," said Sandy, "but I never knew it was here."

Jenny had been groping her way round, touching the rocky walls, scuffing her feet in the leaves and raising an acrid dust. Now she turned and said, "We'll meet here."

"What?" said Sandy.

"We'll meet here; for the spells. No one ever comes. And it's not all that far from the houses. And if we pick our way, not hard to get to."

"That's a daft idea," said Sandy.

"No. It's a good idea," said Grizel, and Sandy was over-ruled.

The next time the group met it was in the cave. They reached it excited by the scramble among the frosty trees and stones and dead bracken; and sitting in the cave, among the leaves, round the guttering candle, with the tinkle of water from the half-frozen burn outside, and the Devil's Cradle a dark blotch in the starlight, they were moved by tides of feeling stranger and deeper than they had ever known.

At this first meeting Jenny dominated them more than ever. She had a darting intelligence that found no outlet in the conventional family routine. She was chronically bored by the daily round, and the gatherings for the spells and necromancy which were no more than a ploy, albeit a compulsive and gripping ploy, for the others, were becoming for her the most important thing in her life. For Jenny was not only bored; she was grieving. The cholera had killed a young worker at the bleach-field who had been Jenny's first love. She had spoken to him only a few times; he had danced with her on the Knowe on the night of the Reform bonfire; but she had loved him, and his death had been a deep hurt, all the more so, perhaps, because no one knew of it. But it was not Jenny but Jean Stott, stolid and stupid, who suggested that there was something new they could try.

"My cousin was here from Edinburgh staying with us. And she's been to a place, and they all joined hands roond the table, and—and she says a spirit spoke tae them—a dead man's spirit."

There was a silence in the cave, and eyes flickering from one to another. Jenny said: "No," but some of the others said:

"Why no' try it?"

"Nothing would happen."

"Hoo d'ye ken?" Jean saw her chance. "Are you feart, Jenny?"

It was the challenge that always worked.

"No."

"Then why not?"

So they arranged themselves in a circle on the ground among the rustling leaves, and held hands.

"We'll hae tae blow oot the candle," said Jean, savouring her brief authority. "My cousin said it had tae be in the dark."

"What do we do?" said someone.

"Ye juist sit still, and wait, and ye hear a voice."

They sat with linked hands and waited. The tenuous light filtering from the entrance could only show them as shadows. The silence magnified each rustle of a shifting leaf, each ripple of sound from the burn. Tension tightened the grip of their fingers almost to pain. Some had their eyes closed, listening. But some, and Jean was one, had their eyes wide, and it was Jean, when the cave was full of terrified expectancy, who cried:

"There's something there! I see something!"

And the circle dissolved into hysterical crying and laughing. Someone lit the candle, and one of the boys re-established order.

"Be quiet! I didna see anything. Are you sure, Jean Stott, that you saw—saw a spirit?"

But Jean, now that the candle was alight and the silence broken, was not sure.

"I *thought* I did. Mebbe no'. It—it was just a kind of thicker black over there in the corner. . . ."

"Ach, that's just your imagination. Isn't it, Jenny?"

But Jenny had drawn back from the light, not wishing that any should see the tears on her cheeks.

For she too had seen something, though she knew it was all within. Clear as in life, she had seen Walter holding his hands to her, his hair ruffled by the wind, his eyes laughing as on that night at the Knowe. She did not answer the question, and Sandy Todd, who was next to her, turned to look, and saw her hand brushing her cheek, and with a rush of tenderness moved back and put his arm round her, saying nothing. At first she sat rigid: then her body relaxed and she leant against him, turning her head on his shoulder, and sighing. Then suddenly she was her usual self and moved into the light.

"We'll have no more calling up the dead," she said. "What would you feel like if someone you knew came back?"

"I think it micht be interesting," said Dougie Johnston, putting up his usual defence of facetiousness. "There's one or two I could think of micht hae tales tae tell . . ."

"Aw, be quiet, Dougie," said Sandy. "If ye cannae help makin' a fool of everything, stop coming."

"But I think Dougie's right." This was Isabella Farquharson, a fairly new recruit to the company. "We spend our time on things tae raise the devil and tell the future—but tae meet someone you know, who's over there . . ."

"I say no," said Jenny. "And anyway it's time we went. And mind, no' a word tae a soul aboot the cave."

210

They told no one: but after their move to the cave, things changed. The place itself laid its compulsions on them. At every meeting they now had a fire. The two or three who arrived first would light it, watching anxiously as the spark fell on the little heap of paper and dead leaves and the thread of smoke led the flame to the twigs and onto the branches laid reverently across them. The late-comers arrived to the heady smell of woodsmoke—and years after, in sober middle-age a whiff of it from a garden bonfire could bring a quickening of the pulse—and the fire, as they sat round it, put on them its age-old spell, drawing them to itself and to one another. They began to dabble in deeper things than predicting the future. Someone whispered the words "Black Mass" but, as none of them knew anything about Mass, they had no idea what was involved. Grizel's book had a description of the Hand of Glory—"the hand of a murderer taken from the gallows and pickled in brine and brimstone" and used for all manner of evil. They were happy to agree that this was beyond their reach. But what about a little clay figure stuck with pins and put in a burn to waste away? "By this means," said the book, "the witch or warlock will cause his enemy to dwindle and pine into a mortal sickness".

"I don't think we should try to make people ill," said Grizel.

"Why not?" said Jenny. "Just to see if it works."

211

"You would have tae hate someone real sair tae dae that," said Dougie Johnston.

"I'll dae it." They looked in surprise at the speaker. Billy Neal was a quiet boy who had come as an orphan to Dyplin to live with his uncle and aunt. "I hate my aunt—she's an ill-tongued bitch."

Billy made his image with clay taken from the bank of the burn. They hardened it in the fire that they always had in the cave. And Jenny brought pins to stick in its shoulders and arms. "But not in its heart. We're not wanting to kill her." Then they put it in a little pool in the burn for the water to wear it away; and waited.

In three days the image was a shapeless lump; and Billy's aunt was in bed with a sharp attack of shingles. Surely here was proof of the power of a spell! It frightened and exhilarated them. Chance they ruled out. They began to experiment with others; to bring rain, to make the cattle ill, to raise a storm. (After this effort they sat in awed silence watching the rain slash down past the mouth of the cave while the wind, roaring down from the hills, tore the twigs and branches from the trees.) They exulted in the successful incantations and explained the many failures as being "no' richt done" or "spoilt by some silly body laughing". Annie Baxter, an insignificant girl, treated by the others with casual contempt, startled them and won their interest one day by going into "a kind of dream" as she said, speaking in a high strange voice and uttering menacing and barely comprehensible half-sentences, transmitted to her, she claimed, by "a wee black man with bright bright eyes" who was whispering into her ear.

There was all the difference in the world between Grizel's garden shed and the cave by the Devil's Cradle, with its darkness and its drifts of leaves. Some of them took to going there at other times than their meetings. Going into the cave was to leave behind the known world and enter an earlier time; beyond family and parents; beyond precepts and rules. The boys' exploring hands were resisted no longer; the girls yielded. Not all of them. Jenny blankly refused all Sandy's pleadings, and Grizel, bewildered by what she had started with her grandmother's old book, kept herself apart. The idleness imposed by the frost gave opportunities; the pressures were too great. Seeing them of a Sabbath, happed up well against the bitter cold of the church, faces solemn, eyes downcast, none of their elders could have imagined what currents of complicity and desire flowed between them.

17

MARY went only once to watch the curling, being much more interested in her skating. But Alison went several times, and on her third appearance there, Daniel Rutherford greeted her.

"Good day, Mrs. Campbell. Is Miss Tullis not with you?"

"No. She had things to do."

"I've only seen her here once."

"She's no' very interested in curling." Alison was determined to say nothing about Mary's skating, convinced that the less Daniel knew about Mary's activities the better.

But Daniel found out for himself.

One Sabbath—the last of the keen frost, when the skies were clear, and the air biting, Mary, after their mid-day meal, came to her father sitting by the fire with the big Bible on his knees, and said, "Father, I'm going to the pond to skate."

David looked at her in blank astonishment.

"But it's the Sabbath, Mary. You know it wouldn't be right . . ."

"I *don't* know, Father. I've been to church—we'll be going again, though it's so cold in the church I dread it. Do you know some of the ladies take hot bricks in their muffs to the church, it's so

214

cold? What is wrong if I go out into the air and sunshine? Didn't God make them?"

"Aye. But it says in the Book tae keep the Sabbath Day holy . . ."

"There will be no one there. I will be all alone. No one will see me. And I'll feel a better person there than being cooped up inside."

She had her way, of course, and was soon striding up the hill, her skates tucked under her shawl out of sight in case Alison's sharp eyes, peeping from her back window, might see them. The lochan was, as she had known it would be, deserted. There was the tedious business of fastening the complicated leather thongs of her skates, and then she was on the ice. She was quite steady now on her skates, could turn without shuddering to a stop, could feel the delicious freedom of speed.

Daniel Rutherford, coming over the crest of the hill on the homeward stretch of his Sunday walk, saw the small dark figure circling on the clear sky-reflecting ice, and knew at once it was Mary. When he was half-way down the slope she saw him and waved, and continued skating. Even when he stood at the edge of the ice, she did not stop but went on circling.

"Aren't you going to speak to me?" he called.

"I can speak when I'm moving. If I stand still I might fall."

She skated past him, laughing.

"I can't shout all the time."

"Why not?"

"Someone might hear." He looked round at the empty hills. "Besides, I can't shout the things I want to say."

"Better unsaid then." And she sped away from him.

"It's not fair. I can't come to you," he called.

"You could slide."

"But I should fall, and you would circle round me like a bird."

"You run after a stone on the curling-ice."

"But the stone goes where I send it. I'm in control."

"And this is different."

She flew round the ice, showing off her new skill, and then slowed down beside him. "I must stop now."

She hobbled onto the bank and sat down on a clump of heather to undo her skates.

"Let me help you."

Daniel knelt before her and began to untie the thongs. She looked down on his bent head, the strong red hair curling from under the bonnet he wore, and had such a longing to touch her fingers against his cheek that she had to clench her hand tightly in her lap. He untied one skate and lifted it from her foot.

"There, that's one off."

His look met hers as he glanced up. He dropped the skate, and took her in his arms, and kissed her. Mary did not resist.

216

As they drew apart, she laid her hands in his and said, "Do you love me?"

"Yes. Yes."

"Truly?" She sighed, smiled at him, and said, "And I you. But now I must go home."

"Now?"

"Yes. We shall meet again. You must come and see me—often."

He took off her other skate, helped her to her feet, and they went down the hill together, not speaking. At the garden wall Daniel said, "I'll leave you here."

"Yes. That would be best. Otherwise Alison might see you, and scold me. She does not like you."

"But that's of no concern."

"No indeed."

She raised her face to his, and after a moment's hesitation, he kissed her gently on the cheek, and watched her go down to the house. He was puzzled. She was like no other woman he had known. But then, had his experience of women been so very wide? There was his wife, whom he had at first desired, but scarcely loved, and whom, to be honest, he had found boring. There were the women he had lain with; exciting bodies and no more; not even Meg. Striding down the road, he frowned, thinking of Meg, for Meg was beginning to make demands, not just satisfy them. The wives of his colleagues he scarcely thought of as women at all—and now Mary—Mary, cool and book-learned, demure even, admitting with complete frankness and none of the coquetry he had come to take for granted with women, that she loved him.

Ah! But did he love her? That was the question he faced as he reached his own gate and went into the house, where he knew the Sunday tea-table and Susannah and the children awaited him. As he sat at the table, he tried to visualise it with Mary there instead of Susannah. But the prospect gave him no pleasure. It was not Mary in house and home he wanted; it was Mary in his arms, in bed: not bookish Mary with her eager solemn talk of authors and poetry, but Mary the slender, light—oh, so light body. He had to force himself to listen to Susannah.

"I don't suppose you'll be coming to the church tonight, Daniel. You don't think enough of what you owe to your position. You should set an example. I'll go, though it's so cold in the church these days I feel stiff and aching when the sermon's over. Though I notice Mr. Glendinning has been cutting down on the sermon. Only half an hour this morning. . . . Daniel, are you listening?"

"Yes, Susannah. The Minister cut his sermon: much to everyone's relief. He has some sense in him, for all his priggishness."

When Mary came in, the skates swinging from her hand, David looked up and shook his head.

"You're back. Was anyone else there?"

"No one on the ice. I saw Mr. Rutherford coming down from the hill. He walked back with me."

She had her back to David but the tone of her voice made him say, "Mary, Mary, be careful."

She swung round and faced him. "What do you mean?"

He faltered before her bright and angry eyes. "Well—you're not getting fond of him . . . ?"

"And why not? Didn't you say you hoped some day I should marry and have a home? And is he not free to marry?"

"Aye. But Mary—" he had to say it—"are you sure he's a good man?"

She was silent a moment, astonished.

"A 'good man'? I never thought otherwise."

"Aye." David shifted in his chair. "It's juist that Alison there aye has a tone in her voice when she speaks o' him. . . ."

"Alison's as big a gossip as any in Dyplin." Her voice was sharp. "You know yourself that nobody ever says a good thing about another here!"

"I don't think that's fair to Alison," and David was silent.

That night the wind shifted, clouds came up from the west; by morning the edge was off the cold; the sun had gone and a bitter mist filled the valley.

"The frost has taken the air," said Alison over the hedge. "The thaw will soon be here."

She was right. By the end of the week it had all gone. The mist was back on the hills, and a relentless rain falling for three days washed away all traces of ice and filled the burn with curling waves of foaming fawn spate. The exhilaration of the frost

219

went too. The houses smelt again of wet wool, the faces took on the old glum look: the groups huddled over the fire and grumbled and scandalized. The library, closed during the frost for lack of custom, re-opened. Daniel walked home from it with Mary, carrying her books. Battling through the rain, he with his plaid wrapped round him, bonnets over his eyes, she in a long black cape, they were noticed from behind curtains and through shop windows, though only Alison knew how often Daniel went in with Mary, how long he stayed.

She would offer him a seat by the fire, take off his wet things and hang them up, then make tea. They seldom touched each other—Daniel got the impression she avoided contact; was she afraid of it? But she had a way of gently fussing round him, which was something he never got from Susannah, nor from Meg either. Now and then her hand would brush his cheek, or for a moment she would lay her head on his shoulder. She was like a bird, fluttering just out of reach, enticing the pursuer on. They talked a lot, mostly about books. Her eyes would glow as she spoke of something that had moved her in her reading. He liked to see her face light up as they talked, and she would forget to withdraw her hand from his grasp. Her happiness in his presence was evident. In his home he had never even wondered if he made people happy. Nothing, he was convinced, would make Susannah happy. And his children? He provided for them; that was about all. But simply his presence could set Mary shivering. What would it be when it was more than mere presence? He began to think marriage would not be too high a price for possession. Meanwhile, there was Meg.

One morning, Meg in the dry-salter's heard some tittle-tattle, delicately spiced with scurrility, about Daniel and Mary and went home with rage and sorrow in her heart. She said nothing to Daniel when he came to her that night but teased and yielded and provoked as in their first days together. On the Sabbath, she went to church.

Meg had never been to church since she came to Dyplin, understanding well enough that it was "not for the like of her" to be seen there among the respectable upright and godly. That some of the men who made their way to her door under cover of night should solemnly make their way to the kirk on Sunday she did not find at all strange. That was how things were. But since the sickness, she had felt that the barriers between her and the rest were less rigid; though just why she chose to go to church at that particular time she would have found it hard to say.

She planned it carefully: dressed herself soberly in black, bought herself a plain black bonnet; found a pair of white gloves and washed them spotless; made her way to the churchyard and waited in the shade of a clump of yew trees till the last strokes of the bell, and then slipped up the outside stair to the gallery and into a back seat, so that very few knew she was there. Joseph Harvey, from his seat beneath the pulpit, saw her, and the solemnity of his Sabbath face momentarily fell apart under the shock. Matthew saw the woman in black with the red hair glowing under the austere bonnet and thought, "Has she come to repentance?", being not so unaware of Meg's reputation as Alison would have him. It was after the service, which was longer than of late, Matthew having reverted to his usual length of sermon, that the congregation became aware of Meg's presence. Worshippers in the gallery, unless prepared to pick their way over the grass of the graves, had to take a narrow gravel path round the gable of the church and so join the main approach. Meg was first down the gallery steps, but by the time she reached the front of the church there was already a group of people standing exchanging the usual Sunday greetings and comments. When they saw her, silence fell, and there was a drawing back, so that a path was left for her through the group. Those still coming out of the church stopped still too, and Meg was left, the only figure walking down the path. Even the children were still, held by firm parental hands. The only sound was the crunch of gravel beneath Meg's feet. She looked once or twice to either side for a nod or a smile. There were only blank stares or downcast eyes. Then she heard hurrying feet behind her, and a voice saying, "Good morning, Miss Annan," and when she turned, it was Mary.

Meg could say nothing.

Mary said, "I'm sorry the frost has gone, but it is

certainly less cold in the church now," and they walked together to the forking of the paths, Meg saying no more than "yes' or "no", Mary prattling of the weather and, finally, saying, "I should be much obliged if you would call some day about altering a dress for me."

"I will," said Meg. Then awkwardly, "This is my path home. Good morning."

Mary walked on slowly till she was joined by her father and the Campbells. No one spoke; and none of them ever mentioned the incident to Mary. But over the Sabbath mid-day meals the tongues in Dyplin wagged to some tune that day. In the Manse too there was mention of it.

"Did you know Meg Annan was in church?" said Matthew over the cold meat, for only the minimum of cooking was ever done in the Manse on the Sabbath.

"No, but I saw her afterwards."

"So you saw what Mary Tullis did."

"Yes."

"Mother, was not that a fine thing? There was that woman, left alone, scorned you might say, by all, and only Mary extended to her the grace of charity."

"Aye. Mind you, it maybe wasn't scorn kept us all back. I was dumb-founded. Maybe the rest didn't know just what to do."

"But Mary did. She alone extended a welcome to the repentant sinner. . . ."

"Now Matthew, dinna juist jump at things. How

do you know Meg's a repentant sinner? She might have other reasons for coming to the kirk forby repentance. I thought masel' she was ower soberly dressed—all that black, and the pure white gloves—as if she's taken mair care over her appearance than a woman deeply repenting might have done."

Matthew's knife and fork clattered on his plate. "Mother, I do not understand you. You are a good Christian woman, but sometimes you seem to lack charity. If you believe in repentance, you should believe that Meg Annan has by the grace of God come to a sense of sin and repented."

"Aye. I'm not saying it's impossible—forby, Meg's particular sinning takes two, and where's the repentant men? If all I hear is true, there wouldna be juist one or two. . . . But you're right, Matthew. If Meg is truly set on a new life, then she should be welcomed into the fold. It's juist I think human nature's a very tricky thing, and whiles I think you ministers mak' it sound simpler than it is. . . ."

Matthew looked at her, and she wondered if he was angry. Then he half-smiled and shook his head. "Perhaps we do sometimes. In the cholera I learnt a lot about people. And in the cholera too Mary was a shining example. . . . Anyway, I shall visit Meg Annan."

"I suppose you must."

"Of course. It won't be the first time. Oh yes," in answer to her look of near-horror, "I went before to try and show her her error—but she was obdurate,

obdurate. But you see perhaps my words have borne fruit in time."

Matthew did visit Meg, and found her all meekness and downcast eyes, and "Yes, and no, Minister". Not quite as soberly clad, with a green shawl round her shoulders, and her hair flaming. But then, she could scarcely help her hair, which, after all, must be held to be a God-given attribute. . . . Nothing she said, which was little—was in any way likely to offend. Neither could she be described as shattered by a sense of sin; yet, on the other hand, she could not be described as obdurate. Matthew was moderately satisfied with his visit, until the very end when, as Meg gave a little curtsy and said, "Good morning", he for the first time saw into her dark, bright eyes: and what he saw there was not a sense of sin.

Meg waited three days before Daniel came to her. Daniel had, of course, seen the incident outside church, and had been forced to listen to Susannah's angry comments all the way home. "That umbrella-maker's daughter—setting herself up as better than the rest of us." "Do you mean you should have walked with Meg Annan?" "No, I do not. I know what is what, if others don't." "What do you mean, then?" "She always has to be different—like the time she took the cholera woman's purse to pay her messages, never thinking if she would be spreading the sickness; and you watch out, Daniel. I've heard about her and you in the library. She's setting her cap at you," and Susannah flounced into the house.

The children's presence at the dinner table kept her silent, for it would have been impossible to explain to them why Meg should have been left alone. Daniel escaped after the meal, but at night had to listen to it all again.

He met Mary next day as she changed her books, but said nothing. No one ever did mention the incident to Mary, and she herself thought little of it, having simply felt sorry for Meg as she saw her walking on her solitary way.

When Daniel did at last go to Meg, he found her in a strange mood. She was silent and unwelcoming, and when he sat down as usual by the fire, she sat on a chair opposite him, not on the floor by his knee. He stretched out a hand to her, but she ignored it.

"Are you angry about something, Meg?"

"No."

"I saw you at the church."

"Yes."

"Why did you go, Meg?"

She flashed a look at him. "Why should I not?"

"No reason. Only I have never seen you there before."

To which her reply was: "You're seeing a lot of the umbrella-maker's daughter. Aye walking back up frae the library with her."

Daniel frowned. "It's nobody's business who I walk with."

"Is it no'? You wouldn't walk up the street wi' me, Daniel Rutherford. Ye're quick enough tae come tae my bed; but ye'd no' be seen in the street wi' me."

Daniel looked at her in astonishment. Of course he wouldn't walk up the street with her. That was impossible. And Meg knew that very well.

"Meg." He tried not to sound angry. "You wouldn't expect me to walk up the street with you. How can I? Because you . . ." he stopped, suddenly realizing that he was about to speak the unsayable.

Meg spoke for him. "Because I'm a 'bad woman'. I ken fine. Though these last months there's not a man touched me but you; oh aye. They've been at my door, coming in the dark like yoursel'. But I turned them away because of you."

Daniel could say nothing.

"I thocht it might be different after the cholera. Things were different. They still are, to a point. Folk speak tae me that before would have crossed the road when they saw me coming. . . . Daniel—" her voice lost the bitter note, and became coaxing— "gin I were respectable, would you marry me?"

"Marry you? I've never thought of it."

"Of course you haven't. But suppose I was respectable, would you?"

Light dawned on Daniel. "Is that why you went to church? To start being 'respectable'?"

"Why not? There's naethin' against it in the Bible, is there? Though the church-going folk are no' for it. Drew back as if—as if I was dirt."

"Miss Tullis didn't."

Meg's eyes flashed. "Dinna speak tae me o' her!

227

Coming tae walk sae kindly by the poor fallen woman tae show she wisna' wi'oot charity like the rest! I hated her afore—and I hate her waur noo! I'm not to be behaulden tae her for onything!"

She had risen and was pacing up and down the little room, her skirts swinging against the furniture. Daniel rose too, and put his arms round her. "Meg! Meg! What's got into you? Come, sit down by me here beside the fire. Let down your hair. I like to see the firelight in it."

But she pushed away from him. "They say you'll marry her."

Now he was angry. "I told you before, after the Reform Ball, that they'll say anything in Dyplin. Yes, I walk home from the library with Miss Tullis and carry her books. I like books too. She can talk about them. Sometimes I go in and talk with her father; he is a knowledgeable man, and it's a change from talking with the teachers. . . . And you are not going to tell me who I walk and talk with and who I don't. . . . Where's my hat and plaid?"

"No, don't go, Daniel. I didna mean tae make ye angry." She pulled the pins from her hair and it fell round her shoulders. "See? We'll sit by the fire as usual. I'll pit oot the candles and poke up the flames in the coal . . ."

Sitting by his knee, looking into the flame, while his hand stroked her head, she said, "Gin we were married we could do this every night." Then she turned her face to him, the old teasing Meg. "But

228

gin we were married, it mightna' be sae pleasant," and she drew his hand to her breast.

But Daniel, when he made his way cautiously home that night, was frowning. For Meg, clinging to him as he said goodnight, had clutched his plaid and whispered, "Daniel, I love you. I've never loved a man but once, long ago; and now I love you."

Love between himself and Meg was the last thing Daniel wanted.

18

ALTHOUGH no one mentioned the incident at the church to Mary, there was much talk in Dyplin and, just as it was dying down, there appeared in the *Inverforth Gazette* a bitter set of verses castigating the hypocrisy and cruelty of a community which, coming out of a Christian service in which it so happened that the text had been "Charity suffereth long, and is kind", could leave a woman to walk on her solitary way because it judged her a sinner. It could have come from the pages of Crabbe's *Parish Register* and, though carefully non-localized and with not a name mentioned, it set the tongues hammering again. Meg heard of it, got a copy of the *Gazette* and read it, and went into a blaze of fury that lasted for days. Nothing Daniel said could calm her.

"It's me it means, ye ken that. I could kill the man that wrote it. And it's someone in this place. I ken that fine."

"Not necessarily so, Meg. Someone could have heard about it. . . ."

"Aye. Me a thing for a clash a' aboot the country. Oh aye, I ken fine fowk are talkin'—Meg Annan gaun tae the kirk; juist imagine!" She exaggerated the gossipy tone of the words. "But I dinna believe that. It's someone here. Maybe it's the umbrella-maker's daughter hersel'. They tell me she writes poetry."

"It's not her." Daniel was genuinely shocked. "What she writes is not like that at all. It's sweet pretty stuff about waterfalls and trees and the countryside."

"Oh aye. Ye'd ken that nae doot. But if ever I find oot whae made a mock o' me like that, I'll kill them!" She paused. "Mebbe it's daft auld Craig frae the hill. They say he's besotted wi' books tae."

"Meg, Meg. You don't know. It's not all that important. Outside Dyplin no one will think of you."

"I ken that. But it's being made a thing tae be written aboot that riles me; it mair than riles me. It makes me boil wi' rage."

Perhaps no one else boiled with rage in Dyplin, but more than one wondered whether Craig was the author of the offending verses. No one thought of Mary; it was unimaginable that the umbrella-maker's quiet, unobtrusive, rather dull blue-stocking daughter could have written like that. The speculation was short-lived, ousted from public interest by a much more disturbing event.

One day there was a sad little funeral in the kirkyard. An old ploughman from one of the upland farms was buried, attended by the farmer and his wife and none other, for he had lived for thirty years in the bothy and never a soul kin to him had been seen there. He was simple-minded, came seldom to Dyplin and, when he did, got roaring

231

drunk and had to be put somewhere dry and sheltered to sleep it off. Everyone knew George frae Gartgunnock, and no one wished him ill. The morning after his funeral, one of the workers at the bleach-field, hurrying in the morning twilight by a short cut through the churchyard, saw George's grave gaping wide, the earth hurled in untidy dollops round it. A more timid soul might have turned and fled; not Andrew Rogan. "Ah got a bit o' a start, but Ah juist went ower and looked in. And there wis the box, empty as a used egg shell, the lid tae ae side, wi' the wid a' cracked whaur it had been wrenched off puir George. Ah'll admit at first Ah had a wee shiver thinkin' maybe George had got himsel' oot, but a' roon the earth was trampit doon wi' fit marks, and Ah guessed it maun be the wark of the resurrection men."

There could be no other explanation; and no one could remember when such a thing had ever happened before in Dyplin. In Inverforth, yes; and even in one or two of the villages near Inverforth. But it was easy to take a body from Inverforth down-river to the Queensferry and on to Edinburgh and the ever-hungry anatomy rooms. But Dyplin had been too remote, transport too difficult; or so it had seemed, though as David Tullis pointed out, it was not so very far to Kincardine, and there were boats there too to take a cargo to the Queensferry. And indeed, on the very night when George had been lifted, Dr. Munro, coming back from delivering a baby in a house on the Kincardine road, had passed a gig driving rapidly towards Kincardine with three men sitting in front, one of whom, wrapped in a dark cape and with a hat well over his brows, he had taken to be drunk, so awkwardly did he lean on the man next to him. . . .

It took a day or two for the full implication of the incident to be appreciated. Then, out of the welter of deliciously horrifying clash about lights having been observed near the church, of the sound of a horse's galloping hooves, of a black shape seen gliding through the kirkyard gate, the soberly nasty truth emerged that someone in or near Dyplin must have contacts with the resurrectionists, for it was certain no one outside the district could have any knowledge of poor George's passing; so who could it be? And a vicious little breath of suspicion blew round the place. It also became clear that in future watch would need to be kept over a new grave to protect it from similar desecration; and that for three nights. It was done in other places—relatives of the dead took on the task as a duty. And from now on it must be part of the routine of death in Dyplin too.

The men held a parish meeting. The matter was soberly discussed. It was decided that male relatives of the deceased would perform the duty, and if there were none such relatives, neighbours or friends would be called on. The very fact that a watch was known to be kept would, it was felt, be sufficient to stop any more desecration. And indeed the next two funerals produced no incidents. But then Mattie Maclaren, an old woman who had lived alone and very secluded in a little house three or four doors down from the Campbells', died. She had no kith or kin that anyone knew of, and so it was arranged that neighbours would take on the duty of watching. John and David were to take the third night watch; but on the day before, John came to see David with a plan which would not only prevent a grave-robbing, but might even bring about the discovery of the robbers.

"I thocht we would let it be kent there was juist tae be a two nights' watch. And on the third night you and I would go vera quietly, and no' showing ony lichts or onything, but keep a real sharp lookout. And if it's someone here in Dyplin is sending word, like as not they'll try something, thinkin' there's nae watch. And we micht catch them; if no', this business o' watching is going to have tae gang on for long enough. There was a resurrection at Inverforth last week, and one at Inchbogie."

David agreed to the plan, but when John called in for him after darkness had fallen on the third night, he found Daniel Rutherford with David, and learnt that Daniel was to share his watch. David explained why.

"I've an order for two unbrellas that I promised for tomorrow; but I've been kept back by the handles not coming in time. I've never been late with an order yet, and I can get them done if I work tonight. So Mr. Rutherford here says he'll take my place. And if I get finished in time, I'll come and

234

relieve him, for I'm not wanting you to think I'm dodging my turn, John."

"I wouldn't think that. But I'll be glad of Mr. Rutherford's company, fur it's no' the cheeriest place tae spend a night, and if the resurrection boys do come, I wouldn't like just to fall on them single-handed."

"Let's hope they don't come," said Daniel. "They can, I believe, be violent and even dangerous."

"Oh weel, there's twa' or three guid cudgels doon there in the session-hoose, sae I guess we could mak them run."

They left, and David went on with his work, which he had brought down to the house from his workshop. Mary sat quietly reading. She made him tea, and then went back to her book. When he worked late like that, which was seldom, she generally sat up to keep him company. About half an hour after midnight, he finished his task, put away the umbrellas, and said, "Make me another cup, Mary, and I'll away down to the churchyard."

She did so, and then, as he took his plaid, she said, "I'm coming with you."

"Mary! It's not a job for a woman."

"Oh, I won't *do* anything. But I want to see what it's like being in that little building in the dark, and waiting for something to stir outside—yes, I must see it."

David knew better than to argue. "You're a queer girl, Mary. Sometimes I wish . . ."

"You wish I was a good little domestic puss like the rest of womankind? Then I wouldn't be me. See, I'm ready. And we must go very quietly and keep in the shadows—not that that will be difficult. There's no moon, just starlight."

She took her father's arm and they walked as softly as possible down the steep slope of the street, and on to the churchyard gate. It was closed, but they managed to open it with no more noise than a faint rasping of the rusty hinges. The session house, a small stone building with a slate roof and two little windows, was on the far side of the church. Their feet crunched on the gravel, so they moved onto the grassy verge and walked in single file. There was just sufficient light to show the bulk of the trees, the church, and the shapes of tombstones. The night was still and windless.

The only sign that there was anyone in the session house was a thread of light under the door. David knocked, and almost at once John's voice asked who was there.

"It's me, David; and Mary's with me."

They heard a muffled exclamation; the light vanished, and then the door opened and John's face loomed pale in the darkness.

"Canny as ye come in. See, here's my hand."

He guided Mary into the thick darkness; David followed; the door was closed, and then John re-lit the candle in the lantern on the table.

Daniel was seated at the far side of the table, and was evidently much surprised to see Mary. John was looking not too pleased, and David said:

"She would come. I couldn't stop her."

"I'll not do, or even say anything," said Mary. "I just wanted to see what it was like. And look, I brought something for you."

From under her cloak she took a small basket. "Scones and butter," she said, "and some seed cake. And a bottle of black-currant cordial."

John shook his head. "Hoo can we be angry when ye bring us that?"

As they ate and drank, David asked if anything had happened.

"Not a thing," said John. "We've kept a lookout from the window, and whiles opened the door to listen, but there's not been a sight or sound o' anything."

"I wonder if they'll ever be caught," said Daniel and, while the three men talked, Mary looked round the little room.

The session house had been built at the same time as the church, about 1700. The room had bare stone walls, and a fireplace, but no fire burnt in it tonight, and the room was chilly and had a dampish smell behind the reek of the candle smoke. At one end was a large dark oak cupboard; in the middle of the room was an oak table with benches on either side and a heavy wooden arm chair at one end. The window-sills were deep, almost the full thickness of the wall, and on one stood a big hour-glass, and on the other a clutter of ironware—a round collar with chains. Beside the fire was a low rough wooden stool, and in one corner were three long thick cudgels. In the opposite corner was an ironbound wooden chest about two feet square, with a heavy cumbersome lock. The floor was wooden and worn with much usage, so that the knots stood up in little shining blobs.

John saw Mary looking round, and said, "That's the auld hour glass they used tae time the sermons by. An' yon iron contraption is the jougs—they used tae be fastened in at the church door, and the session would sentence a scolding woman tae stand there wi' the iron collar roon her neck—an' if ye ask me, a gey wicked thing it wis, tae. Thon's the auld puir-chest, whaur they kept the money. Aye, an' yon's the stool o' repentance. Ma faither could mind seein' lads and lassies sittin' on it—M'hm." (He changed the subject with a little clearing of his throat and an involuntary flicker of the eyes towards Daniel.) "In the cupboard there are the communion vessels, and the records—and gey queer readin' some of them are tae!"

Daniel had risen and was peering out of a window. "It's unfortunate," he said, "that Mattie's buried at the bottom of the slope there. We can't see to the actual spot. And anyway, it's too dark. They could be working down there now, and us not know."

"That's true," said John. "I'm thinkin' it mebbe wasn't such a good plan efter a'. But you'll be going hame noo. You can tak a bit look doon there."

Daniel hesitated. "To tell you the truth, I should

238

prefer to go down the path just there to the burn." His shoulders shifted a little. "It's foolish, I know—but I hate the very thought of walking alone among the dead at night. . . ."

"Do ye now!" John was genuinely surprised. "I wouldn't have thought it o' ye. What about you, David?"

"Me? I don't much like a graveyard at any time; night time or day time, they're, to me, sad places; but not fearful."

"Not by day," said Daniel, "but at night. . . ."

"I wonder why night time is the ghostly time," said Mary. "If I were a spirit, I'd rather come up in the daylight, than change one dark for another."

John was a little scandalized. "If you ask me," he said, "fowk see ghaists at nicht because their imagination has mair freedom at nicht."

But Mary was in a fanciful mood. "Perhaps," she said, "perhaps they're there outside, clustering round this little building, wondering why we're intruding—pressing against the window there."

John frowned, Daniel looked at her wondering if she was serious, David shook his head. But they all started when there was a gentle tap at the door.

"Losh me! Whit's that?" said John. He moved to the door. "Who's there?"

"It's me. The Minister. Let me in."

"A minute, Meenister." John blew out the light, opened the door, and a dark figure slipped in. When the candle was re-lit, Matthew spoke.

"I was coming through the kirkyard a minute ago

239

on my way back from Andrew Soutar's—they sent for me, thinking he was dying, but he's rallied—and I'm certain I heard something from the direction of Mattie's grave—a clink of metal and, I thought, voices."

"Noo's oor chance!" John reached for the cudgels. "Come on!"

"Wait a minute." It was Daniel speaking. "We can't just rush at them. They might even be armed."

"There's been no word of that in the papers," said David. "I think they do not want to add killing to their crimes."

Matthew was impatient. "We must go now. Here, give me a cudgel."

"You, Minister?"

"Yes, John, me. I consider the disturbing of the departed an abominable crime, and I want a cudgel. And the rest of you may do as you please, but I am going now."

And the Reverend Matthew Glendinning grabbed a cudgel, and went to the door.

"Hey! Bide a wee, Meenister. If you open the door, the light will shine out. Here, Mr. Rutherford, here's a cudgel. There's none for you, David."

"It's my watch," said David, "and I'll take the third cudgel. Mr. Rutherford, you can stay here and keep Mary safe."

Daniel didn't protest. John blew out the candle and he, David and Matthew went out over the uneven turf in the direction of the sloping ground.

Mary stood up and said, "I'm going too."

"But there might be danger."

"I'll keep back. But I'm going."

She stepped out into the still night air and Daniel followed her. They could dimly see the other three weaving their way through the headstones. Just at the top of the sloping bank, and still out of sight of anyone below, they stopped. Mary and Daniel halted too. In the silence they could hear a muffled thud of metal on wood, a softly spoken word or two. Then one of the three ahead—she thought it was Matthew—sprang forward and down and out of sight, followed by the other two. There was shouting and the sound of heavy blows. Mary began to hurry forward, but Daniel caught her arm.

"Don't be foolish, Mary. You might be hurt."

"I must see what's happening. I must."

He drew her to him. "I won't let you. There's a risk. . . ."

"Not if you're with me."

She smiled up at him, broke loose, and caught his hand so that he could not do otherwise than follow her. At the top of the slope they stepped into the shelter of a tall headstone. Mary clutched Daniel's arm and they looked down to Mattie's grave. She caught his hand, and pulled him forward.

"We'll keep out of the way. But I must see what's happening."

The turf and earth had been scattered round it, and a dark figure in the grave was holding up a pickaxe to ward off a hail of blows from John Campbell's cudgel. David had seemingly knocked a spade from the hands of a second, who was retreating before him with his hands over his face and, even as they watched, stumbled back over a table-stone and fell sprawling across it. David stood over him, unwilling to strike, and suddenly the man turned over, scrambled down on the far side and ran off in the darkness towards the church gate. Matthew was having a hard fight with a short thickset man with a shovel. It was hard to see what was happening, but Mary could hear hard-drawn breath and the sound of blows. Then there was a cry and at the same time the crack of bone. Matthew fell, and his opponent loped off among the graves, holding a leg and cursing. John turned to help Matthew, and the man in the grave scrambled out; they saw him supporting the other towards the gate, but no one went after them. They were all round Matthew, who was lying with eyes closed and blood trickling from a wound in his head and a gash on his cheek. But even as John was groping for his pulse, Matthew opened his eyes.

"We'll tak ye tae the Manse, Meenister," said John. "David here will go on and tell your mother what's happened."

"My mother's not there. She's gone to visit her sister."

"Weel, we'll tak ye there onywey."

At the Manse door, Daniel left them. David and John supported Matthew into the hall and onto a chair. Then there was the bustle of lighting candles and finally they got him into the kitchen and into the old sagging leather chair by the fire. Mary got water and with her own handkerchief began to wash the blood from his face. John put coal on the fire, which was almost out, filled a kettle and set it to boil. Then he looked at Matthew's head. There was a swelling round the cut, and it was very painful to the touch. The cut on the cheek was not deep, and the bleeding had stopped.

"Ye've had a lucky escape, Meenister. It could have been a lot worse. You should get off tae bed noo. Would you want me to get Dr. Munro?"

"No. There's no need. I'll see him in the morning."

He tried to stand up, but sank back with a little groan. A fresh little trickle of blood ran down his temple.

"Don't try to move," said Mary. "Do you know where I could find anything to tie up your head?"

"In the drawer there—in the dresser—my mother keeps clean linen strips. . . ."

Mary opened the drawer and found neat rolls of torn up sheets and pillowcases. She gently bandaged Matthew's head, and then, the kettle having boiled, made tea for him. Then John and her father helped him up to bed.

Once they had him between the sheets, David looked with concern at the wan and suddenly very youthful face beneath the bandages.

"Will you be all right, Mr. Glendinning?"

"Yes, thank you. Matilda will be in in the morning; she's at her mother's tonight. And if I feel no better, I will send for Dr. Munro."

So they left him with the candle flickering beside him and went downstairs, to find Mary waiting for them in the kitchen, having cleared up the clutter caused by her attending to Matthew.

As they walked back through the dark and silent town, John said, "Man, yon was a bonny fecht o' the Minister's wi' yon ill-faured rascal! I didna think Mr. Glendinning had it in him! Mind you, I kent he was brave enough in the cholera—but that's a different kind o' bravery. I didna think he had the other kind—whaur a man gangs ding-dong wi' another at the risk o' a broken heid or limb. It's no' juist whit I expect o' a minister—tho' in the killing time there must have been mony o' them ready tae swing a sword wi' the best. Ye did no' badly yersel', David."

"I was angry. And anger makes it easier. But I could not hit the rascal when he was sprawled on the grave-stone; it was too much like battering a cornered rat."

"Aye, aye. Weel, it's been a guid nicht's wark. I dinna think there'll be mony more resurrections." Then, more soberly, he added, "But it's clear noo someone in the place has been passing on the word—and I'd fine like tae ken whae."

"When we came down from the session house," said Mary, "I thought I saw a figure slipping away

244

from the grave over the stile in the wall that leads to the burnside."

"Aye, aye, like enough that's our man. He'd be keeping watch but no' taking an active part. . . . Aweel, we'll mebbe never ken noo. But the three we saw were all strangers."

As they climbed near home, they saw a light from John's house, and at the sound of their steps and voices the door was opened and Alison called them in. Over whisky for the men and mulled claret for herself and Mary, she heard the tale of the night's doings, but did not share John's approval of Matthew's exploits.

"The Minister's fechting wi' a resurrectionist! That's naethin' tae be proud of. It's no' becoming tae his cloth."

John stared in genuine amazement. "And what would you have him dae, wumman? Turn the ither cheek till an ill-faured scoundrel that's howkin' up puir Mattie? Forbye, there's Bible warrant. The Lord himsel' wisna backward wi' the money-changers. And furby—" for whisky and the exhilaration of battle were working on him—"If ony of the pious wee gnaffs on the session say onything against Mr. Glendinning for this night's wark, they'll hae me tae reckon wi'."

Sleep would not come to Mary that night in spite of the mulled claret. Her mind raced with visions of the gloomy little session house, the faint starlight outside dimly revealing the tombstones, the presence of the quiet sleepers in the earth all about

245

them, the violence by the open grave. She felt again Daniel's arms round her as he tried to keep her from the risk of hurt, and how she had felt safe and secure as he stood beside her while they watched the struggle.

Then she turned restlessly and buried her head in the pillow, remembering how Matthew had laid his hand on hers as she busied herself dressing his wounded head; only for a moment, but as if he could not help it, and looking at him in surprise she had glimpsed such a strength of longing that the memory made her jerk rigid beneath the sheets. She was not to blame if the Minister loved her—no, in no way. She had never given him a thought, except in half-mockery. Nevertheless, her last conscious thought, before she slid into slumber, was of Matthew rushing down the slope in the church-yard like a small avenging deity, brandishing his cudgel.

19

THE story of the night's doings gave Dyplin material for talk for many a day. On the whole, the matter was approved of. Matthew's part was, on balance, regarded as being almost praiseworthy. The unregenerate and godless chuckled at the revelation of the old Adam in the Minister. The godly, mindful of smiting Amalekites and other warlike episodes of the Old Testament, came down for the most part in favour, all the more so as his action had been in defence of the helpless dead. Censoriousness found an outlet in criticism of Mary. There was pursing of lips and the drawing-down of eyebrows, and sage noddings over the counter in shops; and little silences as Mary passed, with false smiles to greet her, and low murmurings after. "Aye, aye. She was at the session hoose tae. Wi' three men. At that 'oor o' the nicht." "Ah well, but she was wi' her father." "Oh aye. *And* Rutherford the schule-maister. An' ye ken whit he is. They say they're gey freendly—ower freendly." And a meaningful drop of the eyelids and a screwing of the mouth supplied the unspoken meaning. There were even some who would have it that Mary herself had wielded a cudgel and been in the thick of the fray. "Laid a man oot, they say."

But the more judicious decided this was going too far. "Fowk will aye exaggerate."

But spring was coming. The snowdrops were out—great masses in the policies of Griffton, little clumps in the gardens of Dyplin. The daffodil spears were piercing the ground; the snow on the hills was no more than the patch in a corrie on Grey Wisp that always lingered till early summer. It was the time for the washing of curtains and the cleaning of cupboards and the scrubbing of floors and the sweeping of chimneys. Even Mary felt the impulse and swept into a passion of cleaning and scouring. If Matthew had visited the Tullises he would have found her entirely the prudent domesticated housewife. But Matthew, since the encounter at the curling, and having heard of Daniel's attentions, had stopped his pastoral calls, except to come and thank Mary for her care of him on the night of the struggle in the kirkyard. She had been out, and he had left a message with David.

Daniel teased her a little about her zest for cleaning and polishing, and Mary answered gaily:

"But I can be a good housewife if I want. I hate a dirty or untidy house. I like orderliness."

She could not tell him that her cleaning of the house was a rite of thankfulness; when she looked back at her wretchedness of the previous spring, she could not believe in her happiness. Every time she saw Daniel she knew that she was nearer and nearer to being in love; and as she scrubbed and swept and polished she thought of life with Daniel—cherished and protected, not with the anxious uncertain protectiveness of her father, but with a cherishing that left her free to be herself. . . . True, Daniel did not talk to her of love, nor she to him. But she knew he desired her; and was content to wait until he spoke out, and leave everything beyond that vague.

Normally, at this time, Dr. Munro would find himself called to deal with strained backs, and broken wrists, what he called "the cleaning illnesses". But this year it was not so. The curtains were washed, the chimneys swept, but the great zestful rivalry of the cleaning was not there. Perhaps the returning life in the fields and gardens renewed the sense of loss of the non-returning dead. Dr. Munro, going his rounds, sensed the mood and was concerned. He spoke to Matthew, but found it hard to put into words what he felt.

"Do you sense anything out of usual among the people, Minister? They seem to me to be still apathetic, as if the burden of the sickness still weighed on them."

Matthew considered. "Perhaps so. It was a great scourging."

"The women, for example—at this time they would be in a rare whirl of cleaning and polishing, grumbling at the work, enjoying it all, and triumphant at the end. Not this spring."

"Perhaps," said Matthew, in all sincerity, "it is a cleansing of the heart they need, an acceptance of the workings of Providence. And then the cleansing of the outward habitation will follow."

To which the doctor's answer was a grunt, and he went away wondering how someone he knew to be brave and kind—"and with a temper too,"—could so often sound forth pomposity. "And yet I believe he means it. And maybe there is something in it. Rid of the anger and sorrow I daresay they might get down to the scrubbing . . ." and the doctor went off to deliver yet another scrap of humanity into this vale of tears. He was unsuccessful. Sarah Jamieson, young widow of young Walter Jamieson who had died trying to rescue the sheep, did not much want to live, and in spite of Dr. Munro's skill and the help of Margit Boyd, the skilliest howdie-wife in the district, she died and the baby with her. They buried them close to Walter and for a day the town spoke softly of them, and went quietly about its business.

None thought to watch over them: it was taken for granted the resurrectionists had been frightened off for good. But on the second morning after Sarah's funeral, those going early to work found the grave open, the coffin gone.

The rage in Dyplin was beyond bounds. The other two incidents had been horrifying enough; but after all, the victims were old, worn-out, their bodies no more than cast-off raiment. But Sarah—bonny, dark-eyed Sarah, young and sorrowful—and her baby—that they should become mere material for the knives of the anatomists, be pored over, and doubtless jested about by medical students, known to be a set of coarse devils—no, it was too much.

250

And someone, someone in their very midst, had betrayed Sarah, had told the brutes who lifted her. Here was a focus for the dumb resentment of the past months to centre on and justify itself. Dark threats were voiced as to what should be done to the miserable wretch when found. Even the teachers of the New School, who tended to maintain an Olympian detachment from popular feeling, were perturbed. After all, resurrectionists were no respecters of persons: there was old Mrs. Wardlaw, mother-in-law of Dr. Duffus, not expected to last another winter: suppose she—? Or any of them, for that matter, life's uncertainty being what it was. . . . So the wave of fear and anger swept over all Dyplin.

But who was the informer? No one had an idea. So their rage found no outlet, and people glanced askance at each other, and there were fisticuffs in the Thorn Bush.

But the truth did come out. A little to the south of Dyplin there was a cluster of wretched clay houses. The poorest lived there—those who did the least skilled jobs at the bleach-field, those "on the parish", those who did any odd bit of work that came their way. Among them was Rob Little. Rob was "no' richt in the heid", and had spent his life in a bewildered haze of incompetence. He was married to a crooked, plain woman, who bore him six bewildered whimpering children, as unable to cope with life as their father. Maimie, his wife, battled hard to feed her brood, and keep them at least decently covered with clothing, though they ran barefoot. Rob clung to her as the one stable factor in a puzzling world; and though she let him have the sharp edge of her tongue, she would defend him against any jeering or teasing from anyone else.

For some time Maimie had been coming to the shops more frequently, buying more bread, more oatmeal, and once some butter. Mrs. Walker, serving her, had said:

"Rob's working the noo?"

"Aye. Up the country. On a fairm."

But a week after Sarah and her child had been taken, Maimie slid into the shop, bought her meal and bread and three slices of bacon, and put down for payment a golden guinea. Mrs. Walker looked at it in astonishment, and then at Maimie.

"And whaur did ye get this, Mistress Little?"

It was desperation had made Maimie use the coin, for she had none other left in the house, and the children had not eaten for twenty-four hours. Guilt made her lower her eyes and murmur:

"Rob did extra work on the farm. It's—it's a' I've got."

Mrs. Walker stared under bent brows, bit the coin, turned with an ill grace, and gave the change. Then as soon as Maimie was out of the shop, she locked the door, drew down the blind—though it was half an hour before normal closing time—and went to find her husband.

"A golden guinea! Rob Little never got that from a farmer. He's stolen it—or—or . . ."

He looked at his wife. "Aye. Ye're thinking what I'm thinking. The resurrectionists!"

Mrs. Walker nodded. "Aye. I'm awa in tae George Matheson."

The word went round. In an hour an angry group of twenty or so were gathered in Walker's back shop. Loudest among them was Johnny McIndoe, who had lost a wife and two sons in the cholera, and had taken to drink.

"We maun get Rob and mak him pay."

"Hoo that?"

"Gie sic a threshin he'll no' can walk for mony a day."

"Burn his hoose."

"His wife and weans are no' tae blame."

"Are they no'? She kent a' aboot it. Aye, and tellt lees."

"But are we shair . . . ?"

"Aye we're shair. Come on, the day's drawing in. Let's awa' tae the Biggins,"—for so the little settlement was called.

Willie Little, Rob's eldest boy, ferreting about behind John Campbell's sheds to see if he could pick up some kindling wood, heard the tramp as the group of angry men went down the street, and someone calling across to a passer-by:

"Hey, Tam, we ken whae did it. Rob Little. And we're on oor way tae mak him pey. Are ye fur coming?"

Willie didn't wait to hear the answer. Fifteen minutes later he was panting out a garbled tale to his mother, of men on the way to get his father. Maimie, who had been living in a dread of this for weeks, put her hands to her mouth, was silent for a minute, and then said:

"Yer faither's settin' snares in the Black Wood. Rin tae him, and tell him no' tae cam hame—and no' tae bide in the wood, either. Tell him—och, tell him tae gang onywhere. Mebbe tae the glen—there's corners there he could hide. And—and tell him ye'll gang up the Glen and whistle when it's safe fur him tae cam hame—if it ever will be."

Then she shut the door, gathered the other children round her, and waited in the low-roofed room that was always dark because of the tiny windows and the clay plastered walls.

Presently she heard a gathering buzz of voices, an irregular trudging of feet. Soon the house was surrounded by a wave of angry sound. There was a hammering on the door and Maimie opened it. In the wretched little ashy garden the men were trampling the kale stalks and brandishing heavy sticks. Johnny McIndoe was in the front rank, reeking a little, his reddened eyes full of rage and misery.

"We want Rob."

"He's no' here."

"We'll see."

He pushed her aside and staggered into the house. The children began to whimper, and Maimie shrank against the door post. But a glance round the room, which held nothing but a table,

254

four chairs, a sagging sofa, the bed in the recess and a little dresser, showed that Rob was indeed not there. Johnny came back to Maimie.

"Whaur is he?"

"Settin' snares."

"Whaur?"

"Up thon wey,"—and she pointed southward to the Braes.

"She's telling lees again," said a voice. "Rob sets his snares in the Black Wood. That's where we'll find him."

"Let's after him, then."

They turned to go back the way they came, Johnny bringing up the rear. At the garden fence he halted and called, "Someone should bide here tae get Rob if we miss him in the wood."

But Maimie had closed and bolted the door. No one was prepared to wait on the doorstep.

"Ach, why bother? Noo we ken it's Rob we're seeking, we'll get him sooner or later. Awa' tae the Black Wood!"

To reach the Black Wood quickly, they crossed the grounds of the New School, where the boys, kicking a ball about, stared in astonishment. Just as they left the ground to join the Old Road at the foot of the Black Wood, they met two women walking back to Griffton. One of these, recognizing Samuel Walker, said:

"And where's the lot of you off to?"

"We're looking for Rob Little. He's in the Black Wood setting snares."

"And why are you seeking Rob?"

"He told the resurrectionists when to come. . . ."

"Oh." She drew her breath sharply, for she had been a neighbour of Sarah's.

"Weel, ye'll no find him in the Black Wood. We saw him no' that lang syne makin' his wey ower the hill there, like as if he was going tae the Glen."

"Ah." Johnny was exultant. "Noo we've got him. We'll split in twa, some of us'll gang up the hill there, and doon intae the glen frae beneath the castle, And you, Samuel Walker, you tak the rest and go up the path fraw the Mill Green, and we'll catch him between us like a hunted beast."

Soon Rob, scrambling desperately along the path, with a half-formed idea that he must find a hole or hollow among the tree roots and hide there, heard shouts from below and answering cries from ahead, swerved, and began clawing his way up the steep slope to the road above. Rob was good among trees: his skill with the snares had kept his family from starving more than once: and he might have got away, had he not dislodged a great lump of stone that bounced down through the trees and crashed on to the narrow path just as Samuel Walker edged himself round a bend.

"He's up there," cried Samuel. "After him!"

The slope was steep, and they had not Rob's sure-footedness; so he had a good start and reached the road well ahead of them. He began running up the road, afraid to go back among the houses, forgetting there had been men ahead of him in the glen. But as

256

he rounded a bend, the breath rasping his throat, he saw them running down the road towards him, hallooing as they came. So he tumbled over the low dyke on his right, and began to gallop shamblingly down the grassy slope.

Mary was alone in the house. David had gone to Perth on business and was to be away overnight. She was reading by the fire when the back door shook under Rob's wild blows. When she opened the door, he stumbled in and said, "Dinna let them get me. Dinna let them get me."

He was dirty and earth-stained, and smelt of dirt-sodden wool; and his eyes were like a frightened dog's as he pawed at her. Mary looked up towards the hill. The first of his pursuers were already over the back fence. She pushed down his hands and said, "Bolt the door behind me," and stepped outside.

When the first of the pack reached the house, Mary was facing them, her back to the door.

"Let's in, woman," shouted Johnny. "We ken Rob's in there."

They gathered round her, puzzled and angry, unwilling to lay hands on her.

"Why are you hunting him?"

Several answered. "He's the wan that's been telling the body-snatchers."

"How do you know?"

"We ken."

"His wife had a golden guinea."

"I have a golden guinea but I'm not an informer."

"Ach, woman," and Johnny stepped forward, "dinna be smairt wi' us. We want Rob Little, and by God we'll get him."

"Try. The door's bolted."

Again they hung back, then someone said, "There's a front door!" And three or four ran round the end of the house.

But the front was barred. Mary had barred it earlier. And they came back, furious.

"It's lockit. But he's there-coorin' doon beside the dresser. We could brak a windae. . . ."

"Na, na." This was Samuel. "Nae damage tae property." He pushed himself forward. "See here, Miss Tullis. Rob Little maun be taught a lesson. We'll no' dae mair than let him feel whit he deserves. Noo, juist let's in."

"I can't. The door's bolted."

"Tell him tae open it."

"No."

Johnny McIndoe thrust his raddled face into hers.

"Why not? D'ye approve whit he did?"

"No. But you're many, and he's one, and this is not the way to do it."

"Awa' wi' ye," and Johnny pushed her aside, began battering on the door. The others moved forward, and Mary was afraid. She pressed herself against the stone wall of the house, and said:

"Leave him alone, leave him alone," and Johnny

turned and struck her across the mouth. There was a mutter, half of growling approval, half of shame, and for a moment all movement ceased. Then Mary, looking despairingly up towards the hill, saw Daniel striding down the slope beyond the fence, and shouted his name. He seemed to be looking down towards the house, but did not quicken his pace. At the fence he stopped, stared down at the crowd, and then strode away down towards the road and out of sight. Mary's second cry died in her throat, and someone said:

"The schulemaister kens better than interfere."

Johnny was battering the door again, and another joined him. When they stopped, they heard a high-pitched whimpering from within.

Mary cried: "Don't! Don't! Let him be!" Someone put a hand over her mouth, and another shouted: "Here's an axe," and brandished David's wood axe. Johnny seized it, and had it raised to strike the door when a cool, strong voice said:

"Whit's adae?" and John Campbell stepped through the gap in the hedge. Alison had rushed down the street to where he was mending a broken door for Mysie Smith, and told him what was happening.

He knocked down the hand over Mary's mouth, put his arm round her shoulders and said, "Since when did Dyplin fowk fight wi' weemen?"

"She's got Rob Little in there, and he tell't the body-snatchers. . . ."

"So." He looked over them. "Ye maun be gey

259

feart o' pair shauchly Rob when it taks that mony o' ye tae catch him."

"She's nae richt tae keep him awa' frae us," said a voice, "an' forby it was her that brocht the cholera, takin' in yon man frae Perth."

Johnny gave a low growl and said, "Is that the truth? Did she bring it?"

John Campbell put Mary gently behind him, and faced them with folded arms. "It's not true. I was the first tae be near the cholera. When I coffined a puir lad and his sister at the Torlinn Inn."

There was silence, and he went on, "Ye'll get nae guid oot o' batterin' doon David's door. Ye'll pit yersels in the wrang—damagin' property. Awa hame, and the morn we'll tak' Rob afore the Kirk Session, and see whit's tae be done."

"He'll rin awa'."

"I dinna think so. Whaur would Rob wi' six weans and a wife rin tae? I'll tell him he's naethin' tae fear in the wey o' a broken heid or skin . . . and we'll dae it all in the proper wey."

Johnny still growled dissent, but the fire had gone out of the others, and they turned with low mutterings and drooping heads, and went round the end of the house and down the street. When they had gone, Mary called through the door, "They're away, Rob. Let us in."

There was silence, and then feet shuffling, and the sound of the bolt being drawn, and Rob peered round the door. The room was full of his sour smell and John shook his head in disgust. Mary moved to

260

the window, and stood looking out, not speaking.

"Weel, Rob," said John, "whit's this ye've been up tae? Telling these wicked body-snatchers when tae come. . . . Did ye no think whit ye were daein'?"

Rob whimpered again. "The weans wis that hungry—the fairmer gies me three and sixpence, and it's no' enough. Thir men gied me guid money—but I said I widna lay a haun' on onybody in the kirkyard—juist tell them. I never pit a spade in: I juist tellt them."

He pulled at John's jacket, whimpering again.

"Aye, aye. Weel, noo, Rob, I'll tak ye hame, and the morn we'll gang tae the Meenister, and some o' the Session, and see whit's tae be done. Fur ye did muckle wrang, Rob, ye knew that. Tae be the means o' the deid being howkit up—it's an evil thing."

"I didna touch them: I didna see them takin' them oot—and the weans wis hungry."

Mary turned. "Give him to drink before he goes," she said, and they watched as the whisky brought some colour to the clay-coloured face.

John took Rob home, and tried to explain to Maimie that she must see that he was there in the morning when they came to take him to the session house. But by morning, Rob and Maimie and the children, and such of their possessions as they could carry, were gone, never to be seen again in Dyplin. On the whole perhaps this was a relief. In the morning, the rage of the day before had abated, and most of those who had been so hot on the trail of

261

Rob had had time to ponder the question of just what, after all, they could do to him. . . . There were still the embittered few who raged at Rob's disappearance, and they headed a general feeling that Mary had interfered with a well-founded attempt at rough justice and robbed them of a sweet revenge.

Mary herself was made wretched by the whole thing. Alison, coming into the house as soon as she had seen John taking Rob down the road, found her sitting slumped in a chair, staring into the low fire. Alison clucked her tongue disapprovingly at the lingering traces of Rob's presence, and said:

"It's cheerless here. Come in wi' me, Mary."

Mary shook her head. "No, thank you."

"Well, ye'll let me build up the fire?"

Mary nodded, and Alison put on coal and poked and riddled till the flames were flickering again. Then she sat down and said, "What was ado?"

Mary stirred impatiently and Alison added: "No, I'm not going to leave you alone. It'll do you good to talk it out. What was ado?"

"Rob was the one who'd been telling the resurrectionists when to come . . . and they chased him to my door. So I took him in. Well, what else could I do? He was like a frightened animal."

"Did he admit doing it?"

"Oh yes. He did it for the money. He said his children were hungry—but guilty or not, I couldn't let them get him, could I?"

Alison shook her head. "No, you couldn't.

Though it was a wicked thing he did. What's to happen how?"

"John says they'll take him before the Kirk Session."

"Aye. That's a better way tae it. Aweel, all's ended fine. You did right, Mary."

But Mary turned her head aside, and said nothing. Alison looked closely. Mary was struggling with tears.

"Mary, are you hurt?" She rose and laid a hand on Mary's tightly-clenched fingers. "Ye've had a shock. See, will I make you tea? The kettle's singing."

"Yes, please."

While Alison fussed with the tea things, Mary stood by the window, looking up the hill. From time to time Alison glanced at her. When they were sitting with the tea, she said slowly, "When I was coming up after John frae Mysie's—I ran doon there tae tell him what was happening—I thought I saw Daniel Rutherford coming down off the hill."

Mary looked down into her cup, and then at Alison. "Oh, Alison!"

"Tell me, lass, tell me."

"When I was out there, trying to get them to go away, Johnny McIndoe—" she gave a gasp almost of disbelief—"struck me on the face, and pushed me against the wall—and just then I saw Daniel coming down the hill towards the crowd, and I called to him—he stopped at the fence, and then he turned and went down towards the road. . . ."

263

Her voice died away. She gulped at her tea, and Alison said, "Maybe he didn't hear you."

"He could see me."

"Not necessarily, Mary."

"But he could see the men battering on the door. He knew my father was away."

Alison looked into the fire and said nothing. The clock ticked, a little gust of wind blew in the chimney, and a coal fell. She had been putting the case for Daniel because Mary's distress grieved her. Herself, she thought Daniel quite capable of turning a way from the angry crowd, remembering John's comment on the affair that night in the kirkyard.

"Daniel Rutherford wisna forward in the fight. Mebbe he thocht he was needed tae protect Mary. Aye."

But to talk further with Mary about Daniel meant raising topics that Alison found hard to deal with. Love was a thing Alison knew, but found hard to speak of: as most of her contemporaries did. But looking at Mary's bleak and unhappy face, she made the effort. "Mary, tell me, do you—do you—" she stumbled over the word—"are you fond of Daniel Rutherford?"

Mary answered the real question. "I love him."

"Oh Mary!"

"Why 'oh Mary'?"

Alison, who had learned to know Mary, could hear the danger signal in the sharpness of the question, but blundered on. "He's—I'm not sure

264

he's a good man, Mary." It was out, and she waited for the tornado. But it didn't come. Mary sat silent, looking into her cup. Alison made another effort.

"Is he fond of you?"

"Yes."

Alison probed a little farther. "Has he said so?"

"Yes." (But only after I'd asked him. Does he, really, really?)

"Well then . . ."

"Well what?"

"He's free to marry you. . . ."

"But he hasn't asked me to. If he had, I would have said 'Yes'. But don't you see, Alison—" and she looked straight at her—"don't you see, how could I marry a man who left me like that? It was cowardly."

Alison, who disliked Daniel but was distressed for Mary, could only say: "You must see him and talk with him. . . ."

Not long after Alison had gone back home, Daniel Rutherford knocked on Mary's door.

"May I come in?"

"My father's not back yet."

"Still, may I come in?"

Once in the room, he took off his muffler and made to take her in his arms.

Mary drew back. "Daniel, this afternoon, when you came down the hill, did you hear me calling to you?"

This was an easy lie. "No, I didn't."

"Did you see me?"

He looked under his brows. "I saw a crowd of men at the door. Were you there?"

"Yes. I had Rob Little inside. You have heard how they chased him."

"Yes. But why did you not stay indoors too?"

"I thought I could turn them away, but I couldn't. Johnny McIndoe struck me. . . ."

"Mary!" He took a step towards her, but she put out a hand to stop him.

"And I called out to you, but you just turned aside . . ."

"Do you think I'd have done that if I'd seen you?"

"But you knew I was alone in the house. You saw them battering the door. . . ."

Daniel walked over to the window and looked out over the trampled and disordered garden.

"I didn't know you had Rob in here. I didn't know they were trying to break in. . . ."

"But you didn't try to find out what they were doing."

"I told you I hate violence. Johnny McIndoe was always a quick-fisted man. They'd have turned on me—and I thought they would soon leave battering on your door."

"You didn't wonder why?"

"Of course I did. But it was no concern of mine. . . ."

"No? If it had been the other way round, if I had seen them at your door, I would have thought it concerned me."

She had sat down on a chair by the fire and he came now and stood behind her, a hand on her shoulder.

"Mary, don't let us quarrel. I misunderstood the situation. And I am sorry you were so badly treated."

"If it hadn't been for John Campbell they would have broken the door open with an axe."

"Ah yes, the good John Campbell." He could not keep the sneer out of his voice. "You're lucky to have such vigilant neighbours."

"Don't speak like that about them."

"No, I will not." He moved round in front of her and took her hands.

"Let us be friends again. I did wrong perhaps. But I know the people here. They can be cruel and wicked. When my wife died, they said I had killed her; and one dark night, outside the Thorn Bush, they surrounded me and threatened . . . and I was afraid."

He turned away from her and said: "You see, I admit it."

He waited for her to speak words of understanding. Instead she rose from her chair and stood behind it so that it was between them, her hands resting on the back.

"Daniel, do you love me? Really love me?"

He had not expected this. "I've told you I do."

"I know you desire me—but do you love me?"

A little ripple of irritation ran through him. He remembered another fire-lit room, but the woman in it was not asking these oddly stilted questions. "There is the bed," said Meg, with no wordy probings into what he really felt. . . . He countered Mary's question with another:

"And you?"

"You have not answered."

"Do I need to? Come on, Mary, you feel for me as I feel for you. I know it. I knew it the first time I saw you in your long black cloak. I knew that beneath it there were fires. . . . Admit it, Mary."

He made to step round the fire and hold her, but she said sharply:

"No!"

"Why not? Are you afraid? Of yourself?"

She still faced him. "Daniel, do you love me?"

"What do you mean?"

"Would you risk yourself for me? Would you cherish me if I were ill? Would you forgive me if I did wrong?"

There was an intensity in her words that made it not easy for him to brush them aside: that made him, for a moment, aware of something he had never known and never could. So he hesitated a moment before he said:

"Why yes. But it is you I want, you in my arms, you in my bed."

"No more?"

"More too." But she knew he was lying.

"Daniel, did you know I was there, this afternoon, at the door there? Did you see me?"

Suddenly, his irritation rose in him. This silly

talk of love and cherishing—the girl lusted for him as he for her: she must have known that all their bookish talk together was just a screen, elaborate courting-play such as he'd read certain birds performed before mating. He had even thought of marrying her if that was the only way to possess that small delicate body—but love? Bodily innocent she might be, but her reading must at least have taught her enough of the passion between men and women to know what he wanted—here and now.

So he moved round, caught her by the shoulders and said, "Yes, I did see you. And did not come down because I was sure they would not harm you, and my interfering would have made things worse."

He drew her to him and said, with his face nuzzling her hair, "You may call me a coward. It doesn't matter. I want you now—now."

For a moment she let him hold her; then broke away, as if by some violent effort, and said, "You care nothing for me—not *me*, just this," and she flung her hands wide and looked down over herself. "You left me out there—you were afraid— you thought of yourself alone." She drew her breath in a half-sob. "I don't want to see you again."

"You don't mean that."

"I do, I do. If all you want is—I thought you loved all of me."

She kept her face turned, so as not to see him standing there so close to her.

"What else is worth 'loving'?" he said, anger

swelling in him. "Oh, you mean our talking of books? Those conversations about the poets and the novelists—the great Sir Walter? Little Miss Austen?" He wanted to wound her and found his weapon. "I'd as readily have talked with you about the price of eggs and butter."

He wound the muffler round his neck.

"Good-bye."

But before he left, he held out a hand to her. She shook her head, turned aside, and did not look at him again.

That night, when darkness had fallen, Daniel went to Meg. She was in a brisk mood, quick-voiced, sharp-tongued.

"I hear your Miss Tullis has been playing the heroine again. Saving that wee runt Rob Little frae his just deserts. That'll no' make her verra weel-likit. But I daresay she's no' minding, her with her book-learning and a'."

Sore and bitter and guilty as he was, Daniel was struck by the venom in her voice, but all he said was, "She's not 'my' Miss Tullis; never was, and never will be."

"Aha! Flung you over, has she?" Then as she saw his face darken, "Who cares for her? I won't throw you over."

20

WHEN Mary heard the door close behind Daniel, she stood for a moment quite still, and then quietly and methodically prepared for the night, bolting the doors, smooring the fire. Not until she was in bed, lying in the dark with her eyes on the pale uncurtained square of the window did she allow herself to feel the wound.

For wounded she was. Her cheek was still tender from Johnny McIndoe's blow, but the greater hurt was elsewhere, and deeper. Into the security and contentment she had built in Dyplin, after the disaster of Glasgow, had come Daniel, with his kind interest in her reading, those quiet walks back from the library, and then the ball, and then the skating, and then she was in love again, but this time a love that, she had thought, comprehended all of her, mind and body.

And yet, and yet—she had not told him of the poetry-writing. Lying rigid beneath the bedclothes, she pondered the reason. Lack of trust, remembering his earlier betrayal of her secret? Or was it that she would always have to keep some little bit of life entirely to herself? It was unimportant. For the brute fact was—she sat up in bed, clasped her knees, and laid her head on her folded hands—she had been living with an illusion.

271

Daniel was a coward; with an ugly mean cowardice that could leave her alone facing a group of ugly men; and then try to justify the expediency of it. And those talks that she had treasured so much—he had flung them in her teeth. He only saw me as a willing body—her thoughts groped—as a Meg Annan. She gave a little gasp into the bedclothes, wondering if, after all, it was not better to be a Meg, and not a Mary Tullis, burdened with a mind and a stiff-necked pride.

But Mary Tullis she was: and in the dark, tossing till light began to brighten in the window, she knew that whatever there might have been between her and Daniel was dead and finished: and knew that his presence would have set her trembling like a taut violin string.

The next morning she woke with an angry bitterness in her heart. As soon as her household tasks were done, she pulled a shawl over her shoulders and climbed up Gloom Hill. It was the first time she had been to the crest since that first encounter with Daniel. It was a clear, windy, coolish day, with cloud shadows pacing the landscape. She sat on the crest and looked down on the town and remembered how she had sat there when she first came and thought how beautiful it was. Now she knew how much the beauty meant—and her hand touched the bruise on her cheek. She remembered how Daniel had come on her there and spoken to her. The pain of it made her spring to her feet and stride across the battered grass of the summit. "I hate them all. No—not all—" remembering kind Alison and John—"but most of them. They're cruel and stupid and mean, with little, little minds."

She had her face lifted to the sky, not watching where she trod, and she almost fell as she stumbled against the chain and stones that marked the place of the witch-burning. She looked at the stones, and thought, "Mean and stupid and cruel. Poor girl, poor tormented girl. But I can fight back."

She walked back to the house almost gaily; and that night sent a poem to the *Inverforth Gazette*. It was a blistering account of the pursuit of poor Rob and of the meanness of the farmer who could pay a man such a derisory wage. Names were disguised, and all mention of Rob's having found refuge in a house omitted. Nevertheless, for the first time, one or two in Dyplin began to wonder if she could be the author. Alison even suggested something of the kind to John, who poured scorn on the idea.

"She's ower gentle for that."

Alison opened her mouth to answer and shut it with a snap. She recognized wilful blindness when she saw it, and herself soon put the idea from her; for Mary, who had always seemed to Alison too aloof and detached from the life in Dyplin, began to linger more over cups of tea and encounters in the garden, showed more interest in what was going on; became, to Alison's way of thinking, more human. And Alison was quite ready to tell Mary what she knew—which was much—of the intricacies of life in

Dyplin: with certain reservations. She never spoke
of Meg or Daniel; nor did Mary ever mention them.
But she learnt much of Dyplin, of wrongs inflicted,
injuries unforgiven, reasons why the As never
spoke to the Bs—births too early, marriages too late,
secret shames and hurried departures; people
missing, and once a skeleton found in the woods
after a winter's weathering. Alison, who had her
scruples, was careful to differentiate fact from
supposition. "They say" prefaced the conjectural,
"I know for a fact" the authentic.

Alison "knew for a fact" that poor Sarah Smith,
the Walkers' serving-lass that had died in the
cholera, was fathered by old Dr. Gillies's nephew
on Mary McArdle's sister who had afterwards gone
to Canada with a sailor she'd met at Inverforth Fair.
"And a fine speculation in the parish it was, what
with the Manse being involved and the McArdles
such a respectable family." And there was Bradley
the shoemaker's wife; he'd married her for her
money; and was the most henpecked man in the
place. She was a queer woman. She came to
Griffton as a governess, and she married as a second
wife childless old Shawcross that used to have the
Thorn Bush and had a mint of money. She took
him off to London for their wedding-jaunt—and
next came word that he'd died awful suddenly.
They said it was in a duel defending her good name;
well, some said that. Other's said she'd got rid of
him—with poison. Anyway, she came back cool as

you like and married Bradley; they said he was in terror of her.

It was after this story that Mary said, "All the stories are of wickedness and shame. Is there no one good in Dyplin?"

For a moment Alison looked blank. Then: "Oh aye. You might say most o' the folk are good; or mebbe it would be truer to say the most o' folk are honest and respectable most o' the time. Whiles some of them have their lapses. Not many are what ye would call 'bad' all the time. I grant ye, the clash is mostly about the wickednesses and the sorrows— but it's aye been that way, has it not? Your books that you set such store by, are they no' full o' orra on-goings? The bad and the strange and the sad, I'm thinking, make the best stories."

Mary could not deny this, but it was not the point she was after. "In books yes, but in Dyplin it puzzles me. Here are the people going about so douce and respectable and underneath . . ."

"But you're not thinking straight, Mary. The fight in the kirkyard, you saw it yourself; Rob Little; there's always been fierce doings. Not so much now-a-days, now that we're supposed tae be that civilized and with the Reform and all. When the New School came, some, like John thought the old roughnesses would go, wi' all these scholarly folk coming tae the place—but some o' them have played their cantrips tae—the old doctor himsel', the first Rector, he did some queer things in his time. And now the cholera has upset everything. I

275

think folk feel that come what may in the way of the New School, and Reform, and the gentry suddenly very friendly and keen for the votes, life's still hard and uncertain, and the feeling boiled over the other day wi' Rob Little."

David's coming in put an end to the talk for he refused to gossip. But Mary brooded over all that Alison had told her. To her, it confirmed that Dyplin was mean and cruel, hypocritical and sly, and her anger and hurt over Daniel expanded to take in the whole place. The next day, she wrote to Torrance of the *Inverforth Gazette*, and asked what was the likelihood of his publishing a volume of poems in the style of those she had been sending him. It could be, she suggested, a Scottish parallel to the works of Mr. Crabbe. If he agreed, she must ask him to maintain the anonymity under which she had written the others. . . .

Torrance, who cherished dreams of becoming another Ballantyne and an influential Scottish publisher, and who had already decided to print a volume of *Tales by a Schoolmaster* from a village in the Fintry hills, was delighted with the suggestion. He wrote to Mary. Including the poems he had already printed, a small volume, to be ready as soon as possible, first of a series perhaps? And of course he would respect her desire to remain anonymous.

"She could not write them any other way," he said to himself, as he sealed the letter, "and mebbe I'm taking a bit of a risk myself—but nothing venture, nothing win. And so far there's been nothing as strong as some of Aeneas Clarke's stories—" for the schoolmaster from Fintry wrote out of a robust, realistic eighteenth-century tradition.

No more poems appeared in the *Gazette*, and those that had slipped to the back of the Dyplin consciousness. The days were lengthening to summer; the green mist of growing corn lingered in the folds of the fields, there were lambs on the hill, and Dyplin was quiet. Perhaps a kind of shame troubled the people for the pursuit of Rob Little. Perhaps they drew back from the impulses that had set them hallooing after him: perhaps these were just waiting for another chance to break out. . . .

One night, late enough for it to be dark, Meg, working at the fire brewing up a mixture of herbs, heard a timid knock at the door, and knew it was not Daniel. She put down the jug from which she was measuring water into the pot, and went to the door. A woman, apparently young, with a shawl wrapped round her head half-hiding her face, stood on the step. Meg was used to such visitors—generally servant lasses come for a love-potion—which Meg gave them with cheerful cynicism, perfectly aware that it was a harmless mixture of dandelion root and wild thyme. So she stood aside and said, "Come in", but her astonishment was great when the girl dropped the shawl to her shoulders, and she saw it was Jean Stott, for the Stotts were among the ultra-respectable families of Dyplin. Never had any breath of even innocent gossip been voiced about the Stotts. Andrew Stott was a saddler, with a snug business among the farmers and gentry; himself a good craftsman, he had in his employment a tradesman and two apprentices. He was an elder in the Kirk, punctilious in all his religious duties, a ruler in his household, but not an oppressive father. Ishbel Stott, his wife, was a model housewife, quiet, discreet, not mixing overmuch with her neighbours. There were five children in the family—two girls, and three boys. Jean was the eldest child. She and her sister had been educated at the Misses Blellochs' little school for young ladies, which had survived the setting-up of the New School because certain parents felt the New School was too big and too rough for the nurture of their daughters. Grizel Wauchop and Jenny Niven had attended classes in the New School for writing, Arithmetic and Literature, and had not graced the Misses Blellochs' establishment, but they were nevertheless friendly with Jean, who had been allowed to play and go to the dancing class with them because they too came of "godly homes".

Jean stood in Meg's room, looking round uncertainly, faintly nauseated by the pungent smell from the pot hanging over the fire.

Meg waited for her to speak, and then, growing impatient, said a little sharply, "Well, what is it, lassie? If it's a love-potion you're wanting, I have none. I've stopped making them."

Jean shook her head, but said nothing.

"What then? Come, the likes of you doesn't come tae see me fur friendship's sake."

She saw the girl's lips move but could hear nothing.

"Ye'll hae tae speak up."

The words came in a half-shout. "I'm in trouble."

"Trouble? What kind o' trouble? No—you're no' meanin' . . ."

But Jean had fallen into a chair by the fire, and with her face in her hands, was sobbing bitterly.

"My God!" Meg spoke softly to herself. "It's no' possible". She moved to the door and bolted it. "Fur we're no wantin' onybody else coming in." Then she went back to Jean, laid a firm hand on her shoulder and said, "Noo, stop that noise, which'll dae nae guid tae onybody, and tell me whit ye're wantin' frae me."

She kept her hand firmly grasping Jean's shoulder till the sobbing stopped. Then she sat opposite the girl and said, "Ye're expecting a baby."

Jean nodded wordlessly.

"Whit dae ye want o' me?"

Jean glanced at her, looked down again and whispered, "I've heard it said that you—that you have a stuff that'll tak' it awa'."

"And whaur did ye hear that, my lass?" And, to herself, "And whatna kind o' talk has they godly girls being haein' amang themselves?"

"I heard it."

(Coming back from the cave one twilight, four or five or them together, and Thomasina Brown, a small dark girl with a smooth little body and a bad reputation, had told them her older sister said Meg Annan could get you rid of a baby with stuff that she sold in a bottle.)

"Aye, and what else did ye hear o' Meg Annan? I wonder ye daur come here—tae a sinfu' woman like me."

The girl looked at her in silence, her eyes beseeching, and Meg's mood changed.

"Ye havena told yer mother?"

A violent shake of the head.

"Weel, do ye no' think ye should?"

"I can't. She would tell my father—I think he would die with the shame."

"Hoots awa', lassie, it's no' the end o' the world. Tho' mebbe for a family like yours it would seem it. But I canna help ye. Oh aye, I'll gie the lasses something tae try on the lads tae mak' them in love—but it's mair a joke than onything else. And I have never—and never will—gie onything tae a lass tae tak awa a wean. A' my stuff is just things fur a sair stomach or a stappit bowel, or tae mak yer hair brighter or yer face bonnier; or rub intil an achin' back. And that's a'."

But Jean was on her knees beside her, and had caught her hands, and was pouring out a torrent of tears and choked words, half-sentences, half cries of pain. "But you must help—I'll get money—please, please. . . ."

280

Meg seized her shoulders, shook her and shouted, "Be quiet! Sit down there and try to talk about it wi' some sense. Here, drink this—" and she poured a half cup of brandy from a bottle high on the shelves by the fire and made the girl drink it.

"Ye just must tell your mother. Aye, it'll hurt them, but gin they love you they'll look after you."

Again the shake of the head.

"Weel, can ye no' marry the man?"

Another shake of the head.

"Why not? He's not married?"

No, he wasn't married.

"Lassie, I canna advise ye if ye'll no' speak. Does he ken aboot the wean? Weel, does he?"

"No. Nobody knows. Nobody at all, but you now."

"Aweel, I'll no' tell. But you must let him know."

"I can't."

"Oh, but ye can and ye must. And ye can get mairrit."

Jean was steadier now, as the brandy took effect, and she said, "But it's not the getting married. My father will never forgive me or get over the shame. He'll never hold his head up again. He won't even let us speak the name of anyone who . . ."

"Ye'll no' want tae tell me how it happened? I canna think how a girl like you . . ."

"It was in the cave—" she stopped, but the drink was blurring things and it didn't seem to matter what she said, so when Meg exclaimed:

" 'The cave'?" she went on:

281

"The cave in Spootie's Glen. That's where we meet to cast the spells—Grizel has a book—and we tried to raise a spirit—we've been going all winter."

"I wondered whiles whit the lads and lasses were doing this winter, wi' all the auld ploys stopped after the sickness. But I never heard sic rubbish. Spells and witches indeed—in the cave—nae wunner ye're the wey ye are. . . ."

"You'll not tell—about the cave?"

"No. I'll not tell. I'm no' one fur being in the public eye mair than I can help. But as for you, Jean Stott, I canna help you. I've telt ye whit I think ye should dae."

Jean rose from the chair and wrapped the shawl round her head again.

"Then I'll be going."

Something in her voice made Meg look at her. "Keep calm aboot it; there's a lang while ahead o' ye. Things can happen. Hoo will ye explain at home the reek o' brandy on yer breath?"

Jean gave a little smile, very different from her earlier hysteria. "I'll manage."

She waited quietly till Meg unbolted the door, and stepped into the darkness.

As she walked back to the house, Jean thought how strange it was that she had been able to tell Meg Annan, the bad woman, what she could not tell her father and mother. This was surely proof enough how far she had fallen into sin. A phrase of her father's came into her mind: their portion is with the ungodly. That was her now; her portion was with the ungodly, with the Meg Annans. A quiet despair settled on her, and the only hopeful thing she could think of was Meg's advice that she tell the father of her child what had happened. He was Ninian Stewart, a fair handsome boy, a friend of Sandy Todd's, who had come late into the group. His father, the blacksmith, ruled his family of four sons with a rod of iron. They were all afraid of him. The eldest was apprenticed to his father; the next had been sent to sea; Ninian was to go to his uncle, who had got on in the world and owned a small woollen mill in Yorkshire. Perhaps, thought Jean, perhaps they might get married, and move to Yorkshire, and then no one outside their families would ever know.

Her father and mother were out visiting friends. Jean let herself in, said goodnight to the serving lass, and went to bed, with at least the possibility of some way out of her despair. She lay awake most of the night, thinking it all over. In the morning she had persuaded herself it could all be worked out. She would see Ninian at the next gathering in the cave, and tell him, and surely together they could face their parents. With a lighter heart than for many a day, she went off to do the shopping for the household, this being her daily task. In the grocer's she heard Ninian's mother telling Mrs. Walker that she had been up very early that morning to set Ninian on the road to Inverforth, where he was to get a coach that would take him to Edinburgh and thence to Yorkshire. "His uncle is taking him to learn the trade, and a great chance it is for him."

Calmly Jean got her provisions, took them home, left them in the kitchen. Then she told her mother she was going to see Grizel, and went out.

Later that morning, Mary too went out, and walked down to the Martyr's Bridge. She stopped as usual to look over into the black deep pool. Down in the depths something light shimmered and moved in the slow swirl. It was a shawl caught in a submerged root. That afternoon they took Jean from the water.

There was talk, of course, but subdued and unsubstantiated. Never a word of conjecture or doubt came from the Stotts themselves. Jean had lost her footing, trying to reach some primroses growing on the bank, and slipped, and fallen. If any of the men who struggled to get her body out noticed that there were no traces at all of slipping or falling, they said nothing, overawed perhaps by Andrew Stott's stony grief, for Jean was his favourite child. Grizel, Jenny and the rest of the group were much moved. Death was not for them: death was for the old or the very young. In the cave, on their first gathering after the tragedy, a timid voice was heard to suggest that perhaps this was God's way of punishing them for what they were doing—but Jenny firmly rejected this. Accidents were accidents, and had nothing to do with them. All right, let them stop their gatherings, if that was what they felt. No one was forced to come. But let them remember how dull and monotonous life had been before—at least this gave them something to do.

And of course they went on; the secrecy, the sense of dabbling in forbidden things; of having moved outside the rules laid down; of leading a second existence unknown to parents and family, was too strong a drug to give up. But the drug had to be strengthened. One night, one of the boys brought a miserable scraggy cockrel to the cave; they cut its throat above the fire and watched the blood spit in the ashes. The reek of burning feathers stuck in their throats, and two of them were sick.

That night they walked home in total silence, each apart; a boundary had been crossed, and they were afraid.

21

SOME three weeks or so after Jean's death, Craig made one of his rare trips to Inverforth to the market, and as usual went to Johnston's bookshop. It was a small dark shop, kept by David Johnston and his sister, and at first sight seemed a poor enough place. But it was the only bookshop between Perth and Stirling and the Johnstons, while keeping to a sober and frugal way of life, made a comfortable living from it; being wise enough to hold a range of books from the weightier topographical and historical works that the gentry liked for their shelves, to the lighter fare preferred by romantic young ladies. Craig was an honoured customer and Mr. Johnston took him into the back shop to show him his newest stock.

"I've not much in your line just now, Mr. Craig. There's a book here, *Domestic Manners of the Americans* by a Mrs. Trollope."

Craig grunted. "I'm no' that keen on books written by women."

"I've the latest volume of Mr. Southey's *History of the Peninsular War*."

"That's a bit mair tae my liking. Aye, I'll tak it. It'll be fine fur the lang winter nights."

"You'll not be much interested in a new volume by Alfred Tennyson, poetry not, I think, having much appeal for you. . . . But wait, I have something just come in from the *Gazette* office. Torrance has taken to publishing and the first two books are *Tales of a Schoolmaster*—and not bad they are; very masculine, I'd say—" with a knowing little twinkle—"and a volume of poems, anonymous, rather like the late Mr. Crabbe's work. One or two have already appeared in the *Gazette*. I have been told they are fairly closely based on actuality." He lifted a small volume bound in grey pasteboard and held it out to Craig.

He glanced into it. "Aha. I read this one on Reform in the *Gazette*." He turned the pages, read a few lines, chuckled, raised an eyebrow and said, "I see what you mean by actuality. Aye, aye, I'll tak' this tae."

And so Mary's poems came to Dyplin.

Craig read them as he ate his dinner in the Inn at Inverforth, and thought about them driving home through the rain under the misty hills. For all that he lived up the hill, he knew as much of the life of Dyplin as anyone: and had no difficulty in piercing the thin disguise of the verse to the realities beneath. Whoever wrote these must have known Dyplin for a long time; who of the older inhabitants was capable of the book? Had old Dr. Gillies been alive, he would not have put it past him. . . . Could it be Dr. Munro? No. He didn't know the doctor well, but there was a bitterness about the work that was alien to the doctor as far as he could judge. Then who? A master at the New School? He had heard there was a versifier among them—but who of them could know Dyplin so well? "Whoever he is, he's not frightened. This book'll have them all by the ears. And I ken hoo they can get on a man's heels and drag on at him," for there had been a time when Craig had known the blistering power of malice and rumour.

At Andrew Stott's, where he stopped to pick up a horse-collar that was being re-stuffed, he met Walter Fraser and said, "I've a book here ye could weel pit in your library. Of strong local interest, I'm thinking."

Walter glanced at the volume, looked up at Craig and said, "You didn't write it yourself?"

Craig looked at him astonished, and then guffawed. "Na, na. I'm a reader o' books, nae a makar. Ye ken whit the Book says, 'O' makin mony books there's nae end', and I'm no' one tae add tae the number. To tell ye the truth, I was wondering which o' ye schulemaisters micht be responsible, and, dod, I think ye're as likely as onybody yersel'."

Walter Fraser gave a perfunctory smile in acknowledgement of the jest, returned the book, and went home. Next day he drove to Inverforth for a copy. Within a week every household with any pretension to an interest in books had its copy; and within a fortnight, almost every house where the inhabitants could read. Torrance was delighted with the success of his books. *Tales of a Schoolmaster* was also selling well in the Fintry

288

hills, but producing nothing like the effect of *Verses from a Northern Parish*.

For Dyplin was outraged. The protective coverings were ripped off. The stories, the scandals, the truths and half-truths that eddied and flowed from ear to ear, whispered and nodded over, now caught in cold print were suddenly outrageous. Even those not directly depicted felt their life together was at risk. Old scandals, old feuds raked up and made plain opened up old sores, revived vanished dissensions. A great anger swelled against the writer of the poems. And no one knew who it could be.

Certain things seemed evident. It must be someone who had known Dyplin for a long time; so it was in all probability a native of the place. No one thought of Mary, a mere incomer; not even Alison. She knew how deeply shocked Mary had been by Daniel's weakness at the time of the Rob Little incident; but Mary, tranquilly carrying out the daily round, going to and from the shops as usual, exchanging the customary greetings, revealed nothing of her fierce revulsion against Dyplin and its people. Alison was inclined to think Daniel was the author. This would account for there being no echoes in the book of the whispers that had sped round Dyplin at the time of his wife's death.

Meg also noticed this. She was among the most furiously angry, for the poem about her reception in the churchyard was reprinted in the book.

"Ye're no' in it," she said to Daniel. "But I

289

would have thocht there was enough kent aboot you
tae mak' verses on." She was silent for a minute
"Are you shair it's no' the umbrella-maker's
daughter wrote them?"

"Yes, quite sure."

"Hoo that?"

"She hasn't lived long enough here to know all
the tales."

She looked at him. "It's no' yersel'?"

"Me? Of course not."

"Mind you, if it was her, if I was her, I'd hae pit
you in. . . ."

"But why?"

She put up a hand and tugged at his hair. "Fur if
ye were tae gie me up, I'd dae onything tae get me
ain back. Mebbe she's different. Aye, but I was
forgetting. She gave *you* up, is it no'? God, I hate
her."

The venom in her voice startled him.

"But why? She's never harmed you."

"No. It's just I canna bide her—wi' her airs and
graces and her books and her mimsy weys—and her
giving you up. I canna—but she had the will tae dae
it . . ."

She turned aside in the darkness and he could feel
her draw a long, harsh breath.

In the Manse too the book was talked of. Mrs.
Glendinning got a copy and left it where Matthew
could see it and waited for his comments.

"Mother, I do not like books of idle verification
in the house. Are there not books of sober fact and

290

interest at hand without wasting substance on such as this?"

"Aye, Matthew, I daresay. But you must be almost the only man in your parish who can read that hasna read this. And it's my opinion, for what it's worth, that you should read it. It'll tell you a lot about your flock that I'm thinking you don't know. And forby, Matthew, I'm past the age at which any book is likely to turn me frae the path o' righteousness—always supposing I'm in it."

Matthew looked a little foolish.

"Aye. I know that. It's just—it's just . . ."

"I ken. You feel that the Minister's family maun keep tae the highest standards—and I wouldn't have you different. But you should read the book, Matthew."

Matthew did, and was troubled.

"Can all this be true, Mother? Because if so, I have a heavy task ahead of me."

"And what's your meaning, Matthew?"

"I can't let wickedness go unreproved."

"Matthew, laddie, you're no' thinking of going round the parish reproving the fowk for the ill-doings that's set out here? For all that you're the Minister, you're an incomer here, and you canna tell what in all this is true and what made up. Forby, these are past things. And mony a sore heart there'll be among fowk who have mebbe stepped aside and tried to get back tae the path, and noo are finding the past raked up again. Aye, and there'll be

291

anger tae. I wouldna like tae be the man that wrote this gin it's ever found out who he is."

Matthew had to agree. "But maybe it's a good thing that the hidden wrong-doings have been brought to light," he said finally.

"As far as I can mak' out," said his mother, "they werena hidden. Maistly everyone kent aboot them. And fur the sake of living together, they let them be. . . ." She saw Matthew's face grow stern. "Oh aye, you're thinking they should all have been rebuked and made to acknowledge their sin publicly—at least, that's what some of your friends in the Presbytery would say. I'm no' sae sure. Gin you point out the right way tae them—as you dae—I've heard you preach on sin and repentance mony a time—then I say it's up tae them tae dae the rest."

Her voice changed, and she spoke hesitantly. "It's between them and God, is't no', Matthew? Whiles I think some ministers think it's between them and their people. . . . But I'm just an ordinary woman, and no' versed in these things."

Matthew, and this was rare, kissed her gently on her forehead. "Perhaps that's why you keep me right so often, Mother."

She put her hand on his for a moment, and then went on briskly, "What interests me, is whit made the man write a book like that? Why should he suddenly want tae shame the fowk?"

"He is someone bitter and lacking in charity, I think. But who?"

Matthew was silent for a moment.

"Could it be Daniel Rutherford? I think he is a cold and bitter man. And there doesn't seem to be any reference to him in the book."

Matthew was not the only one to wonder whether Daniel was the author of *Verses from a Northern Parish*. Some of his colleagues in the New School thought he very well might have been. The School itself had not escaped mention in the book. An old story involving the young wife of the first writing-master and the French master of the day had been evoked in a coolly malicious poem. The French teacher had long since returned to his native land, but the lady, now a stoutish widow, still lived near the school and acted as assistant sewing-mistress. On the whole Mrs. Manson took the matter calmly; having weathered the original storm she was prepared to ride this one out: which she did by blandly accepting the disguised names at their face value and insisting they bore no reference to herself or anyone else she knew. But her brother, drawing-master at the school, and a quick-tempered puritanical man, actually struck a colleague who made some jesting reference to the matter. Mrs. Grueber took up an irritatingly sophisticated and "French" attitude to the whole affair, and purported to find Daniel Rutherford a much more interesting man than before. But on the whole, the staff at the New School felt that if Daniel had indeed produced the book, he had gone too far, and many remembered the whispers that had crawled round at the time of his wife's death.

"He should never have done it," said Walter Fraser, "when you think there were those that thought Mrs. Rutherford's death was no accident."

A cold hostility grew against him. At first Daniel was not aware of it, for the Infant School was in a building separate from the main body of the New School. But one day Susannah came in from her shopping almost in tears. Mrs. Duffus, who had always been cordial to her, had passed her in the street with the frostiest of nods. Mrs. Drysdale had cut her, and it was only when Mrs. Grueber had stopped to say with poisoned sweetness and a deeper-than-usual rolling of her rrs, that "Mr. Rutherford had been very naughty to write such wicked things" that Susannah had realized what it was all about.

"They think you wrote that book." She looked at him. "Did you?"

"No."

He said no more and Susannah asked no further. But she had alerted Daniel. He made a point of going into the New School, and there encountered a chilling ill-will. He went to the Library and tackled gentle Walter Fraser, who was incapable of cutting anyone.

"Why is everyone so hostile?"

Walter was uneasy, avoided Daniel's eye on the pretext of arranging books on the table, and said, "They think you wrote the book."

"Well, I didn't. Tell them so."

But the denial, faithfully repeated by Walter, carried no weight at all.

In the town, Daniel's authorship came speedily to be accepted. Anger flared, for old wounds had been re-opened; and old jests, too, re-born. The victims of old laughter, now renewed, were as bitter as those who had scandal about them revived. Folly has less dignity than sin: ridicule is perhaps harder to bear than reproach. So it was that among the most furious was Johnny McIndoe. Johnny had always been something of a butt for mirth in Dyplin, being a feckless man. In the book there was retold a ridiculous episode in which Johnny, poaching the river in the Griffton policies, had ended up in a tangle with the gamekeeper's wife. It was an old jest, largely forgotten, and Johnny, whom the loss of his wife and family had endowed with the dignity of bereavement, and who, in his more sober moments, felt he had attained a certain position in Dyplin, was furious at the revival of the jest, with a blind fury not lessened by his drinking. There were others angry too, and so it happened that one day when Mary was out doing her household shopping, she came on a little crowd gathered in the central square where the roads from the Thorn Bush and the Burnside met. Mrs. Walker and Mrs. Robertson and other shopkeepers were on the pavement looking at a cluster of men led by Johnny McIndoe, all having drink taken, shouting a jumble of accusations and curses at a man with his back against the gable end of

Bradley's shop. Fear had bleached his face; his hands were raised to push back the menace and he mouthed denials that were unheard and unheeded. It was Daniel.

Afterwards, Mary could remember a spurt of cold triumph as she watched; a sense of justice working out; and, too, anger at the crowd's bullying.

"What's wrong?" she asked Mrs. Walker.

"He wrote yon book."

Mary did not stop for thought. "He didn't. I did."

And she stepped quickly from the pavement till she stood behind the group. Then, as Daniel's eyes, flickering with fear, met hers, she raised her voice.

"Stop. Stop, I say."

They turned in dazed surprise, and she said, her voice clear in the sudden stillness:

"I wrote the book."

Then she turned and walked steadily up the road to the house, her back straight, her dark dress blown a little by the breeze from the hill, leaving behind a deep silence in which no one moved.

22

THAT same day, Meg had gone off in the afternoon on a herb-gathering expedition up the Glen, beyond the castle and into the hills. When it was already drawing to twilight, she came down through Spootie's Glen to look for wood sorrel. Picking her way down the tiny stony track she was suddenly aware of the scent of woodsmoke, and stopped to sniff the air. Could it be tinkers? Everyone knew they shunned Spootie's Glen, preferring to pitch their black tents on the flat land by the river. But who else could it be? She went on. The scent grew stronger, and presently, looking to her left, she saw a thin little whisp of smoke trailing up into the fading light that filtered through a gap in the trees. She left the path, scrambled up the crumbling bank, and noticed that others had worn a track there already. Of course, this was the Highlanders' Cave. Poor Jean Stott's half-forgotten tale of the spell-casting in the cave came back to her. She pushed through the bushes, found the entrance, stooped, went in.

They were kneeling round the fire, and turned white startled faces towards her. There were two candles lit, stuck in the sheep skulls which Sandy Todd had found up behind the castle. Between the candles was the fire, a glowing mass of wood and ash. Behind the circle of figures round the fire, a young girl was standing, almost beyond the reach of candle- and fire-light. She was standing straight up, her arms rigid by her side, and she was wearing only her long white cotton shift. No one spoke or moved.

Meg moved forward to the fire. The light played on her red hair; she held her basket in one hand, her other lifting her black skirt. To the kneeling group it seemed as if they had at last conjured up some dark figure from the past. Then she moved into the light, and a voice said:

"It's Meg Annan."

"Aye, it's me. Whae did ye think it was? Meg Merrilees hersel'? This is a queer-like place tae be meetin'. This is whaur ye dae your spell-castin'? Oh aye—" as they looked at each other in alarm—"I ken. Puir Jean Stott tellt me."

Still they said nothing, but seemed to draw together a little, still watching her, like sheep when a dog comes close.

Meg stepped farther into the light, and peered beyond it into the dimness, to the white-clad girl.

"And whit's this? A lassie in her shift?" She leaned forward, looking, screwing her eyes.

"I dinna ken you. But you're a gey young lass tae be standing in your shift fur the lads to be gauping at."

Still not a word had been spoken from the group. Dismay and guilt hung heavily in the air as Meg turned her eyes on them.

"If it's just to be lookin' at the lass? Nae mair? Or will ye be liftin' up the braw white shift when the fire's smoored and the candles oot?"

And now they moved, heads turning, their eyes dropping before her contempt. Only Jenny Niven did not turn aside but faced her and said, "It's no' for you to be rebuking us, Meg Annan, if all we hear is true."

They waited for her anger, but it did not come. Meg put down her basket, folded her arms over her breasts and gave a slow smile of scorn.

"And whit hae ye heard aboot me? Naw—dinna tell me—I ken. That I tak men tae my bed. But they're grown men—aye, and ye'd mebbe wonder at some o' them, fur they'll no be unkent by you. But they're grown men and I'm a grown wumman. An' you're a cleckin' o' silly weans, playin' aboot wi' your candles and your bit banes and a reeky fire, and stirring up things ye ken little aboot. De ye no' ken whit ye're playin' wi'? There's one amang you is deid already, and there'll be mair if ye dinna stop this nonsense."

They were all looking at her again, and the child in the shift was sobbing.

"Who's dead?"

"Jean Stott put hersel' intae the river because she was cairryin' a wean, begotten here amang all yer stupid spell-raising."

"It's not true." Grizel's voice was desperate.

Aye, but it's true. She tellt me hersel', puir thing. An' I'll tell ye this. If you dinna stop a' this rubbish wi' spells and fires and candles and young lassies shakin' in their shifts, I'll tell the parents o' every wan o' you that I ken—you, Grizel Wauchop, and you, Jenny Niven, ye impudent besom. Aye, and the laddies tae—tho' some o' you's mair than laddies and should be shamit tae be meddling wi' sic silly young things." She picked up her basket. "I'll wait till I see that lass happit in her claes, and then I'll go. An' ye can mak up yer minds whit tae dae. But if I hear o' ony mair goings-on in the cave, I'll tell the hail toon."

She said no more, but stood waiting as the girl went back, whimpering, into the darkness. There was a rustling of leaves under her feet, a sniffing and sobbing, and then she came back to the light, buttoning up her dress. Meg swung round, her skirts fanning behind her. For a moment her body, as she stooped to go out, darkened the cave. Then she was gone.

The boys looked down at their hands awkwardly planted on their knees. The girls looked at one another across the fire. Two of them moved aside to let Phemy Aird, still sniffing, kneel by the glow. It was Jenny who spoke first.

"Mebbe it's not true."

"Don't say that." Grizel's voice was sharp with the pent-up unease of weeks. "Don't say that. What we've been doing is wrong. We all kent that. I wish I'd never found the book. And I'll not come here again."

"Ah, but you will. We're all in this equally. And

300

if we're going to stop, we must all stop, and together, and never tell anyone."

"But who can stop anyone doing that?" This was one of the boys.

"Because we'll put a curse of hell on anyone that does."

In the half light her words held conviction. No one murmured a doubt.

Phemy spoke.

"A curse of hell is on us all noo, seeing we killed Jean."

For a moment they looked at her in horrified disbelief. Then there was a chorus of denials.

"That's not true." "We had naethin' tae dae wi' it." "That's a wicked thing tae say." "It's a lie."

"It's no' a lie." Sandy Todd had risen to his feet and looked down on them, frowning. "It's the truth. Jean would be here the day if it wasn't for all this."

He waved an arm that indicated not only the cave but all that happened in it, and when Jenny made a move to speak he silenced her with another gesture.

"In the old days they burnt the witches and I aye thocht that was a bad thing tae dae. But now I think I can see a reason fur it—if they were daein' wickedness like us." He pointed at Jenny. "If you'd lived twae hundred years ago they'd have burnt you, Jenny Niven."

And suddenly all the hidden guilt and the resentment at her domineering was out and they turned and looked at her with hatred. For a moment, a little moment, Jenny felt panic. Then she was on her feet and looking now across at Sandy, now in scorn at the white upturned faces.

"Aye, aye. Perhaps we went a wee bit far. But we didna kill Jean—that's just a bairn's havers. So we'll stop it—the summer's coming and we're no' wanting tae be spending the lang days in a cave. So we'll stop. And never say a word to anybody. And that's that."

"But it's no'." Sandy was firm. "If we hadna been having all this going on in the cave, Jean wouldna be dead."

"We killed Jean," whispered Phemy again, rocking to and fro.

"But we canna do anything about Jean," said Grizel.

"We could do a penance." This was from Tommy Davidson, a slender, dark boy, a comparative newcomer to the group.

"What's a penance?" said a voice.

"I've read in books—and an aunty tellt me—that in some places when folks have done something wrang, they do a penance—like, like walking up a stair on your knees."

They looked at the idea in silence. Grizel spoke.

"It wouldn't bring Jean back."

"But it would make us feel better if we did something to show we were sorry," said Tommy.

"We could tell what we had been doing: tell everyone. That would be a hard thing to do. That would be a true penance."

"We canna do that, Grizel." Jenny's voice was sharp. "We canna tell our fathers and mothers."

Silence again as they accepted the truth.

Phemy sobbed.

"Then we'll always feel it was our fault. For ever and ever."

There was an uneasy shifting of positions round the fire. Jenny looked down at them and found the answer.

"We will do something. Sandy Todd says he sees why they burnt witches for their ill-doing. Sae we'll burn a witch."

She savoured the startled switch of their gaze from the fire to her face.

"Oh, no' a real wumman. We'll make a witch and burn her. We'll burn her here, in the cave, at the time of the May Burning. And that'll be our penance, and that'll burn away the bad feeling."

There was a clamour of voices but in the end they agreed. It was an easy way out. They would make a witch in the cave and burn it there and never go back. They would swear it over the fire. Would they swear it over the blood of a cockerel? Yes, said Jenny. No, said Grizel. They decided not.

So they began building the guy that was to be a witch. One or two had built scarecrows on a farm. They knew how to make the wooden framework. They got straw and old clothes; they painted a crude face on a stuffed sack. They worked hard and finished it. Then Meg got to hear of it.

23

MEG had gone from the cave straight to her cottage, walking quickly and angrily down through the bracken and trees of the glen, and then over the slope below Gloom Hill. She was strangely upset by what she had seen in the cave, aware that it was sinister as well as silly. "Raising the de'il indeed. He's no needin' fires and can'les in sheeps' skulls tae be raisit in this place. An' yon lassie in her shift—Och! it's no' richt. But I'll see that's stoppit."

But in the morning when she went to the shops and heard the tale of Mary's claiming authorship of the book, the doings in the cave slipped to the back of her mind.

For Dyplin was agog with excitement. Not only over Mary's authorship, but even more over the dramatic way in which it had come to light.

In her shop, Mrs. Walker told and re-told the tale: "There the schoolmaster was, wi' the men round about him, and that Johnny McIndoe ready to grab him by the throat, when her ladyship steps forward cool as a cucumber. 'I wrote it' says she, and away up the hill, stately as a duchess. Oh, she's a bold one, yon."

"And what happened next?" This was Madame

Laporte, who normally maintained an air of superior detachment towards local gossip.

"The men just looked after her and said naething. I think they couldna believe it. And the schoolmaster picked himself off the wall, and straightened his coat, and made his way through them with a face like thunder. He'd been made tae look kind o' small, you see."

"I canna think Mr. Rutherford could ever look small," said Leah Beattie, who worshipped Daniel's height and fiery beard from afar.

"Ah, but you see, it seems when they were chasing Rob Little and she was keeping them off from getting him, Daniel Rutherford came down the hill, and she called tae him fur help—fur Johnny McIndoe struck her such a blow she was on her knees and fair desperate—and the schoolmaster never heeded but just went on his way."

"I don't believe it," said Leah Beattie indignantly.

"Aye, but it's true. For Willie Johnston tellt my man in the Thorn Bush."

"Personally," said Madame Laporte, picking up her basket and straightening her shawl, "I think it is a storm in a tea-cup. Not that I approve of what Miss Tullis has done. Old scandals should not be raked up. But as they were largely forgotten before, so they shall be again. Besides, the book is really a record of trivialities. In my position, I get confidences from people which I shall never reveal, but from which, I assure you, I could make a book that would quite put Miss Tullis's out of mind. . . Have you finished your shopping, Miss Beattie? Then we might walk down the road together," for since the Reform Ball the two ladies had become friendly, and Leah was frequently invited to partake of a glass of Madeira and a slice of cake in Madame's cosy parlour—and to share, under pain of strictest secrecy, some of Madame's confidential tit-bits.

Meg had been standing in the shadow at the back of the shop for some time, and it was only when Madame Laporte, who acknowledged her presence with a stately dip of the head, and Leah, who smiled at her timidly, had gone, that the other ladies realized she was there and dropped the subject of Daniel.

But Meg would have none of it. She moved up to the counter with her customary composure and said, "And what will happen to the umbrella-maker's daughter now?"

"Naething, I suppose. The men canna very well lay hands on her," said Mrs. Walker. "And mebbe Madame Laporte is right, and it's no' worth bothering about."

"That's all right for you," said Joan Rennie, "there's none o' your lot in the book. But what about us, wi' yon old story about Jock's brother and the sheep-stealing? That's not a nice thing for a decent family to hae raked up."

"That is true," said Mrs. Walker smugly, "and it's not for us who have never had anything to hide—" her eyes flicked over Meg's unsmiling face—"to make little of the sore feelings of the less fortunate. Now what can I do for you, Meg?"

Meg made her purchases, went home and left them, and then set off up the road to the castle, soon leaving it for a little path that led into the glen and down to the level of the burn. There were tasks to be done in her house, but it was too small for her in her present angry and exultant mood. She had never seriously thought of Mary as the author of the verses which had so angered her; and her dislike of Mary now boiled up into hatred: a triumphant hatred, for Mary had put herself outside the world of Dyplin; and Meg, sharing in Dyplin's righteous indignation, was for once inside it.

But what would happen to the umbrella-maker's daughter? Would public outrage be positive and visible? Or would she too be quietly cold-shouldered, subtly rejected, implacably barricaded out by the self-righteous and respectable? It had taken the cholera to make a small breach for Meg.

"I could tear her eyes out." She spoke the words against the noise of the burn tumbling into the dark pool beneath the castle, her finger curling into the wool of her shawl. "I could tear her eyes out."

She had not gone to the glen with the intention of meeting Daniel, but, it being a Saturday and he free of school, she was not surprised when she came out from the shelter of the trees to see the tall figure on the skyline as he came down the track to the castle gate. She wondered whether to call to him or not, but he saw her, and left the track to stride down the path towards her.

"I didn't think to meet you," he said. "It's early in the day for you to be out."

"I couldna bide in the house." He heard the edge in her voice, noted her flaming cheeks and the clenched hands.

"Is something wrong?"

"Wrang? I've juist learnt that yon book—and yon ill-thocht piece o' verse aboot me—was written by the umbrella-maker's daughter."

He looked sideways and said, "I thought everyone knew that by now."

"Weel, I didna. Come under the trees here. I want tae talk tae you."

They moved into the shelter of the trees, and Meg leant against the rough trunk of an ancient birch-tree, while Daniel stood on the path and poked about among the loam with the stick he always carried on his walks.

Meg waited for him to speak, but he said nothing. So, her brows drawn over her eyes, she said, "I hate her, I hate her. But I'll not be the only one to do that. They tell me fowk thocht you wrote it. And she rescued you in the nick o' time frae bein' struck doon by Johnny McIndoe."

Still he said nothing.

"Made you look small, was what Mrs. Walker said."

Daniel struck savagely at a branch and split it across.

"Aye, so you're angry tae. Wi' yoursel', or wi' her? Why should you be angry wi' her for rescuing you from an angry lot o' men? Verra good o' her it was, seein' you'd no done the same for her."

"Damn you!" and Daniel turned to go back to the track.

"Na, na, Daniel. Dinna be angry wi' me. I dinna care whit ye did or didna dae. I'm juist tellin' you whit they're sayin'."

He turned back and caught her arm. "Don't. Don't do it. I wish I'd never seen her."

"We're agreed on that. But I want to know whit's tae happen tae her."

He looked puzzled. "I don't know. Nothing, I suppose. What can happen to her?"

"I dinna ken. But something should be done tae a body wha rakes up and pits intae cauld print a' the wicked clash that fowk's pit up wi' and that's been forgotten. I have pit up wi' plenty frae the awfu' guid fowk—mair especially the weemen—o' Dyplin. An' whit I did didna cause hauf the misery she's caused."

He shook his head again. "I don't see what can be done. Perhaps it would be better to let well alone, and it'll all die down."

"Oh, that's weak, weak. I'd like tae see her burnin' on Gloom Hill, like the witch lang syne. Whit richt had she tae come here and upset everyone?"

"Meg, Meg, calm yourself. She's done you no harm."

"Hes she no'? She *pitied* me—and I'm no' fur onybody's pity. An' she made a bonny fule o' you."

"Do you think I don't feel that? But I didn't think you would cast it up at me."

Meg had calmed down a little.

"It maks nae difference tae me whit they say aboot ye. It's no' fur your reputation I want ye. It's fur your reid hair, and the big beard on ye an' other things no' tae be spoke o'. But gin I was you, I would be bitter, bitter fur whit she's done. Na, na—" as he stepped towards her—"I'm ower angry fur ony play. I'll up the hill a bit, and then hame. Ye can come tae the hoose the nicht."

She swung past him and up the path with her usual bold stride, and Daniel went on the path that would take him through the trees to the road.

He had kept a calm face towards Meg, but he was humiliated and bitter: and of course angry with the woman who made him so. He had always carried himself with a certain self-sufficiency that had something of the arrogant in it. He was an outstanding teacher of young children and had a concern for his pupils that extended beyond the schoolroom: and for which he was greatly respected. But there was a coldness in him towards his colleagues and fellow-townsmen; he did not join much in the various doings of Dyplin. There was always a reserve in him. So they had been ready to believe he had written the book; and perhaps some of them were not sorry to have a good reason for sneering at him. And to be rescued by a chit of a woman, whom he knew to despise him, and who had rejected him—it was too much! Not that anyone had said anything to him since the events of yesterday. But he imagined there was a slyness in the customary greetings as he went about the street, a little smirking, a change in attitude.

He exaggerated the reaction of Dyplin, but was not altogether wrong. There was a certain satisfaction that Daniel Rutherford had been shown to be less than admirable, but there was too much concern for the revelation about others for much attention to be given to Daniel. Yet the reactions to Mary's admission of authorship were curiously muted. There was no precedent in Dyplin. The aggrieved parties could not physically assault her; and cutting her in the street, or serving her coldly in the shops—though both were tried—were ineffective against her quiet and altogether unaltered manner. Besides, some of the more thoughtful pointed out that showing too much indignation was tantamount to admitting the truth of the episodes in the book. No one, they said, outside Dyplin, would know who was meant. Better, perhaps, to ignore the whole thing.

But Torrance of the *Inverforth Gazette*, being a good businessman, had sent copies of *Verses from a Northern Parish* to places well beyond Inverforth. Someone on a trip to Edinburgh saw it in a bookshop; and at the thought of strangers reading it, a slow irrational rage began to gather. It was no use anyone's pointing out that outside Dyplin no one knew the truth or otherwise of the subject matter. Then a letter came from Willie Johnston's brother: he had spotted the connection. So now "the haill world wud ken aboot it a'."

Mrs. Glendinning came back from the village to the Manse one clear spring morning, put her basket on the kichen table, gave a few brisk orders to Matilda, and went to knock on the study door—an almost unheard of thing to do, for it was understood that the Minister, unless called out on pastoral duty, spent the morning in uninterrupted study and meditation. When his mother entered, Matthew was not at his desk, nor at his bookshelf, but standing by the window which looked out over the Manse garden to the church. Mrs. Glendinning loved her garden, and primulas and a few tulips were bright in the little border beyond the grass; and the old gean tree was just coming into bud. He turned to his mother a little wearily, and she had a sudden glimpse of him as imprisoned in the square, sombre room.

"Matthew," she said, "there's a lot of ill-feeling blowing up about Miss Tullis's book. Apparently they're reading it in places away from here—and folks are getting letters about it; and they're angry."

Matthew had sat down at his desk. "I'm sorry to hear it."

"She shouldn't have done it, Matthew."

"Perhaps not." He lifted a pen, and drew it through his fingers—a habit of his when puzzled or worried. "But she did not write it down as truth.

She changed the names. Perhaps she did not know the people would be recognized."

"Then she's more of a fool than I thought. She should ken how people here ken all about each other."

"She was brought up in Glasgow, where people do not pry on each other so much."

"Aweel, if it wasn't the people, I mean the real people, she was getting at, it was the place. And it's not for an incomer to be crying down a place they ken little about."

"Yes, I know. I wish she had not done it." He put down the pen, pushed back the heavy black chair and went back to the window. "But I think, since she writes verse, she thought only of the stories as material and did not consider . . ."

"Havers." Mrs. Glendinning was unwontedly heated. "If you ask me, she wrote that stuff in a rage after breaking off with Daniel Rutherford."

"What do you mean?"

"Oh Matthew, surely even you ken that she and Daniel were—very friendly. Folk all kent it."

"Yes, I did know."

"Aweel, it's all finished. If you would juist let me tell you mair about what goes on . . ."

"I will not have vain babblings bandied about in the Manse."

"Verra weel, verra weel. But you have heard that when the men were chasing poor Rob Little, and Mary Tullis was facing them, that Daniel Rutherford turned aside and wouldna help?"

313

"Is this true?"

"Aye it's true. A'body in the place kens it's true. Except the Minister." Mrs. Glendinning's discipline over her naturally sharp tongue slipped. "I sometimes think you keep yourself far ower unspotted from the world!"

Matthew let this pass. "He did that? I would not."

"I ken that. Yon man, for all he's so big and gallant looking—aye, and good at the sports too—he's a cauld, selfish cratur inside."

"Mother! 'Judge not that ye be not judged'."

"Aye, aye. Weel, my conscience is clear. I've told you what's going on, and it's not 'vain babblings'."

She was turning to go, when Matthew said, "I will go and see her."

"And what good will that do? She canna un-write the book."

"I could warn her about what people feel."

"She's no' a young woman to take warning of any sort kindly."

"Nevertheless I shall go."

There was an underlying determination and eagerness in his voice that told his mother much. The Reverend Matthew Glendinning would not be going only as a pastor to see Mary. His mother said no more, but went out closing the door quietly, troubled for her son.

Matthew did go to see Mary one evening. She greeted him composedly, made tea, sat quietly with a piece of darning while he and David talked.

314

At last Matthew found an opportunity to say, 'Are you happy here in Dyplin, Miss Tullis?"

She looked up from her work, her dark eyes a little surprised.

"I am neither happy nor unhappy. There are worse places to live. I like the hills and the woods."

"And the people?"

She shrugged her shoulders. "People are the same everywhere."

He plunged on, the pastor taking over. "In your book you appeared to—to have no high opinion of them."

She put down her darning, her eyes flashing. "It was not the people of this place I was writing about. I changed the names. I wrote these stories as—as types of the way people act."

"You have no high opinion then of humanity."

"No, I do not."

She snapped the words, and then picked up her work again.

David had been listening uneasily. "She meant no harm to the people here, Minister. But I wish she had not done it."

The two men looked at Mary, who kept her eyes on the darning and said nothing.

"People are angry," said Matthew. "They do not understand that it was not a personal attack. . . ."

"I attacked no one. I told what people had done. If people are wicked and foolish, I did not make them so."

"But they are hurt and angry."

315

"I am sorry if that is so. But what can they do? You do not want me to stand up, perhaps in the kirk, and say it was all lies? Because it isn't."

"I do not ask you to do anything. Except perhaps to think long before you write more of that kind. It might provoke the people."

"On the night they were hunting Rob Little, I was struck by one of the people you are so concerned about. Have you rebuked him?"

Matthew went pale. "I did not know . . ."

He was so manifestly distressed that Mary's anger vanished and she said more gently, "No harm was done. And I do not want you to say anything to him. I am told he suffered great loss at the time of the cholera."

"Nevertheless, he should be spoken to. . . ."

"No, you must not. Better let it be forgotten. Let us say no more about the matter—or the book."

"Very well," and he turned to David.

As he walked home half an hour later he was angry with himself. He had been the rebuking pastor when his whole desire was to be the protecting lover. Looking at her and she had sat with her mending, her dark head bent, her hands slender and a little work-roughened, he had momentarily seen her at the Manse, the Minister's wife, her price above rubies. And he had had to spoil it all and call out the hard, scornful Mary who had no respect for him as a minister and little liking for him as a man. His visit had been a waste of time. He had not warned her strongly enough that the anger of Dyplin might spill over into definite action. He had not told her that at the May Burning, now not far off, Dyplin was changed.

The May Burning was a ritual peculiar to Dyplin, found in no other village along the hills. No one knew how old it was, but there were records of it back into the fourteenth century. It centred on an enormous fire which blazed from dawn till dusk. What it commemorated no one knew, and no one cared. It happened on the last Wednesday of May and, until Dr. Gillies came to the parish, had been a time for dancing, drinking, fornicating—an abandonment of all the accepted rules by most of Dyplin—even those normally douce and respectable; though a few managed to resist the pull, shutting themselves in their houses, with their children round them, closing and bolting doors and shutters, and sitting with open Bibles to add a spiritual protection against whatever forces were abroad. For it was not like Hallowe'en and Hogmanay, which the whole country shared. This was something very close, very private. It was not talked about and looked forward to. Only a day or two before the due date, the fire was finally built, by silent men who scarcely spoke to one another. It was a vast release for all that had to be battened down for the rest of the year, and would be battened down on the morrow.

The "old doctor"—Dr. Gillies—changed all that. Worldly he might be, a toper he might be, but he could recognize evil when he saw it, and his first experience of the May Burning shocked him. It was manifestly evil, a relic of pagan superstition, an occasion of the grossest godlessness. So he set about changing it. Being worldly-wise, he knew better than to abolish it entirely. It had its innocent side. He had noted the wide-eyed wonder of the children watching the towering flames. It would become a children's ploy, a bonfire, games, perhaps a procession: but no more.

It had not worked out quite like that. The bonfire was not lit till late evening, when dusk was falling; the children had their procession and games; but the day was a holiday for everyone; the Thorn Bush did a mighty trade; and what happened among the trees of the glen and the thickets by the river was as pagan as in the old days. Matthew had come to expect that on the Sabbath before the May Burning there would be a diminished congregation; and that the church would be packed on the Sabbath after. Each year he preached against the May Burning. Each year in vain.

He himself never went near the fire. He was always uneasy at the time of the May Burning, discouraged, feeling he fought a losing battle. If there was to be any action against Mary, would it not take place then? But no, he could not see anyone actually attacking her: evil might be abroad at the May Burning, but not that. And besides, David was much respected; and according to his mother, the general feeling was that David was to be pitied for being unwillingly involved with the book. Nevertheless, Matthew went uneasily about his work, conscious of tensions accumulating, and whisperings at street corners abruptly dying as he passed.

About a week before the May Burning, Meg Annan met Grizel on the road just above her cottage. Grizel, tormented by misgivings and remorse since Meg had told them how Jean had died, had taken to going on solitary walks. She smiled uncertainly at Meg, and was passing when Meg stopped her.

"I want to talk to you. Come into my house for a minute."

Grizel looked alarmed, and Meg said:

"It's a' richt. There's naebody tae see you darkening my door. And I'll mak' shair naebody see you gang oot. But I must hae a word wi' you."

Inside, while Grizel looked round with uneasy curiosity, Meg went on, "Sit doon, lassie. I'll no bite you. I juist want to ken if all that nonsense at the cave is ended. I should have askit sooner, but it kin' o' slipped ma mind. Hae ye finished wi it?"

"Yes. Well, almost."

"Whit dae ye mean, 'almost'?"

"We—we did a penance. We made a witch—to burn in the cave—because of Jean."

"I dinna understan' a word you're sayin'. Noo, will you juist tell me whether or no' all that nasty nonsense is finished?"

The whole story came out, and when Grizel had finished, Meg sat for a while and said nothing.

Grizel stirred uneasily, and Meg flashed a look at her.

"I'll no' keep ye lang. Juist let me think a while. Ye've made a guy, a witch, tae burn in the cave? It seems a kin' o' daft-like thing tae me—but aye, I think I unnerstaun' whit wis behind it. But I'm thinkin' noo, why burn it in the cave? Why no' at the May Burning bonfire?"

"But people would ask why . . ."

"Aye, but ye could say it wis juist a ploy—juist something fur the bonfire. Besides, there's no' much o' a—whit did ye ca' it?—penance aboot burning it in yon cave and naebody kennin' onything aboot it. But burnin' it oot there—an' mebbe wonderin' if somebody wud guess, or find oot—*that's* a rale penance!"

She looked slyly at the girl, and waited.

"But it's all made—how could we get it there?"

"I tell ye what. Ye can bring it here—in bits if ye like—and I'll keep it, and no' tell onybody. An' on the day o' the Burning—juist afore they all gather fur the fire—the lads could cairry it there and set it up. It's no' far frae here, and ye can cross the burn by the stanes, and it's no' likely onybody will see."

"I'll have to ask the others. . . ."

"Aye, aye. You do that. But mind ye tell them tae that there's nae choice. I have ye a' in my haun'—" she stretched it out and closed it slowly—"fur I can tell the haill warld whit ye've been up tae." Her voice suddenly wheedled. "But I swear by God himsel' and the deil tae I'll no breathe a word if ye

cairry oot a richt penance and dae as I say. And noo'
I'll juist mak' shair there's naebody aboot tae see ye
leaving."

She opened the door, looked out, and beckoned to
Grizel. But before the girl stepped out, Meg laid a
hand on her arm.

"I'll need the answer by the morn's nicht."

She got it. The next night, when it was dark,
there was a knock at her door, and when she opened
it, the candlelight shone out on four boys carrying
bundles wrapped in sacking.

Sandy Todd spoke. "We've brought the guy."

She took them in, and they unwrapped the
grotesque body, the straw limbs, the primitive face.

"Ye can pit it in there," and she showed them the
lean-to at the back where she kept two chests of
material and other clutter.

"Can ye pit it together easily?"

"Aye." They spoke in monosyllables, ill-at-ease
in the house that they'd often whispered and
sniggered about.

"Then come tomorrow and dae it."

They came, and when they had finished, Meg
looked at the result critically.

"It's mair like a heathen idol than a wumman,
witch or no'. Never mind, I'll redd it up a bit, and
it'll be a rale guid guy. Noo mind—no' a word. And
I'll say naethin'—ever—and ye can come when
fowks are at their supper afore the Burning, and set
it up." She looked at them. They were sullen and
anxious. "And when ye watch it burn, ye can tell

yersels—and the lassies tae—that ye're burning awa a' that dirt ye were at in the cave—and forget it."

Once they had gone, she went to stand in front of the thing propped against the wall in the little low-roofed room. The light played over the bulging body, the flaccid arms, the black gashes of mouth and eyes, the rags of the clothes.

"Aye, aye." She nodded at it familiarly. "We'll hae tae smerten ye up a bit," and she set down the candle, opened a chest, drew out a roll of material, spread it on the floor, and knelt with the big scissors in her hand to cut it, while the flame cast her shadow on the wall.

24

O N the Knowe the pile of wood and rubbish for the May Burning was beginning to take shape. There was no organized building of it; a fortnight or so before the day, someone would place the first little heap on the spot; the word would go round: "They've started building the fire", and in a secretive off-hand way it would be added to daily: and more by adults than by children. Dr. Gillies, when he "reformed" the ritual, had laid it down that the games for the children and their procession through the town should be organized by the beadle of the kirk. Joseph Harvey enjoyed doing it, recruited helpers from friends and parents, and threw himself into it with enthusiasm; not lessened by his awareness of the fact that Daniel Rutherford thought that he, as teacher of the Infant School, should be in charge. There had indeed been an acrimonious debate about this when Daniel was first appointed to his position. But the old Doctor was still alive then, and Daniel's claim had been very firmly put down; so nowadays he pointedly ignored the preparations. Daniel was a bitter, unhappy man these days, conscious of coldness on the part of his colleagues, an unsmiling hostility on the part of the townspeople. He had come as a young boy to Dyplin, when his mother, early widowed, came to live with her sister. For years he had nursed a secret sense of superiority, holding himself aloof: but holding himself aloof was very different from being set apart at the will of others. He spoke again to Walter Fraser in the library:

"So the mystery is solved. Miss Tullis wrote the book."

"Yes, so I heard. I wish for her sake she had not."

"At least everyone knows now I did not. Though some people still behave as if I had."

"You are imagining things."

"Perhaps." And Daniel had to leave it at that.

"I could not say to him," said Walter to his wife, "that the story of his cowardice when the girl was being mobbed is more damaging than being suspected of having written the book!"

One day, Florrie, Daniel's second daughter, came back late from school her face scratched and her eyes full of angry tears. When Daniel asked her what was wrong she burst into sobs and said Charlotte McMurdo had said that he had told the woman that wrote the nasty book all the horrid stories about people in Dyplin, and it was all his fault. "So I told her it was not true, and I pulled her hair and she scratched me—and I don't want to go back to school if they're saying things like that."

Daniel comforted her—he could be a kind parent—and then went out to walk off his rage that yet another grievance had been pinned on him. He took the road down to the Martyr's Bridge, walking with long strides, switching the stick he always carried against the tall plants on the verge of the road. To his annoyance, as he came in sight of the bridge, he saw a man leaning on the parapet looking into the water. Beyond, a van was drawn up at the roadside and a grey horse was munching grass. It was Peter Robertson. He turned at the sound of Daniel's steps, recognized him, gave a stony stare, and turned back to look in the water.

Daniel's first impulse was to walk past him in silence. But instead he stopped by the parapet beside him and said, "A fine day."

"Aye." Peter did not look at him. He was normally a sociable man, always ready for a crack.

Daniel took the plunge. "Mr. Robertson, I want to ask you something. My girl Florrie came home from school today much distressed. She says the children are saying that I told Miss Tullis the tales that she made into the book."

And now Peter did look at him. "And didn't you?"

"No, I did not. How she got to know them I cannot say. But not from me."

"Aye, but ye were verra freenly wi' her."

"I knew her quite well. We never talked of Dyplin."

"Whae did?"

"I don't know."

"Aweel, you see, fowk noticed there was nothing aboot yerself in the book. And it's no' that there havena been plenty tales aboot yersel'."

His little eyes—Daniel had never noticed before

what small eyes he had—were bright with speculation, and Daniel could say nothing to this.

Peter went on. "There's those that hae been made a mock o', and they're angry. E'en masel—yon bit aboot the mice in the bakehoose, and the deid yin in the loaf—it happened years syne, in auld Shivas's day; but there's fowk coming in til the shop noo—this verra morn, makin' remarks aboot hoping I've got the flourbins weel covered. . . ."

Daniel struck the parapet savagely. "Words never killed anybody. Why can't people let it die? It's the present that counts, not stories from the past."

"It's all verra weel for you, schule-maister. You're no' in it. Whit would you dae?"

"I'd throw the book in the fire and forget it. But at least, Peter, you'll let it be known I am not responsible for the book or anything in it. And I will not have my children tormented."

And he marched away up the hill, past the van, while Peter leant on the wall and looked after him.

"And I believe he is speakin' the truth," he said to his horse as he pulled the beast's reluctant head from the grass. "I do believe he is."

That night in the Thorn Bush Peter spoke of his encounter with Daniel. His words received a mixed reception; some accepted Daniel's assertions; others did not, and loudest among these was Johnny McIndoe, banging the counter and shouting:

"It's easy fur him tae say 'burn the book' and forget it! He's no' in it. By God! It's the wumman we should burn, no' the book."

"Johnny, Johnny, ye're no' tae say things like that in my inn." Jock Bishop, the owner, appealed to the company. "Can ye no' keep him quiet? He's had ower much."

Johnny thrust aside the hands seeking to restrain him. "I'll no' be quate. The schule-maister tellt a' they things aboot me and you and you—and noo he says 'just burn it'."

"I did not tell any tales about anyone." No one had heard the door open, and in the silence following his words they gaped at Daniel standing there. He seldom came to the Thorn Bush, and then only seeking the parent of a child, but he had decided to follow up his encounter with Peter Robertson by going to the inn that night. He stepped up to the counter and said to Jock, "A small whisky."

Johnny McIndoe lurched forward and pushed an uncertain finger in Daniel's chest.

"You're the man whae wants tae get rid o' the haill affair by 'just burning the book'! Aye, but you werena in the book. We wis. An' pittin' it in the kitchen fire'll no' put it richt."

Daniel looked at them, and thought how he hated them: not just wretched drunken Johnny, but the others, the respectable little men coming in for a decorous dram; worried about their little reputations; and able to make his life and his family's a misery. He found the necessary gesture.

"I do say burn the book. But not in the kitchen fire, one by one. Why not at the May Burning? In the fire on the Knowe? All at once. Burnt together, forgotten together.''

He lifted his glass and drank as the hubbub rose around him.

When it had died down again, Peter Robertson said, "We'll dae it. We'll gather a' the copies o' the book we can, an' tak' them tae the bonfire. But mind—keep a' this as dark as ye can. There's mebbe some wud want tae stop it.''

"Let them try,'' said Johnny. "There's naethin' wrang wi' burnin' books. But the wey we'll burn them'll show what we think o' it.'' He sought Daniel's hand to shake it. "A verra guid suggestion, schule-maister. I see we've been wrangin' ye a' the gither.''

There was still light in the sky when Daniel came out shortly after, sick with self-disgust, angry with everyone. He and Meg had reverted to meeting up at the Castle when the days lengthened and the risk of his being seen going to her cottage increased. But now he went straight to her house, lingering for a little under the trees at the foot of the glen to make sure no one was about, and then slipping to her door and quietly knocking.

She was surprised to see him, but stood aside at once to let him enter. She had been working: a half-finished brown calico dress was draped over a chair, her basket with thread and needles beside it. She swept them all up and put them in the back room. Daniel sat down and gazed morosely into a small early-summer fire, so different from the blaze of winter.

Meg stared. "Whit's wrang?" She stooped. "Ye've drink on your breath."

"I went to the Thorn Bush—" and he told her why and with what result.

"So they're gaun tae burn the umbrella-maker's daughter's book? I'm richt glad tae hear it." She took a swift step across the room and lifted something from the sideboard. "Here's my own. You can tak' it and gie it tae Johnny tae burn."

He thrust her hand aside. "No, I will not. I don't wish ever to be near Johnny McIndoe again. I wish I'd never said anything about burning the books. I wish Mary Tullis had never come near this place!"

"Ye're no' the only one to wish that. As fur burning the books, it's whit they deserve. You werena in it, Daniel." She looked at him with narrowed eyes. "Why did she miss ye oot? Ah weel, I'll no' ask mair. But ye'll see, once the May Burning's ower, fowk'll forget aboot it—and ye'll hae nae mair worry aboot it either. See here, will I mak' ye a bowl o' punch? I hae all I need."

Daniel, normally an abstemious man, agreed.

"I'll juist get the water boiled. And we'll no' say anither word aboot books or the umbrella-maker's daughter either. You and me hae better things tae dae."

Daniel might manage to clear himself of suspicion that he had supplied Mary with the material for her verses. But for Alison, it lay heavy on her conscience that she had given the stories to Mary. One day she spoke to her about it.

"I didna think you would be making a book oot o' what I told you aboot the folk here, Mary. I thought you were just interested in them, not that you were wanting to hold them up and make a mock of them."

Mary brushed this aside impatiently. "I wasn't making a mock of the people here. I changed the names."

"Maybe, but folk are angry."

"Then they are stupid. Why should I try to hurt them?"

"Aye, that's what they say. Why?"

"It's a stupid question. Yes, the stories did interest me. They show people as foolish or wicked—and that's how people are."

Alison looked at her in astonishment. "You're verra young tae think that, Mary."

"But it's true. Don't you see, what you told me about the goings-on here prove it? When I came, I thought Dyplin was a beautiful place, a good place. My father had to warn me not to think it too beautiful and too good. And he was right. In the book it wasn't Dyplin I was writing about. I was using the stories about Dyplin to write about people anywhere and everywhere."

"Ah weel, they don't see it that way. Nor do I." Alison was a little nettled by a note of impatient superiority in Mary's voice. "Are you sure you werena getting some of your own back on Dyplin,

330

for what happened here at your own back door?"

She regretted the words at once, for Mary flushed, her lips closed tight, and she turned away in silence.

"You shouldna' hae said it, Alison," said John, when she told him.

"I ken. I wish I hadna. Though it's true, I'm sure of that. Not just Johnny McIndoe hitting her, but Rutherford turning away. . . ."

"Maybe, maybe, and I'm no' sorry if she's rid o' him. . . . But, Alison, I ken whit she means aboot no' meaning Dyplin."

"Weel, I don't."

John sighed, knotted his brows, and said, "See yon picture there, the one I got at Jamie Macphee's sale?"

He nodded towards a dark little oil-painting of a fishing smack under sail on a stormy sea.

"I see it."

"Weel, it's Jamie Macphee's faither's boat. But I didna buy it because it's his faither's boat, though it's interesting enough that it is. I bocht it because it minds me o' a' the boats that fights wi' the sea. . . . An' Mary wud be usin' Dyplin, meaning fowk a' ower the place."

"Aye. That's what she said. But I'm not clever enough for these fancy ideas. Nor are the maist o' people." Alison rose and went through to her back kitchen, pausing at the door to say, "All I ken is, she put down all the old clash and folk are gey angry." She stalked out, but put her head round the door to add, "And I doubt Mary'll hear more about it."

25

THE May Burning drew near. The children's excitement mounted. They tormented their parents into concocting disguises for the procession. They practised running and jumping. They ran in and out of one another's houses, comparing, squabbling, envying, full of activity. They had been deprived of their fun at Hallowe'en, Ne'erday had been darkened by the solemnity and grief of their elders; but the May Burning was to be theirs for fun and ploys. There was an exuberance, spilling over into lawlessness, about their activity that made Joseph Harvey shake his head and speak to parents.

"The weans is getting a bit oot o' haun," he said to Rabbie Paterson, having just found Rabbie's two small boys hammering away at each other with enormous bones they had cajoled Willie Johnston into giving them. When he'd separated them and asked why, they had said they were going in the procession as "savage cannibals" and were practising.

Rabbie, however, was indulgent: "Och, they've no' had much fun this while back. It's time they got enjoying themselves."

The children's behaviour might verge on the outrageous, encouraged by unwonted indulgence on the part of the grown-ups, but otherwise a great calm settled on Dyplin in the days before the Burning. There were none of the usual little flurries of excitement or gossip. People met, exchanged greetings, passed on. In the Thorn Bush, all was decorum. And yet, there were sly glances of understanding, noddings and winkings. By the day before the Burning, practically every copy of Mary's book was neatly stacked in two big baskets in an out-house at the Thorn Bush and, though no one spoke of it openly, almost everyone knew that something out of the ordinary would happen at the Burning. The Minister didn't know, of course, and Dr. Munro only heard two days before: but even the masters and wives of the New School knew something was a-foot—and indeed, several of them had handed over copies of the book. John was among the last to hear, and came home to tell Alison, only to discover she knew already.

"Aye, I ken. They're going to burn the book."

"But that's a wicked thing tae dae."

"So you say. But there's nothing you can do to stop it."

"I ken that. Whit's worrying me is—will Mary be gaun tae the Burning?"

"No. She says she doesn't want to go. And David's not going. If you ask me, he's a worried man, and he doesn't look well these days; he looks awful tired."

"He worries aboot Mary. Whiles I dae masel'."

On the day before the Burning, Meg lingered

over her shopping until she saw Jenny and Grizel coming down the street. As they met, she said, "If ye want tae see yer guy, ye can come the nicht tae the hoose. But dinna bring the laddies. Juist yersels."

They came in the late twilight, and Meg took them into her room. "Before ye see it, I'll tell you whit the laddies are tae dae the morn. The fire's lichted aboot ten o'clock. I believe it's a graun' fire, and the weather's been fine these last days sae it'll burn fine. The laddies'll hae to climb up, and pit a big branch in the middle, tae tie the guy tae, sae that it's stannin' up. Let them come aboot nine o'clock. There'll be naebody aboot then. Ye'll tell them?"

They nodded.

"That's fine. Come awa ben, then, and see your guy."

She opened the door to the little back room, and stood aside for them to enter. Grizel went in first, and stood still, her hands clutching her skirts. Jenny followed, and stood too.

Behind them Meg spoke. "Weel? Do ye no' like it?"

"It's—it's like a real woman," Grizel said in a whisper. "It's like—"

"Dinna name her!" Meg's voice was harsh. "Dinna name her! Guys shouldna be named. Pittin' a name till them can pit a life till them! She's a guy." Her voice changed. "Juist straw and claes, lassies, juist straw and claes."

335

Jenny's eyes were bright. "It's very well made," she said and, moving up to the figure propped against the wall, she laid a hand on the dress. "Very well made."

But Grizel turned on her. "We can't burn that," she said. "It's too like a real woman. It's just like—" she glanced at Meg. "It would be cruel."

"Havers," said Meg. "It's just a guy."

But Jenny still had a hand on it. "The more like a real woman, the more like a real witch; and the better."

Grizel turned to leave.

Meg stood aside to let her pass, but said, "You'll no' be thinkin' of saying onything tae onybody? Remember whit I said."

Grizel said nothing, but caught up her skirts, hurried to the door and ran from the house.

Meg turned back to Jenny with a question in her eyes.

"She'll not tell," said Jenny. "They're all afraid to tell. I'm not afraid, but—" she stroked the figure again—"I'll not tell either."

She went back to the outer room and stood looking round with interest. Her eyes lingered for a minute on the curtains drawn across the bed-recess. Then she opened the door to leave.

"Thank you for helping with the guy, Meg." She glanced over her shoulder, then leant forward to whisper: "Why are you doing this to her?"

Before Meg could answer, she was gone.

The morning of the May Burning broke clear and

sunny. The hills were honey-coloured under the bright sky, splotched with the young green of the bracken. The fine weather of the last week or so had not only put the bonfire in good burning order, it had brought the trees into full foliage and set the gleans flowering in the glen. The children's races took place in the morning on the level ground known as the Miller's Ground by the burn below the Knowe. A crowd of parents and aunts and uncles and grandparents came to watch and sit on the grassy slopes in one of the first really warm days of the year. Some did not come, unable to face the ghosts of children who had run and jumped the year before; but the children themselves thought only of the present. It was the first time, Matthew thought, since the cholera, that the shadow had been lifted. He said so to Joseph Harvey.

"They are happy again, Joseph. I thank Providence the shadows are lifting."

"Aye, indeed, Minister." Joseph sounded a note of whole-hearted agreement which was far from his true feelings. For Joseph had heard rumours of things to come which he did not mean to pass on to the Minister; and besides, for the moment at least, the shadows had lifted; and even the dourest of the grown-ups were smiling.

The set order of the celebrations was that, after the children's races, everyone went home for dinner, and then came the procession, which started from the front of the New School, made its way round the town, and came back to the level ground beneath the Knowe where the children received sticky cakes baked specially by Peter Robertson and drinks of sweet lemonade. Then the procession re-formed and marched back to its starting place, preceded by the piper who had led it on the outward march. The children went off home: some went to bed: most waited, getting more and more excited, till it was time to see the bonfire lit. Then they too were firmly herded home, to lie, unable to sleep, listening to the laughter and shouting, the piping and fiddling that began on the Knowe and then seemed to flow all through the town like water spilling from a cistern.

Always, at the May Burning, the atmosphere in the afternoon in Dyplin was different from the morning. By that time, the Thorn Bush had been busy. There was tension as fathers tried to seem soberer than they were, and wives and mothers scolded, and the children looked on, either solemnly or with giggles. Nevertheless, it was understood enough decorum would prevail to let the procession form and re-form. The disguises were much the same from year to year: Robert the Bruce, Wallace, Jack the Giant Killer, Little Miss Muffet, Red Riding Hood—an odd scarecrow or witch, or soldiers and sailors, or fairies. Many of the costumes were handed down in families; or exchanged between neighbours: and Robert the Bruce, in the same tin and cardboard armour, had become a traditional feature. The same fond relatives who had turned out to watch the sports urned out again, to gossip, applaud and smile.

But this year, as the procession made its roundabout way from the school to the Miller's Ground, a silence fell. For this was a different procession. The historical and fairy-tale characters were almost invisible in the throng of bogles and witches, scarecrows, skeletons, devils with horns and tails, and small white ghosts dancing and gibbering. Matthew, standing by Dr. Munro, whose own children had gone as Prince Charlie and Flora Macdonald, was appalled.

"This is dreadful," he said. He pointed to a prancing devil. "To make a mock of the Evil One is not far from making a mock of the Almighty! And to see children. . . . It should be stopped."

But the doctor put a hand on his arm as he stepped forward. "You can't stop it. The children told me that bogles and ghosts and suchlike were, so to speak, to be in fashion for the procession this year. And is it surprising? Think back, Minister, think back to what they saw and heard, these children. Maybe now they've turned it into a game they'll be able to forget it."

The procession passed silent spectators all the way to the Miller's Ground. It had seemed a harmless enough thing when a child had insisted on dressing up as a "ghaistie" or "a bogle", or, more daringly, "a bony man—a' the boys is going as bony men". But to see these posturing skeletons and prancing shrouds, to hear the laughter more fearful than merry struck cold on those watching. Thin

339

clouds drifted over the sun and dulled its brightness. The eating and drinking on the Miller's Ground were cut short; the children themselves seemed cowed, and trailed dejectedly back on the return walk. By six o'clock Dyplin's few streets were empty of life, and indoors meals were served and eaten in an uneasy quiet, though the normal practice on the day of the Burning was for the children to run between one another's houses, and for neighbours to "drop by" for food and drink.

But towards the time of the lighting of the fire, movement returned to Dyplin. Doors opened, people came out, there was a sound of raised voices and loud laughter. Down in the Thorn Bush, Johnny McIndoe, who by an effort had kept himself sober enough for the work, took a sack and went to the outhouse and filled it with the books they had been so stealthily gathering. Johnny's attempt to carry it on his back failed, so Peter Robertson took it instead; then they found the others making their way to the Knowe. There was, as always, shouting to and fro, and banter, and teasing of the girls, walking in groups of five or six, arm-linked. For the country-people from round about came to the Burning; even the teachers and wives from the New School were there, and young Innes and a friend or two from Griffton. By ten o'clock, the ground round the great piled-up fire on the Knowe was thick. To reach the Knowe they had to climb up a steep slope from the level ground by the burn: so that they did not see the bonfire properly till they reached the top of the slope. And as each caught sight of it, the talking and the laughter died.

For Sandy Todd and the others had done their work well. On the top of the huge pyramid of wood and boxes, old furniture and rubbish there was a figure, tied to a strong upright post. At first all they saw was that it was the figure of a woman: and then as they moved nearer, and stared up, they saw it wore a brown dress that stirred in the breeze, and a light straw bonnet with roses under the brim. It was very real-looking, horribly real-looking to be hanging up there on the fire: and some thought it had a familiar look, but couldn't say who: and one or two thought they did know. But it was Johnny McIndoe, peering up with drunken eyes, who guffawed, pointed, and said thickly:

"Yon's the umbrella-maker's daughter!"

He turned to the young man who was waiting with a blazing torch to light the fire, and said, "Set it going, man! It'll be a bonny blaze. An' we've stuff tae burn here as weel." And he dragged the sack of books from Peter Robertson's shoulders and, swaying and staggering, emptied it to the ground.

Young Fisher thrust the blazing torch into the pile. It caught a heap of shavings and the flames rose flickering brightly and ran in and out of the heap of fuel. There was a moment's silence, and then a shout—but not the usual deep roar of applause, for the sight of the figure there made for uneasiness, and stirred memories of old old tales of horror; and Johnny's words of recognition passed

341

from one to another, so that it was no longer a guy they saw, but an individual: the name had given it life. And now Johnny had lifted a book from the pile at his feet and hurled it on the fire, and was offering others to the by-standers. "Here's yer chance tae show whit ye think o' this stuff"—and there was a surge forward of people, hands clutching in frenzy for the hated book and throwing it. Johnny thrust an armful on Daniel, and watched him drop them on the flames. It was almost dark now, for the sky was overcast and the night coming. The flames leapt, the smoke wreathed round the figure at the top, and the crowd began to dance round the fire.

Mary saw it all. Restless and unhappy, she had left David sitting by the fire, and gone up onto the hillside behind the house from where she could watch the fire as she had done on that first day in Dyplin. David had tried to dissuade her and, when she insisted, said:

"Aweel, I'll go to the workshop for a while. I dinna want to sit by myself."

"I won't be long." A weariness in his voice made her glance at him. He looked tired and drawn, and she felt a little spasm of guilt, knowing that he had been greatly anxious and very unhappy these last weeks. "But I must get out for a little."

From the hillside, she could clearly see the mass of the unlit fire and the figure on top: this surprised her, for no one had told her there would be a guy. Straining her eyes, she saw it was the effigy of a woman—and suddenly it was imperative to see it more clearly.

From the road to the castle a path led down to the burn and stepping-stones: and then she could climb up among the trees of the glen to a point above the Knowe, where she could see the fire and yet be hidden in the trees. The crowd was gathering and she could even hear the sound of the voices.

By the time she had crossed the burn and climbed up to her vantage point, the fire had been lit, and the smoke blowing in her direction, hid the figure. She leant against a tree panting, with her eyes closed. When she looked again at the fire, the smoke had cleared, and she saw herself bound there above the busy tongues of fire.

The shock turned her cold and stiff and she clung to the rough bark of the tree for support. She could recognize some of the people down there. There was a man with a sack, and someone dragged it from him and tipped something out onto the ground. At first she was puzzled; then she saw what it was: books; they were burning her book. She watched, standing rigid until she saw Daniel throw his armful on the fire. Then she slid to the ground and hid her head in her hands and covered her eyes.

So she did not see Alison leave the Knowe and hurry down to the level ground and over the bridge and up the path to the Manse. From his study Matthew heard the banging on the front door, and his mother opening it. Then there were hurried footsteps, and Alison herself opened the door and said:

"Mr. Glendinning, you must come. To the fire. They're burning her—Mary—oh, it's cruel, cruel. You must stop it."

He jumped to his feet, white with dismay, and caught her outstretched hand.

"What are you saying? About burning? It cannot be true."

"It is true—no, don't look like that, it's not Mary herself, it's a scarecrow made like Mary—everyone can see it's her. It's cruel and wicked—you must stop it."

He was already out of the room, and she heard his feet scattering the gravel as he ran.

From the Manse gate, Matthew could see the glow from the fire in the sky. He ran down the road and scrambled up the slope to the Knowe almost on all fours. The fire was blazing hard, and the flames wee beginning to lick round the feet on the top. It was unmistakably Mary—Mary in a brown dress and wearing a copy of the frivolous little bonnet that had caught his eye in the church the first time he had seen her. The crowd was dense, but they had stopped dancing to watch.

He pushed his way to the front, turned to face them and said, "This is wicked and cruel. You must stop it—pull it down with poles." But even as he spoke the words, he realized their futility. As it was, the men he was facing laughed at him.

344

"We canna touch that bleeze wi' polies, Minister. Ony mair than we can pit oot noo."

"It's the May Burning, Mr. Glendinning. An' ye'll no' interfere wi' that, Minister or no Minister."

Their faces were flushed, and not the men's only. And now they had joined hands and were dancing round him—he could recognize them, men and women who had sat under his pulpit week after week. He knew them, but they looked at him as if he were a stranger. And now he was being pushed and buffeted and dragged from one to another, and nothing he said made any difference. They did not even try to hear him. It was like a nightmare. All they wanted was to push him out from among them, and be left to watch the May Burning.

Now he was on the outside of the crowd. Near him was a group of young people. He recognized Phemie Aird, Jenny Niven, Grizel Wauchop and, among the boys Sandy Todd and Dougie Johnston. They were in a group apart, not dancing or singing with the rest, but staring at the figure on the fire with a kind of expectancy that he found puzzling. The flames reached the hem of the dress, and caught the straw beneath. In a moment the guy was one huge flame and the crowd was still and silent. There was a sickening moment, then the head fell into the blaze and vanished. It burnt very quickly, and when nothing was left there was a shout and the dancing started again: and this time Grizel and the rest were dancing too, almost, it seemed to

345

Matthew, as if the burning of the figure had been some kind of signal. He turned his back on the crowd and the fire and looked up at the hills. His eye caught a movement at the edge of the trees, and he saw Mary scrambling down towards the stepping-stones. She had seen it all, then. In a moment he had left the Knowe and was making his way to the Tullises' house.

When he reached it, it was in darkness. No one answered his knock. He pushed open the door and went in. By the glow from the fire, he could see the room was empty. From the back window he saw that there was a light in David's workshop and, as he stood looking out and wondering whether to go to it, he saw Mary come down the path from the gate onto the hill. She was holding her hands crossed on her breast, but it was too dark for him to see her face clearly. She stopped at the workshop door, hesitated, and went in. A minute or two later, he heard her give a wailing cry. When he reached the workshop door, he saw her kneeling on the floor, the light from the candle in the lantern hung on a nail above the workbench falling on David's head as he lay slumped across the worn wooden surface. She heard Matthew's step and looked up.

"My father is dead," she said.

26

THE day after the May Burning was always an unofficial holiday in Dyplin. Traditionally no one was a-stir much before mid-morning, and then women with shawls over their heads scurried out to "fetch milk" for the porridge slowly cooking over the late-lit fires. The men woke to sore heads, furred tongues and brittle tempers, which improved as the day wore on.

But this time they woke to a nagging uneasiness, a sense of having shared in something shameful, of a darkness over the memory of the Burning. It was felt even among the staff of the New School. It was customary for the staff of the New School to attend the Burning till the fire burnt low and then withdraw and continue the festivities discreetly in their houses. But even they awoke with a sense of self-reproach.

Dr. Duffus, morosely sipping his late breakfast tea, said to his wife, "Things got out of hand last night at the Burning. Whose idea was the guy? There was no such thing other years."

"Some of the young people of the village, I think, put it up." Mrs. Duffus had had a word or two with Annie in the kitchen—a weary-eyed and chastened Annie, who had her own weight of uneasiness to carry, quite apart from guilt over a guy. "Annie

347

says there's talk of them wanting a witch-burning—some kind of silly nonsense. I tell you, Henry, Dyplin hasn't been right since the cholera."

"Hmph." Dr. Duffus grunted, being in no mood to discuss the moral state of Dyplin. "It wasn't the guy that worried me so much as the throwing of the books onto the fire. Burning books," said the Doctor, who cherished every volume he possessed as if it were a living creature, "is a wicked thing; and barbarous; like the Inquisition."

"It was Mary Tullis's poems they were burning."

"She should never have written them. She went too far. But burning books is bad. I saw with my own eyes Daniel Rutherford throwing some into the fire."

"Yes. Well, you see, there was something between him and Mary Tullis. . . ."

"Hmph?" The Doctor gave an interrogatory grunt, twitched an eyebrow and said: "Even so, it's no excuse for burning books. And what do you mean 'something between' them?"

"There was talk that he might be thinking of marrying her. But she threw him over—they say."

"Did she now? She's probably well rid of him—I tell you—I've got new thoughts about Daniel Rutherford. He's a good teacher—but to burn books . . ." and the doctor lapsed into a frowning silence.

Daniel himself slept late and heavily, after a night in which he had thrown precaution to the wind, had danced round the fire, flung in the books, felt a vicious pleasure in seeing Mary's effigy burn, and drunk hard—so hard that, when he made his stumbling way to Meg's door, he had slumped across the threshold and lain at her feet, while she jeered at him and, finally, flung cold water over him.

"G'wa hame, Daniel. You're nae use tae me the nicht. Man, you're a fearsome sicht tae be the maister o' the Infant School!"

So Daniel had made his way home through the streets echoing with broken songs and faint shrieks and laughing, and tumbled into his bed, unaware of Susannah's censorious eyes through the crack of her bedroom door.

Meg did not go to bed at all and in the early light was out on the hillside walking away the exultation that had kept her awake.

"I've had my own back on her noo!" She spoke the words aloud. "A'body must hae kent it was her—and oh! the flames licked at her!" But as she climbed up the steep slope of the glen, and stood where she could look down on the cold embers of the fire stirring in the keen morning air, her mood changed. "And yet whit's the guid o' it? I'm still the Meg Annan that's tae be kept oot on the edge of things. Like her tae. I'll awa' hame tae ma bed."

By mid-day, Dyplin was coming back to life: and the tongues were wagging. Burning the books wasn't a bad thing—they should never have been printed—it was a justifiable revenge. But the guy? Wasn't that going too far? Mind you, the umbrella-maker's daughter had brought the cholera, hadn't

349

she? Still, mebbe it was ower rough, putting her up like yon—it had spoilt the Burning, hadn't it? Fowks' feelings had got out of hand—not but what she'd mebbe deserved it. . . .

And then came the news of David's death; and a guilty hush spread from house to house.

When Matthew had heard Mary's words: "My father is dead", he did not believe them. But when he gently lifted David's head and looked at his eyes, and felt the chilling hands, he knew them to be true. Mary, standing quite still, watched him dry-eyed, her face showing no trace of feeling.

"I'll go for help," said Matthew. "Let me take you to the house." But to this she made no response by word or gesture. So he left her, and hurried back through the house to the street. Once there, he stood still. Where was he to go for help? John Campbell he knew to be out of Dyplin. The doctor? The doctor was almost certainly at the Burning, or at a friend's house. But would surely have left word where he was to be found. . . . It would be best, perhaps, to go back to the Manse and get Alison.

So back he went, and found Alison and his mother taking tea, and told them the news. Alison rose at once. "I must go to her," she said, and snatched up her shawl.

"You must go with her, Matthew," said Mrs. Glendinning. "I will go to the doctor's house."

Alison and Matthew said not a word to each other as they hurried back. They went straight through the house to the workshop. David was as he had been when Matthew left. Mary was sitting on the bench beside him, with her hand laid over his, her face still, her eyes dry. She turned her head at the sound of their footsteps, but said nothing.

Alison put out a hand towards her, then drew it back.

Matthew spoke. "We must carry him into the house. He cannot stay here."

Between them, they carried David into the house, and laid him on the couch in the little parlour. Then Alison busied herself building up the fire, and putting on the kettle. She drew Mary forward.

"You're cold, Mary. Come and warm yourself at the fire."

At the word, a shudder went through Mary, and she shrank back. But Matthew took her other hand, and between them Alison and he got her seated by the warmth. In a little while, Alison put a cup of tea between Mary's hands, and told her to drink it. She took a sip, and then sat with her hands curved round the cup as if for warmth: and still she had not spoken. Alison looked a question at Matthew, who shook his head and laid a finger to his lips. His heart was aching for Mary. It seemed to him she had withdrawn into some secret refuge in herself, and shut out what had happened; and he was afraid that a word or act on his part might rouse her to agony. Alison, for certain, was expecting him to utter the words expected from a minister of the gospel at such a time. But she did not know that Mary had seen the Burning. . . . Helplessly he

351

bowed his head and prayed silently and desperately.

The silence was broken by the sound of steps coming up the hill towards the house.

Matthew opened his eyes, and Alison said, "The doctor?"

But the steps stopped at her own door.

"It's John. He said he might be home tonight."

Matthew followed her to the back door, and said, "Mrs. Campbell, Mary saw the Burning. She was among the trees above the Knowe . . . she saw it all."

Alison said nothing, but gave her head a little shake as if she were trying not to hear.

She slipped through the gap in the hedge, and into her own kitchen.

John was taking off his coat, and said, "I thocht you would still be out, seeing it's the Burning."

"Oh John, I'll never go to another Burning in my life. This has been a terrible night—but the worst of it is, David's dead."

"What are you saying?"

"It's true. Mary found him in the workshop. The Minister's there now. Oh John, you should have been here. Maybe you could have stopped it. . . ."

She was half-sobbing, and clutching his sleeve, and John, in alarm, caught her by the shoulders and said, "Alison! What are you talking about? Pull yourself together, woman."

Alison gave a great gulp, swallowed hard, and told him.

John flushed with anger. "And naebody stopped it? Gin I'd been there . . ."

"But you werena. And Mary saw it all. And noo David's dead. And John, she hasn't said a word—she's like a stone. . . ."

But John had already left the house. Alison followed, and entered the Tullises' room in time to see John lay his hands on Mary's shoulders and say:

"Eh, Mary, lass!"

Mary looked up at him, gave a little moan, and laid her cheek on his sleeve for a moment: and then went on staring into the fire, still clutching the cup. John took it from her and drew up a chair beside her, laid a hand over her cold fingers, and sat in silence.

Matthew drew Alison to the back of the room. "As Mr. Campbell's back," he said, "I'll go now. I'll be back in the morning. I—I cannot say the usual words to her—I am afraid of distressing her. . . ."

He was a puzzled and bewildered young man, and Alison felt a surge of kindliness towards him.

"I'm sure your presence has been a comfort, Minister. Words could have done harm."

"I thought so. Now I will go to David."

He went into the parlour, and she heard his voice raised in prayer. Then the door opened and closed, and he was gone.

Alison set about the task of getting Mary to go to bed, but this she refused to do, shaking her head every time it was suggested. It was with great relief that Alison answered a knock at the door and found Dr. Munro on the step.

She told him that Mary had found her father when she came back from the Burning.

"So she saw it? I wasn't there, but I heard about it. A most disgraceful business."

"Aye, it was. I cannot get her to speak or lie down—she hasn't uttered a word since she found him. . . ."

The doctor took John's place beside Mary and said gently: "Miss Mary, this has been a great shock to you. Your father came to me some weeks ago because he had not been feeling well. I found his heart was not good—but he said I was not to tell you, for he would not have you anxious. . . ."

She looked at him and said nothing.

"Now you must go to bed. Mr. and Mrs. Campbell will stay here—" he looked at John, who nodded—"and I will give Mrs. Campbell some medicine which you must take. Otherwise, you will be ill."—"As she is already," he added to himself.

Mary shook her head.

"But I won't leave this house till I see you in bed."

Finally they persuaded her to go upstairs, and Alison put her to bed. Then the doctor gave sleeping draught, and watched till she slept.

Her sleep was long and heavy. When she woke Alison was sitting in a chair by the window.

"How are you?" she said, and waited to see Mary would speak.

Mary put her hands to her head. "My heads feels muzzy—" she paused. "I remember. My father—he's dead."

At least she was speaking: but still with a dreadful calm that made Alison shudder.

Mary sat up, and flung back the bedclothes. "There are things to do. . . ."

Alison said gently, "Don't distress yourself, Mary. All is in order. Flora Martin has been, and your father is lying in his room."

Flora Martin was a small meek little woman who could act as a sick-nurse if required, and who was always called on to "lay out" the dead.

Alison went on, "John will help you, Mary. Don't distress yourself."

So the accepted pattern established itself. A letter was written to David's brother in Ayrshire. A lawyer from Inverforth arrived, offered condolences, told Mary that her father had left her well provided for, and left, puzzled and interested by her unnatural composure, all the more so after he heard something of the events at the Burning when he called in on his old friend Dr. Duffus after his professional visit. Then came the day when Matthew spoke the words of comfort to a little group of Mary, the Campbells, Dr. and Mrs. Munro and Mrs. Glendinning, gathered in David's house. And then they carried him away to the churchyard and the women were left. Mrs. Munro and Mrs. Glendinning left soon after the men. And Alison returned to the room where Mary was with a

355

heavy heart. For Mary had not shed a tear or shown a sign of grief all this while. Nor had anyone referred by a word to the Burning. So it was with mingled distress and relief that Alison saw the tears streaming down Mary's cheeks when she turned from looking up at the hills to face her.

"Oh Alison . . ."

Alison put her arms round her, murmuring comforting words, letting her weep her fill.

When John came back, she was calm again, though her eyes were red and swollen. Alison made a meal, and then Mary said:

"I cannot thank you for all you have done. But tonight you must go back to your own house. I am not afraid to be alone here. And you are just next door."

"The Minister will be coming to see you, Mary," said John. "He told me to tell you."

"Will she be all right?" said John, when he and Alison were back in their own house.

"Aye, I think so. When I saw the tears I felt happier aboot her."

"There was a good number o' fowk in the kirk-yard."

"What? After whit they did tae Mary?"

"Aye. It made me angry tae see them, a' wi' their solemn faces and their black claes. Hypocrites."

Alison was thoughtful. "Mebbe it wasn't hypocrisy. Mebbe they were feeling sorry. . . ."

"Weel they micht. But has it occurred tae you, Alison, that the girl has tae gang on living here, gaun aboot amang the fowk that burnt her books and burnt her image—hoo can she dae it?"

"Of course it's occurred to me, John Campbell. And I dinna see a way out either—except that I'll help all I can. Mebbe she'll leave Dyplin."

Left to herself, Mary wandered round the house. She went into her father's room, and looked at his watch lying on the chest of drawers, and his boots neatly ranged on a shelf under the window. In a cupboard hung his clothes; and in a box on the top was his tile-hat, that he wore to church—that he had worn last Sabbath to church. Suddenly the desolating sense of loss returned to her, and she sat on the bed, looking out of the window, trying in vain to keep down the tears. Better to let them come; and she laid her head on the pillow. Then she heard a knock at the door, and had to rise, dry her eyes, go downstairs and open. It was Matthew.

She stood aside to let him enter, and said, "There's a fire in the kitchen," and followed him there. She sat down and Matthew took the chair opposite her.

This time he was there as the Minister, and he began to speak of David, his character, his sure and certain hope of salvation, the comforts of religion that Mary could rely on. He did it earnestly and sincerely and with an authority that Mary had not seen in him before. Remembering her past pertness, she felt a prick of shame, and when he asked her to kneel and pray with him, she was moved and touched by the conviction of his words. When he rose to go, he took her hand. He had meant to tell her that he had seen the Burning, but a sudden widening and darkening of her eyes warned him that she feared he might be about to do just that. So he merely said, "I want to tell you to remember that you have friends—John and Alison Campbell and myself. I will do anything I can at any time to help you."

He took up his hat and was gone.

27

ALISON had been right. The presence of so many of the men of Dyplin had been a gesture of penitence. There was nothing formal about it: but on the morning of the funeral, man after man had said:

"I think I'll just pit in an appearance at the kirkyard the day. You can look oot ma blacks." And the wives, for the most part making no comment, had done so, and watched their men in twos and threes go to the churchyard gate, before retreating into their houses to discuss things among themselves. Dr. Duffus himself was there, conspicuous for the immaculateness of his funeral blacks and glossy tile-hat. And there were those with wit enough to know that his appearance at David's funeral was an adverse comment on the doings at the Burning.

In the days that followed, there was much discussion; and out of it came a consensus that, while the burning of Mary's book was justified— "she'd nae business, an incomer, tae rake a' that up"—the effigy was inexcusable; and the condemnation was the stronger as they remembered the feelings of glee rather than horror with which they had watched the flames embrace the figure on the fire. Everyone knew the valley had had more than its share of witch-burnings in the old days; there were the stones on Gloom Hill to remind them—and the faint and flickering taste of what their great-grandparents must have felt watching a real burning appalled even Johnny McIndoe in his sober hours. And yet in a sense there had been relief too—as if the fire licking round the figure had been cauterizing and cleansing the blind resentment of months.

Besides, there was the mystery of who had put the guy there. Dyplin hated mysteries, but this proved insoluble, even by the well-known technique of spreading such preposterous rumours that the (approximate) truth was flushed out. So Johnny McIndoe was blamed, boys from the New School ("aye up tae some nonsense"), Craig from the hill, because he was the outsider *par excellence* in Dyplin, and a gang of the displaced miners, angry at the cholera that had driven them away, and which had been brought by the umbrella-maker's daughter. At one session in Mrs. Robertson's parlour someone did tentatively mention Meg's name, but this suggestion was firmly squashed. "Meg Annan kens better than dae onything tae mak' hersel' conspicuous here—mind when she turned up at the kirk?"

Jenny, Grizel, Phemy and the others held one last meeting together a few days after the Burning, in the shed where it had all begun. They were subdued and guilty, and relieved too that it was all over.

"We'll never meet again," said Jenny. "No' like a group, I mean. It's finished. We've done oor penance. So it's all burnt away."

"Ye mean we needn't feel bad any more about Jean?" quavered Phemy.

"Just that. As I said, we've done our penance. It's finished."

"I don't think it is," said Grizel. "What have we done to the umbrella-maker's daughter? Everyone says it was her up there."

Jenny flashed on her. "Well, we didn't do that. That's not our blame. Besides, if it was her, she deserved it. She brought the cholera."

"Aye, and wrote a lot o' lees aboot fowk in a book. You should hear whit my mither says aboot her." This was Sandy Todd.

"But it wasn't lies," said Grizel. "It was true. That's why people are angry."

"That's nothing to do with us," said Jenny sharply.

"But it made it more—more—more—" Phemy was groping for words—"it was more awful it being like a real person." She found the words. "It made us feel more. Not nice feelings," she added in a whisper.

There was silence while they contemplated her words. Then Jenny dismissed them with a jerk of the head.

"There's one thing. Nobody is ever to say that we made the guy. Never. It would all come out—about the cave and everything. We must swear."

So they did. And no one, not even Phemy, broke the promise. And in the end, it was Jenny, as an old woman, who told the truth.

Mary knew nothing of the changes in the tides of feeling in the village. She put to the back of her mind all memory of the Burning, taking refuge in her grief for her father. A letter came from Ayrshire, a kind letter, offering her a home with David's brother. She delayed answering for a few days, and then wrote gratefully, but saying she must have time to think over her future plans. About her future she had not thought at all. She went through the mechanics of housekeeping, cleaning and cooking small meals for herself. Alison did her shopping, for she refused to go into the village. When Alison, after a week, suggested she should make an effort, she simply said:

"I will never go among them again."

It was the nearest she came to referring to the happenings on the night of David's death; Alison said no more.

"It's as if she was shut away inside a box or a cupboard," she said to John.

"Ye're getting imaginative," said John, "but I ken whit ye mean. It's a pity the Meenister's no' weel. He could mebbe have been able tae talk tae her."

For Matthew had been struck down by what Dr. Munro called winter influenza on the evening of David's funeral, having indeed forced himself to be there, and for a fortnight was confined to the

362

Manse. He had been forced to hand his pulpit over to young Mr. McIhone from Hillfoot, a student of divinity, who preached sermons of vast length and vaster irrelevancy, displaying as much of his newly-acquired theological lore as he could pack into them.

Joseph Harvey, reporting to Matthew, said, "The fowk'll be glad tae see ye back, Meenister. An hour on the imperfection of sanctification is a sair trial."

Matthew felt compelled to rebuke such an uncharitable judgement on a young aspirant to the ministry, but was too weak to do more than utter a deprecatory word or two. Nevertheless, he could not help feeling pleased when several of the congregation, unwontedly demonstrative, waited to shake his hand on the first Sabbath back in the pulpit, and say they were glad he was back. He had preached a mild sermon on trust in God—and perhaps the congregation were relieved, for the word had gone round they were to be castigated for what had happened at the Burning. Matthew had indeed meant to preach rebuke and the necessity of repentance, but Mrs. Glendinning had brought word from the village that people were feeling self-reproachful and guilty: and Matthew, experience begetting wisdom, decided that he should leave repentance to the working of conscience; and that a sermon of rebuke might not, in any case, help Mary. For John, when he heard the Minister was improving, had gone to see him, and told him of his and Alison's concern.

"She'll no' set a foot ower the door—I mean, tae gang among fowk. Alison sees her often enough takin' the path up the hill. Sae mebbe if you could see her . . ."

Matthew needed no urging. On his first day out, he went up to Mary's house, though the pull up the hill left him panting, and feeling his legs weak. Mary had heard of his illness, but was nonetheless shocked by his white face and the way he was leaning on the doorway. So there was more warmth in her invitation to him to enter than perhaps there would have been had he been in his usual health. When he was seated back from the fire, for the day was warm and bright, she offered him some of David's whisky, but he refused. Looking at her, now that she was silent, sitting opposite him, he in his turn was saddened by what he saw. She too was pale, her eyes shadowed, the sheen gone from her hair, her head drooping.

"Miss Tullis," he said, "you are still deeply sorrowing for your father."

"Yes." She looked at him. "Do not tell me it is wrong to grieve. I loved him very much; and did not show it enough."

"I would not say it is wrong to grieve; and few of us do show our love enough. I only say we must try to accept God's will and the sorrow it brings."

"Yes." It was a polite assent. He had a sense of a blind being drawn down, shutters being shut. He went on, trying not to feel he was blundering, "You must try not to be driven into solitude. . . ."

364

Her head jerked up, her face flushed, and she said, "Whether I am solitary or not is my affair. Do you know . . ."

"Yes, I know. I was at the Burning. I saw it. Didn't you know? Alison Campbell came for me. I tried to stop it. They wouldn't listen. Didn't you see? I saw you, going down to the stepping stones. That was why I came to the house. Didn't you wonder why I came?"

Her hands were tight on the wooden arms of her chair. "I thought of nothing but my father—but before—before I came down from the hillside, I saw the crowd surging and dancing round someone—it was you?"

"As I said—yes. But it was no use—they wouldn't listen. They pushed me away. . . ."

Mary had turned her head aside, and said, without looking at him, "I do not know how they could be so cruel."

"It was cruel. But perhaps less so than you think."

She looked back at him in anger, and he added quickly, "Wait. Don't be angry. No one in Dyplin knows who put the—the figure on the fire. They were astonished to see it."

"But they knew it was meant for me?"

"Yes."

"Then why did they leave it? Why did no one pull it down?" She stood up and walked over to the window, trying to control her tears. Then anger flared in her again, and she swung round, "And they burned my book! They knew very well what they were doing then! You cannot say they were innocent there!"

"No, they knew what they were doing. It was a bad and a stupid thing to do. But . . ."

" 'But' what?"

"They felt they had a grievance."

Now she was facing him with her head high, and her eyes very bright. "Do you think they had?"

"You want to know if I think you should not have written the book? I am sure you did not write it as an attack on the people—I don't know why you wrote it, but I am not versed in the ways of poets. Perhaps something compelled you. . . ."

"Then you do understand. I thought no one did. Yes, I felt compelled. I suddenly saw that the lives that people led here, that seemed so—so small and uneventful—dull in fact—were not so. That all kinds of things went on—that they didn't need to be great or powerful—or live in big cities—that they were part of the human pattern, and that evil was as much a part of life here as anywhere. I did not write it in scorn. It was more—it was more in sadness. I was not putting myself outside it all." She stopped suddenly. "I have never put this into words before. Do you understand?"

"I think so. But there is more than evil in the lives lived here. Perhaps you gave a one-sided picture?"

But Mary was angry. "I think not. I told you—I

was struck by that drunken Johnny McIndoe—and they chased poor Rob like a beast."

"I do not excuse it."

"And then they did that to me. They didn't come face to face and tell me what they thought. They did that."

Her anger left her. She sat down again, and said, "And I do not know where to go or what to do. I am alone."

Suddenly, she was quite defenceless, and very fragile. Matthew had never seen her like this, not even in the days immediately after David's death. In a moment he was beside her and had caught her hands in his.

"There's no need for you to be alone." And, as she looked up at him in astonishment, "I want you to be my wife."

"Be your wife?" She did not seem to understand, gave a half-smile, shook her head, and said, "But that's impossible."

"It's not, it's not. Don't you know I love you? I have loved you from the very first day I saw you."

Mary drew her hands away from his, shook her head again, and repeated, "It's impossible."

"But why?"

She simply shook her head.

"You don't love me. I know that. But with time. . . . It is not impossible."

"I can't think of it." She groped for some way to

make the refusal less stark, avoiding his eye. "It's only three weeks since my father . . ."

"Of course." He moved away from her. "I always seem to say the wrong thing at the wrong time to you. Very well, I'll say no more for the present. But I want you to marry me."

He made to go, but before opening the door, he said, "But I didn't come here to tell you that. I came, as your minister, to say I think you are wrong to shut yourself off, not to go out. People, I am certain, are sorry for what happened. Besides, it is not like you to show yourself defeated. Good-bye. God be with you."

And he was gone.

Mary sat on the chair, staring at the fire. Her main feeling was irritation. Here was another burden laid on her, for of course she could not marry Matthew Glendinning and would have hurt him by saying so. And she did not want to hurt him. That he loved her she believed—she had known it ever since the night when she had helped him after the fracas in the kirkyard. But it had never entered her head that he would actually tell her so, still less that he would ask her to marry him. That was quite, quite out of the question. But for a minute or two she let herself think what it would be like, remembering the warm fire and the gentle candle-light in the Manse on that dark winter's afternoon which now seemed years gone, when she and her father had been entertained there. Perhaps that was waiting for her—a warm gentle life, sheltered,

humdrum, with small joys and griefs muted by
ordinariness; and no longer feeling outside things,
but part of the pattern. . . .

She jumped from the chair and began busying
herself with preparations for her evening meal. For
of course such day-dreaming was nonsense.
Nowhere was there a warm cosy refuge from life, of
that she was sure. Had not her book, her troublesome book—and she wondered now if she had been
right in making it—been proof of just that? No
matter how small and humble people were, life
would swoop—as the cholera had swooped and
shaken up Dyplin. And besides, to marry Matthew
for the sake of finding a cosy shelter for life was
dishonest. Chopping up potatoes and onions,
grating carrots, she thought of Matthew, and how
wrong she had been in her first thoughts of him.
She had seen him as prim, narrow, dull. Now she
knew him to be courageous, willing to see, anxious
to see, other ways of looking at life, but firm in his
grip of his faith and principles. Too firm, perhaps.
But kind and selfless. Her father had once applied
to him one of his stock phrases of approbation:
'He's a good man''; and that surely summed him
up. But as for marrying him—no, that was not to be
thought of.

But she went on thinking of it till Alison, who
was of course aware of Matthew's visit, tapped on
the door.

"Can I come in? Here's the things you asked me
to get, Mary." Then, as they settled up payment—

"But is it no' time you began going out yourself?'

"That's what Mr. Glendinning said." She knew Alison must know of Matthew's visit.

"He's right, Mary. You shouldna let them get th better o' ye that way."

"He said that too. Alison, that night—" It was th first time she had mentioned it to Alison—"Mr Glendinning said you went to him to stop it. . . ."

"Aye, I did."

"I didn't know. Thank you, Alison."

"Nae need for thanks. You should just put it out of your mind. Forbye, the folk are not happy aboo it either. If you put it behind you, I'll guarante nobody will ever speak a word o' it."

"But every time I go among them I wil remember."

"Ye canna spend your life cooped up in th house. You don't want tae leave Dyplin? Weel, y must just accept what's happened and go on. Mos o' the folk have to do that when things happen."

Mary said nothing; but the following day, whe Alison asked if she needed anything from the shops Mary said, "I'll come with you."

She went round the shops with Alison with cool, a slightly frosty, calm and dignity tha surprised Dyplin. "Ye would have thocht efter whi happened, she'd hae been a bit doon-cast. No' her Cool as a cucumber. 'Thank you, Mrs. Walker' when she took the change and oot the shop wi' na mair ado! She's a queer yin!'"

370

But when they were back, and Alison said, over-eagerly, "Ye see, it was all right, Mary."

Mary, setting down her basket, said, "I hated it. I could feel them watching every movement. I could feel their dislike."

"Och, that's nonsense. Shall I come in for you tomorrow?"

"Thank you, Alison, but tomorrow I'll go alone."

Meg had seen Mary with her basket from a distance, for the first time since the Burning. That evening, up at the Castle, she spoke of her to Daniel. "The umbrella-maker's daughter has come oot o' hiding. I saw her at the shops the day."

Daniel said nothing. He was always uneasy when Meg talked of Mary.

"I wonder she can show her face after a' that's happened." She propped herself on an elbow to look at him. "You were throwing her books in the fire wi' the best o' them, I hear."

Still he said nothing. She dropped back again.

"I was hearing Dr. Duffus was no' awful pleased aboot that."

"Who told you that?" he spoke angrily.

"Oh, different folk. I'm no' sae much on the edge o' things that folk dinna speak tae me. They say Dr. Duffus wanted tae tak' the job o' infant schule-maister awa' frae ye."

"That's a lie! There was never any question of that. If you want to know the truth, what he did say was that he thought the burning of books was not what one expected from a teacher—and maybe he's right."

"Havers! The books deserved tae be burnt. But I'm glad there's nae question o' ye losin' yer job."

She put out a hand and caressed his neck. "Whit wud ye dae gin ye did lose your job?"

He thrust her hand down savagely, and sat up. "There's no question of that."

"Aye, but suppose . . ."

"I'd get another."

"Aye, but would that be all that easy? Gin ye'd lost it fur burning books. . . ."

"Why do you ask, Meg? I'd go overseas maybe—but this is meaningless. There's no question of it."

"I ken. But whiles I think it would be a great thing if you and I could go away overseas taegether—whaur naebody kens us. . . ."

Daniel's heart sank. "Meg, I've told you before, such things are not possible. You forget I have children—and a sister."

"I'm remembering. It was juist a thocht. Noo ye're angry. Dinna be angry, Daniel. Ye ken whiles I like tae tease. . . ."

But, striding down through the fresh green of the trees bordering the road, Daniel felt angry again. Meg was beginning to presume. Perhaps he should break with her—no "perhaps"—he should break with her. But even as he said the words to himself he knew it was not possible for him to give her up.

28

AS the days and the weeks passed, the Burning sank gradually, not into oblivion, but into the vast chest of past history; and Mary, going quietly up and down the streets, became more accepted into the scheme of things than she ever had been. The Burning, with the destruction of her books and the effigy, had made her part of the Dyplin lore; and the resentment against her and the book had been cauterized away. The cholera, too, was becoming past history, smoothed into memory, just as the turves on the graves in the kirkyard had knit themselves together and were part of the whole once more. It would soon be a year since the triumphant Reformists had celebrated the passing of the Bill and the beginning of the Golden Age of Justice and Democracy. The more ardent among them thought of celebrating the anniversary, but the idea wilted and died. For the Golden Age was not here yet, and General Wedderburn in Westminster was a distant figure, and hard to visualize as the rubicund gentleman whom they had so cheerfully carried on their shoulders last December.

Meanwhile it was midsummer; the long days had come; and a spell of bright weather to match them. The New School broke up; after the final ritual of

373

The Examination, in which all the classes were questioned by a body of learned professors from St. Andrews and renowned clergy from Edinburgh, august men with impressive whiskers and black suits and flowing, ample gowns, all guaranteed to create a mute awe in the examinees. The Examination took place in the school hall on the last afternoon of the session. Before it, the Examiners were treated to a lunch by the Governors at which no expense was spared, and where cold salmon and roast duckling and strawberries and cream were washed down with more than adequate supplies of good wine. The menu and speeches were faithfully reported by the *Inverforth Gazette*, which added, as by an after-thought, a brief paragraph declaring that, meantime, the "young aspirants in the groves of Academe" were regaled on succulent mutton pies and lemonade in the school grounds. The Examiners were in benevolent mood by the afternoon, and The Examination, as always, "was passed with credit by all, not least by the Infants who, as in previous years, demonstrated the skill and thoroughness of the teaching they had undergone".

The performance of the Infants was impressive, and one of the professors from St. Andrews went out of his way to speak to Daniel and tell him so. His comments in the same vein to Dr. Duffus met with nothing but a grunt. Professor Ogilvy, mildly surprised by this reaction, decided the Doctor was suffering from indigestion. But the Doctor had not forgotten Daniel's behaviour at the Burning and had heard other whispers too. Dr. Duffus would have given much to remove Daniel Rutherford from his staff, always provided that it could be done without scandal; for the Doctor knew how disastrous scandal would be for the New School, now well set on a course of success and renown. He had even thought of having a quiet talk with Daniel on the advantages for an energetic teacher of going off to, say, Canada, where emigrant Scots would surely welcome a schoolmaster to carry on the tradition of a good Scots education. On the other hand, it might be better just to let things be and wait for the rumours to die—as they surely would. The Doctor could remember many a rumour that had swept Dyplin like a forest fire and died down into cold ashes. Like the rumours about Craig, originating mainly, as far as the Doctor had been able to discover, in the fact that the man preferred books to people.

So the School broke up: the boarders going off in two special coaches to catch the Mail at Inverforth, the local children to pack away their books and settle down to enjoying long days of idleness. Most of the teachers took themselves and their families to the sea-side or to visit relatives. A relaxed somnolence settled on Dyplin, undisturbed by the few summer visitors who came to occupy "rooms with attendance." Even John and Alison went away—to spend two weeks with John's married sister in Glasgow. Daniel sent his children to the Borders, but Susannah refused to go with them. If Daniel went on holiday, she would go; otherwise she saw it as her duty to stay and look after him. Among such of her friends as remained in Dyplin, this gave her a satisfying touch of the martyr; and she had a pleasant time attending a round of tea-parties with other ladies whose responsibilities also kept them in Dyplin, though some of her friends saw her self-sacrifice more as self-preservation.

"I'm glad to see Susannah Rutherford has had the wit to stay at home," said Miss Methven. "Otherwise she might find her brother had vanished for good when she got back—with a certain person!" For rumour had at last caught up with Daniel's friendship with Meg.

Matthew and Mrs. Glendinning stayed on in the Manse, and Matthew set about his wooing of Mary. Meeting her one morning walking up to the house with a heavy shopping basket, he took it from her and carried it to her door. On another day he came with a present of new strawberry jam. He said it was from his mother, though Mrs. Glendinning had protested she saw no reason why she should give jam to Mary Tullis.

"I want a reason for going to see her," he said, so letting his mother know what was in the wind.

"Surely a minister doesn't need the excuse of a pot of jam to visit a bereaved home," she said tartly.

"No indeed. But I was there yesterday."

"Well, you can't go there every day with pots of jam."

But Matthew found other excuses. He took one or two of his books of travel to Mary. This touched her. She knew he found it hard to share her reading habits, her passion for novels and poetry. He was trying to find a common ground in books. She thanked him gravely, and when he had gone, set about reading them. She found them dull but set herself the task of going through them out of a sense of—it was more than obligation, perhaps gratitude.

Love, however, had given Matthew new perceptions.

"You find these books uninteresting," he said, after a week.

Mary looked guilty. "It was kind of you to bring them. . . ."

But Matthew was not offended.

"I see there is no wooing of you from your novels. And I have been thinking that perhaps I have been too harsh in my condemning of them. They could— they do, perhaps—teach us more of the ways of men."

"Oh, they do! they do! But, to be truthful, I do not read them for that, but for pleasure." She smiled at him. "Is that wrong?"

"No, surely not. As long as you remember they are not true." He shook his head ruefully. "I find it hard to understand why you prefer what is not true to what is."

"But didn't you ever listen to stories when you

were a child? Hop o' my Thumb and so on."

"Why yes, my mother told me them. But these are for children. We must put away childish things."

He was suddenly solemn, a way he had, which Mary privately called "putting on his pulpit". But it had ceased to irritate her; she accepted it as a part, and a genuine part, of him.

"But could there not be a truth in untruth? What about the parables?"

She waited for his answer, for she had never before introduced anything of religion into their talk, accepting Matthew's pastoral activities with queer passivity.

He looked grave and said, "You cannot compare the parables of the New Testament with the fictional tales of love and hate which you read."

Mary opened her mouth and quickly closed it. He had been kind, very kind, and this was no time for a Biblical argument. She only said, smiling, "But you do not call my reading sinful?"

Matthew shook his head, and caught her hands. "You are, I think, the least sinful person I know."

Mary drew her hands quickly away and turned aside. "We are all sinners," she said. "You know that."

A few minutes later Matthew left, carrying his rejected books.

But after two days, he was back, this time with Mungo Park's *Travels to the Interior of Africa*.

By now, Alison had realized what was happening. "The Minister's taken to lending Mary books," she said to John. "I'm telling you, he's going to marry her."

"Hoots, woman," said John, "can he no' len' her a book withoot you thinking o' weddings?"

But Alison was not to be put off. "It's no dacent. He's up there every second day. He'll be getting her talked aboot."

John pushed back his plate.

"I canna fathom you women. A'body would think ye'd be glad if Mary wis settled. What does it matter if she's talked aboot? Furbye, ye ken fine that here it's juist no' possible fur fowks no' tae be talked aboot. I've nae doot they talk aboot us—though guid kens there's no' such excitement wi' us!"

"He should be mair discreet, him being the Minister."

"But if he's a man in love, discretion'll no' be the first thing in his mind. He's a man tae, wi' a man's feelings. . . . A' richt," (as Alison looked scandalized) "I'll say nae mair. But there's a bit o' the Daniel Rutherford in us a'. An' noo I'm awa' tae the workshop."

And he seized his bonnet and was gone.

The next day they left for Glasgow. But Alison was right. The tongues had begun to wag. No one, or only the irretrievably bawdy-minded, and they not seriously—suggested anything immoral in the relationship. It was rather a pursing of lips and a shaking of heads. Oh aye, they'd been sorry for her yon time. But they needna hae been. A hard young wumman, grabbing the Minister like yon, when he was daein' his job at the time o' puir David Tullis's death; an' him hardly cauld in his grave. Even the ladies of the New School found it an interesting topic.

"She has been very clever, the little *précieuse*," said Madame Grueber. "She has snatched the handsome young pastor from all the good and sober little girls. She is a deep one, that one."

Mrs. Glendinning came back from the shops tight-lipped, and curiously silent. But one morning, smarting from a series of insinuatory pin-pricks, on her return she rapped smartly on the study door.

"Matthew, I must have a word with you."

"Yes, Mother?"

Her observant eye flickered over the desk. Normally—it being a Thursday—it would have been stocked with books as he settled down to writing his sermons. Today there was only one book beside the big Bible and Concordance which were always there. A glance at the pages sufficed.

"Mattha! Are you reading a book of poetry?"

Matthew turned guiltily. "The poems of Mr. Wordsworth—yes."

"That's the effect of your visits to Mary Tullis! Matthew, the whole place is ringing with you and her."

Matthew looked surprised. "Why?"

"Because you're never away from the lass's door."

"That's not true. I haven't been for two days."

"Matthew, don't make a jest of it."

"I'm not jesting." He saw she was distressed and rose to his feet and laid a hand on her shoulder.

"I have told you before, Mother, I want to marry Mary. I love her. I hope I shall persuade her to love me. And—" his voice hardened—"it is my concern and mine alone. I am the servant of my people, but not to the point that they dictate what my private concerns must be."

"Aye, aye. But a minister's not just like other fowk, Mattha, and a minister's wife is a kenspeckle figure; or rather—" she floundered a little—"just because a'body kens the minister's wife, she has to be that much mair careful no' to be kenspeckle. . . ."

"And who made Mary Tullis 'kenspeckle' as you call it, who made her a conspicuous person in this town, but the people themselves? And now you hold it against her. But, with God's help, I will make her my wife." He smiled at her. "Don't be distressed, Mother. Mary is a good woman."

There was clearly no more to be said but, as Mrs. Glendinning closed the study door, she nodded her head to the solemn grandfather clock ticking against the wall, and murmured, "It wasna just the folk made her conspicuous. She did her bit too."

Matthew disregarded the talk; Mary was unaware of it. He came to the house nearly every day, and she came to look forward to his visits. When he talked of his travel books, his face lit up, and he spoke with as much enthusiasm as if he had actually been to Arabia or to India. She discovered he had a quite deep knowledge of botany, and could name all the flowers he saw on the few walks they took up the hill road. He responded as much as she did to natural beauty. One day, as they stood looking down at a huge beech tree in all its early-summer splendour, she said:

"This is your poetry."

And it was then she lent him her Wordsworth.

But he seldom smiled; and never laughed. There was a solemnity about him which at first made her a little uneasy. It seemed as if he were afraid of laughter; as if he felt it was wrong to laugh in the face of existence and the great facts of sin and redemption. But as time passed, she came to accept this as part of him.

One day, coming down from a visit to a lonely shepherd's cottage in the hills, he overtook her walking on the slope of Gloom Hill. It was a breezy day, and there was colour in her cheeks and a sparkle in her eye which he had not seen since David's death. They walked side by side, and suddenly she said:

"I feel I could fly," and, catching up her skirt with both hands, she began to run down the slope. Matthew hesitated for a moment, took off his hat, and followed, his black coat-tails flying. He ran with long awkward strides, passed her, placed his foot awkwardly on a tussock, fell and rolled over,

ending up sprawled on his back while his hat
bowled on downhill. Mary stopped, saw he was
unhurt, and began to laugh. Matthew sat up, looked
at his hat, looked at her, and laughed too, hearty,
unthinking laughter. She offered him her hand, but
he sprang lightly up without her help.

"I couldn't help laughing," she said. "I'm
sorry."

"You need not be." He was still laughing. "I'm
not hurt. But I suddenly thought, what would
Joseph Harvey think if he saw the Minister
sprawled on the hillside and his hat rolling away
from him."

"Do you know, I have never seen you laugh
before."

His hat had come to rest and he picked it up and
ran his hand over it.

"I did not think I was so solemn. But it is true, I
do not laugh much. I don't think I've laughed like
that for years."

He was about to put his tall black hat on again,
but Mary said quickly:

"Don't put it on."

He looked surprised.

"You will stop laughing if you put it on. Why
must you always wear a hard black hat like that?"

He turned it slowly in his hand. "It is expected of
me."

"But why?"

He stood looking into it, the laughter gone. "It is
part of the uniform of my calling." His eyes met

hers, appealing for her understanding. But all she said was:

"You need not wear it out here. Besides, you have to hold it on all the time for fear the wind lifts it."

So Matthew carried his hat, and Mary watched the wind blowing through his hair.

They parted at the gate in the wall of her garden, and Mary went into the house, not letting herself look towards David's workshop, knowing that she could not put off for ever the task of going in to clear it. Out on the hillside she had for the first time felt free of her grief. Now, entering the silent house, knowing that John and Alison were away, that she was quite isolated, the emptiness smote her, and she shivered, and crossed her arms and tried to hug the chill away.

But the sense of loss weighed heavily. She could not keep down the tears, and wandered through the house seeing her father at every turn. In time the mood passed; she dried her eyes, and made herself a meal of porridge and eggs. She drew the table to the window so that she could look up to the hills as she ate. She thought of Matthew. There was a refuge from loneliness: into the warm firelight of a life in the Manse and with Matthew's love to shield her. She knew now that she could marry him as far as loving went. It was not the loving she had felt for Daniel—if that was love at all and not mere desire. But yes—she could envisage life as Matthew's wife, and it was no longer an impossibility. But there was the other thing: the other thing that had to be told:

that made it impossible, and that she could not bring herself to tell. Perhaps she would never have to—perhaps Matthew could be brought to see that marriage was not possible without her having to tell him.

"But you are not making it clear to him that it's not possible," said her inner voice. "You should not have allowed him to come about you as he has been doing. You are making the final hurt worse and worse. You are being cruel."

But she silenced the inner voice. Perhaps Matthew would never ask her again (though she knew this was untrue), and so the matter would not arise. It was only now, when she thought of the bleakness of life without Matthew's visits, that she realized how much she depended on them to keep at bay a great black wretchedness. Then she began to think that perhaps her speaking need not be the end of it all. She was too honest ever to think of not speaking. But if she was honest with Matthew, that was surely enough. No one else need know. If Matthew could accept it—then perhaps she could enter that warm and sheltered life she imagined with him.

So Matthew went on coming; and read Wordsworth; and began to make unspoken plans for a life with her.

By the time Alison and John returned it was taken for granted in Dyplin that the Minister was to marry the umbrella-maker's daughter.

John's gig had been driven by an apprentice to

meet them off the mail coach at Inverforth. When he and Alison reached the house, they could see smoke curling from the chimney—Mary had been in to light the fire, and on the table in the kitchen was a little pile of provisions she had bought for them and a plate of freshly-baked scones. But she herself was not to be seen. While John carried in their box and parcels, Alison threw off her shawl and bonnet, and opened the back door and looked up the garden, clucking her tongue at the weeds that had grown. The kettle that Mary had set on the hob, and which was gently singing, she brought to the boil on the fire and made tea.

John, sitting down at the table, drew a deep breath and said, "I like being home. Glesga's an interesting enough place but I couldna live there."

"Nor me neither."

"I see Mary had the fire lit."

"Aye. She's a good neighbour." Alison put down her cup. "Oh John, what are we to do about her?"

"Why, naething. Whit had ye in mind tae dae?"

"I dinna ken. I wish you had never gone tae see old Robert Macfadyen, even though he is your father's cousin."

John gave a sigh. "I kind o' wish it masel'. And maun say that what he telt me aboot Mary upset me—aye, it upset me a lot. But when ye think o' it Alison, the fact that we noo ken that Mary had love-bairn afore she cam here doesna make her different. She's still the lass that we've come tae-tae like; and that saved my life."

"I know all that, John. But it does make a difference. It shouldna, but it does. And John, we've learnt aboot it. Suppose other folk do?"

John sat silent for a moment. "I dinna think it's likely. It was just a chance that David Tullis's name came up when I was talking tae Robert."

"Aye, but . . ."

" 'But' what?"

"But Robert's daughter is married tae Andrew Stott's brother. And the Stotts were tae be in Glesca too."

John pursed his lips and raised his eyebrows.

"Weel, we can only hope they hear naething. Stott's a self-righteous auld deevil—and ye needna pretend tae be shocked, Alison, ye ken it' true. And Ishbel Stott isna much better—though mebbe no' sae much since puir Jean's death."

"What do you mean?"

"I shouldna hae said that. But when I—when Jean was being pit in her coffin, puir lassie, I heard her mother whispering tae hersel', 'Jeannie, Jeannie, why did ye no' tell me?' An' I'm thinking yon was no accident. . . . But I shouldna hae said onything—I hear mony a thing that's no' fur telling. And we'll never, no never, tae onybody, say a word aboot Mary."

Later, when the long clear twilight lay over the hills, Alison heard voices and, looking through the curtains, saw Matthew saying goodnight to Mary at her front gate. They shook hands with quiet decorum, but Matthew's light-hearted step as he swung his way downhill told Alison much, and she shook her head and sighed.

Next morning she saw Mary. She was certainly less woebegone than when John and Alison had left on holiday; but quiet and composed as usual. Alison now knew her well enough to realize that Mary kept her feelings very much to herself. But next day, when John came in for his dinner, he found Alison flustered and worried.

"They're all saying that the Minister's going tae marry Mary."

"Who's 'they'?"

"Everybody."

"Hmph. You mean all the clashing weemen in the place."

"Maggie McArdle say he's proposed."

John laughed.

"Did Mary say onything? No? Weel, d'ye no' think she'd tell you if it was true?"

"I don't believe it myself. But John, supposing he does? It wouldna be right for him tae marry a girl who—who . . ."

John pushed back his chair. "It's nane o' oor business."

"But he should ken."

"The only person whae has a richt te tell him is Mary hersel'."

"Suppose she doesn't?"

It was seldom John ever showed anger to Alison but now it broke forth. He did not shout—John never shouted—but when roused he had a harsh grating way of speech that Alison hated.

"Alison Campbell, do ye no' ken Mary weel enough yet tae be shair that she'll tell him? She wudna dae a thing like that—marry him and no' tell. She's honest as the day."

"She wasna honest as the day aboot her book."

"She was—as soon as she saw someone else getting the blame, she was. An' I tell you she'll no marry the Meenister withoot telling him. An' then it's up tae him."

Alison said no more. The long days passed with the weather set fair. Matthew's visits became daily: all his stiffness went; he talked freely and easily; and seriously too; but not weightily, not ponderously; not "putting on the pulpit". Mary saw the danger—and every night said to herself she would tell him tomorrow; and then could not do it. She began to take it for granted that it would not make all that difference, he would understand; for she had found in him a charity towards people that she had not thought him capable of. But, though she kept putting off the moment of speech, she never varied in her resolve that the words must be spoken; only now it was to be "when" he asked her once more to marry him, not "if".

The holiday-makers began to trickle back. Matthew had been waiting till his elders were all once more in Dyplin. When Andrew Stott came back, a Session meeting was called.

On the day of the meeting, the weather broke,

thick mist covered the hills; the steady summer rain drummed down, battering the flowers, sluicing off the leaves. John, who hated meetings of any kind and usually sat dumb from start to finish, went off grumbling.

"The session house'll be cauld and damp. Joseph never lights a fire in it frae April till October. And it'll be that dark we'll need candles, and there's naethin' mair dreich than candlelicht mixed with darkened day. Forby, I met Andrew Stott, and he telt me he was 'going to raise a certain matter' at the session—an' I couldna help wonderin' whit it micht be. . . ."

Alison found it hard to settle while he was away. At last, after two hours or so, she heard his footsteps on the path, heavy and slow. He came in shaking the water from his hat and hanging his coat over a chair to dry. Then he moved to the fire and stood with his hands on the mantelpiece looking into the flames.

"Something happened," said Alison. "Andrew Stott . . ."

"Aye. We got through the meeting, and at the end, when the Minister asked if there was anything anyone wanted to say, Andrew Stott said he wanted to bring up a matter. Ye ken he's aye bringing up things—generally something somebody's done or not done that's against—or that he thinks is against—the true doctrine. He kens the catechism backwards, a' the reasons annexed included. . . ."

"John, I'm not interested in Andrew Stott and the catechism. What did he say?"

"Aye. Weel, he looked a' roon the table, and then he stood up, and said he was shair we a' agreed that a minister should be circumspect in a' his doings, and no' given tae conduct that would provoke ony talk that micht no' be in accordance wi' the dignity o' his office. I could see the Minister stiffen, and his jaw set and a cauld steely look in his e'en—I canna think hoo I ever thocht he was a kind o' softish man—and he said: 'Are you referring to anything in my conduct, Mr. Stott?' There was a rasp in his voice that put me in mind o' a heavy file on iron. But it didna hae ony effect on Andrew. He went on in that calm voice o' his, saying that only a desire for the good o' the Kirk was making him speak. What he wanted to say was that he thought it was unbecoming in a minister to let his name be linked to a young woman's so that—and these were his very words—'in every shop and on every street corner, they're spoken together'. Then he sat down, and there wisna a sound, till the Minister got to his feet and said, awful quiet-like, but I could see his chest heaving under his black coat, and his hands held the edge o' the table like vices: 'I deny you, Andrew Stott, or anyone else, the right to remark on my conduct in such terms. But as a matter of courtesy to my session, I will tell you that I intend to ask the lady in question to be my wife'.

"There was a kind o' sigh went roon the table as a'body sat back and breathed again. And then Stott was on his feet again, and leaning over the table, and wagging his finger at the Minister, and saying: 'That you must not do. You cannot take to the Manse of Dyplin a fallen woman, who has borne a child out of wedlock!' "

He stopped. Alison put a hand on his arm. "Go on."

"Ye've heard folk say that so-and-so was 'stricken', Alison. Weel, that just describes what Stott's words did tae the Minister. He staggered—I saw it—went white as if all the blood had left his heart. And then he drew himself up, and began the Benediction, and not a word was spoken and we came away, and no one even said a 'Goodnight'."

"Oh John! Poor man! Poor Mary. And there's nothing we can do."

"Nothing. I think he's with her now. I thocht I heard steps behind me coming up the brae, and it's no' likely tae be onybody else."

Mary was surprised when she heard Matthew's knock on her door, knowing that there was to have been a Session meeting that evening. She opened the door eagerly, saw his face white under the black hat, stood aside to let him enter, and followed him slowly into the room. He stood in the middle of the floor, clutching his hat, crushing the brim. He said:

"Is it true? Mary, is it true?"

She did not need to ask what he meant.

"Yes."

"Then why, why didn't you tell me?"

"I was going to. If you had asked me again to

392

marry you I would have told you." She paused and looked at him. "You must not think I would not have told you."

He looked very earnestly at her. "Yes, I believe you. But oh! I wish you had told me before—before I had made such plans—before I had gone so deep in love."

"You have stopped loving me? Since this afternoon?" Her hurt made her scornful. "That was a fine love, Mr. Glendinning."

"You would not say that if you knew what I feel at this moment. It is agony." She could see the sweat glistening on his forehead. "But if I had known before, I would have fought it down; I would have kept away from you. You have been most cruel."

"Has it made so much difference? Shall I tell you how it happened?"

He shook his head, but she went on:

"Yes, I shall. You are not the only one to know pain in love. I loved a man in Glasgow—oh, but deeply, deeply. And he me. His father was a great merchant, and wealthy. We were to be married, but his father sent him on a long trading voyage before we were to be married—I think he was disappointed that his son was marrying an umbrella-maker's daughter. And before he left, we lay together; and his boat was lost in a gale off Cape Horn; and I bore his child and it died. Don't talk to me of the pain of love!"

Tears were bright in her eyes as she turned her

head aside. Tenderness and pity swept over him, and he reached for her hand. But she snatched it from his touch.

"No. You have stopped loving me."

"Mary, Mary, I have not stopped loving you. I do not think I ever shall. But I am not my own master. I cannot do anything that would bring reproach on the Church I serve."

It was only afterwards that the brutality of what he had said came home to him. At the time he could think only of his own cruel dilemma.

At his words Mary flushed scarlet. In a low, calm voice she said, "Now you must go." She turned aside and did not look at him again.

When the door had closed, she stood rigid in the room, battling against black desolation. She could not even weep, so deep was the hurt. The low cloud over the hills darkened the room, and the rain trickled down the little window panes. Suddenly she felt as if she were choking. She locked the front door, went to the back kitchen and put on her heavy boots. Then she found her heavy cloak, pulled the hood over her head, and stepped out of the back door into the coolness and wet. She locked the door, and put the key, as always, in a niche under the flagstone. Then she gathered her cloak round her and went up the path towards the freedom and consolation of the hills, rain and tears trickling down her face.

29

MARY went straight up the slope to the crest of Gloom Hill. The long grass was heavy with rain and soaked her boots and weighted the hem of her skirt. She concentrated on making her way up, striding from tussock to tussock, trying to avoid the soft green grass between, now spongy with moisture; and all the while, tears ran down her cheeks. She reached the crest, drawing sobbing breath, shuddering as she passed the witch's chain and stones, and made her way down the other side. The hill-tops were invisible behind the cloud: even Craig's farm was blotted out; and the rain slanted down. She crossed the track and entered the trees above the glen, found the shelter of a huge oak-tree whose leaves reduced the rain to a gentle trickle, and leant against the trunk to draw breath.

Her first feeling was one of relief and solace, to be away from people, house, chairs, tables, pots, pans, alone out here. The air was full of sound—drumming of the hard rain on the trees, the gentle patter and plop of the drops from the branches just above her, and the distant growling of the burn below, beginning to fill with the rush of water from the hills. She was no longer crying. The fierceness of her grief and anger had died down. She was numb with a bleak despair that she had never felt before, as if she had been battered into passivity. Perhaps if Matthew had not come so quickly after David's death, after the other thing, she would not so easily have brought herself to think that it might be possible for her to find a haven and a refuge in marrying him and settling down to life in what she still visualized as a warm firelit room, hushed against storms outside. Had she had time to battle through the pain and sorrow on her own, she might have seen it was hopeless. But he had been like a life-raft to a drowning man—pulling her out of the depths of loss and rejection; she had clung to him, almost unaware of it, until it seemed impossible to give him up. She had spent long hours arguing with herself that what had happened in Glasgow need not mean the end of it; there was the story of Mary Magdalene in the Bible; and the woman of Samaria; and had not people pointed the finger of scorn at Mary the Mother of Jesus herself? Matthew knew all this too; and if he loved her as he said, surely it would be all right.

When she heard him say, "I cannot do anything that will bring reproach on the Church I serve," it was as if he had lifted a great cudgel and struck her across the face.

Even now, remembering, she turned her head aside as if from a blow. She felt the bark of the tree against her cheek, and gave a little twisted smile. She had dreamed of a warm firelit room; and here she was, under a tree with the rain-drops pattering.

She looked up at the hills darkening under the twilight and mist. The rain was less fierce. She held her cloak round her, stepped out from the protection of the tree onto the road, and went up towards the castle, bending her head under the rain. She had no purpose, except to be alone, and let the rain and the effort of walking through it numb thought and feeling.

The road dipped down and then swung round to the castle. She took the path up to the hills. It ran close by the Burn of Sorrow that came down from the hills and joined the Burn of Care below the castle. As she climbed up the path she heard the sound of a little waterfall which she had often stopped to watch. It had a full and angry note, and she left the path and picked her way over the slippery grass to the little path that ran along the bank just above the burn. The waterfall, upstream a few yards, fell into a very deep pool between sheer cliffs of shining rock. The water here was still and black, and the stretch was known simply as the Black Pool; but tonight there was movement in it as the spate of water from the hills drove through and the rain dimpled it. Mary clung to a young birch tree and peered down.

From her earliest years she had been fascinated by deep water, at once attracted and repelled. On the Ayrshire farm where she had spent her childhood holidays there was a little burn where she played for long hours in the shallows. At one point it ran in a deep pool through an outcrop of rock. She would ask her father to take her there, and she would stand on the brink, staring down, clutching his hand, never daring to go alone. The pool under the Martyr's Bridge drew her in the same way; but there she had the reassurance of the high stone parapet. Here was nothing between her and the water but her hold on the tree. She stared down. In the half-light, the pool was a black pit, with a gleam at the foot where the surface stirred. Her muscles contracted; little shivers passed over her; but she could not lift her eyes from the dark sliding movement. Suddenly, with a shudder, she left hold of the tree and turned to scramble back to the security of the path. Her foot caught on an exposed root and she fell back. Her cloak spread out like a bat's wing, and billowed round her as she struck the water; the rain and the waterfall drowned her cry of despair.

The rain died out overnight. By morning the sun rose. Old Betsy Black up in the castle, opening the door at the foot of the tower, found the courtyard full of puddles but a clear sky above. From a lean-to shed opposite came a plaintive "moo". Bluebell, her cow, was hungry and her udder heavy. "I'm coming, lass," called Betsy, and was soon milking her into a wooden coggie. That done, she untied Buebell from her stall, and led her to the castle gate, talking to her, as she always did.

"Whaur'll I tether ye the day, ma bonny beast? Eh, but last nicht's rain was fearsome. Ye've pretty well cropt a' the gress roon here. Wull we try yon fine patch ower the burn, below the Black Pool? If the steppin' stanes is nae covered—fur I'm thinkin, there'll be a fine spate in the burn the day."

Bluebell followed her meekly on the end of the rope, and Betsy led her down towards the Burn of Sorrow. But before she left the track to take the little path down to the water and the stepping stones, she stopped.

"It's nae use, Bluebell. The stanes is covered, and I'm no' juist prepared tae kilt up my skirts and paddle over. Sae ye'll hae tae be contentit this side."

She moved a few steps down the path to view the spate. "Aye, I've seen it waur. But it's a lot fuller than yestere'en."

She bent forward, peering under frowning brows. "Guid sakes! Whit's that?" In her excitement she dropped the rope. "It's a wumman. Ma God? It's a drooned wumman."

She scrambled down the path, muttering amazement. Mary lay prone on the shingle at the edge of the water, her shoulders and head out of the stream, her face turned sideways, one cheek in the mud, the other shining under the sunlight, her hair a matted tangle, and the rest of her body held against the stepping-stones. The surge of the spate when she fell had carried her out of the pool to the shallows and, in her last gasp of consciousness, she had clawed her way to the shingle—her hands were still clutching the mud and pebbles. Betsy put her hands under Mary's armpits, hauled, and managed to pull

399

her a few inches up onto the verge. Muttering and grumbling, she heaved and pushed, until Mary was out of the water, and lying in a patch of sunlight on the grass. Only then did Betsy feel for life—fingering her wrist, holding a blade of grass to her lips. She thought it stirred, she thought she felt a tiny pulse. She straightened up.

"I canna get her up tae the castle. Whit's tae be done?" She looked round vaguely. Bluebell's brown and white rump was just disappearing round a bend in the direction of Craig's farm. Whenever Bluebell broke loose, as she frequently did, she made for the good pasture round Craig's steading.

"Eh! the canny beast. Craig's the man tae help. I'll juist awa' after Bluebell." She looked at Mary, drew the tangled hair back from her face, and folded back her sodden cloak.

"That'll let the the sun warm you, whae-ever ye are. Guid ken's whit's at the back o' this." And, shaking her head, she set off after Bluebell.

Craig had just finished his breakfast porridge when there was a knocking at the door, followed by Betsy's appearance beside his chair.

"Ma certes, Betsy, but ye startled me! Whit dae ye want? Is it that coo o' yours again?"

"Na, na, Craig. Oh aye, she's here, but that's no why I'm here. There's a drooned wumman doon there at the Black Pool. No' richtly drooned—I think there's life in her. But I canna shift her masel'."

"What?" He was staring at her incredulously.

"I'm tellin' ye. Come on, Craig, harness yer powny tae yer cart, and we'll fetch her up." She pulled his sleeve. "I'm nae that doited, Craig. I mebbe speak tae ma coo, but I'm no' at the stage o' seein' drooned fowk that are no' there!"

Craig did as she asked, harnessed his sturdy Highland pony to the cart and led it down to the stepping-stones. Mary had not moved at all, and at first Craig thought she was dead. But then he too felt a movement in her wrist, and between them Betsy and he got her into the cart.

"Ye can tak her tae the castle," said Betsy. "I'll soon hae the fire lit."

"That's a kind thocht, Betsy," said Craig, "but I think I'll tak her up tae the ferm. Mirren'll look efter her. I ken her. She's Mary Tullis, the umbrella-maker's dochter."

Betsy's old small eyes widened. "Her that they burnt? Puir lassie. Mebbe that's why she did it."

Craig said nothing, being indeed greatly shocked at finding the woman was Mary. He helped Betsy into the cart, and then led the horse back to the farm. He halted the cart at the door, opened it, and shouted, "Mirren!"

Mirren came through from the kitchen, and looked not too welcomingly at Betsy, who had climbed from the cart and was standing by it.

"See here," said Craig, "help me get the girl oot."

Mirren looked at Mary in blank surprise. "That's

the one cam' here afore. What fur are ye bringin' her back, Craig?"

"Because she's juist been dragged oot the burn, and is mair nor hauf drooned. We'll tak her tae the wee room, and then you and Betsy here'll tak' the claes aff her. Ye'll hae a goonie ye can pit on her. An' I'll awa' and pit bricks tae heat in the oven, and we'll pit them roon her in bed and get some warmth in her."

So it was done. In a surprisingly short space of time Mary was in bed with hot bricks wrapped in flannel at her feet and sides, and Craig was trying to get whisky between her lips with a little horn spoon, while Betsy and Mirren hung her clothes by the kitchen fire.

"It's no' the first time I've done this fur that lassie," said Mirren. "She cam' here afore—oot o' a day o' mist naebody in their sense wad hae been oot in." She shook out Mary's cloak. "She's a queer one. But whit fur did she dae it, that's whit I'd like tae ken."

She and Betsy looked at each other knowingly, but before either could speak, Craig shouted:

"She's coming round. She's opening her eyes."

30

IT was two days before Betsy went down to Dyplin for her weekly shopping, and could tell the story of her finding of Mary at the Black Pool. For once, and gratifyingly, she was the centre of attention in every shop she went to. She did not exaggerate her story; it needed no embroidery; but by evening it had grown and flourished so that when Matthew at last heard it, he stood for a minute quite still—"I thocht he would fall doon wi' the shock," said Mrs. Walker, who had told him— and then turned and strode up to John's house as fast as the steep slope allowed. He knocked at the door but did not wait for it to open. John and Alison were at their evening meal, and looked up in surprise as he burst into the room.

"Tell me," he asked, breathing fast, "is is true? Is Mary dead! They say—they say she threw herself into the Black Pool and is dead."

John had risen to his feet. "She was found in the Black Pool—that's certain. But I wis speaking wi' Craig frae the hill no' hauf an hoor syne, and Mary's alive, and in his hoose."

"I thank God," and Matthew collapsed into John's big chair, leaned back, and closed his eyes.

"Aye, sae dae we." John's voice was harsh, and Alison looked at him in trepidation. She knew that note. "We havena set eyes on her since the nicht o' the Session. It wis the morning efter that that auld Betsy fra the castle found her. You saw Mary that nicht? Aye, I thocht sae. Whit did ye say tae her, that would mak her, Mary, try tae—tae end her ain life?"

Matthew was silent, and John turned away with a heavy shrug. "I micht hae kent you wouldna say onything."

"No, wait. I find it hard to speak about—about my personal feelings. I loved Mary—I love her—but I told her—I had to tell her—that, as a minister of Christ's Church, I could not marry a woman who—who . . ." his voice faltered.

John stared at him. "Ye tell't her that? Juist like that? Man, did ye no' mind hoo your Maister dealt wi' the woman taken in adultery? The Bible's fu' o' women that nae doot you could ca' 'fallen', but they're no' blotted oot o' the Scriptures—ye'll mind Rahab the harlot? Aye, and ye'll ken—fur I'm juist an ordinary joiner that's read the Book—but ye'll ken there's a Rahab listed amang the earthly forebears o' Christ himsel'. Oh man, man, whaur wis yer charity that suffers long and is kind?"

"Wheesht, John, you're goin' ower far," said Alison, scandalized at the disrespect to the Minister, and obscurely troubled by the fervour of John's defence of Mary.

But Matthew gestured to her. "No, let him speak, Mrs. Campbell."

"I've nair mair tae say. Except that if your words

drove Mary tae dae whit she did dae, meenister or nae meenister, ye hae a load o' guilt tae carry."

"Do you think I am not feeling that? It's less than an hour since I heard—I feel as if it were years." John kept his back to him, and Matthew turned to Alison—kind, troubled Alison.

"You have to understand. I cannot do anything to bring my Church into disrepute—" he saw John's impatient jerk of the head—"or difficulty. And marrying a woman who—think of the talk, the smirking behind hands. The life of the Kirk would be—" he searched for a word—"blemished." He appealed to Alison. "You understand?"

"Oh yes. I ken fine whit it wud be. The Kirk would lose respect. It would lose authority. I—I dinna think ye could dae it, Mr. Glendenning."

John swung round. " 'Respect'! That's a' ye think o'! I thocht the the Kirk wis fur sinners—I thocht there was a parable aboot lost sheep! An, mebbe if a sinner—if ye ca' Mary that—I dinna—was taken as wife o' the Minister, the fowk that really matter wud be encouraged tae think better o' the Kirk. Like yoursel', Meenister, I see fowk when life's gi'en them a dunt—and when life's finished wi' them—and I've thocht a lot aboot the meaning o' things—aye, and searched the Scriptures—but I dinna seem tae hae reached the same answers as you."

"John!"

Alison was near to tears, but Matthew laid a hand on her arm and said, "He's right to speak out. So must I. You, John Campbell, are not the minister of the congregation. Am I to do something that will scandalize and hurt faithful souls who had worked for and grown up in the Kirk? Do you think it was easy for me? I tell you, I love Mary Tullis; I want her for my wife. But I cannot let my selfish desires over-rule my duty as a minister of the Church—I cannot." His voice broke and he fumbled for words. "That is what I say to myself, most of the time. And then another voice says that I am making that an excuse because I am not strong enough to face all the trouble and difficulties that would come if I did marry her."

"I thocht you said you loved her?"

"I do."

"Weel, then . . ."

"I cannot let love blot out duty."

"I give up." John looked at Matthew. "But I see I was mebbe misjudging you. I've tellt ye whit I think. But it's fur you tae decide."

"Yes." Matthew picked up his hat. "You say she is at Craig's."

"Aye, and likely tae be there a whiley. She's gey weak," he said.

"I shall go and see her. Goodbye, Mrs. Campbell." He held out a hand to John. "Goodbye."

John shook his hand and showed him to the door, and came back to a silent Alison.

"Weel, Alison?"

"Weel what?"

406

"Ye're not pleased wi' me."

"I dinna think you should hae spoken like that tae him. For one thing, he's the Minister, and for another—but you mebbe didna see it—he's going through agonies and he didna need you tae preach at him."

John looked slightly uncomfortable. "Weel, I got kind o' carried awa'. But the thocht o' Mary, trying tae dae awa' wi' hersel' made me angry."

"Aye, but ye're taking it that she did try tae kill hersel'. Have ye no' thocht that it micht hae been an accident? I ken Mary as weel as onybody, and I do not think she would dae a thing like that. Men," said Alison with a sniff, "are aye ready to think a woman'll be ready tae die for love o' a man. Some mebbe will. But I dinna think Mary's one o' them."

And she refused to discuss the matter further.

Two days later Mirren looked out of the window of the parlour at Craig's farm, where she was giving Mary a glass of warm milk, and said, "Losh me! That looks like the Minister coming up the path. I dinna ken a'body else wud be coming up the hill wi' a black coat and a hat. It'll be you he's comin' tae see—Craig tellt him a while ago no' tae bother comin' tae see him." She rubbed her sleeve over the table to take away the dust, for caring for such furniture as Craig had came low in Mirren's scheme of things. She put another log on the fire, blew the dust from the mantelpiece, straightened her apron and stationed herself near the front door.

Mary laid down her book and waited, very still, her hands in her lap clasped tightly.

She heard his knock, and Mirren's voice bidding him enter. Then he was in the room, and Mirren had closed the door behind him.

"Mary!" He moved quickly to her chair and held out both hands. She said nothing, looking at him with her dark eyes in which he could read nothing at all; she might have been looking at a stranger.

"Mary!" he said again.

She unclenched her hands and said, "Why have you come?"

Matthew did not answer. He saw that one of her cheeks was marked and bruised, and she was very pale. Her hair looked unkempt. She was so different that he could not speak, choked by remorse and pity.

She frowned a little and said, "Why have you come?"

"I had to see you."

All the words he had prepared went from him and he could only say, "Why did you do it? Was it because of me? Of what I said?"

She frowned again. "I don't understand."

"Why did you—" he could not say it—"they said you had been found dead, in the Black Pool. Why—"

"Ah. So they are saying I threw myself in, that I tried to kill myself. Of course, they would."

Her voice was wearily scornful. "Well, I didn't. I

caught my foot on a root and fell. No one will believe it, but that is the truth."

"Then I didn't—it wasn't—oh, Mary!"

He sat down on a chair by the table and laid his head on his hands.

Mary looked at him and said, "What is wrong?" Then, as he made no move: "I understand. You thought, you truly thought that I had tried to kill myself because of what you said?"

"I did not mean—I did not realize what I was saying. Mary, you must understand—if I didn't love you so much, it wouldn't matter so much. I didn't know what I was saying—I could not choose my words. . . ."

"It was not the choice of words. It was their meaning that was like a blow." Her sense of hurt revived, gave her the means to wound. "Why did you come here? To salve your conscience, worried in case you had driven me to try to kill myself? Except that you can't take back the words you said."

"Mary . . ."

"Yes, now I am being cruel. I am learning to be cruel. You and others have taught me." She had risen from her chair and was walking up and down the little room. Suddenly she stopped and swung round to face him.

"And I was coming to love you: so much that I made myself think it wouldn't matter, that you would understand. . . . Why do you think I didn't tell you sooner? Because I didn't want you to stop coming to be with me. . . ."

She thought he was going to speak, but when he said nothing, she went on, "You didn't come here to unsay those words, did you? You still feel you would be betraying the Kirk if you married me? Do you?—No, do not tell lies."

"I will not lie. I have thought—I have battled—to find the truth, and I have not found it. I want you for my wife; I shall never want another woman as I do you. But—since there must be honesty—you have born a child—and this could be a stumbling-block for my people in the Kirk. . . ." He looked at her, afraid that her anger would flare again. She was looking at him sadly, and suddenly he took her hands and said, "We can go away somewhere; leave Dyplin; I could be a schoolmaster. . . ."

"No, Matthew—" it was the first and only time she called him by his name—"that is impossible—both for me and for you. If I can't be the Minister's wife, I can't be anything else. And even if you ask me now to be the Minister's wife, I should say no. I could not bear it. Goodbye." And she held out her hand.

"I shall see you again."

"Possibly. But I must tell you I shall never spend another night in Dyplin."

From the little window she watched him go down the track, till the slope of the hillside hid him. Then she went upstairs to the little bare bedroom and lay for a long time, sorrowing.

31

WHEN Mary came down, Craig had come in and Mirren was bringing the soup and bread that were the usual mid-day meal. "Mirren tells me the Minister has been here."

"Yes."

He cocked an inquisitive eye. "Just asking after your health?"

"Not quite." She decided to tell him.

When she had finished, he said, "Aye, it's a fine tangle. And it's no' for me tae say what he should do. They tell me he's a good minister."

"He's a good man," said Mary. "He believes that there is no possible higher privilege than being a minister of the Church. I knew that, and yet I hoped . . ."

"Ah weel." Craig was unwilling to pursue the topic. He had an uneasy inkling that this girl, who had twice arrived in his house in a way which made it impossible to keep her out, was a danger to the principle of non-involvement by which he lived. So he went on, "What'll you dae noo? I mean, if you're no' wantin' tae live in Dyplin, where'll ye gang?"

"I don't know. Ayrshire, perhaps. I should like to stay here for a while—" she saw his look of dismay—"I would pay—I'm not poor."

"It's no' a question of paying. But we're no' juist verra genteel here. The hoose is gey ordinar."

"But I like it. I like the books; I like being up on the hillside; I like being away from people. Please, Mr. Craig."

It was true she was little trouble. She talked little, she could sit quiet with a book for hours. But was that because she was still recovering from her accident? Might she become more obtrusive as she grew stronger? And what about Mirren? If there had to be a choice between this girl and plain, stupid Mirren, he'd take Mirren every time. But he and she had this in common. They had both been rejected by the herd. Remembering a time long past, he said:

"Weel, stay till ye see the way clear. I'll no tak' money, but ye could gie some tae Mirren for her extra trouble."

After a week at the farm, Mary felt strong enough to walk down to her house. It was cold and full of sadness, and she shivered, standing in the kitchen with the ashes still in the fire, and withered pansies drooping in the little jug in the window. She set to and cleared things up, tied up stale bread and butter in a bundle and put it on the midden at the top of the garden; chose a few books to take back with her, and put them and John's model boat into a basket; and filled a box with changes of clothes which Craig would lift next time he was down with the cart. There was no sound from Alison's house, but just as she had finished her tasks, she heard Alison in the garden, and went out.

"Mary!" Alison was full of pleasure at seeing her. "So you're back! Oh, I'm glad to see you. Come in and sit down and we'll have a cup of tea and talk."

Mary, as she had so often done, slipped through the gap in the hedge, and was soon sipping tea from Alison's white and gold cups with the big deep saucers. Alison kept up a flow of talk about Dyplin's doings while she made the tea, but when they were seated, she said again, quietly, "I'm glad you're back, Mary."

"But I'm not coming back," Mary said flatly. "I am never going to live in Dyplin again."

"Oh Mary! Where will you go?"

"I don't know yet. I'm staying at Craig's till I've decided. Alison, I must ask you something. You don't believe I tried to drown myself?"

Alison nodded and said, "I never thought it."

"And John?"

"He doesn't know; not since he saw the Minister."

"There's something else I want to know. Was it John who told the Minister about—about the baby? You had been in Glasgow...."

"No. It was Andrew Stott." Alison was reproachful. "You should know John better. He did know, but he would never have said it to anyone."

Mary sighed. "I'm glad. I'll never forget how good you and John have been to me."

Alison looked at the basket. "I see you're taking his boat with you."

"Of course. I couldn't leave that." Mary became practical. "I'll leave the key of the house with you, and when Craig comes for my box, you'll let him in? Please."

"You'll come and see us sometimes," said Alison, as Mary prepared to set off up the hill.

"Of course. It's not all that far to Craig's. Not in distance. But a long way other ways."

Alison watched her go, her basket in one hand, a little bag of necessities in the other. To John she said:

"I kent what she meant. She looked as if she was setting off on a long journey somewhere."

To which John's reply was, "For a sensible woman ye whiles get the daftest notions."

"Do I?" She gave him what he called "one of her deep looks". "She took your boat."

"Did she now?" He looked out of the window to the hills. "Aye. I think she liked it. . . . What's fur tea, Alison?"

But Mary did feel she was travelling to another country. Round Craig's house there was a square enclosure surrounded by a drystane dyke, big enough to hold the ewes at lambing time, and give pasture to the pony. His ten cattle beasts grazed the good grass by the burn. The house was at the hill end of the enclosure. It was a low, white-washed house. A narrow lobby divided it. On the right was the big living-room, with a window looking down to the south. Off it, to the rear, was the bedroom where Craig and Mirren slept. Craig had added another room, entered through what had been the gable end of the house, and here he kept many of his books. To the left of the front door was the little parlour, and off it opened a small bedroom where Mary slept. At the end of the passage was the kitchen. Tucked in under the roof were two attic rooms lit by skylights and approached by a narrow stair immediately to the right of the door. It was a warm, solid house, able to withstand storm and tempest. The stable and byre were part of the building, stretching out to the west. When Mary opened the gate and stepped inside the sheltering wall, she felt as if she were coming into a refuge; like the feeling, she thought, of the pursued who reached sanctuary in the church in the old days. She said something of this to Craig that evening as she arranged her books in the space he had cleared for her. He chuckled:

"Aye, but this is nae Kirk, lassie!"

Life settled into a routine. Craig went about his work as usual. Mary went for long walks over the hills, and came back, drugged with strong air and tiredness into a state of non-feeling which was almost happiness. The long days of summer were still with them; and often she spent hours by the parlour window alone with a book. Sometimes, if it was a dull night, and they lit candles before bed-time, she sat in the big room with Craig and Mirren. Craig and she read; Mirren knitted; or

415

sometimes laboriously read to herself, with moving fingers and lips, a broadsheet Craig brought for her from Inverforth. Mary lent a hand in the house to the extent of keeping her bedroom and the parlour in order. Mirren made it clear she wanted no one in her kitchen, and Mary hesitated to get busy with brush, broom and duster in the other rooms, for fear of offending her. One wet day, however, she took down a book from a shelf in Craig's bookroom—he had told her she had the run of his shelves—and the puff of thick dust as she did so made her sneeze. Craig was away at the market in Inverforth, and Mary decided she would clean the books. So she got brush and shovel and rags, and set to. Mirren, busy baking in the kitchen, did not know what was going on until Mary, having finished, showed her the books dusted, and the floor swept, the window cleaned, and said placatingly:

"You've so much to do, Mirren, I thought I'd save you the work."

Mirren only said: "Aye," and Mary didn't notice the dull flush that crept over her cheeks. Craig, on his return, showed only a modified gratitude till he saw she had scrupulously returned each book to its place. Then he said it was all right, but he did not see why there was so much fuss over a pickle dust. Mary did not mind. She had enjoyed doing it.

Next morning she was wakened by angry voices at the back door, which was close by her bedroom window.

"I'm awa', Craig. Ye can get that besom tae mak' yer pairritch—gin she can. Them that's sae muckle fur readin' is no' a' that great fur kitchen."

"Noo, Mirren, juist haud a wee."

"Guid-day, Craig."

There was a sound of receding steps; a shout of "Silly bitch", the slamming of a door, and silence.

Mary rose, dressed quickly, and quietly made her way to the kitchen. Craig was sitting staring gloomily into the fire. Mary said nothing, but filled a pot with water, hung it on the swee, and took a handful of meal from the barrel.

"Mirren's awa'," said Craig.

"I know. I heard her."

"It's your fault. Ye hurt her feelings."

"I'm sorry."

"She'll be back. I'm shair o' it. She went away once before, and cam' back. Then it was my sister offended her."

"I didn't know you had a sister."

"Oh aye. She lives in Edinburgh. She comes once a year tae see her disreputable brother—and one time she was here, Mirren took the huff and left. But she'll be back. I gie her a week."

"Where would she go?"

"Ower the hills tae Whiteford. The tinkers'll be here the noo. Mirren's a tinker born. Aweel." He rose and reached for his bonnet. "Ye'll juist hae tae tak' ower. I see ye can mak pairritch. When a's ready, call me in."

After one day of cooking and washing, Mary

417

appreciated why Mirren had not much time for dusting and sweeping. Water had to be brought from a spring on the hillside—Craig did this for her; Mirren had been left to get it herself. The big kettles on the hob had to be kept constantly filled. But Mary went to it with a will. On the fourth day, when she set down on the table the big dish of stew, and the bowl of potatoes, Craig sniffed the appetizing smell, and said:

"Ye're doing weel. I didna think ye had it in you. Aye, aye, ye'll mak' a fine wife fur a man some day."

Mary waited for him to pass her her plate. Then—

"Why not for you?" she said.

"What?" Craig laid down his knife and fork and stared.

"Why not marry me? You see I can run your house for you. And then I could stay here for always."

"Ye're no' serious, lass. Or are ye?" He peered at her. "Na, na, it widna dae. Ye've no' lived here through the winter, when fur days ye'll maybe no can see the dyke there; or when the snaw's piled up there on the north side o' the hoose. Ye wud gae daft. Oh aye, I ken there's aye the books—and fur me, efter a hard day oot on the hill, that's fine. But ye wud be shut in the hoose fur days, wi' naebody but me tae see. . . . That's why I took Mirren. She's nearly simple-minded, and gin she's warm and dry by a guid fire, she's content. She was born in a blac'

418

tinker's tent, and left an orphan, and the schule maister's wife at Whiteford took her, and brocht her up, and trained her tae cook and bake and wash and spin—but no' that much about polishing up furniture, as ye've seen, but efter a' that's the least o' it. Gin I could mairry onybody, I'd marry Mirren."

"Why don't you?"

"Because I canna mairry onybody. Because I've a wife already. I dinna ken where, but somewhere in the wide world, I hae, tae the best o' my knowledge, a wife."

He pointed his fork at Mary. "An' I'm no' gaun tae tell you the story, my lass. Ye'll juist hae tae repress yer wumman's curiosity, for I'll no' tell ye, neither noo nor ever."

They ate in silence for a minute or two, and then he said, "That's the queerest thing—gettin' an offer o' marriage frae a lass like you. Ye're no' vexed at my refusing it?"

Mary shook her head. "No. It was just a thought I spoke out loud."

"Aye. But it widna dae. Ye ken, lassie, ye mind me o' one o' thae silly young yowes we get some time. Sheep, ye ken, are no' silly beasts the wey fowk think o' them. They're wise in their ain weys. But noo an' again ye get a silly young yowe that disna ken whaur tae pit hersel'. Noo she's up near the tap o' the hill, noo she's doon by the burn. She doesna plan her grazing like the ithers. Weel, it seems tae me, ye've no' juist found your grazing grun' yet. But up here is no' the richt one fur ye—I'm no' drivin' ye awa'. Stay as lang as ye will. But leave ye will—some time."

Three days later, Mirren came back, walking into the kitchen as if she had just been out picking up the eggs from the henhouse. Mary was taking a loaf from the oven at the side of the fire when she came in. The smell of fresh bread filled the house. Mirren looked surprised.

"Sae ye can mak breid."

"Oh yes," said Mary, "but I can't get the crust like you, Mirren."

"Ye need tae ken the oven. But that's no' bad."

Mary took the bull by the horns. "I'm sorry I did what I did, Mirren. From now on, I'll only keep the rooms I use. You are the one to run the house."

"As lang as that's understood. Noo I'll get on wi' the denner."

32

THOUGH Mary was no longer seen in the streets, her affairs were still of the deepest interest to Dyplin. Betsy's discovery of her half-drowned in the burn was a fine piece of news. That she had escaped with her life was something of an anti-climax, but in no way diminished the force of the question *why* she had flung herself into the Black Pool, the possibility of an accident being instantly dismissed. Had the Minister jilted her? And if so why?

There was a convention in Dyplin that meetings of the Kirk Session were confidential. Elders were solemnly warned against divulging to their wives what was discussed, "for it is not meet that the business of the Lord's House should become the subject of idle clash such as women are prone to". But the wives had their own ways of finding out, and it took only a week or so for Dyplin to learn of Mary's having borne a child, and that the Session had warned the Minister against marrying her.

Here was something to keep the tongues wagging, and true too. The righteous were censorious with much self-satisfaction; the not-so-righteous rejoiced at the revelation of fellow-frailty. There was, here and there, a renewed spurt of anger over her book—that one "no better that she should be" had held up to scorn the misdoings of others. But by and large it all resulted in a more tolerant feeling towards Mary; they could now feel superior towards her.

All this was grievous to Alison, who, though totally upright in her morals, had a natural charity that could understand and forgive. She spoke of her trouble to John.

"I canna stand the way they're all talking about Mary. As if they were glad."

"Mebbe they are; they'll feel she's weel doon tae their level noo. But it'll pass, it'll pass. Something will happen tae tak their attention, and they'll forget Mary."

"All the same I wish . . ."

"Ye wish it hadna happened? Her hae'in a wean? Me tae. But she's no' the first nor will she be the last—and it doesna mak her ony different. She's still the lass that saved ma life."

"Aye. I dinna feel different. But all the same I wish it wasna the way it is."

It was Jenny Niven who told Meg. Jenny had taken to going now and then to Meg's house; at first on the pretext of taking some work to be done; relining the bodice of a dress, altering the length of a skirt; latterly with no excuse at all and in defiance of her mother. She had expected Meg to be pleased, even exultant at the news. But all Meg said after a moment's silence was, "What of it? I only wish the bitch had never set foot in Dyplin."

"I thought you'd be glad to know . . ."

"Tae ken she's nae better than me? Jenny Niven ye ken naethin' aboot things at a'. And noo I've work tae dae, sae ye'll hae tae leave me tae it."

The news might once have rejoiced Meg, but now she was too troubled to care. For Daniel was leaving Dyplin.

Sharp eyes had noticed that the brown dress worn by the guy on the bonfire was a copy of the dress Meg had made for Mary at the Reform Ball. It was easy to take the next step—that it was Meg who had dressed the guy; and there were some ready to take a further step; so that in time it came to the ears of Dr. Duffus that the teacher at his Infant School had persuaded Meg Annan to make the effigy of the umbrella-maker's daughter for the fire.

"This is too much," he said to Mrs. Duffus. "I could overlook the other thing—but this is too much. I won't have one of my teachers behaving like that."

"What are you going to do?"

"Get rid of him. Oh, discreetly. I want no scandal attached to the School. But as soon as I see a way . . ."

A week later he came to Mrs. Duffus triumphantly.

"I have it!"

"Have what?"

"The means to be quit of Rutherford. This is a letter from Jack." (Jack was the Doctor's brother, a minister in Nova Scotia.) "He says they urgently need a teacher for a school they're setting up out there, and can I find him one?" He turned over the letter. "As the matter is very pressing, he will leave it in my hands to choose someone so as to avoid delays over sending letters back and forth. . . . Then he gives the conditions of service, which seem very good . . . passage paid, etc. Don't you see? I can offer this to Daniel Rutherford."

"But surely—if you are getting rid of him because of unseemly conduct—is it right to send him to Jack?"

Dr. Duffus became solemn.

"I have nothing but praise for him as a teacher. He's outstanding. No one there will know anything about the umbrella-maker's daughter—or Meg Annan. One could even say I was doing him a favour by allowing him to extricate himself from a very awkward situation. This letter is providential—just providential. I shall send for the man this afternoon."

Facing Daniel across his wide leather-topped writing table in his room above the entrance to the New School, with the founder's portrait glowering down on them, Dr. Duffus wasted no words.

"You may wonder why I have asked you to come and see me. Unpleasant tasks are best dealt with quickly, so I shall come to the point. I was surprised and disappointed to observe at the May Burning that you took part in the burning of the book written by—ah—by a local young woman—conduct, I feel, unbecoming to one who should be an example to the young of our community. No, let me finish," as Daniel made a move to speak.

"However, that I was prepared to overlook. But I cannot overlook your extraordinary conduct in persuading someone—someone of no good reputation—to make an effigy of that same person for the purpose of having it burned in the fire."

Daniel stared at him.

"I do not understand you, Dr. Duffus."

"It has come to my ears that you were instrumental in having the guy made that was burnt at the bonfire. Do you deny this?"

"Absolutely. This is the first I have heard of it. It is a wicked lie."

"Indeed? You will not deny, however, that there has been, for some time, an—ah—an association between you and Meg Annan, a woman of ill-repute?"

Daniel's control broke. "No. I do not deny it. Why should I? It has in no way affected my work as a teacher. You can have no complaints against me on that score."

"None. None at all. And that is why I am able to offer you a way out of this situation. For understand, Mr. Rutherford, I will not have as a member of the teaching staff of this establishment anyone whose conduct brings scandal on the School. I know well the damage that can be done to a school by scandal, especially in its early days. So I have a proposition to make to you."

And he brought out from a drawer the Reverend John Duffus's letter.

When Daniel left the Doctor's study an hour

later, it was all decided. Every objection he raised
had been dealt with. When he spoke of the certainty
of Susannah's refusing to go, the Doctor promptly
suggested she become the assistant sewing mistress,
for Mrs. Manson was beginning to find the work
too much.

"You have thought of everything," said Daniel
bitterly.

"I have, for I mean you shall go, by one way or
another. But I promise you, no one shall hear from
me why. I shall say you were offered this appoint-
ment and took it."

When he left Dr. Duffus's room, Daniel, instead
of going home, took the old road to the Martyr's
Bridge, as he always did in times of stress, avoiding
the new turnpike. He was full of bitter anger. Dr.
Duffus was not impressive physically, being short
and rotund; in his heart Daniel had rather looked
down on "the little man", failing to detect the
ruthlessness beneath the Doctor's cheerful
bonhomie. Now "the little man" was sending him
across the Atlantic to work in some kind of crude
pioneering establishment. And there was nothing
he could do about the Doctor's plans for him, short
of refusing to consider them at all and condemning
himself to an ignominious and difficult search for a
position. The humiliation enraged him. He hated
being humiliated. That was what had driven him to
take part in the burning of the book—rage at
humiliation—and that at the hands of a woman—a
small quiet woman whom he had desired and who

had rejected him and made him feel his own cowardice. But at the Burning he had felt something like shame seeing that cruel mockery of Mary on the fire. And to be accused of being the instigator! Meg had never mentioned it to him; and it was this which had first made him think she might have something to do with it. But he had never spoken of it to her; he was growing weary of her viciousness whenever Mary's name was mentioned. He was weary of Meg; for Meg made demands, wanted always to be assured that he loved her; never was assured. How often had he sworn to himself that he would be quit of her? Not go back? And then found himself again beside her. Up at the castle, Meg had cajoled and bribed Betsy into opening up for them a little vaulted room opening from the stair and lying above Betsy's kitchen. It had a rusty old bolt on the inside; Meg had gathered bracken and fern, brought a rug, and made a bed. When Daniel wondered about Betsy, Meg scoffed. "She'll no' breathe a word. I've made it worth her while." But Meg had spoilt these encounters of pleasure and desire by talk of love; of being forever faithful; of dreams of being somewhere else where she could be always with him. She never mentioned marriage now; but he was sure it was always in her mind.

He had reached the bridge, and leant as always to look into the darkness of the pool. Dimly it reflected the arch of the bridge and himself, his face a white blurring in the blackness. He had looked down like this with Mary beside him. That was the day he had made his peace with her. That had been a mistake. He should have left the little blue-stocking with her books and poems to go her own way—for all her dark clear eyes and the warm glow of her skin and the small firm curve of her breasts beneath the prim buttons of her dress. And now, because of her, and because of Meg, he must leave Dyplin and all his life there. But at least the Atlantic Ocean would effectively solve the problem of Meg. He would be spared the odium of breaking with her. Dr. Duffus would have to take the blame for that.

He was aware of another white blur down there beside himself. Meg's voice said in his ear: "I didna expect tae see you here Daniel."

When he looked round she drew back from his heavy frown. "Is onything the matter Daniel?"

"I'm going to have to leave Dyplin. Dr. Duffus is dismissing me. And why? Because he has heard that I asked you to make that guy of Mary Tullis for the May Burning."

"But you didna."

"No. I told him so. But there were other things. Tell me, Meg, did you make that guy?"

"Aye. But I didna think—Oh Daniel, I didna think they'd ever connect you wi' it!"

"I wish you had not done it. Now I must go away."

"Where to?"

"Across the ocean. To Canada."

"To Canada!" The words were a wail of despair. "Ye canna! No' that far!" She caught his arm. "Tak me wi' you, Daniel. Ye must tak me wi' you."

He had not expected this, and in a great surge of panic and anger he had a fierce impulse to lift her and drop her into the water waiting beneath them. It passed; but at least he could shake her out of her hysteria. But as he made to grasp her, he heard the wheel of a cart coming down the road beyond the bridge. He drew back a step and said:

"We'll talk of this later."

"Ye'll come tae ma hoose the nicht?"

He nodded and turned away, but she pulled him back.

"See ye dae come. If ye dinna, I swear tae God I'll come doon tae your place and batter on the door till ye let me in."

Daniel had the rest of the day to think things over. As darkness drew in he made his way with his habitual caution to Meg's house. He knew what to do. He must avoid a quarrel with Meg. She was quite capable of creating a scene at his door, and an open scandal which might follow him to his new position must be prevented. On the few occasions when he had been forced to tell lies, lying had come easily to him. So when Meg opened the door, he smiled at her. By the time he left, all was smooth between them, and he knew that as far as Meg was concerned, his departure would be decorous.

Dr. Duffus was determined that no time should be lost in getting rid of Daniel. Assistance was given in the way of booking passages, packing goods, finding somewhere for Susannah to live. A month after his interview with the Doctor all was ready. True to his word that he would do his best to keep any breath of scandal from Daniel's going, the Doctor raised no objection to Walter Fraser's organizing the presentation of a "a handsome black marble timepiece" to Daniel, and even graced the ceremony of presentation himself. (The clock Daniel left with Susannah.)

Mary first heard of all this when Craig, after one of his excursions to Dyplin, said over the dinner table:

"They tell me schule-maister Rutherford's got a new job in Canada, and he'll be awa' afore the month's oot."

He cast an inquisitive eye at Mary, for though he boasted of his detachment from the world at large, Craig had an ear for clash and had heard enough to wonder how Mary would receive the news. Mary appeared to take it calmly, merely saying:

"He is a good teacher, I'm told."

Inwardly she felt a great sense of relief, for she had dreaded that some time she might come face to face with Daniel while walking on the hills. When she thought of him it was with a surge of self-disgust. Their acquaintanceship had begun and ended with treachery from him. She was ashamed that she could have let herself be so blinded as not to see the man behind the brave exterior that had so dazzled her; that still made her shiver when she

430

thought of him. He was something she wanted to blot out as if he had never happened.

A few days later she went down to see Alison, from a sense of duty and because Craig said he had met John in Dyplin and he had been "asking after her". She looked into her house and took a few books. The house was still cold, but not sad; she felt nothing in it; it was an empty vessel, drained and dry. She reminded herself that she must ask John to dispose of the stuff in her father's workshop. Then she went in to Alison.

Alison was of course happy to see her. They sat companionably and Alison gave her the current clash. Mary listened politely and thought how far she had moved from Dyplin and its ways. What she noticed more keenly was what Alison did not say.

Abruptly she broke into a description of the dress Madame Laporte had made for Mrs. Innes for her niece's wedding, saying:

"You haven't mentioned Daniel Rutherford."

Alison stopped short. It was the first time she had heard Mary mention that name since the May Burning, and she spoke so calmly that Alison was at a loss for words.

Mary went on: "I hear he's leaving Dyplin and going to Canada."

"That's so. But Miss Susannah's no' going. She's to be assistant sewing-mistress at the New School." She paused. "Mary, since he's leaving the place, would you not think of coming back here?"

Mary shook her head. "No, Alison." And then, "They'll all know about me?"

"Aye."

"I can just hear them. It might have been better if they'd known from the start. . . . But my father was so sure no one need ever know. He left Glasgow just to protect me. Perhaps he might still be alive if . . ."

"Na, na. You mustn't think that. He was doing his best for you; and seeing you well and happy would make him happy."

"It's as well he died when he did."

"Oh Mary. . . ."

Mary spoke first.

"How—how is the Minister?"

Alison looked at her sharply.

"He's going aboot as usual. But he disna seem very happy. Awful glum."

"I'm sorry," said Mary, and rose to take her leave. Alison watched her go up the hillside.

"For such a small slip of a woman, you've caused a fair upheaval."

"Talking tae yersel' Alison?"

She had not been aware of John's coming in. Now he stood with her and watched the small figure breast the rise.

"I was just thinking that that lassie has caused a fair upheaval in Dyplin."

"Aye, she has that."

Alison watched his eyes linger on Mary before he turned heavily away with indrawn breath. Should she speak? No, it was better to keep quiet. If he was fond of Mary beyond friendship, it was better it should not be admitted. She knew the strength of silence.

She also knew when to speak. Meeting Matthew next day at the gate, and seeing the drawn misery on his face, she said, "Mary Tullis was visiting me yesterday, Minister."

At the mention of her name, his look became eager. "How is she?"

"Well I think."

"Has she any plans? What is she going to do?"

"She only said she would never come back to Dyplin."

"Oh. I am glad she is well. Good-day, Mrs. Campbell."

He strode on up the road remonstrating with himself. He had known she would never come back—so why should Alison Campbell's words have been like a blow? He had tried his hardest not to make visible his unhappiness, going about his work as usual, taking much time to prepare his sermons, reading new books on theology which he had sent from Edinburgh, and chiding himself when his attention wandered from long dissertations on effectual calling, justification, sanctification and adoption to thoughts of the time when Mary was enticing him towards less arduous and more seductive books. Now he was on his way to visit Ruth, wife of Tom Saunders, a small sheep-farmer whose land lay close under the hills. He had

married them just two years ago. She was a
beautiful young woman, and had been wooed by a
well-to-do brewer from Inverforth. But she had
chosen Tom and now was dying of consumption
and not likely, so Dr. Munro said, to last out the
week. He would take what comfort he could to
them; Tom had at least had his wife for two years,
whereas he, the Minister, would never have Mary.
He stood still on the road, appalled that such a
thought should have come to him on such an
errand, and uncovered his head to ask forgiveness.

When he came back down the road he had no
thoughts for himself or his concerns. There was a
stretch of the way from which almost all Dyplin
was visible, sloping down into the valley, and he
lingered for a little, leaning on a wall and looking
down on the town and the bell-tower of the church.
He had left approaching death up at the little farm.
But next Sabbath in the church he was to baptize a
child into the body of Christ's people. In the days
ahead people would come to him with complaints,
with requests for help, material and spiritual. He
would see sinful man in all his weakness; and sinful
man striving for good. It had been so for centuries
in Dyplin; it would be so for the years to come. His
own hurt must in time be annulled. But the basic
movement and fluctuations, the ups and downs of
the place, remained constant. After all, what
necessity was there for his dreary theological books?
He needed as his tool no more than the Book itself
which summed it all up, and he quoted aloud:

434

"A time to be born, and a time to die . . . a time to weep, and a time to laugh; a time to mourn, and a time to dance. . . ."

He went on towards Dyplin.

33

A WEEK later Craig brought the news that Daniel had left Dyplin.

The next morning, Mary said to him over their porridge, "I think the time has come when I must make plans to go."

Craig poured some milk into his bowl before answering. "Ye needna hurry awa'. But I'm pleased ye're feeling weel enough tae think o' it. Had ye onything in mind?"

"No. Perhaps I could teach little children."

Craig shook his head. "I dinna see ye as a teacher." He laid down his spoon and put his hands on the table. "Why no' bide here till ma sister comes? I tell't ye she comes here every year aboot noo tae visit me fur a week. She's aye fu' o' talk aboot the peace of the countryside when she comes. Efter a week she's fair hotching tae get back tae Edinburgh."

"Why should I wait for her?"

"Did I no' say? She's mairrit, but she's the editor o' a paper fur weemen—*The Ladies' Friend* or something like that. I wrote tae her aboot ye—fur ye've been in ma thochts—tae see if mebbe she could give ye something tae dae. Mind you it would mean going to Edinburgh and leeving there. But from what Christina tells me, ye can be mair yersel' amang a crowd in the city than in a wee place whaur a'body kens a'body."

"My father said that."

"Aye. Weel, dinna hurry awa'—wait till Christina's been here."

Before Mary could answer, he had risen from the table and gone. It had cost him no little effort to, as he put it, put an oar into Mary's business, and now as he went to bring the sheep down from the high slopes, he wondered why he had done it. "I've lived contentit enough wi' the books and Mirren, and the sheep and cattle beasts. Why I'm lettin' masel' get mixed up wi' yon girl I canna think. Except she minds me o' things past, when I could hae done wi' a helping hand. Forby thae fowk doon there in Dyplin hae been gey sair on her. Wi' Christina she'll be in amang writing bodies an' the like that'll mebbe understand her better. . . . Aweel, we'll juist hae tae wait an' see."

Later that morning Mary went down to the castle to take Betsy some scones and oatcakes from Mirren's weekly baking. The little door set into the great gate of the castle was open, the door of Betsy's kitchen unlatched, but there was no answer to Mary's knock. She called, but got no reply. But this was not surprising. Betsy was probably in pursuit of the errant Bluebell. Mary put the scones on the kitchen table and closed the door. The stair of the tower curved up into the darkness, and Mary began to climb it. She had only once before been up the

437

tower, and then on a misty February morning. She did not much like the castle; it spoke to her of sorrow and violence; and she secretly wondered how Betsy could live there, apparently quite unperturbed by the looming stone walls and the rushing of the burns of Care and Sorrow always in the air. But today was bright and clear, the bracken beginning to colour, and the view from the top would be good. On the way up she looked into the three great rooms that made up the tower. They were cold and gloomy. She tried to think of them with fires blazing in the huge fireplaces, hangings on the walls, torches smoking in the sconces. The vision of flaming torches made her shiver, and she stepped with relief into the good air.

The view to the south was beautiful: the green tree tops of the glen running down to the flat valley below—a few houses—the Braes beyond, and then a gleam of water and distant hills hazy on the skyline. It was very much the view she had been looking at from the hillside when she had first met Daniel. Remembering, she turned abruptly away and walked round the little square central turret to look at the hills on the north. When she rounded the last corner, she stopped and gave a startled exclamation. A figure was standing looking over the parapet. It turned and faced her. It was Meg Annan.

She had not seen Meg at close quarters since the incident at the church, and now she was struck by her look of desolation. Her hair was unkempt, strands blowing in the wind, and she was hugging her light shawl round her as if she were bitterly cold.

The two women looked at each other. Meg spoke first.

"It's the umbrella-maker's daughter! I didna think tae see you here, though now I mind me they said you were living wi' Craig up the hill."

Mary said nothing, startled by the ill-feeling in her voice.

"They say he rescued you when you flung yourself intae the Black Pool."

"I didn't fling myself into the pool."

"No?"

"No."

"Aweel, whit dae I care whether ye did or ye didna?"

She turned away, and looking up at the bare empty hills, said, "Ye ken Rutherford's awa'?"

"Yes."

"Ah, but dae ye ken *why* he's awa'?" She turned to face Mary again. "He's awa' because the wee fat man that's heid maister o' the New Schule sent him awa', because he'd been tellt that Daniel got me tae mak' the guy—the guy o' you—that was burnt at the May Burning."

Mary put a hand on the wall of the turret to help control the sudden shivering that shook her, in spite of the mild September sunshine. Her voice was very low as she said, "Did he?"

"Did Daniel ask me tae mak' it? No. He kent naethin' aboot it. I did it."

"But why, why? How could you be so cruel, do such a wicked thing . . . ?"

"Because I hate you, you and your books and your mimsy ways. And because folk said he was going to marry you. And because you pitied me."

She spat out the words, and Mary drew closer to the turret wall.

"But I still don't understand. Why should that make you hate me?"

"Because Daniel was my man. Oh aye, he carried your books frae the library, and drank tae in your hoose, and you went yer walks taegither, and I'll swear ye thocht ye loved him—if ye ken whit it means. But whaur dae ye think he spent his nights, efter he'd said a polite guid-day tae you on your doorstep? He spent them wi' me. Aye, that's shaken you, has it no'?"

Mary could say nothing. Meg turned away to look at the hills again.

"I loved him. Dae ye understand? I loved him. Oot o' a' the men I've kent—and bedded wi'—I never loved but two and nane like him. An' noo he's been sent awa'." She turned back to Mary. "But afore he went, he promised me that I would gang tae. Oot there, whaur naebody kent us, we'd be mairrit. He said, when he was in Glasgow, afore they sailed, he'd book me a passage on a boat tae follow—mebbe in two-three months."

She turned her head and dashed a hand across her eyes. Then she drew the other hand from beneath her shawl. It held a letter.

440

"I got this this morning. It's frae him. He says he couldna get a passage; he says on thinking it ower, he doesna think it would work fur me tae follow him. He says—he says he disna love me that wey, and we'd best no' hae ony mair tae dae wi' each other."

There was such blank despair in her eyes that Mary forgot her own bitterness.

"Oh, Meg," she said. "Oh Meg."

"Dinna pity me! I'll no' hae your pity!" She lowered her voice.

"D'ye ken why I came here the day? I thocht tae fling myself frae this tower. But I thocht, mebbe I wouldna be killed, but juist broken, and I couldna dae it."

"You won't kill yourself, Meg. That would mean he'd won. He's a bad man, Meg. A bad man."

"I kent ye didna ken aboot love. Aye, he's a bad man, and weak, an nae a thocht for a'body but himsel'. But it maks nae difference. D'ye no' understan'? It maks nae difference."

She paused. "An' I'll never see him again."

"But you won't kill yourself, Meg. You're too strong. You won't kill yourself."

And Mary turned, went down the stair and up the track to Craig's, and did not look back.

From the tower, Meg watched her, realizing with a shock of dull surprise that she no longer hated Mary. She looked down from the parapet at the ground. The umbrella-maker's daughter had said, "You're too strong to admit defeat", but she knew nothing about it. "Defeat's no new thing for me. I've lived with it for many a year." She walked down by the edge of the glen in a state of numbness, refusing to think. She had work to do and she sat by the fire sewing fiercely till the light failed. As she was folding the material, there was a knock at the door, and her heart stood still, remembering Daniel. When she opened the door, she saw a young, dark-haired man. He smiled at her.

"I'm back, Meg."

"Tam Oliphant." He was a ploughman from a farm up on the Braes.

"I didna like it in the Borders, and noo I'm back wi' auld Gloag—at a better fee."

"Aye."

His smile died. "Have ye been ill, Meg?"

"No. Why?"

"Your face is thinner. But your hair is as bonny as ever. Can I come in?"

Meg made no movement, looking at something beyond him.

"Meg?"

"Aye." She stood aside.

Next day Betsy found Meg lying on the rocks at the foot of the castle tower: and Meg was dead.

34

THE morning after she had heard the news of Meg's death, Mary came to Craig at breakfast and said, "Craig, I want to go and climb Ben Suidhe."

"So you're feeling all right again? Ye gave us—me and Mirren—a fricht last nicht."

For when Craig had blurted out the news, Mary had turned so white he had caught her, fearing she would fall. Then she had gone to her room, and had not come out to take food or to speak to anyone for the rest of the day. Now she was still pale, but otherwise seemed as usual.

"I feel quite all right in every way. But I want to get away by myself—and you once told me it was quite easy to climb Ben Suidhe from here."

"It's easy enough, meaning there's nae rocks or precipices tae climb. But it's a fair distance. It'll tak ye near a whole day. I'm no shair I'm just happy aboot yer gaun by yersel'. Whit aboot Mirren ganging wi' ye?"

"No thank you. I want to be by myself. I've always wanted to climb the highest hill in the range—and this seems the right time."

He looked at her. "Aye, aye. There's times when the hills can be a help. . . . I'm not asking why you want to go, and I'll not stop you." He raised his

443

voice. "Mirren!" And when Mirren came through he said, "Mary here's wanting tae climb Ben Suidhe. Is it safe, d'ye think, tae let her go by her lee-lane?"

"Aye. It's a clear path. It's the same path I tak tae reach Whiteford. But when you reach the Moss, at the back o' the Queen's Mount, the path divides. Fur the ben, ye tak the left haun—and follow it till ye reach the tap. I'll pin up yer skirts fur ye. An' I'll len' ye my lang stick—that'll be a help wi' the climbin'. And I'll pit some breid and beef in a bag fur ye."

"You see," said Mary, "Mirren doesn't think there's anything outlandish about my going."

"Nae mair there is," said Craig. "The only thing tae worry aboot is mebbe the mist coming doon. But I dinna think that'll happen the day. If it does, you must juist sit doon at the side o' the path and wait—and I'll come tae find you." He went to the front door, and looked out. It was a still, clear day, with a haze over the distances and not a cloud. "But I think ye'll hae sunshine and clear skies."

By nine o'clock, Mary was on her way, her skirt pinned up, wearing stout boots, Mirren's staff in her hand and a small bag with bread and beef and a little bottle of milk slung over her shoulder. Craig had shown her the path, running up into the hills above the Burn of Sorrow. It was narrow, not much more than a sheep track, but well defined and easy to follow. From time to time it dipped into a fold in the ground to cross a little rivulet running down

444

from the heights to join the burn. Soon she was out of sight of Craig's farm, and alone in the wide landscape, the only living creature besides the sheep scattered on the slopes. In the little glen which the burn had cut for itself bracken and fern grew, and the bracken was yellowing. There were some clumps of late bluebells in sheltered nooks, and golden moss, and dark-flowered grasses. If Matthew had been there, he could have told her their names no doubt. But she would never never again walk with Matthew and hear him name and discuss the flowers they saw.

Soon she had climbed above the bracken, and there was nothing but the long hill-grass, lion-coloured, and thick. These hills had no heather; they did not blaze in autumn as she had been told the hills to the north did. On her left across the burn, a great gash had opened in the huge mass of the Queen's Mount, as if some gigantic pick had been hacking into the rock. It was full of blackness, in spite of the sun, and she saw a bird, some kind of hawk, rise from its depths and circle in the air above.

She walked steadily on. Apart from the momentary dipping of the ground to the runlets, it was a steady pull upwards, but gentle enough to do no more than make her draw her breath more deeply. The sun was warm on her back, and she took off the knitted jacket Mirren had insisted on her wearing and tied the arms round her waist and let it hang. The hill air was cool on her throat and she pushed up the sleeves of her bodice to feel it on her arms. The hills were closer now: on her left the great mass of the Queen's Mount, and on the other the slope leading up to the long ridge of Grey Wisp: these were gentle hills, rounded and quiet: not like the hills of Switzerland she had seen pictures of in one of Matthew's books: where the snow never melted, and sharp peaks stabbed the sky. Scornful mountains: but here they were kind.

The burn was smaller now, and ran close by the path, very clear over sparkling pebbles. She stopped to cup her hands under one of the many miniature waterfalls, and drink. Her ear caught with pleasure the small sounds of the water, and she said out loud:

"And beauty born of murmuring sound
Shall pass into her face,"

and smiled, at herself and the poet. "Beauty" was not so easily got. She was not beautiful, except perhaps her eyes. But her hair was straight and brown: Meg was—had been—beautiful. Even with her face torn by scorn and grief, she had been beautiful, and her hair was splendid. Mary dragged her eyes from the tiny pool below the little ledge of rock, dried her hands on the grass, took up her stick, and walked on.

In another hour, she had reached the Moss, and stood where the path branched. The Moss was a level boggy hollow among the hills, and in it the burn disappeared. The wider path led ahead; that

446

must be the one to Whiteford. And this, the narrower one, leading up to the left in the shadow of the Queen's Mount, was the one she must follow. It was very silent in the hollow, very still. There were no sheep; no longer the ripple of the burn to break the hush. When a bird rose scuttering in front of her, she gave a little cry, and for a moment her heart beat even faster. She was not afraid, not at all, but the loneliness and silence produced a sharpening of senses, a quickening of awareness, that could have companioned fear; and effectively numbed conscious thinking.

She went on steadily but more slowly. The slope was much steeper now. She came out of the shadow of the Queen's Mount and the sun was pleasantly warm again. Ahead the path wriggled up and vanished into the sky, not too far away. She knew the hills well enough to be sure that was not the top. When she reached that place, there would be further climbing to do; and indeed the final ascent was up a gentle slope. She was aware of the landscape unfurling round her, but she did not stop until she had reached the indubitable crest, and stood, leaning on her staff, panting, and amazed.

The haze had lifted from the horizon, and it seemed as if the whole of Scotland was there before her. Away to the west, far away, was a dim peak, pearly grey; could it be one of the Arran mountains? Perhaps Goat Fell itself? To the east there was a distant glint of sea, and a little nubble where the horizon dipped, which could perhaps be North

Berwick Law, of which she had heard her father speak. And could that little smudge beneath a craggy outcrop be Edinburgh itself? She remembered her father had once said it was a haunted city. Why? If she went there would she find it haunted? If so, it would be by a mightier past than her own. Were the people who lived there aware of this past? Or did they live out their lives unheeding? She imagined it a place teeming with life and ideas. Perhaps before too long she would find out the truth for herself. Her gaze moved from east by south to west, taking in rivers, woodlands, moor and a sea of rolling hills, huge combers of the earth. She turned to look behind her, "It's like being God! Here I am and the whole world there at my feet! I wish I could stay here for ever and ever."

She lay back in the prickly grass, turned her head from the sun, and stared into the sky. Under her fingers she felt the strong grass. If she moved her head sideways, she looked through a forest of stems and twisted blades; there was a little golden beetle twisting its way through them. She and the beetle, the sun, the grass, the sky and the huge world beyond . . . everything blended into a sudden burst of—what? Light? Feeling? Not thought. No. For a moment, a flash of time, she was not aware of herself; but it wasn't sleep, for all the while she saw the sky and felt the grass.

She sat up abruptly, reached for the bag, pulled out the bottle of milk and drank, and began to munch the bread and beef. The heady exaltation passed, and as she ate and drank and looked at the world beneath, she thought of herself as she had never done before, clearly, calmly, as if from a great height.

She thought of her love in Glasgow, and her dead child; of her father, who had sheltered her and swaddled her in anxious affection; and Matthew whom she had grown to love because of his gentleness and kindness, and the honesty that had in the end been cruel; and Daniel she thought of, not with the usual self-disgust, but with pity for the man so hollow for all his gifts; and Meg, poor Meg, who had hated her so much: the revelation of that hatred was still raw in her thoughts; she still did not understand it fully, and perhaps never would; but why should she? It was not necessary to understand everything; but it was necessary to accept.

The hills around her had been shaped and moulded by weather and storm. Now, for the first time, in her hill-top serenity, she could look at the May Burning without a feeling of cringing suffocation. It had happened, it was there, like the great gash in the hills she had passed on her way up. She was able to see how it had happened. She had ripped apart the acceptance other people had woven from pain and fear; she had not done it knowingly but through blindness and—yes, up here it was clear to her—through arrogance. And she had run away and found shelter in Craig's farm and Craig's books, like a little frightened animal running to its burrow. Craig himself had done just that; come out of life, run for shelter, built himself a little haven, cowering inside the farm dyke, fenced round with his books. He had tried to tell her, and she had not wanted to listen. How could she have been so blind to the sadness of Craig? She remembered other lines recently read:

. . . the heavy and the weary weight
Of all this unintelligible world.

She pondered the words for a moment and then jumped to her feet. The world was truly unintelligible, but she was young. It was not yet time for her to feel it heavy and weary. It lay there before her, and it was time for her to go out and meet it, and be herself, and no longer the umbrella-maker's daughter.

She slung the bag over her shoulder, and picked up the stick. Slowly she let her eyes travel over all that lay round her, knowing she would never again see it thus. She heard herself say "Thank you", though to whom or to what she could not have said. Then she turned and went down the path with swift sure steps.

THE END

GUIDE
TO THE COLOUR CODING
OF
ULVERSCROFT BOOKS

Many of our readers have written to us expressing their appreciation for the way in which our colour coding has assisted them in selecting the Ulverscroft books of their choice.

To remind everyone of our colour coding—
this is as follows:

BLACK COVERS
Mysteries

*

BLUE COVERS
Romances

*

RED COVERS
Adventure Suspense and General Fiction

*

ORANGE COVERS
Westerns

*

GREEN COVERS
Non-Fiction

MYSTERY TITLES
in the
Ulverscroft Large Print Series